A CURSED SON

REMNANTS OF THE FALLEN KINGDOM
BOOK 1

DAY LEITAO

SPARKLY WAVE, MONTREAL 2024

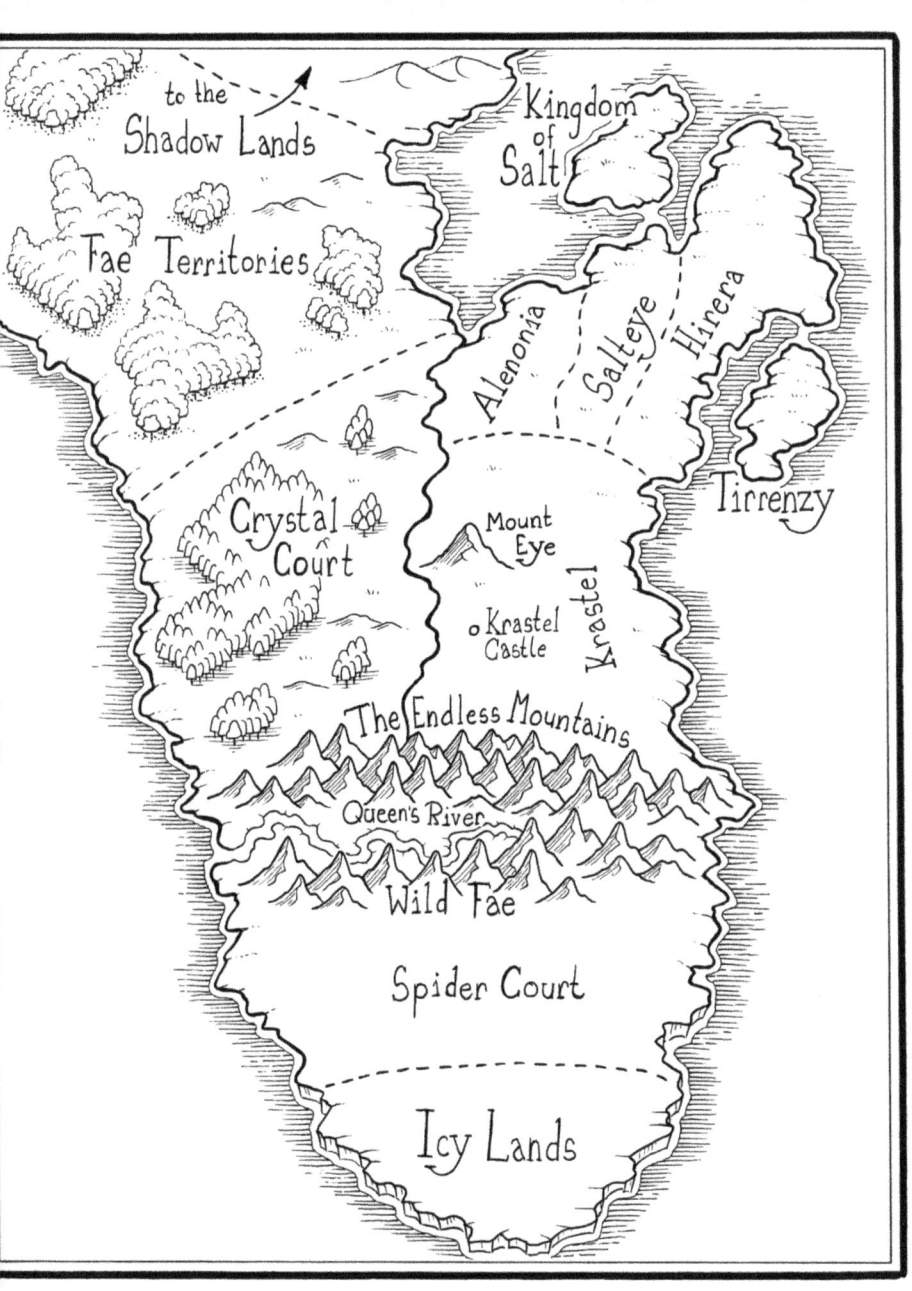

Copyright © 2024 by Day Leitao

All rights reserved.

No part of this book may be reproduced in any form or by any electronic or mechanical means, including information storage and retrieval systems, without written permission from the author, except for the use of brief quotations in a book review.

Cover design by Selkkie Designs. (@selkkiedesigns)

Chapter header illustration by Jwitless (Natalia Sorokina).

Map by Angel Perez (@simplefantasymaps)

Chapter divider by PetiteMarket on Creative Market

Illustration on the back of the front cover by Natalia Sorokina (Jwitless)

Illustration on the back of the back cover by Cebanart.

To all those part of us hiding in the shadows, and to everyone who's brave enough to let them step into the light.

1

Love makes people stupid. And irresponsible.

Barefoot, standing on a thin ledge ten floors above the ground, I'm glad I praise intelligence above all else. But then, perhaps love is what drove me here. A different type of love, the best type of love.

Just a few more steps, and I'll reach Tarlia's window. At this height, the guards' murmurs down in the outer gardens of the castle disappear, drowned by the wind's lullaby. The trail of stars in the sky seems closer than the lanterns on the ground, whose light can't reach me, can't reveal me, even if someone was curious enough to gaze upward.

Sometimes, I wonder if the Elite Guard is housed in the upper levels of the castle's highest tower to remind us of our importance or to render us insignificant, separated from the rest of the world.

Few venture out here, afraid of an impossible fall, even though the ledge is wide enough for my feet. What can I say? Fear distorts reality. Not mine. At least not concerning heights.

Quin's question and his smile flash through my head. *Are you going to Lord Stratson's wedding?* The echo of his words bounces in my head, disarranges thoughts, unveils buried wishes.

Why is it that we can't dissolve thoughts? Can't forget things on purpose? I'm not in love with Quin. I don't know if I'll ever be.

Now, love can lead to stupid decisions, but what about non-love? What about a wisp of hope that maybe this could become something... I don't even know what. And yet that smile...

I clench my hand holding the bag with the drusils, the dessert Tarlia loves so much. Even as a little girl, her eyes would glimmer at the sight of the roasted coconut sweets. I want to bring her some of that joy tonight, perhaps remind her that I'll always love her like a sister. It doesn't matter if she's been failing the tests.

Yes, I study and study, but for me, it's different; I have to be perfect. I don't think it's fair to ground the royal substitutes who miss some questions on our tests, especially when it's about a minor fae court. We don't even have any dealings with the fae, not even with the Crystal Court, right beside us. Of course we need to learn about other kingdoms. And yet, why deprive Tarlia of this little joy? It's not like we have a ton of it.

Quin's smile hasn't left my mind. He's a member of the Elite Guard, trained to impersonate the oldest prince when needed, just like I can stand in for the princess. A little different, I guess. The male substitutes play more of a protective role, while we... Let's just say our job is a thorny tangle. They are also older, in their early twenties, while we are all nineteen.

The thing with Quin is not his obvious good looks. He's brown-haired and brown-eyed like the elder prince, and fit, too, but they're all like that. What makes him different is his relaxed, disarming smile, and perhaps how often that smile is directed at me.

I shouldn't be thinking about him.

Using one hand, I hold on to the grooves of the stone wall and inch faster, aiming to reach my friend's room before my thoughts veer to dangerous paths.

Three more careful steps, and I'll get to Tarlia's window. That's what I have to do, before that sweet smile melts my mind.

One, two, three. There.

As my fist approaches the glass for a knock, the Almighty Mother reminds me to look first.

In shock, I almost drop the bag, but I manage to catch it before it slips. I shouldn't be looking. I should turn away.

Sayanne's words are the ones that cross my mind now. *She's a slut.* Slut. Slut. Slut. A word for women only.

Almost like a reply, I remember Tarlia in a rare moment of honesty. "You think we'll survive this?" Her bitter laugh still echoes in my mind.

Tarlia doesn't seem bitter now, she seems... Blissful. On all fours on her bed, it's as if nothing matters but that moment, a pleasant abandon lulling her into satisfaction. Perhaps it's like me, when training, when only my movements matter, and there's nothing outside the training court.

Of course, in her case, there's something *inside* her, filling her, pushing into her, and judging by her face, it's better than all the drusils in the world.

Her face. It's funny to see her like that, considering how much she looks like me, from her wavy burgundy hair to her upturned nose. A nose that was sculpted, like mine. Burgundy hair that's artificially colored, like mine. Unlike me, though, she doesn't have to fear death if her roots appear, and I've glimpsed some light brown a few times.

I have no idea what my true hair color is like, if it's light lilac or dark purple, bright or muted, as it has never been given the chance to emerge. All I see is dark burgundy, like Tarlia's hair. Our eyes are both brown, although mine are slightly smaller than hers.

I should look away, but my eyes are frozen in place, fascinated by their primal, animalistic movements. Did I look like this? I never did it in my bedroom, though. Instead, I climbed down to the outer gardens, where only hedge walls protected me. I want to bury the memory, bury the shame. Tarlia doesn't have any shame, and it's funny that Sayanne thinks she should have some.

Shame is dreadful.

Behind her, pumping fervently, is Fachin, one of the guards in the Elite Tower, his muscular body contrasting with Tarlia's soft curves. It's odd because I thought she was involved with one of the substitutes. And then, perhaps she was. Perhaps she still is, but likes some variety. These guards should be protecting us, though. Will they start thinking we're all fair game, ready to invite them into our beds?

Great. Now I hear Sayanne's words again. *She's sullying our names. Men talk. They'll think we're all sluts. A slut's value is zero.*

Not always zero, but I never told her that. I never told anyone.

The schism between my friends is uncomfortable. We always promised to treat each other like sisters, and now Sayanne and Tarlia barely talk to each other. I hate being stuck in the middle. Sayanne thinks I'm taking sides, but I'm not. I wish we could all be sisters again, but I guess there's no return to the time when drusils were enough to bring us bliss.

Sayanne. Will I let her spend an entire day with Quin and his beautiful smile? After her spiteful words?

I notice Fachin leaning over and grabbing Tarlia's breasts, his hips moving faster and faster, and I avert my gaze before I see too much. All the endurance training is paying off, I guess. Or else my standard for comparison is terrible. I know it's bad, and I'd rather not remember it.

Would I want an evening of pleasure with Quin? Not really. I want more. I know I want more, and the Almighty Mother told me there's nothing wrong with that.

In my dreams, I lean against a chest with a star, enveloped in a tender hug filled with love and affection, feeling so safe in those arms. They are just dreams, but what if they're a sign? What if it's Quin? I know he doesn't have a star on his chest, but these things are symbolic.

Great. Here I go, swarmed by hopeless delusions. But what if?

I decide to leave Tarlia's window and bring the drusils another day. This is her room, her private moment, and I've already breached her privacy much more than I should have.

As I step on the ledge to return to my window, Quin's dreadful smile comes to mind again. Could I risk ruining my reputation and all my hard work just for the opportunity to spend a few hours with him? Alone with him, traveling in a carriage to a remote region. An evening away from the castle. We would get the chance to spend time together, without ears overhearing us. I would see some of the kingdom, some of the forest, the River of Tears.

And what if Quin is my kindred soul, the one in dreams, the one I hear whispering those soft words my mind can't comprehend, but my heart can?

See, there's the nonsense talking. But what if? Can I

make a stupid decision based on a tiny, tiny chance that going on this mission could bring us together?

That smile.

I step into my room and don't recognize my thoughts anymore. That's a different, crazy Astra, not the Astra who needs to be perfect, the one whose life depends on it.

But it's just one day. One trip. One chance.

A plan forms quickly in my mind.

Who am I fooling? I've had this plan for a long time, but kept burying it deep, ashamed of those rebellious thoughts.

I reach under my mattress and take the small bag with the forty silver ducks. Who would guess that shame could take the form of coins?

They are my reminder never to open my heart again. Never to be silly again. And yet. Yes, it's foolish, but I can't help it. Love, or rather, the possibility of love, is like a strange hot iron. You touch it, get burned, but then want to touch it again.

I open my door, thankful that the hallway is empty. We're not supposed to leave our wing at night, but there are always cleaning maids passing by, usually collecting laundry. Indeed I see Sofia trailing my way, carrying a pile of towels, and I beckon her.

She frowns, but approaches me. "Yes, my lady."

Lady. I wish. Oh, I wish.

I pull her hand and put three silver ducks in it. I've clung to these coins for so long, treasuring my pain, and yet all I feel now is relief to get rid of some of them. "Convince the kitchen to make passion fruit custard tomorrow for dessert at lunch, and I'll give you three more ducks."

She stares at the coins, then back at me. "I don't choose the menu, my lady."

With my hands around hers, I close the coins in. "Certainly the ducks can do some talking. I'm just... craving it." I give her an innocent smile.

Sofia looks at me up and down, in a calculating gaze, then whispers, "Seven more. For the cooks. And I want them now."

No, I can't give her my coins now. What if she doesn't do what I ask? Odd how this part of the plan, which should be the easiest, is already encountering obstacles.

I decide to remain firm, instead of trying to be friendly. "Tomorrow night. Five more." I show her the palm of my hand, as if to take back the coins. "But if you don't want the deal, I understand."

I'm applying some of what I learned in our personality class. In a negotiation, you can't show how much you care for something, or people will exploit you. You need to act as if you are ready to give up at any moment, that you don't care.

Sofia lowers her head. "You'll get your custard, my lady."

The reason I want passion fruit custard is that it's going to disguise the taste, and Tarlia doesn't like it, so only Sayanne will eat it. This is disgraceful behavior, for sure. But then, don't I deserve to give destiny a push?

The woman disappears down the hall and I ready myself to walk on the ledge once more. Am I truly going to break into my master's study and steal some poison?

The question is odd, considering I'm already outside the window.

See, there are two versions of me. One of them is giddy with excitement, willing to do whatever it takes to go on this trip, while the other is horrified, facepalming and shaking her head. I'm both of them, so I have the awful experience of being stupid and aware of my stupidity at the same time.

But then, I don't hear the Almighty Mother censoring

me, so my conclusion is that I'm on the right path. A very crooked, immoral path, but right nonetheless.

For a trip. For a chance. Perhaps a foolish chance, but I'd rather seize it and see what happens than bemoan what could have been.

I'M LEANING on his chest again, tracing my fingers over that strange star. His voice is a low, comforting rumble in my ear, while he caresses my hair with gentle strokes. The movement is so soft, so soothing—

The bells ring outside, jolting me back to my bed, where I'm alone, and yet they can't erase the feeling of his hands holding me. A phantom touch, still there, still protecting me.

These dreams have been my solace for a while now.

When my heart was broken—which was my own fault, but that's beside the point—the priestess told me about this trick of faith to see my kindred soul. I knew it wasn't dark magic, and indeed I felt the Almighty Mother's presence as I lit a candle on my windowsill and burned a strand of my hair, visualizing the sacred cords connecting souls.

Since then, he's been in my dreams. Not always, but often enough that I can close my eyes and recall his comforting presence, his warm touch.

I've never told anyone.

Master Otavio would freak out. He insists that I, more than anyone, need to show that I praise the Almighty Mother, need to show that I'm not a heathen, and yet he doesn't want me talking to the priestess. My sisters... I know they would say I'm foolish, and plus, Otavio always told me to hide my tricks of faith.

But I don't need to tell anyone. My kindred soul brings

me peace at night when I sleep. Brings me joy, even when I do something so irresponsible. If anything, I felt him closer than ever tonight, almost as if he had been truly lying beside me.

Perhaps it's a sign.

I don't want to think he's Quin, I don't want to raise that hope, but I can't help but wonder.

I just... I can still feel that love, a cocoon of protective light surrounding me, and there's no way to ignore that calling.

OUR TRAINING GROUNDS are on the roof of our tower, since so much of what we do has to remain a secret. A canopy covers part of it. Under it, there's a long table for our masters, and a small open area for training. I should consider myself lucky that on a hot summer day like today, I have to remain in the shade. It's not that I have some special privilege, but that my skin can go from beige to brown in the blink of an eye. Princess Driziely is only moderately tanned, so her substitutes have to be about the same color. I'm not going to complain that I get to train in the shade.

Neither Quin nor Sayanne are here. There's nothing unusual about that, as we are sometimes taken aside for individual training and advising, but I know they are being briefed on their trip. I also know that my plan is despicable, but I've gone too far to step back now. Step back. I'm doing quite a lot of that now. Dodge, dodge, step back, try to attack, dodge again, and dodge some more.

I need to focus on my movements because my partner is Fachin and I have to bury my memory of what I saw last night.

I'm wearing a heavy dress and wielding a training dagger, while he's mock-attacking me with a training sword. It might seem odd, but we need to mimic a real-life scenario, and Princess Driziely is not going to carry a sword or wear trousers. The idea is just to find an opening to attack, or at least get good at dodging.

I try to bury my anxiety, but it's like an itch, reminding me that I might be caught. And then, perhaps some of the anxiety is because I might *not* get caught and then I'll spend time away from the castle walls, away from this tower, close to Quin. I have absolutely no idea what's going to happen, and this lack of control is unnerving.

When the noon bell rings, I walk to the dining hall, mindful not to show any anxiety or anticipation. People tend to give themselves away, as they don't know what it means to *act natural* because they never bothered learning. I had a lot of training on that, so it shouldn't be a problem for me—at least in theory.

The dining hall occupies the entire top floor of the tower and has vaulted ceilings and tall windows. I wonder if one day this room held extravagant parties and balls, despite our isolation from the rest of the castle.

Nowadays it has some ten small round wooden tables, and it's where the Elite Guard eats, always at the same time, and if we're even ten seconds late, we'll just have to skip a meal. Our instructors and masters sit at a larger round table, from where Otavio and Andrezza are always watching us. They're already there, in fact, but I don't pay attention to them because it's not something I'd usually do.

The three princes and the princess have a table here too, even though most of them never come. Princess Driziely used to eat some meals and study with us, but she hasn't been around much lately. I feel that she doesn't like us, which is unfortunate, since our job is to protect her. But then, I don't think I would appreciate my parents training other girls to replace me in public ceremonies and even in a potential marriage, as if I were an incompetent idiot. Well, I would like to have known my family. Would like to find out who they were, at least. No point in stirring this pain.

I sit at the table reserved for the three female substitutes, where Sayanne and Tarlia are already sitting in silence. Between them, an invisible wall I can't manage to break.

From the corner of my eye, I glimpse Quin entering. I turn and give him a friendly nod, even if my natural impulse would be to ignore him, but then I wouldn't be acting natural and it would be even more suspicious. He gives me that gorgeous smile that warms my heart. I'm not crazy; it *is* for me.

And he told me he'd been assigned to Lord Stratson's wedding. Isn't that a subtle hint? Perhaps not even *that* subtle.

My life's already too complicated, considering I might have to replace the princess in a marriage alliance. It's something I try not to think about, even if I yearn for an opportunity to prove my value. And then there's that other complication about hiding who I am. I can't forget it, obviously.

Still... Do I have to look that far ahead? I should, but perhaps I can't help being foolish.

The kitchen staff comes in, pushing trays of food on metal carts. There's a chance they never made the custard, but I have a workaround for that, too. A little more complicated, but it should work.

Your plan should never depend on somebody else. See? I pay attention to what Master Otavio says. In fact, I'm just putting into practice a lot of what he's taught me. If anything, he should be proud.

Sometimes I wonder if he thinks I'm only good inside the walls of this tower, if he fears my nature will take over and then I'll spoil everything, but I won't. I know it's an honor to serve the kingdom, and I take my job seriously. One more reason why going on this trip is a brilliant idea; I'll prove my worth.

As they remove the covers from the trays, the plate with the yellow dessert emerges like a sun from behind clouds. Yes! The silver ducks ended up being useful, after all. I take my plate to serve myself, and then I think the Almighty Mother is indeed watching over me, as the perfect distraction is coming into the hall—and walking in our direction.

Prince Ziven has an odd position in the kingdom, or maybe no position. His father was the former king, but when he died, the crown went to his brother, Ziven's uncle, now King Leonius, protector of the Kingdom of Krastel.

Ziven... sometimes I wonder if he's shrewd and knows the mess he could cause if he decided to step up and demand the throne. That's hardly a problem, of course, considering most of the time he can't even step forward without stumbling.

Like the other princes, he wears a bracelet with a blue opus stone on his wrist. That stone, if activated properly, with training and meditation, can become a conduit for elemental magic. There are two common types of opus stones; water and air. There used to be one for earth as well, to help grow plants and crops, but I guess it's not destructive enough, and fell into disuse. Fire magic is too dangerous and unpredictable, said to have a will of its own, so there aren't beacon stones for that. Air magic is volatile, but some sailors have air opus stones to move their ships. In Krastel, a few royal members and rich merchants carry water opus stones.

The joke that goes around is that if his opus stone controlled alcohol, Ziven would be an expert at it. Alas, his stone controls water—or should.

In Prince Ziven's case, it controls nothing, since he never learned to use his magic.

Despite being a useless drunk, there's something about him that's strangely fascinating. I swear I tried to read the *Book of Seduction*, but it says girls like powerful, strong, confident men. Ziven is a skinny mess of wasted potential, and yet perhaps it's his almost golden, light brown hair, or his hazel eyes. None of that is unique or uncommon, but on him, it looks fascinating. His secret is a mystery to me.

I ignore him because he has never acknowledged my existence. Fascinating or not, there's nothing appealing in someone who can't see the difference between me and a wall.

Sayanne keeps staring straight ahead, her shoulders square, as if he didn't exist. Tarlia glances at him, her jaws slightly dropped, her expression wistful. I don't think she's flirting or even aware of the look she's giving him.

And that's the perfect time for me to grab some custard.

As I'm serving my plate, Ziven collides with our table and laughs. "Ladies, ladies. I'm used to seeing double. But triple?"

I take the opportunity to spread the calapher powder over the dessert, my plate covering my hand, and say, "I know, right? With me, it's my ears. I'm hearing the same joke echoing for the tenth time now."

Rude, sure, but I've always wanted to say that, and it diverts attention from my hands.

Unfazed, he laughs again and walks away.

Sayanne still ignores him, while Tarlia's eyes follow him. Would Tarlia want to bring him to her bed? For some reason I conjure the image of Ziven and her together. It doesn't look bad. I've seen him shirtless, making a fool of himself on the training grounds, and even though he's slim, he's quite fit.

"Astra, that's disgusting!" Sayanne's words startle me. "You're going to eat custard with your food?"

True. My plate has rice and chicken stew, as well as the custard, but I had no choice. I wanted to make sure I also ate it, so I had to take some before poisoning it. "I was craving it."

Sayanne raises an eyebrow. "Careful with your cravings."

"Stop it." Tarlia places her cup on the table with more force than needed. "At least she does something to appease her cravings, instead of annoying the rest of us."

Master Andrezza shoots us a glare all the way from her seat.

"Better annoying than sullying." Sayanne's tone is calm, but she's looking only at me. "When I say something, it's because I care."

"It's just custard." I pretend it's the most harmless thing in the world. "They haven't served it in months."

Tarlia eyes the plate with the dessert. "It's usually leftover from banquets, and we didn't have any lately." She taps a finger on her chin, thinking.

"More reason to enjoy our luck." I manage a relaxed chuckle, even though I'm rattled to realize I had forgotten that Tarlia is always sharp on details.

To ensure Sayanne has some of the dessert, I take a spoon and close my eyes, trying to convey a sense of bliss. "It's incredible."

Now I'm thinking about Tarlia's face last night and

wondering if I'm doing that. I really need to stop thinking about what I saw last night.

Sayanne watches me, her eyes sparkling with amusement. "Who could have guessed that chicken stew was the missing ingredient?"

It isn't.

Some of the sauce mixed with the custard and now the whole thing tastes like puke. I just wasted one of the few good desserts they serve, and now my entire lunch has turned nasty. A suitable punishment, I suppose.

They both turn quiet, that strange wall between them still standing. I hate it that every time I speak to one of them, it's as if I'm betraying the other. And then, the truth is that I *am* betraying Sayanne. If she eats the dessert, she'll be spilling her guts ten hours from now. It's quite hypocritical to even try to pretend I'm a good friend. All for a guy. And the only reason I'm not feeling guilty is because I'm still worried whether the plan will work, and maybe annoyed that she's been calling Tarlia a slut. Well, that is horrible, but then, I'm not much better.

And yet, when Sayanne finishes her meal and takes some of the dessert, I delight in the joy of seeing my genius plan unfold, instead of wallowing in any sense of guilt.

Then, to my horror, Tarlia also takes some passion-fruit custard. I want to scream *no,* and yet I can't. I can't. But I have to say something.

"It's not good," I mutter, hoping she'll take the hint.

Sayanne stares at us, while Tarlia takes a spoon, then says, "Chicken-flavored custard does sound awful, Astra."

Calapher-poisoned stew is much worse. "I thought you didn't like it," I say.

She shrugs. "Changed my mind."

I'm sure Tarlia's eating it just to spite Sayanne and leave

less for her. Why, why? The upside is that now there's no way I won't go on this trip, with the two of them sick. The downside is that guilt is chewing my insides and getting to my bones, since I can't find a way to justify what I'm doing to Tarlia.

But guilt won't change what I've done, so I try to at least appreciate my achievement and the certainty of spending hours with Quin and his gorgeous smile. I glance at him sitting at his table with the other male substitutes, his laughter lighting up the hall.

All my regrets dissipate. Instead, I take a moment to appreciate my resourcefulness. For a crazy moment, I even hope someone will uncover my plan, learn that I've broken into a study, opened a locked cabinet, come in and out, and left no trace.

See? I did pay attention to our classes on opening locks.

2

Fuzzy memories are all that remain from my dream, and yet I can still recall his hug, his chest, the feel of his skin. I let the comfort of that embrace envelop me. Nothing can shake me when I'm so deeply loved.

Before I reach the dining hall for breakfast, an attendant tells me I've been summoned to Otavio's study.

Uh-oh.

Fine. Some things *can* shake me.

It might mean nothing. Perhaps he wants to make sure I'm ready to go to Lord Stratson's wedding.

What nonsense. Had it been the case, he would have waited for me to eat. My breath stills.

When caught, there are two main strategies to consider. The first is to deny and keep denying. That's excellent when there is no proof. The trick is not to exaggerate the feeling of indignation but not to act too nonchalant about it either. Will Otavio have any proof?

The other strategy is to confess quickly, pretend to be sorry, and apologize. It sounds so humiliating. It's still the best option—sometimes the only option—when there's no way to deny what you did.

I'll have to figure out in which situation I'm in.

Still, I try to lean onto the thin hope that he doesn't know anything, that my mind is overreacting, which is a dreadful response, as it can cause us to give away our guilt. I tell myself that there's nothing to worry about, and I have no idea why he summoned me.

I descend the stairs to Otavio's study in calm steps, trying to focus on the feeling of curiosity, as if I had no clue why he's summoning me.

This study is cooler and darker than the rest of the tower, since light comes in only through a small window—the same window through which I came in last night. Before I enter, the familiar scent of books, potions, and knowledge greets me. For the first time, it's nauseating instead of comforting.

Master Otavio stands facing his massive bookshelf, his back to the door, hands clasped behind him. His long, graying brown hair is untied, and his plain black robe can't conceal his unusually stiff, tense posture. None of that bodes well.

Before I even say anything, and without turning, he says, "Close. The. Door."

His tone gives me chills. I've seen him angry before, but now his voice sounds like a blade about to slash my neck.

I can't let it intimidate me, though, and do as he asks.

"Lock it," he adds.

I could swear there's smoke coming out of his head. I face the door and turn the key slowly, reminding myself that he can't have any proof of what I've done and that everything is going to be fine. If I show even a hint of a reaction, he'll know instantly that I'm guilty.

I close the top and bottom bolts, then turn and face him.

He has also turned around, and is glaring at me. I could

swear I see murder in his blue eyes, but I steady my emotions and focus on puzzlement.

"What's happening?" My voice doesn't tremble or betray me, and I can only assume my facial expression is doing the same.

He stares at me in silence. I mean, I can't say that's a stare. It's more like he's trying to burn holes in me with his eyes.

But then, I know that's a strategy to intimidate me, to see how I react. That only calms me, as it means he's not sure of what I've done.

"I'm furious," he finally says. "And yet say one word to deny your doing, Astra, and I'll personally make sure you'll be forever expelled from the guard. Forever shunned."

That's akin to a forced confession, but I don't protest. Knowing when to remain quiet is also a good strategy.

He advances toward me, and I have to use a ton of self control not to flinch.

Eyes narrowed, he says, "You know what will happen if they find out what you are. I'm sure of that. What I'm sure you don't realize is that I might be sentenced to death for harboring you, protecting you, lying. When you take a wrong step, you risk not only your selfish skin—you risk mine. Your behavior may cast a doubt over the other substitutes too, and you could lead us all to our doom."

Could that be true? But nobody would find out.

"You don't believe it." His bitter chuckle grates my skin. "Well, they're investigating the poisoning right now. Calapher. I bet you think you're smart. Except that very few people have access to that substance. Your carelessness could lead them right to me. Now, poisoning two members of the royal guard is a serious, serious act of treason, Astra. How could you be so irresponsible? Do not deny it. You're the only person who knows about that poison."

The only one? Those classes were private, but is it possible that my sisters didn't get the same training? He might be bluffing to snatch a confession out of me. But then, perhaps I should recognize that the chances of denial working here are minimum.

He frowns, and I see concern on his face for the first time since I got here. "I have only one question. Why, Astra? Why? After everything I risked for you, everything I did to protect you, why?"

I know he has kept me hidden, and never told anyone about me. I know that if he hadn't taken me from the orphanage all those years ago, I would have perished in the fire that took it. And yet none of that has anything to do with this.

I make sure my face is blank, and ask, "What are you talking about?" I know, I know this might be the time to confess and pretend to be sorry, but I couldn't help it. I had to give it a try.

"Gather your things. You're no longer part of the Elite Guard."

He sounds serious. He can't be serious. Can't be. The edges of my vision blur, and I feel as if there's no more floor beneath me, just nothingness. Everything I've ever stood on —gone.

My heart rackets in my chest. No, he can't mean it. He wouldn't be that unfair, would he? I try to recompose myself, but anger bubbles up, disarranging my thoughts, stirring angry words. Words I've suppressed for too long.

"Fine. You want to know why? It's unfair. Unfair, Master Otavio. I have the best scores in combat, better than my sisters—"

"They're not your sisters," he roars.

I'm not sure what's the point of that, but I can change my words. "Better than my friends. I always get my answers right. I do everything, everything right. You tell me I need to be perfect, and I'm perfect. For what?"

"For what?" He laughs, as if in disbelief. "What about being alive?"

"I could have survived outside the castle." My voice is thinner than I'd like it to be.

"You wouldn't have. You would have died in the fire. If by some luck you had escaped, your purple hair would have given you away, stupid girl. Our kingdom kills darksouls. Every single one of them, even a baby, a child, is considered immoral, impure, and dangerous."

I hate to be reminded what a worthless scum I am, and that I'm lucky to be alive, since everything about me is so disgraceful.

His voice rises. "And if you survived, and by some miracle found a way to hide what you are, how would you make a living? An orphan girl. Who would have guessed? An ungrateful darksoul."

Just hearing that word makes me small, insignificant, and even dirty. In the classes we had about my kind, when I learned everything they did to humans, I always had to put into practice all my skills not to cry, not to flinch, not to shudder. And yet shame still clings to me, shame for something I had no control over.

"I just wanted to travel," I confess, my voice trembling, my eyes stinging as if I had poured vinegar on them. If this is all over, there's no point trying to pretend anything. "See a little of the world. Why do you only send my si—my friends? I'm capable too. I can be worthy of my position. I work hard for it!"

And in the end there's that, too. I work hard to prove I can be just as good, to prove that I'm not less, that I'm not tainted. I work so hard... And yet it never seems to matter. Treacherous tears now sully my eyes. Controlling tears of anger is a skill I haven't mastered yet, despite everything.

Master Otavio tilts his head and gives me a look somewhere between scorn and pity. "Are you stupid? Do you even realize why a substitute is sent on a trip instead of the princess? Do you know what's at stake?" His expression contorts in fury. "You might get killed." He takes a deep breath. "I can't allow you to risk it. You matter too much." His voice has a strange, rare, raw honesty.

The thought that he worries about me had never crossed my mind. I've always sort of seen him and Andrezza as father and mother figures, and yet he's always been so cold, so distant, always demanding perfection, always saying I'm not good enough. And yet... He cares.

A different thought then crosses my mind, and it makes me angry. "Why can the other substitutes risk it, then?"

"They're well trained." His voice is flat now.

Great. There it is. He does think I'm incompetent, despite everything. And if perfection isn't enough to prove my worth, what hope can I have? Perhaps life will be better if I leave. But what am I even going to do? Where am I going to go? Can I get a job with my knowledge about courts and kingdoms and lords? Hardly.

A cold feeling settles in my stomach, fear pricking my skin with the realization that my life is about to crumble. All because of a smile. A stupid smile that feels insignificant now that I threw my life away.

I want to double check if he means it, if I'm really expelled, but it sounds humiliating. Odd how I can still fear humiliation when I'm at such a low point.

His expression then changes to a placid calm. "Someone's coming. Get yourself together."

I breathe in and think about my kindred soul again. That's the only thing that can bring me some calm amidst this turmoil.

He opens the door and Andrezza walks in. She's so very beautiful, with brown skin, deep brown eyes, and long black hair peppered with a few strands of gray. I trust her, and her presence puts me at ease. I've often wondered if I should tell her everything, tell her what I am, and yet Master Otavio always said that she'd have me killed if she knew it. Indeed, in her classes, I got to hear her opinion about darksouls, and that should terrify me. It's confusing.

"There you are!" There's relief in her voice. "I thought all the substitutes were sick. You know well about Lord Stratson's state and his family, don't you, Astra?"

"Yes." My voice is still shaky.

She nods. "Get ready, then, as you'll need to go to his wedding reception, and the carriage leaves in forty minutes."

"I don't think it's a good idea," Master Otavio says. "We don't know what they ate, and she might get just as sick as the others."

Andrezza glances at me, then looks at him. "We'll have to risk it. You know how much our king hates failure."

Otavio lifts his shoulder in the tensest shrug I've ever seen. "Well then, let's hope she doesn't vomit on the way."

"I'll make sure she has an extra dress and a bucket in the carriage." She turns to me. "Go to your room. The attendants will get you ready."

Really? I'm not expelled? Or is Master Otavio going to wait until I'm back? My stomach then growls and I have to say something about it. "I didn't have breakfast."

Andrezza gestures at me to keep going. "I'll ask them to send something light for you in your room."

I bow and prepare to leave. When I reach the door, I hear Otavio's voice.

"Astra."

I turn.

There.

It's coming.

His face is calm, but I can see the contained rage beneath it. "Just because you were spared of whatever caused their nausea now, it doesn't mean you will be spared again. Be very, very mindful of what you eat."

I know what his words mean, and yet I need to give a reply. "We don't choose what we eat, master."

Andrezza shakes her head. "He's saying nonsense, little Astra." I never know if that's endearing or demeaning. "We still don't know what happened, and it's probably not their fault. Now go!"

I don't wait even a second.

When I reach the hallway to my bedroom, it strikes me: I did it!

I secured my place on the trip. And if Otavio's behavior in front of Andrezza is any indication, he's not going to have me expelled or punished. At least not publicly punished.

Evil deeds sometimes pay off.

TA-TUM, ta-tum, ta-tum. My heart is the loudest sound I hear.

Sometimes we practice jumping from a platform, considering one day we might need to escape through a window or balcony. I love jumping. The moment I'm in the air, with nothing beneath me, is exhilarating but also scary, since I can't guarantee I will land properly and distribute the force of the land into a perfect roll.

It's how I feel now, except that descending the tower's spiral stairs takes much longer than a second—and my anticipation mounts with each step. So many interminable stone steps.

Two guards escort me, and a servant follows with my bag and a bucket. We're always watched, always escorted when stepping away from our tower. I'm wearing a thin, dark blue linen dress with short sleeves. It's a cool, practical dress, perfect for travel, but it's still adorned with expensive rose-shaped embroidery.

The carriage is a simple black thing by the side entrance, lacking the opulence expected from Krastel's royalty, but the idea is to be discreet when traveling. Sure, in theory the substitutes' lives are expendable, but it's going to be too obvious if they put us in a pompous carriage, with a sign on top of it saying *attack me*.

Then again, there are no attacks and no dangers. Krastel isn't at war with anyone. I don't know why Master Otavio is so worried.

Right. He's not worried, he just thinks I'm incompetent. How easily my mind plays tricks on me, constructing a fictional version of events and trying to convince me that people care more about me than they actually do. Sometimes I'm an idiot.

Is that what I'm doing with Quin? Well, at least I'll find out. He's not here yet, so I enter the carriage and wait.

And that's why my heart is making such a ruckus in my chest. It's the anticipation, fear, and also the judgemental part of me still shaking her head in disbelief. She's going to ruin her neck like that.

Of course I feel bad for what I've done, for making my sisters sick, but I don't believe for a moment that I could have gotten Master Otavio killed. It was all lies. Nobody knows what kind of poison was used because the healers aren't familiar with calapher. At least that's what Otavio told me, and he wouldn't be lying when teaching me about poisons.

See, I might have to assassinate or incapacitate someone one day, probably my husband, if I marry in place of Princess Driziely, and I can't leave a trace or raise any suspicion. My master would never claim that a poison is rare if it isn't. At the same time, I doubt he has never taught my sisters about calapher, considering they might be the ones who'll need to assassinate or incapacitate someone one day.

It's odd. While the idea of killing a person is revolting, I wouldn't mind an opportunity to be useful to my kingdom, to prove my worth. Sometimes, I even hope that an act of bravery might change the way they see me, that I might be accepted despite being a darksoul. I know it's nonsense, but I still yearn for the chance to prove my value.

As murderous thoughts of glory cross my mind, the door of the carriage opens and I remind myself to act natural. Act natural, act natural, and yet, my stomach flutters at the anticipation of spending so much time with Quin.

I turn—and realize it's not him.

My stomach lurches, even my heart slows down under the weight of such enormous disappointment. I can't believe it.

Prince Ziven sits there, his light brown hair somewhat messy but still beautiful, giving me a smile that's a hundred times warmer than Quin's, giving me the look that I've always dreamed someone would give me. His hazel eyes are full of adoration, joy, intimacy.

Of course, none of that is for *me*. His expression sours in less than a second, and he turns and stares at the window.

Surprising. Was he... He and Sayanne... Could it be? Really?

I remember then how he bumped into our table yesterday, how much he's been having lunch with the Elite Guard lately, and it makes sense. Even then, I'm surprised that Sayanne would manage to seduce him. Or maybe it's something mutual, something real.

I feel that I have to explain what's going on. "Sayanne's indisposed."

He turns and looks at me like I'm an insect. "Did I ask? I don't care."

Rude, rude, rude. I wish I could get near his table and poison his food, add something for diarrhea. Maybe there's a way.

"Great, then." I smile and turn to the window. There's nothing to see, just the side wall of the castle, and yet it's more interesting than the interior of the carriage with that grumpy prince.

Still, his words make me feel small and insignificant and worthless. Why would an opinion from a drunk, useless prince bother me? It shouldn't.

I'm quite impressed with Sayanne, though.

I recall her a few years ago, her eyes shining with an odd fervor, her arms grabbing the *Book of Seduction*. We were so young. And yet, I'll never forget what she said. "This is the key. For everything."

I can still see the determined glint in her eyes, her certainty.

Was it the secrets in the book that got Prince Ziven interested in her? I'll have to read it again, if that's the case. Perhaps her feelings for him are genuine, but she definitely must have applied what she learned. Stupid me, ignored all that, and now I have to cling to the faint hope that a friendly smile means more than it seems.

But the worst is that my carefully, masterfully enacted plan flopped. All my effort—for nothing.

"Why are you here?" I ask. I don't bother being polite because he doesn't deserve it.

He leans back in his seat, all relaxed and aloof, not once turning in my direction. "Why do you care?"

"It should be someone standing in for Prince Aramel."

"Isn't that what I'm doing?" He points at his chest. "Here as myself."

He's not drunk and doesn't smell of alcohol. Well, it's early, and perhaps he had no plans to drink on this trip. What were he and Sayanne up to? The worst is that I can't ask him.

I snort. "I'm sure Lord Stratson will be delighted to see you."

Ziven turns to me, a cutting smile on his face. "Yes, he'll be so happy. He'll say, oh, they sent the useless bum. But at least I'm the real thing. Of course, there's always a chance our carriage gets attacked, in which case our king will be the one who'll be more than delighted."

He might have a point—a dreadful point—but I can't change any of that, so I try to focus on our assignment. "Did you bring the wedding gift?"

He blinks. "Gift? What gift? Oh, the stupid drunk doesn't know what he's supposed to do. Is that what you think?"

I just stare at him, and then he pulls something from his coat pocket. It's a golden chalice decorated with a large, clear stone.

"Here, a special magical gift!" He holds the chalice with

one hand and waves another over it, making a dramatic voice. "It can tell you if there's poison in your drink!"

The carriage moves, and there goes my hope that someone would get this wacko out of here and call Quin.

Ziven laughs. "The perfect gift for when you want to kill someone, since beacon stones don't work."

True. They're supposed to change color and turn red to indicate danger, but the few remaining beacon stones are clear and never do anything. I think they need to be activated, like the opus stones, but the knowledge on how to do that has been lost. And yet...

"They're still rare relics," I say.

He stares at the chalice. "Useless, rare relics. A symbol of something that's gone. Of course, a dandy gift to please a small lord."

Small, but somewhat important. "Stratson's state is near our northern borders. That's a key area."

Ziven puts the chalice back in his pocket and waves a hand. "Yeah, yeah, yeah. Please spare me your useless knowledge."

"At least I have *some* knowledge, Your Highness. Do you also tell Sayanne that?"

His face is placid as he blinks. "I have no idea who that is."

Interestingly, he truly sounds like he doesn't know her. Still, he doesn't convince me. He could have taken some personality classes. Would he, though? Who would teach him that?

I can lie well, but I practiced that a lot.

The day I first heard Otavio explaining that humans, like fae, can't lie, is a day I'll never forget, as it changed my perception of people.

While fae can't lie with words, humans can't lie with

their tone of voice, expression, gestures. We tend to give ourselves away. This is why fae excel at tricking people. They can twist words to make you think you hear something that's not there. Since they speak confidently even when misleading, human ears and eyes, trained to notice tone and gestures more than words, get tricked easily.

Now us, we can say anything we want, but our face, voice, and movements betray us. We're at a bigger disadvantage than the fae, unless we train to lie and not show. For the substitutes like me, who might one day have to pretend to be someone else, it's an imperative skill, drilled through hours and hours of practice.

Ziven doesn't give any indication that he's lying when he says he doesn't know who Sayanne is. Perhaps he has learned how to lie on his own. But why? That doesn't sound like the action of a mindless drunk. Who could have guessed that there's so much more behind that fascinating, pretty face?

***

EXCITED AND EXHILARATED, I keep my eyes out the window, my ears alert, as we slowly leave the city by the castle, and then travel through farms and fields. And then more farms and fields. After some time, everything looks the same, and all I want is to puke the dry toast I ate. Good thing we have a bucket.

As to Ziven, no face is fascinating after three hours in an enclosed space, without even talking. I eye the bucket on the floor, wondering if carrying something like that is normal, since he never asked about it, or if it's because he doesn't want to talk to me.

A small retinue with four guards accompanies us, the sound of hooves clopping on the road making me drowsy.

Ziven is quiet and grumpy. Well, too bad. It's his fault he took Quin's place. Now we have to barely tolerate each other for hours and hours. My plan now seems so foolish, and the worst is that I betrayed Master Otavio's trust for nothing.

Not nothing. For a nausea-inducing boring trip with a prickly prince.

Perhaps this is the punishment for my deeds. At least I learned that there's something between Prince Ziven and Sayanne, not that the information serves me for anything.

If I had known it, I would never have gotten in the way. But then, he's being such an idiot, perhaps it's deserved. Destiny can be weird.

Ziven taps on the window, and a guard approaches.

The prince asks, "Where are we going?"

The guard is a young lad, no more than seventeen. "Lord Stratson's estate, your highness."

"I know that." Ziven grunts. "Why aren't we taking the shortcut?"

Shortcut. Does he mean... I look outside, and see a high mountain on our left. This is the road north, and that must be Mount Eye. The road surrounds it, unless...

The guard swallows. "My lord, our orders—"

Visibly irritated, Ziven huffs. "I'm not traveling for two extra hours. Let's take the bridge. It's an order."

The carriage stops, and I hear murmurs of disagreement among the guards and the coachman. Prince Ziven outranks them all, but I don't think any of them is too pleased at having to obey him.

The guards don't return to talk to the prince, but I sense the carriage moving forward, then turning onto a smaller road.

Excitement bubbles up in my chest. We're going to cross the River of Tears and enter the fae territory. Our side has a mountain by the river, so the road has to go around it, but the fae side is much quicker. Merchants have taken this shortcut for a long time now without any issue.

Since King Renel assumed the throne of the Crystal Court, the relationship between fae and humans has been friendly. True that he has never been to our castle or invited anyone from our kingdom to visit his court, but then, fae are so different from us. Plus, his castle is said to move from place to place, so it's never in the same location. Personally, I'd love it if our castle could travel. Alas, it's not the case.

In Renel's case, people say that his magic can't ground his castle, or else that he's hiding from his evil brother, the disgraced Prince Marlak. It's a horrific story.

From what I learned, the younger and now disgraced prince looks human despite being a full-blooded fae. An aberration, some claim. According to rumors, he possesses all four types of elemental magic, an incredibly unique gift. Too bad that his gift was squandered. Twelve years ago, Prince Marlak burned alive his mother, sister, and adoptive father, getting burned with his own magic in the process. He escaped, but not without emptying the Crystal Court of all its relics. Among them is the shadow ring, an artifact that can make him impervious to any magic attack.

I think I'd run away from him too.

But the disgraced prince hasn't been seen in years. The path is safe, and the Crystal Court has never cared about us stepping into their territory to avoid detouring for hours.

I'm going to see the Fae Kingdom! This is so exciting.

That's one upside of poisoning my sisters. The horrible thought makes me squirm with guilt. As if guilt or shame could change anything. Well, I'm here. My company is dreadful, but I'll get to cross the River of Tears.

The carriage then slows down almost to a halt. I ignore all my training on how to act princessly and stand up, or at least as up as I can in this carriage, keeping myself steady with one hand on the ceiling and another on the seat. There's a bridge up ahead of us, but it's so... improvised. Decrepit. I'm guessing Krastel or the Crystal Court never officially built a bridge here, for some reason. What I see ahead of me are some long wood planks put together that fit only one carriage. There aren't even any railings on the sides.

Either the planks squeak or I imagine that they do when the carriage goes over them. I look down and see the river, deep down within its shallow canyon. The height is not too much from here, but it's enough to mark a chink on the soil, a true division between human and fae lands.

It might sound funny how I see myself as a human, but it's how I was raised. Master Otavio always told me that darksouls are human, a bit different perhaps, but the same race. I know that I heard something different in our history classes, but it's not like we have pointy ears. And we can lie. So that's why I say *us* when meaning humans. I know it's an *us* to which I don't really belong, but I don't think anyone sees themselves as *the other*. I can't belong to something unfamiliar, and yet I feel that I belong to a group that would never accept me.

I know. Makes no sense. My solution to avoid thinking about it is to practice, study, memorize facts. Tons of facts. For instance, this river is some ten feet deep, even though it's so narrow.

I'm glad when I can only see dirt under us, and know that we've crossed the bridge. From here, the road turns and borders the river, edging grasslands on the other side. I try to look into the distance, see more of the fae land, but all I glimpse are some green hills. As we move further along, the grasslands are slowly replaced by a forest, and what an incredible forest. Perhaps it's my imagination, but I can swear the colors here are more vivid, with leaves a deeper green than on the Krastel side.

The forest gets closer and closer to us, fig trees spreading their twirly branches, golden and rose tree trumpets flowering, filling the landscape in color. There are also tall kapoks and eucalyptus, so many other types of trees, and so much ground vegetation. It feels untamed, wild, unpredictable, and yet I can feel a quiet power emanating from all that greenery.

When I look back and think about Krastel's side, the farm fields feel dead. I know they are food and life and work, and yet there's no power of nature there, as if it had been buried. And then, I like to eat, so I'm thankful for all the farms. The fae have farms on their side too, although some of it is within forest grounds, but then I doubt it would look so wild.

I wish I could get out of the carriage and step foot in that untouched soil, but that's a pointless wish, and would ruin my perfect princess dress. I still have a job to do here, and I'd better do it fantastically well. Maybe there's still a chance Otavio will change his mind about me. If not him, perhaps Andrezza will let me take assignments more often.

Still, the earthy, fresh smell of flowers and leaves is relaxing, invigorating, and being here, by this magnificent forest, feels like a gift.

I'm drinking in the view, when something feels amiss.

It's as if a cloud covered the sun, and yet the sky is just as bright as before. The air feels heavier, strange. I'm about to turn to Prince Ziven to ask if he noticed something, when one of the horses neighs, then gallops away, followed by more horses. From my window, I see that our guards are disappearing down the road.

The carriage stops abruptly, and then two more horses run away, one of them with the coachman. I guess he detached the horses pulling the carriage and we're stuck here.

What are they running from? It could be robbers, but on this side of the river? And why would the guards just run? Unless it's something they planned.

No, I can feel something different in the air, something chilly crawling under my skin.

I turn to Ziven to see his reaction.

He laughs. "Impressed with the bravery of our guards?"

"Why would they do that?"

"Why?" Ziven's hazel eyes are wide. "Why would they risk their lives for us? If I get killed, they might get a medal or something." His tone is playful, but he can't hide the hint of fear bubbling under his words.

I try to think, recall everything I learned in our defense and combat classes, but nothing makes sense. Robbers wouldn't just approach a heavily guarded carriage—and wouldn't spook the horses like that. There's something magical outside, but what?

At the risk of sounding stupid, I voice my question. "Any idea what's out there?"

"We're screwed, fake cousin, that's what we are."

No kidding. "I'm glad you're telling me that. It really hadn't crossed my mind." Then I change my tone. "We'd better get out."

Yes, because a carriage is usually a big target. It can provide a fast escape, but not when our horses are gone, and any protection from arrows won't make up for the risk in remaining here like sitting ducks.

I touch the handle, meaning to open the door, but it's so cold that I have to pull my hand away. There's ice around it, ice keeping the door shut, ice locking us in. Someone's using elemental magic against us—but who? And why?

Ziven is looking down, thoughtful instead of scared. I take my dagger and try to pry open the door, but the layer of ice covering it is too thick. At least I'm holding a dagger. Right. As if it could do anything against magic of this caliber.

The frosted and fogged window doesn't let me see much, but I hear slow steps coming toward us and strong wind. No, not wind. Air magic.

The ice then cracks and breaks in less than a second. I'm about to open the door, when it's removed from its hinges by a gust of wind.

A young man stands outside. Human, not fae, wearing a black tunic, his shoulder length curly black hair parted on the side with some of it shaved around his left, round ear, showing tattoos and a scar on his head. A long burn scar, in fact, going down to his neck, then his exposed forearm and continuing until his left hand, which is adorned with rings.

All my hours of study aren't even necessary now. Human looking, in fae territory, scarred, able to wield both air and water, that has to be King Renel's brother, the disgraced Prince Marlak. Yep, he's wearing a ring with a stone that looks like a stormy sky—the Shadow Ring. The sight chills my bones.

I use all my self control not to tremble or flinch, and yet all my mind can do is echo Ziven's words: *We're screwed.*

3

Calm down. Calm down. When facing danger, we should keep our heads in charge, instead of giving in to panic.

What is Prince Marlak doing here?

Why is he targeting us?

These questions are important, I know they are, and yet, for a fraction of a second that feels like an eternity, I'm enthralled by the disgraced prince's eyes, so dark they look like a bottomless lake.

The prince is neither ugly nor beautiful; he's strangely entrancing like a too heavy cloud, filled with thunder and lightning, holding a destructive tempest. We know it's deadly, and yet… Perhaps the word indeed is *beautiful,* except that it's not usually used like that. And then, he's also terrifying.

Terrifying. Enough to pump my heart into action and break me out of that daze. I need to do something. The priestess comes to mind, and her tricks of faith. *My* tricks of faith, and I surrender to the Almighty Mother. Light. She's the light in the dark.

Light. Light. Light.

A ball of it materializes in front of Prince Marlak. At the same time, a jet of water hits him, I'm not sure from where. I seize the chance and hurl the bucket at him. It doesn't hit the target, as the fae prince blocks it somehow, perhaps with air magic, but I don't have time to look because I slide to the other side and jump out the door Ziven has opened. Is his magic finally being triggered into working? That won't defeat Marlak, but could buy us some time.

My only guess is that the disgraced fae prince wants to kidnap Ziven, and I can't let that happen. My honor as a member of the Elite Guard depends on it.

Ziven is running by the river canyon, heading towards a large tree lying across it. An improvised bridge! All fae magic is weaker on our side, so crossing the river might save us.

My princess shoes are terrible for running, despite all the training I've had with them. It's just that the ground is uneven, with loose gravel and small rocks.

Ziven turns and extends a hand toward me. Maybe it's weird, but right now, everything is, and I let him pull me closer, until our chests are almost touching, and we're soon enveloped in a round wall of ice.

This is definitely not a spur of magic driven by panic. Still, the wall is already cracking. His feat might only grant us a few seconds.

"We need to plan," Ziven whispers.

Plan. Plan. In less than a second. "Can you encase him in ice?"

"It won't hold."

"Do it. When he breaks it, I'll dazzle him with light, and you throw an ice dagger." That would require an incredible proficiency in magic, but somehow, I'm sure Ziven has it, and the fact he doesn't argue confirms it. "We then run in opposite directions. Go to the river, cross it, and I'll head to the forest. Give me the chalice. He could be after that, and I'll let him chase me."

Ziven frowns, but gives me the relic. I hide it in one of my dress pockets.

"It's my job," I add.

"It's wrong," he protests. "We—"

Our ice wall shatters, and I turn to see Marlak staring at us, an eyebrow raised. "Apologies for disturbing your romantic moment."

Ugh. I'm pretending to be Ziven's cousin—but the fae prince might not know that. I see a wall of ice forming around Marlak, and yet I know that it's not going to work. Why did I suggest that stupid plan?

I bolt towards the trunk over the river. It's not that I want to escape, it's that I have a new plan. Glancing behind me, I see Ziven surrounded by ice. Even his opus stone is covered, which means he's defenseless. Now, Marlak would want to kidnap, not kill him. But I have a hunch that's not what he wants.

"You want this?" I raise the chalice. "Come and get it."

I step onto the makeshift bridge. To my dismay, Ziven falls down, unconscious. I hope Marlak used his air magic to make him pass out, but didn't kill him. Please don't be dead. I can't imagine what Master Otavio will tell me if a prince dies under my watch. I can't imagine what Sayanne will feel.

I need to hold on to the hope that Ziven just fainted, and not dwell on the fact that this disgraced prince is a family murderer.

A wall of ice blocks my way forward on the bridge, and I feel a gust of air lifting me. I need to focus and call upon the Almighty Mother.

Light. Light can break magic.

A brilliant bubble surrounds me, shielding me from the

wind, but I'm not even sure what I'm doing at this point. My plan had been to draw Marlak away from Ziven, but it might have been in vain. Am I going to risk my life for a useless relic? Then again, if the fae prince is after it, there must a reason.

My moment of doubt ruins my shield, and I feel air enveloping me and bringing me back to the riverbank, towards the disgraced prince.

Since he has the Shadow Ring, magic won't affect him, which is why a wall *around* him could work. The physical effect of magic can work too. I focus and channel my inner faith, my connection with the Almighty Mother, and create a burst of light right as I throw my dagger.

Even with one hand shielding his eyes, Marlak stops the dagger at the very last second, and all it does is graze his shoulder—and rip his tunic.

What I see horrifies me.

His chest is covered in scars, a continuation of the burn marks covering his arm and neck, some of them adorned with tattoos. But it's not the fact that he's scarred that shakes me—it's the shape of the scars.

I've seen it—many, many times.

On his chest, they form a star.

I'M LYING on a warm chest where I feel so safe, my fingers caressing his skin, tracing a beautiful star on it. Some of it is scarred tissue, some of it are tattooed lines forming a delicate pattern.

His hands caress my hair, that soothing touch, and I meet his deep, dark eyes. Eyes like a bottomless lake.

No, no, no. I'm in the dream, enjoying it, and at the same time watching it, horrified.

Perhaps if I yell I'll wake myself, or at least the bizarre version of me who's been dreaming about this murderous maniac.

"No!"

My eyes snap open, and I bottle down the remaining scream, even though I still hear it echoing in my head. I'm lying on a strange bed of leaves, in a small cave. Rock walls surround me except for an opening ahead, from where sunlight comes in. My wrists and ankles are restrained with ice, and yet I don't feel its cold biting me.

Prince Marlak is crouched, staring at me in puzzlement, twirling my dagger. He doesn't wear a tunic anymore, and his chest is quite visible. There's no doubt that it's the chest I've been dreaming about, and now I just want to dig a hole and hide until the end of all eras.

"You. You tried to kill me." At least his voice is not like the one in my dreams. It's anything but soft or smooth.

This has to be the world's strangest coincidence. Or some curse. Maybe there is someone with the same star and I'm overreacting. I need to stop thinking about these visions—right now. Especially when so much has happened. So much. I think about Prince Ziven and my body coils with rage.

"You killed my friend!" Perhaps he didn't, but I want to see his reaction.

Marlak snorts and waves a hand. "I didn't kill that useless prince."

Useless prince. So he knows who he is—and likely thinks I'm Princess Driziely.

"They'll pay you well to return me."

He laughs and tilts his head. "Except they won't. Because your job is to die to save a spoiled princess, isn't it?"

He can't know. There's no way he would know. The secret about the substitutes never leaves the Elite Tower. "I *am* the princess." I need to stick to that, as it might be the difference between life and death. "And I was just trying to gain time, not kill you. I don't even have the skills for that."

"If you want to pretend, pretend." He shrugs and the movement reminds me of my dreams again, how he sometimes moves his arms and holds me tighter.

Not him. The dream man. Ugh. I had never truly understood the meaning of *awkward* until now. Why? Why?

He extends a hand with the chalice we were taking to Lord Stratson. "Take this. I don't want it."

Well, that's just nonsensical. "Why then would you attack a royal carriage from a friendly kingdom?"

"Friendly? To me? I'm not part of the Crystal Court, in case you didn't study that."

Study? That could be a normal assumption about what a princess does, but it seems that he knows I'm a substitute and even some of what I do.

He adds, "Also, you're not in your territory, and had no indication that you were royalty—fake or real. For all I know, you could be a threat to our land. So I'm not breaching the River of Tears Treaty."

At least his voice is completely different. Baritone, like in my dreams, but harsh, not soothing and loving. I need to forget those dreadful dreams—or rather, nightmares.

"What do you want, then?" I forget to hide the anger in my voice, which is quite stupid.

His eyes widen in mock surprise. "So much bite for someone whose hands and feet are restrained."

I notice that there are strips of fabric between me and the ice, and wonder if he did that to make me comfortable. Make me comfortable, right. I'm hallucinating here.

Well, it feels like it, when everything is so ludicrous and doesn't make any sense.

"Let me go, then. Are you afraid of me?"

"It's not fear." He raises the dagger. "Although I have good reason to be cautious. It's to make things easier."

Make what easier? Oh no. No, no, no.

For the first time I realize I'm alone with a strange and dangerous man, away from anyone who could help me. I also realize I completely forgot to control my face, as he raises his hands, showing his palms.

"Hey, hey. I'm not going to hurt you. Or force you to do anything. I'm not *that* kind of monster."

I'm startled and terrified. His *hey, hey* almost sounded like... No, I'm imagining it.

"What do you want?" There's no more threat in my words, just frustration, or perhaps hopelessness.

I give up trying to understand what's going on. He doesn't want the chalice, and he can't be meaning to kidnap me, if he thinks I'm worthless. I hate it when things make no sense, when I can't predict what's about to come.

"Information," he says. "It won't hurt."

His words chill me as they sink in slowly. Does he have mind magic?

Can he peer into my thoughts?

I feel as if an ice storm forms in my lungs.

Panic. Sheer panic takes over me. He'll see it. I just know he'll see it. I have to stop him.

I relax my face and attempt to erase all traces of fear in it. "Isn't it easier to ask? I doubt I have any secrets that would interest you."

"Apologies, but I don't have time to sift through your lies. I'll be gentle." And his voice *is indeed* gentle, just to make everything even more awkward.

His hand approaches my temple. Involuntarily, I flinch and move my head, but then a layer of ice holds it in place.

"Stop it. I told you it won't hurt." He sounds exasperated but kind at the same time. "I won't see anything private. I'll just glimpse something small. Don't be afraid." Now he sounds like Otavio when I was a child and he had to inject something on my face.

But I'm terrified. Because I know it. He'll see it.

Then I sense his index and middle finger touching my temple—and all my fears vanish at once.

The feeling is the most wonderful ever, soothing, calming, as I'm lying down on his chest. Marlak's chest. He holds me tight with both arms, and I feel enveloped in an energy of love, so strong that it could make me invincible. Here there's no fear, no strife, no suffering. It's pure light.

He kisses my forehead, then my cheek, and our lips meet. So much love in that kiss.

Something snaps, and I open my eyes. Prince Marlak has one eyebrow raised and stares at me, partly in surprise, partly in bewilderment, as if he can't make sense of what just happened.

Well, neither can I.

I realize that embarrassment can't kill a person, but I'm not sure staying alive to deal with the outcome is that much of a tradeoff.

He still stares at me. Perhaps it's horror on his face. Well, I'm horrified, too.

At least he's the one to break the silence. "I'm... flattered. That's..." He frowns, as if searching for the words. "Incredibly sweet, Astra."

How does he know my name? Not that it's the most pressing issue right now.

He smirks, then. "Your talent is quite phenomenal, but you're still no match for me."

Talent? He thinks I'm doing it on purpose? That's disturbing. I don't have time to protest, as he touches my temple again.

All discomfort is gone. We're lying down on a bed of stars and kissing.

Thankfully, this time the awkwardness lasts just a few seconds, before I open my eyes again.

He scoffs and shakes his head. "You think your tricks are impressive, don't you? You think you're smart."

Tricks? Of course. He doesn't know I'm not doing it on purpose and thinks this is a distraction, to hide whatever nonsense I would want to hide.

Odd, but you know what? I think I prefer this much-less embarrassing explanation than the truth.

Yes, take that, evil prince! You won't overcome my powerful mind shield.

As if. But I'll run with it.

I smile and try to raise one eyebrow, even though I can't raise it the way he does. "Oh. So did you find what you were looking for?"

He looks away, sighs, then stares at me and narrows his eyes. "You're forcing my hand. I was *choosing* to be gentle. One more time, and if I were you, I'd drop this pretense."

I can't do this anymore, or maybe I'll truly die with embarrassment. "Just ask what you need to know. Like a normal person—or fae."

"I'm anything but normal. And you have one more chance."

I shut my eyes and try to think about something else. Drusils. Passion-fruit custard. Yikes, vomit-tasting passion-fruit custard—and then it's all gone.

45

There's a light surrounding me, and part of me knows it's not good, not good, I have to stop it, but a bigger part of me knows that this is the real truth.

Marlak is lying down on a bed of dried leaves, slanted rays illuminating his beautiful chest, his lovely arms. I'm on top of him, and lean down to kiss his soft lips, my nipples touching his warm chest and the thin hair covering it. I feel him harden between my legs, so warm, so perfect.

The image stops and yet my eyes are still shut. The only reason I don't beg the Almighty Mother to kill me right now is because that would be blasphemy.

Did I just picture me and this prince almost having sex right in this cave? The light in the vision was prettier for sure, and his scars shone from within, looking magnificent. *He* looked magnificent.

I'm feeling mortified, but I can't let him notice it.

I dare open my eyes and smirk. "So my skills are no match for yours?"

He's looking away, his expression a mask. "No clue. I think you almost tried to check *my* skills." Finally he turns to me, frowning.

Puzzlement, frustration, annoyance. I'm not sure what to make of his face, but I'm glad he didn't mention what he just saw. Despite the sexual image he must have seen, I don't think he's going to take advantage of me or use the vision as an excuse to make any lewd comments, and that's a huge relief.

By the Mother, our standards are so poor that I'm glad I'm not at risk of being raped. But I *am* thankful for that. That said, I don't know what he's going to do now. Perhaps I made everything worse by teasing him, but that's still better than letting him think I'm attracted to him.

I mean, he does have something fascinating going on,

but there's no way to put *sexy* and *family murderer* in the same sentence. Not to mention he attacked our carriage, hurt Prince Ziven, and is holding me captive now. At least he thinks this is some kind of smart trick to prevent him from seeing my thoughts. Let it remain that way.

His face could be made of stone for the way he glares at me. "I warned you. Unfortunately, I won't be as gentle."

Frankly, I don't care. *Here, see all my thoughts, just make this embarrassment stop.* This is the most mortifying experience of my life, and when he touches my head again, it's a relief. I'm ready to lay all my thoughts bare for him. My ability to care, my sense of duty, my honor, they're all gone.

Light surrounds me, but my hands are on the ground, over soft leaves and lavender flowers. I feel safe, protected, powerful, even in a position that should convey powerlessness. Marlak's hands cup my breasts, and they're so large that they cover them completely, while his teeth bite my ear, sending shivers down my spine. I feel his length by my slit, teasing me, a strange kind of agony and delight. I want him more than anything in the world. My thoughts, my feelings, they disappear. All that's left is my body and that aching need.

Then, in one swift stroke, he enters me. There's pain, but it's subtle and delightful, soon turned into pleasure, a raw, wild feeling of being taken like an animal, like the wild fae forest I love so much.

Delightful pleasure, as I feel him inside me, then moving back slowly, and shoving in again hard, each time harder, each time faster. Every thrust dissolves me, undoes me, uncoils me.

His beautiful, fascinating power enters me, breaks me, rips away all my fears. His strength is unleashed, desire unleashed, all for me, out of control, and then it explodes in a ball of light. So much light inside me, light around us. For a moment, we're one. There's nothing more wonderful than this moment, this now. There's no better feeling than this wonderful, magical release, unwinding me open.

I open my eyes and feel that my body is completely relaxed, that wonderful feeling still within me, almost as if it had been real. I had never felt like that when having sex—but then it was never a crazy vision.

His voice startles me. "Impressive. Quite impressive." He then gets up and leaves the cave, his steps heavy.

I want to cover my face with my hands, but I can't because of these stupid ice manacles. It's not shame. The vision didn't feel shameful; it felt wonderful—which is a thousand times worse.

I can't imagine what's going through his mind right now. Well, he's the one who told me he wasn't going to be gentle and maybe got the idea in my head. Why is this happening?

The sound of dry leaves cracking startles me. The ice around me then starts to melt.

Ziven is standing there, and puts a finger over his lips.

***

Stunned that Ziven came to rescue me, I follow him in silence, careful to keep my steps as quiet as possible. He's silent and agile, a far cry from the clumsy, drunk prince who sometimes visits the Elite Tower.

It turns out that we weren't deep into the forest, and soon I see the river and the log across it. Before crossing, I glance back, fearing that Marlak would chase us, but there's nobody, just our broken carriage blocking part of the dirt road.

On the other side, we encounter uneven terrain: jagged

rocks and bushes, making up the base of Mount Eye. I look back again, and still see no trace of the disgraced fae prince. We climb up more jagged rocks until we reach a narrow trail, from where I can gaze down at the river and the vast expanse of the wild fae forest.

Ziven walks ahead of me, his hair almost golden under the sun, and yet for some reason I don't find him fascinating the way I used to.

Odd. Did I only admire him when I thought he was a drunkard? And he saved me!

Then again, knowing that there's something between him and Sayanne might explain my different perception.

Only after we walk some ten minutes, when I don't think Marlak is going to attack us again, I dare exhale in relief.

Ziven stops and stares at me, his brows creased in worry. "Are you all right?"

"Yes."

"What did he do to you?"

Tons of imaginary things. Not that anyone will ever rip that information from me. "Nothing," I say, then realize I need to elaborate. "Well, he tried to see my thoughts, but I didn't let him." The path is wider now, sloping down, and I move beside him, burying all memories of the way I "blocked" Marlak.

"What did he want?"

"I don't know." And it's true. I didn't get a single inkling of what his goal was. Perhaps I should have pressed.

Right. As if I was in any condition to try anything. The worst, the very worst, is that I'm still feeling wonderful. My body thinks I just had the time of my life.

"I got the chalice." Ziven takes it from his pocket and holds it. "Not sure why he left it behind."

"He gave it back to me. Didn't want it."

Ziven frowns. "What was the point, then?"

"Whatever he wanted to get from my mind, but I don't know what."

The prince bites his lip. "Maybe he found something. He left you and went for a swim in a pond. Who leaves a captive and goes for a swim? Unless he didn't care anymore because he was satisfied with what he got."

Satisfied. Oh, dear. Was he? I definitely want to disappear.

"Are you sure you don't know what he wanted?" Ziven insists.

"I don't think he got it. He left the cave annoyed. He's probably arrogant enough that he didn't think you would find me." That's my theory, at least.

Ziven's face is thoughtful. "I don't know." He pauses, then asks, "And what was that magic you did?"

Magic? Oh. "You mean the light? A trick of faith. Any person can do what I did."

"You really think that?" He lets out an amused chuckle.

"It's what the priestess says. You can ask her. And what about *your* magic?"

His face changes all of a sudden, becoming that same indifferent, unfriendly mask he wore before. "You can't tell anyone about it. I won't tell anyone about your magic, either."

"Mine's not magic."

"Oh. You want to put it to the test? Do you know anyone who can cast light like that?"

"I don't know many people." I shrug.

"It's unheard of. You keep doing human magic without opus stones, they'll think you're a darksoul."

I have to control myself not to tremble but I manage it, even if his words have shaken me to the core.

"Darksoul magic needs blood," I say, keeping my tone light and disinterested. "And it's dark. That's not what I did, is it?"

If there's one thing I'm sure of is that I have none of the evil magic of my kind. None of the evil heart.

"I guess not." Ziven stares at me, his expression serious. "We need to agree on a story, tell people something they'll believe."

I was considering telling the truth, omitting all the magic, but perhaps it won't make much sense. "We can say he attacked us and left us unconscious by the river."

His hazel eyes are distant, as if considering thousands of possibilities. "They'll wonder how we escaped. They'll wonder what he wanted."

"Well, *I'm* wondering what he wanted, and wouldn't mind some help figuring it out."

He glares at me. "Do you want to tell them about our magic?"

I exhale. He's right, and there are way too many things I'll never dare tell anyone about my encounter with Marlak.

An idea comes to mind. "We say he mistook us for a fae convoy and attacked it, but let us go once he realized we were Krastel nobles. It explains how we escaped. That said, if Marlak is going to start attacking human carriages using the Fae Path, people need to be warned."

"I don't think he's going to start attacking random people. He wanted something very specific, Astra." I am quite surprised he knows my name. "And royalty aren't supposed to take the shortcut anyway, so there's no risk."

"Fair, I guess." I'm still not sure I shouldn't tell at least part of the truth to my masters. Perhaps Marlak is after beacon stones or some type of relics. Then again, perhaps I could research it myself. There is something else I need to say. "You were brave back there, rescuing me. Thanks."

"Oh, that." He waves a dismissive hand. "My only thought was that he wanted to kidnap me, mistaking me for one of my cousins, but then King Leonius wouldn't lift a finger to rescue me and I would end up floating belly down on the River of Tears."

"You didn't have to go back and save me."

"Of course I did." His eyes widen. "The king wouldn't pay anything to get you back either."

"I know that! But you could have run and saved yourself."

He chuckles. "Don't you find it sad? That the least bit of decency should surprise you?"

"When people are scared, they don't think about others."

"And then they try to fight alone, and it just makes everything worse." His voice is quieter now. "Listen, I still haven't apologized. I'm sorry I was an ass to you when I came in that carriage. I was just... so frustrated."

A prince apologizing to a substitute? That's a first. "Well, I'm sorry I ruined your plans." Truly. I'm not going to confess it was my fault, though, but I can offer a half apology.

"Maybe you didn't ruin anything, Astra. Sometimes things are meant to be."

I sure hope not.

"What do we do now?" I ask.

"We have a wedding party to attend, don't we?"

"You're willing to walk there?"

He shrugs. "Or we can try to get a ride on a cart. What's the alternative?"

True. It's not like returning to the castle would be any faster.

I can't stop thinking about Marlak, though. "We'll need to figure out what he wants. It could be important."

"When we return, I'll help you look into it. But please, let's keep what happened between us."

"I won't tell anyone."

But I'll find a way to understand what's going on—and to get the disgraced prince out of my mind.

4

After an hour of walking, we stumble upon a farmer's cart kind enough to give us a ride. It takes another hour for two royal guards to find us. Two meager guards. It goes to show how worried they were about us. And no sign of our retinue, who are likely hiding in shame somewhere.

Marlak's chest with the star hasn't faded from my mind, opening a different kind of chest full of questions for which I have no answers. And then I recall what happened between us, or rather, didn't happen, but felt like it did, and all I want is to disintegrate and become dust.

I look back a few times, still fearing that he would follow us, but I suppose he won't dare cross the river. My breath stills when I wonder what will happen tonight when I sleep. Will I dream about him again? But the dreams can't be pleasant and comforting anymore, can they? So many questions.

We arrive at Lord Stratson's estate at five o'clock.

I'm exhausted. And starving. And grumpy. Even though I'm used to exercising in a dress, I'm hot. Sunlight has stung my skin, and my cheeks and nose are burning from within, my embarrassment etched on my face. I can hear Otavio's censure already, but what was I going to do? Cross the river and seek the shade of the fae forest?

The manor is perched atop a hill, and resembles a miniature castle because of the thick walls surrounding it. A huge metal gate opens and Ziven and I walk in, accompanied by the two royal guards.

Inside the walls, the ground is all paved with stones, stark and dead. Narrow steps lead to the manor, and I just hope it has some soft place where I can sit.

Three servants greet us, bowing deep, and while Ziven is taken aside to discuss the tribulations of our journey, I'm led to a room to get dressed. *My* opinion doesn't matter. More rest for me.

I bathe and put on one of Lord Stratson's daughter's dresses, a yellow thing covering me up to my neck, with pricklier fabric than I'm used to, but it's nice to change out of my sweaty clothes.

I'm glad when it's time to go to the dining room, so that first, I can eat, second, distract myself from my revolving questions, and third, play the role for which I trained for so long.

This is actually a pre-wedding reception for a few privileged guests, mostly merchants from the area. Ziven sits beside me at a long, heavy mahogany table. Across from us is Lord Stratson, who seems around fifty, and his wife-to-be, a young blond woman who murmurs monosyllables and never raises her eyes from her plate. I don't know if that's her real personality or the way she's been told to act in a formal dinner. It's odd how difficult it is to read people.

On a social occasion like this, nobody shows their true face. But then, do we ever know who we are, or is that the mask we wear for ourselves?

Too much pretending and some seduction classes got my head spinning.

Sitting on Lord Stratson's other side is his daughter, a pretty brunette who seems to be older than her future mother-in-law. It must be awkward, especially when her mother died only three months ago. She never utters a single word, but in her case, it looks like defiance. Her face is as expressionless as humanly possible, as if an enchantment had made her come to this dinner. An order, most likely. I admire her silent protest, and yet wish her bravery could bring her some happiness, even if it won't bring her mother back.

They serve a fire beef stew, a traditional dish from the region. I always thought that *fire* was because of the way it's prepared, but it turns out it's what it does to your tongue. In theory, I trained to eat spicy food back in the castle, but it must have been some fake chili peppers because it was nothing like this.

While I can control my expression, I can't control the tears escaping my eyes, so I raise my cup and say, "It's wonderful to see a happy couple. Makes me emotional."

What a terrible excuse. I stuff some bread down my throat and sip my watered wine. Meanwhile, Ziven suppresses a snicker.

Lord Stratson's daughter disappears after dinner, when it's time to mingle, nod on cue and laugh at boring jokes, just not too much, or some lord will think I'm flirting.

At least Ziven is charming everyone for both of us, relating our encounter with Marlak with excessive dramatics and flourishes, making it sound like facing a prince who let us go and apologized for his mistake was the most terrifying experience ever.

He's good, like a trained actor, drawing interest to a silly story, making it even more interesting because he looks ridiculous, allowing people to laugh *at* him. And how many people can laugh at a prince?

Strangely, it's a powerful display of confidence. And then I realize that *The Book of Seduction* is actually right that confidence is attractive. It's just that it can be goofy and wacky. And yet, now I see his wackiness as a layer, an act.

This can't be the actions of someone merely looking to survive. But what's his goal? The throne? He won't be getting any supporters acting like a fool, and he can't take the kingdom on his own. Perhaps he's biding his time, waiting for an opportunity to strike. It means that he *could* be a threat to our kingdom, and yet I can't warn anyone about it.

When the guests leave, Lord Stratson tells us that our luggage was brought from the fae path. I'm glad they recovered it and even gladder that nobody else was attacked. Perhaps Ziven is right that Marlak wanted something very specific, and this is not the time to wriggle my head trying to figure out what.

A servant leads us to the rooms where we'll spend the night. Ahem—room. Room?

The woman bows. "We were expecting siblings, Your Highnesses, but rest assured there are two beds." She turns to me. "Do you need help changing your clothes?"

"No. It's fine."

Nothing is fine. This is awkward.

The door closes and I'm alone with Prince Ziven, who shows me the palms of his hands. "I swear this is none of my doing."

I sit on one of the beds and rest my face on my hands. "I know." Frankly, I don't know anything anymore, but I don't think he would have conspired to get us into a single room.

He sits on the bed, by my side, and sighs. "Let's hope

there are no assassins."

I shrug. "Nah. Too obvious. But the walls might have ears."

He nods and whispers, "And eyes."

This is the reason it's me here, not Princess Driziely. And it should have been Quin. When I look back at my actions, I realize I was a complete lunatic, acting over something in my head only.

I don't know how I came to that conclusion on my own, how I could have a love story crop up and die in my imagination.

It's not like we would fall in love and get married. I knew that, and told myself I wanted some passing distraction, some passing joy, and yet it would leave me empty in the end —or brokenhearted.

Perhaps a part of me will always remain unfulfilled, and I'll create imaginary stories in my mind. Well, I do have an imaginary lover. A very real imaginary lover who has seen what my mind can conceive.

"Are you all right?" Ziven startles me, but he sounds worried.

"Exhausted." I chuckle. "You?"

He fists the air. "I can conquer the world!" He sighs and whispers, "Yeah. Not right now."

A curtain conceals a corner of the room, and I step behind it to change into my nightgown, thankful that it covers me up to my neck and down to my calves. When I come out, I see Ziven lying on his bed, completely dressed.

"Aren't you going to change?" I ask.

"I usually sleep naked, but I won't. And I'd rather be... prepared. Just in case."

"If assassins enter our room, I'm not sure they'll check what we're wearing."

He shrugs. "I don't want to run away naked. But please don't become paranoid like me."

"No." And if something ever happened, I could escape in a nightgown. "I'll shield the room."

"You'll what?" He frowns, confused.

"Shield. Against evil spirits."

He stares at me for a moment as if I was completely gaga, then shrugs. "Sure."

I touch each wall and say the incantation. "Only light here. Light shields us and protects us from evil. Light shields us, and nothing can pass through this wall."

When I'm finished, he says, "You're truly pious."

He must have been thinking it was an act. "You saw it," I mouth, then add, "It gives me strength. I don't know, hope, courage."

"That's a good thing." No judgment there, which I appreciate.

"It is."

I lie down, ready to fall asleep despite being in this strange house, in this strange room, away from the castle for the first time in my life, or at least the first time in the life I remember.

My mind still bugs me with unanswered questions. What does Ziven want? What's the deal between him and Sayanne?

And then, there are bigger questions. Why did Marlak attack us? What did he want with me? How did he know my name? Am I going to dream about him again? My spine chills with the thought, but it's not as if I can forgo sleep, especially exhausted as I am.

I can't imagine what's going through his mind right now. Has he concocted a logical explanation, or is he as puzzled as I am?

The worst is that a small, thin voice in my head is wondering if he liked it. I'm going to smother that voice with this fluffy pillow, I swear I'm going to.

No, no, no. Not again.

I protest as I see myself in a dream, but gradually, the unease fades away.

I'm in Lord Stratson's state, on a single bed, leaning on Marlak's chest. Moonlight caresses his star-shaped scar and tattoos, making them clearly visible.

Peering into his mesmerizing dark eyes, I ask, "What do you think happened?"

"I don't know." He plants a gentle kiss on my forehead and caresses my hair. How can a simple touch feel so good? "But I'm glad you're here."

The low rumble of his voice relaxes me, soothes me. His smile and gaze are life, love, power. He's more than beautiful, he's magical, and I can feel our love binding us like a powerful light.

I caress his chest, then slide my hand to his stomach, his skin so warm, so soft. I love the way he moans. My hand descends until I feel him hardening in my grip.

I look at him, at his lovely eyes, now closed. "I wanted this so much."

He opens his eyes and gives me an intense look. "It's yours, azalee. All yours now and forever." His voice is solemn, serious. It's a promise, an oath, a gift.

My eyes snap open. I don't have the strength to be embarrassed about the dream. At least it's just mine.

Is it?

Well, of course it is. It's *my* bizarre dream. For once I asked the right question. *What happened?*

But my attention shifted to something else, which apparently is mine. He said it the way someone presents a sword at a ceremony.

Ugh. I don't want Marlak's man thingy.

I have no responsibility over some insane part of me that I have no control over. Who has loving dreams about a family murderer? And that might be the worst part, that it's all with that loving feeling, a sense of deep connection. I'm losing my mind.

I turn to look at the room and see Ziven's exposed butt, his clothes scattered on the floor. It's true that it's hot, and maybe he thought I was asleep. I'll pretend I never saw anything and try to wipe that away from my mind.

The night here feels much different from the castle, and I hear crickets chirping in the distance instead of guards down below, in the castle's courtyard. The fresh smell of leaves from the forest is calming. It feels peaceful being amidst nature, even if a wall blocks us from it.

For some time, I try to remain awake, hearing the sound of wind on the trees outside the walls. I fear falling asleep again, but then I tell myself that my dreams are actually pretty great, and maybe they're not about Marlak at all. It's just an effect of whatever happened today.

A word comes to my mind. *Azalee.* He called me that in the dream.

It's odd that I should know how to write it, but the spelling comes clearly to my mind, as if... As if I'd seen it. But where? I know some ancient fae words, some old incantation words, and yet none of them comes to mind.

It could be a place. No, he wouldn't call me a place.

A name, maybe? But why?

Or maybe it's a foreign word, but I have to figure out if it's old fae or if it's...

Some languages should never be said out loud. Andrezza's words echo in my head. Could it be? And then, it's just a word from my own dream. But it might be a clue. At least I have *one question* whose answer is easy to find. It's something, something for me to look into when I get back.

Rain pours and pours as our carriage strides slowly through the muddy road leading south. We stop at a small village for lunch, but that just makes things worse, as the pieces of fried chicken keep dancing in my belly.

We arrive at the castle at six o'clock, and it's odd that I feel like I'm back home. I never imagined I had any love for my tower, but it's true that it's the only place I know.

Before I have time to rest or change my clothes, I'm summoned to Master Otavio's study. This is normal, as we're always supposed to give updates on our assignments and provide details. What's not normal is that he's alone.

He gestures for me to sit at his desk. Across from me, he leans over, a palm against the dark wood top.

"Happy? Was it worth it? Do you understand why we send substitutes?"

I swallow. "I understand the risks."

"No, you don't." His eyes are so narrowed that they look like slits as he glares at me. "You don't. Tell me something: does that prince know what you are?"

"Ziven?"

"Marlak," he roars.

He knew my name, and that I wasn't the princess, which

is something else I don't understand. But I prefer not to mention this yet, at least until I understand what happened.

Instead, I ask, "You think he would know I'm a substitute?" This is a genuine question, as I truly have no idea how he would have gotten that information.

Master Otavio bangs a hand on the desk. "*What you are.* You know what I'm talking about."

A darksoul. Would Marlak know? I decide to tell Otavio the truth. "I didn't get any indication that he knew that. How would he know?"

"His magic is different, dangerous." He lowers his voice. "It's possible that he could sense you. What did he want?"

"He said he approached our carriage by mistake, but he could be lying or tricking us. Maybe he was looking for something—or someone. I truly don't know."

He leans forward on his desk. "Astra. Be honest with me. If there's one thing, one little thing you're hiding, you could be putting all our lives at risk."

"Everything happened so fast. Is there any specific detail you're looking for?"

"I just want to make sure you're not holding back any information." He stops glaring. "I'm your friend and protector, and I need you to trust me."

Until not long ago, these words, with this tone of voice, would have made me cave in and tell every little thing that happened, but Ziven's secret is not mine, and I'm not going to tell my master the weird thing between me and Marlak. It's awkward enough that the fae prince has to know about it.

"You can also ask Ziven. I'm puzzled, to be honest. Will the Fae King be informed?"

Otavio snorts. "It's a complicated diplomatic situation. But you can bet he knows what happens on his land. From our part, all we can do is send him an apology for the unauthorized intrusion. It's just dreadful." He stares at me. "Did you see the Shadow Ring?"

There's no need to lie now, and in fact, the ring that looked as if it held a cloudy sky was quite impressive. "Yes, he was wearing it. Unless it was a replica. I wouldn't be able to—"

"I know." He clenches his fist. "But I don't see why he would use a fake one." He sighs, and I know the lecture is about to start.

He goes on and on about how I need to protect myself, how the fae prince could have seen my nature, how all his plans could have been ruined.

I don't even know what Otavio's plans are, and the only reason I never ask is because he only mentions them when he's upset. Behind him, on a shelf, a book catches my eye. There's nothing on the cover, but I know what's in it. A Tiurian dictionary, containing the language that must not be spoken.

There's another Tiurian dictionary in the library, as well as language study guides, but I'm not allowed to go there alone, and people would notice what I'm taking. Andrezza has a lot of resources on that language, but I don't know how I could consult them without drawing attention. I need to understand what *azalee* means. It could be important.

"Astra!" His shout startles me. "You aren't even listening, are you?"

I shake my head and pretend to look embarrassed. "I'm so sorry. I was trying to think, master. See if there was any detail I forgot. Something that could matter. This is not the time, I know. I know your words are important, and I'm truly sorry for what I did."

I'm not, but it's better to tell him what he wants to hear

and get this over with.

Then I add, "I'll never do any of that again."

Except for breaking into his study, because that's exactly what I'm going to do tonight, to check his dictionary.

He takes a deep breath. "I'll make sure you're appointed to smaller, safer assignments, Astra. Please don't think I don't notice how hard you work."

"It's the bare minimum." I parrot the words he's told me so many times, then give him a half smile.

"That *is* true." The smile he returns is genuine.

For some reason, that approving smile still hits a part of me starving for approval, starving for *his* approval, as if all that mattered in the world was his opinion. It's a childish part of me, hanging on to the two adults in my life as if they were my parents. They aren't my parents.

The thought is freeing, but it hurts. Waiting to receive crumbs of affection might be pathetic, but expecting nothing, while realistic, is quite bleak.

Perhaps I didn't disguise my emotions as well as I should, as he adds, "And you'll achieve great things—if you have the patience. A small lord's wedding reception is not the greatness you seek, Astra."

"I don't seek greatness." I don't know why I let that piece of honesty slip.

Otavio smirks, perhaps thinking I'm giving the answer expected of me, which makes sense.

But then, what is it that I seek?

I STARE at myself in my vanity mirror as I apply salve on my face, my cheeks warm and red under my fingers. My shame. Otavio warned me that the skin might peel if I'm not careful.

My newly acquired tan means no assignments for me anytime soon—as if they sent me anywhere when I was hiding under the shade. Not much changed.

No. Everything changed, and yet I struggle to pinpoint what *everything* is.

As I stare in the mirror, something catches my eye. A small bag, sitting on my dresser. The drusils! They don't tend to go bad, at least not in two days, so they are still a good gift. I hope Tarlia is alone this time.

Slowly, I take the familiar path on the ledge, steadying myself on the stones on the wall.

Tarlia opens the window for me with a smile that gets even wider when she sees the drusils, followed by a grimace. "I fear I'm going to puke if I eat them, but I want to eat them. What do you suggest?" She takes the package from my hand.

I enter her room and say, "They should still last—"

Tarlia already put one in her mouth.

"Life's short," she says while still chewing, then adds, "If I get sick again, at least it's another day resting."

I glance at some books on her bed.

"You were studying?"

"Had some catching up to do." She then turns serious. "You saw me, didn't you?"

I know what she's asking. She and Fachin. "I didn't mean to. I got the drusils for you, and—"

"It's fine. Just... can you not tell anyone?"

"I wouldn't." I shake my head.

She takes a deep breath. "Do you really think they'll let us go? One day? Give us a piece of land and our lives back?"

Our lives back. As if there had been anything before this castle and this tower. I know what she means, though: their promise of freedom if we finish our assignments. But then there's another possibility.

"If Driziely were to marry, as herself, I believe we could be sent as her guards."

Tarlia rolls her eyes. "As her *maids*, you mean. I just... I wish I could know. I wish I could have an answer. I can't ask someone to run away with me, but I don't want to have just forbidden moments in a bedroom."

"Are you in love?"

"I can't, can I?" She closes her eyes.

"We don't choose."

"We don't choose anything, not even what we eat." She grabs a drusil and smiles. "With some exceptions." Despite her playful tone, I see a tear rolling down her face. She stares at me. "You like Quin, don't you?"

I feel naked and exposed, but decide to be partly honest. "I wouldn't say I *like* him. I don't know him well. Of course he's good-looking, but that's it. And we don't know where our lives will take us."

She takes a deep breath. "Yes, there's no future. But there can be some joy in the present."

"I guess." I smile but feel hollow. I'm not interested in Quin, not really. Not anymore. Maybe too much weirdness numbs one's heart, or maybe I realized my actions were foolish. I'm wondering about Tarlia now. "If you love Fachin, I think you—"

"There's no love," she interrupts me. "When you have no future, you have no love." Her words are flat, as if rehearsed.

And yet I feel love when I think about my visions, and I wish I had never met Marlak, wish the visions had remained pure and perfect and comforting. They were everything I had.

I look at Tarlia and hate to see her so hopeless and resigned. "Trust the Almighty Mother, Tarlia. Maybe you have a future."

She half rolls her eyes but then smiles. "I respect your faith, Astra, but you know I don't believe in made-up stories or made-up people."

Made-up. It seems hard to live without anything to hold on to, without anything to give her hope, but I also respect her choice. Still, I say, "Reality is not that great, in case you haven't noticed."

She looks up. "I daydream, Astra. I'm not as immersed in reality as you think."

I almost ask her what her daydreams are made of, but it might be too personal. I'll never tell her mine, after all.

When I get back to the window, I have made up my mind. Yes, I'm exhausted, but I'm going to Master Otavio's study. Tonight is the perfect opportunity, when he likely thinks I'm too weary to leave my bedroom. I'm going to check his Tiurian dictionary, and I'll see if *azalee* is in it.

It's a small detail, sure, but if I don't look closely at what small clues I have, I'll never get to the main picture.

Getting to Otavio's window always speeds up my heart. It's not like moving to my sisters' windows—it involves climbing down the walls of the tower.

The stones are rough and have large enough fissures for my hand and feet to fit in comfortably, but the height and the absence of a solid ledge for my feet rattle me. It's pointless fear, and if I saw a wall like this in a climbing class, I'd laugh. But then, a mistake here would mean instant death. And then again, the crevices are huge!

I am aware that fear is distorting my perception, and yet my awareness doesn't make it go away, just pushes me into braving it. I hate fearing something so stupid, though.

And then there's that small fear that I could get caught. That I could be expelled. I tell myself I'll be extra careful. If I ever want to hope I'll be assigned to a high importance mission, I can't fear going in and out of rooms undetected. That's the bare minimum.

Before I reach his window, I stop, since I notice a flickering light coming from the study. He could have left a candle burning. But before I get any closer, I hear his voice.

"We'll need to stick to the plan, and be more aggressive if necessary. There's still three months. If we find there's any chance Leonius might want his daughter to be the one to get married, we'll... Change his mind."

"Killing her might ruin our plans." This is Andrezza's voice.

I'm surprised at her casual mention of murder. I shouldn't be surprised, considering everything. But I'm sure this is Princess Driziely they're talking about, and I always thought our goal was to protect her.

"No need to kill. Just worsen her disease. We should have done that a long time ago. Leonius might want his bloodline spread over other kingdoms, but he'll also want to secure a strong alliance, and he won't risk his daughter if she's too frail. Plus, our girls are better suited for that; more beautiful, smarter, more elegant."

Really? Otavio thinks we're smart and elegant? Tarlia and Sayanne, maybe.

He continues, "Do you think Driziely can convince anyone she's the prettiest girl in the world? The kings will laugh in our face."

As if *we* could convince anyone of that. *I'll* laugh next time I see myself in the mirror.

"They don't look much different from the princess." Andrezza is a smart woman, indeed.

"There are tricks, Andrezza, a little more glow on the skin, in the right places. The right clothes. In three months, I'll make them radiant."

Three months for what? It's the second time they're mentioning it, and it has to be a specific date, a specific event. Perhaps Driziely's birthday. She'll turn nineteen, and there should be a big party.

Andrezza sighs loudly enough that it reaches my ears. "We'll only need one of them. Perhaps we should choose and focus on her."

"No. We'll keep training and preparing the three substitutes. Things happen. Just happened, in fact. Two of our girls got sick."

"Did you find out what caused it?" Her tone is concerned.

"Foolish girls, must have eaten something that didn't come from our kitchen." Otavio sounds annoyed.

I, for my part, feel relieved that he didn't even mention poisoning or what I've done. He's indeed protecting me, like he claims. Perhaps I should be more thankful.

"But here? How?" Andrezza still sounds worried.

"The girls get nightly visitors, both you and I know that. One of them might have brought something they're not used to."

"But see, that's troubling." She has that same concerned tone. "Of course they can't be blushing virgins, and I'm glad for the practice our guards and substitutes give them, but if they're poisoning them... You see how that's dangerous?"

Glad for the practice? We aren't forbidden from having dalliances, and yet it feels so cold, so calculated, almost as if the guards and substitutes were instructed to seduce us. A bitter taste settles in my mouth, while the rough stone prickles my hands.

Was it what I did, when Commander Rowe was here

with the Tirenzy prince? Was I practicing, in case I got picked for a marriage alliance? Was I practicing to warm some foreign king's bed?

But I don't even think they'll choose me for whatever they're planning. I think they'd pick Sayanne or Tarlia. They're beautiful and elegant, and won't blush when they're not supposed to. We *can* blush on cue, though, which is useful to show interest without being too direct. Ugh. I hate those classes.

They speak softly now, so I move closer to the window to try to catch their words, but there's only silence. They haven't left the study, though, since I didn't hear steps or a door opening.

Then I hear... Oh, no.

See, I've always thought they were involved, and in my mind it was sweet, but it doesn't mean I want to hear their moans. That's nightmare inducing. Also, if they are involved, why do they keep it a secret? Why not get married? I climb up slowly, my head busy with new, confusing thoughts and questions.

Otavio is the most accomplished beauty master in the world. He can shape our noses, color our hair, give us creams to improve our skin. He even has drops for our eyes, to make them brilliant and captivating.

He treats the queen and has used his knowledge to shape us since childhood. I thought we were doing this to pretend to be Princess Driziely, even if I always suspected he molded her nose too, and perhaps colors her hair. Now, I've always known we could take her place in a dangerous situation, or in a marriage alliance when the goal is not really to have an alliance.

And yet, from their conversation, it seems he has some other plan, that it *needs* to be one of us. Then again, if the princess marries, we would be rendered useless, and so would Otavio and Andrezza. They might be simply trying to keep their positions in court.

No. Otavio would never be useless or out of work. He's too good and his skill is worth a lot. In fact, he could be making a fortune serving other queens and kings. I always believed he remained here, in Krastel, because he had a higher goal.

Well, he has a goal, which is his plan. But what is it? And did I mishear it, or is he making the princess sick? Nausea stirs in my stomach.

Three months. At her birthday party. They plan to have one of us in her place. Then what? Invite many kings and hope we seduce one of them? It makes sense, makes a lot of sense if I add up everything they taught us. But my life will completely change, and I have no idea what's going to happen. The thought makes me dizzy and I hold on tighter to the stones.

I don't know anything anymore.

Plus, I never got close to the dictionary and have no idea when I'll figure out what *azalee* means. Does that even matter, amidst so much?

Well, it was the only question with an easy answer.

No book will tell me why I've been dreaming about Marlak or explain what happened in that cave, and it's not as if I can ask anyone. No book will tell me which of us will replace Driziely at her birthday party, which of us will have to entertain a foreign king in bed. I try to be relieved that it's probably not going to be me, and yet, what's going to happen once I'm rendered useless?

5

My bed feels cold and empty. Even before opening my eyes, I know he's not here. The night is warm, but the satin sheets chill me, chill me in this room with cold marble walls and a huge bed—where I'm indeed alone.

I get up and step onto smooth mahogany planks, then cross a sitting room with white sheets covering chairs, sofas and tables. Large windows lead to a night sky partially covered by treetops.

Marlak's on the balcony, staring ahead, wearing just linen trousers. Even in the dark of night, I can see the brilliant marks and drawings on the left side of his muscled back, while he hunches over, as if looking for something, looking for a solution.

"Husband," I say.

He turns and smiles at me, but the corner of his lips and eyes are tight with tension. "I'm coming right back, azalee." His hair is messy, but still beautiful, and he's wearing golden earrings with crescents and stars.

"You're worried." I reach him and put a hand on his arm.

He nods and closes his eyes, then pulls me closer for a

tight hug. I can hear his heart, saying so much in our shared silence, in our shared moment.

After a while, I look up at his face. "Did you get any news?"

This could be good or bad, and I hope it's not his greatest fear. It can't be, or he would be devastated, and I don't sense any of that.

He takes a deep breath and runs a finger through my hair. "I think I know where the tower is." His dark eyes are tense, his deep voice shaky.

I don't know if I want to hear it, I don't know if I'm ready to learn what dangerous land he'll have to visit, but I try to lighten up his mood and smile. "I suppose it's not in the Crystal Court, then?"

His lips form a line, anguish clear in his eyes. "It's beyond the Pit of Death."

My stomach knots and I fall into a pool of panic. Beyond? Beyond? How can it be? "Can anything survive there?"

He manages a bitter, soft chuckle. "I sure hope so."

What hope does he have to reach that tower? How can he face the dangers surrounding it? Even with all his magic, how can he face those monsters?

There's no point despairing, though. "We'll find a way." My voice is firm.

"I know." He holds me tight and rests his chin on top of my head.

There has to be a way, I know there has to be a way, and yet the last thing I want is for him to risk it, even if it's true that he has no choice.

A sound startles me, and I sit up in bed, my heart racing, a bitter taste in my mouth. Not beyond the Pit of Death, not there, he can't...

DAYLIGHT COMES FROM THE WINDOW, the timid sunrays from early morning, illuminating my room in the Elite Tower, and I realize I'm definitely losing my mind.

I have no idea why my heart's jumping up and down like a maniac.

First, I've never heard of any place called Pit of Death. Second, if there *is* such a place, and if it's indeed dangerous, I should be jubilant to hear that Marlak's about to jump in it. Or over it, to somewhere even worse.

The thought makes me panic.

Great. I have officially gone insane.

Or maybe it's just that if he dies, I'll never know why this is happening.

Right. Because my curiosity is so much more important than my sense of self preservation.

But it is, a thin voice inside me says. I'm going to slap it.

At least this dream had nothing intimate in it. Didn't it? I could feel what he felt. His anguish was my anguish, his worry my worry. If I close my eyes, I can still feel his chin touching my head, his arms squeezing me close, and it all feels so familiar, comforting... And I called him *husband*. Husband, really?

I need to ignore that and focus on what I learned with this dream—if it's even true.

Marlak's looking for something—a tower—and it seems he has found it. What tower? Where? What is he trying to accomplish?

I know that he wants the Crystal Court throne—at least that's what everyone says, and yet he didn't strike me as a power hungry maniac. And then again, he never does, not in these dreams. He's always sweet and loving, almost like a different person. Likely a different person, and maybe I'm just getting things confused. But I saw the star before ever seeing his chest. I saw it.

Perhaps I could use the information I get from these dreams, but the issue is how. It's not like I can walk to Master Otavio's study and tell him I dream about Prince Marlak constantly.

Another sound on the glass. A tap. Someone's there. I rush to it, fearing that maybe Tarlia or Sayanne could be in trouble, but I see Ziven instead. I had no idea he could be awake at six in the morning, or that he knew where my room was.

I open my window. "How did you get here?" It sounds rude. To my credit, I'm still half asleep.

"You don't really think you're the only one who can climb walls, do you?"

He's that observant? "How do you know that?"

"If I want to survive, I have to keep my eyes and ears alert." He then whispers, "Not that I've been in anyone's room before. Can I come in?"

"Sure." I step away to let him enter.

He's wearing a sleeveless black tunic over leather pants, showing off his slim but toned arms. Perhaps he gets so many looks simply because he's handsome, and people don't care if he's drunk or not. At least learning about him and Sayanne ruined all his appeal for me.

He puts his hands in front of him. "You'll need to be calm."

Something happened. Something bad. "What's wrong?" I can't even imagine what's going on, can't even mask the agony in my voice. Is it my sisters?

"It's Stratson's estate." His voice is flat, but slow.

My agony whooshes out of me like the air in my lungs. "What about it?"

He draws in a deep breath. "It was attacked. Completely burned. There are no survivors."

A bitter taste settles in my throat and a ringing sound deafens me for a second. I think about the daughter with her quiet resistance, the servant who prepared my bath, the wife-to-be and her rigid posture. It can't be. "They're all dead?"

"It looks like it. A messenger arrived not long ago." He stares at me. "We don't know who did it. Or why."

"Marlak." I can't believe it, can't believe I let this happen. "He can manipulate fire. I mean, I'm sure you can't burn your family with water magic."

Ziven puts his hands on his head. "Does it make sense, though? If what he wanted was the chalice, he could have taken it."

He could, but... "Maybe he didn't want anyone to know he took it."

Without asking permission, Ziven sits on my bed. "But burning an entire estate is a lot more trouble than just taking it from us, not to mention that we don't even know if his magic works on our side of the river."

The faces of the people who live in that house still keep flashing in my mind. I can't believe it. "You don't need magic to set something on fire."

"True. But it could have been anyone. Anyone, Astra."

I sag on the bed beside him. "We'll need to tell the truth."

He nods. "I knew this would be your reaction. You know what? It was the first thought that crossed my mind. I thought people had died for a stupid lie. But then, if we tell a different story, we might get in trouble. We can't save anyone who died in the fire, but we can still save ourselves."

"Ziven, it could make a difference."

"Could it? Let's suppose we told everyone exactly what happened. What difference would it have made?"

In truth, none. I'm trying to think, trying to find a solution. But there's no solution, only regret. "We shouldn't have gifted the chalice."

"Maybe. But weren't you the one who said he gave it back to you?" Ziven pauses. I can see that he's also shaken and confused. "How could anyone guess he actually wanted it? And in truth, we don't know if it was the disgraced prince. Small lords have rivalries. These things happen."

"They haven't happened in years. Now we're attacked on the Fae Path, and then this happens. Do you really think it's a coincidence?"

"It could be. They'll conduct their own investigation. For all they know, he could have sensed we had the chalice and decided to get it later. It doesn't make a difference whether we fought him or not. We can keep our story."

"So *that's* what you're worried about." It seems so petty, so little.

"Yes. I was worried you'd ruin everything. Worried you would put me in danger." He likely means by revealing his magic.

"I promised I wouldn't say anything about you, and I won't."

His chest rises and falls as he nods. "I appreciate it."

"Is Marlak a murderer, though?" I shouldn't have voiced this thought, but it's too late now.

Ziven frowns. "Is that up for debate?"

"He didn't hurt us." It's not that I'm defending him—or my dreams. I'm just trying to think.

"I know." He shakes his head. "That's also strange."

Then I ask, "How did you hear about the attack?"

"Messengers bringing urgent news aren't discreet. I pay attention."

"While sleeping?"

He eyes me, pauses, then says, "I happened to be awake."

Awake checking messengers coming in and out. He's quite shrewd. "Thanks for letting me know." I then decide to ask something else I've been wanting to know. "Is all the drinking a lie as well?"

Ziven snorts. "What do you think?"

It's a lie, then. An act. "I think you're under the impression that you need to pretend to be powerless to survive."

"My *impression*. Right, it must be my imagination."

"You don't know. And King Leonius is fair."

Ziven bursts out laughing. "Honorable protector of the realm. Of course."

I'm not going to argue with him about our king. "I understand. You're trying to survive, so you need to hide who you are." That sounds familiar, eerily familiar, but it's different because I truly need to hide my nature, and at least I'm trying to do something.

He raises his shoulders. "The fact that I'm sitting here is proof that it's been working."

"Don't you want more, though, more than just surviving?"

He twists his lips in a half smile, half grimace. "Who doesn't want more? And yet how many of us manage to achieve it?"

"Everyone who loves manages to do more than just survive." It's true. I believe that love can take us higher, even if I have my problems with romantic love. I'm not sure how the subject veered in that direction.

"Those are beautiful words, but my heart's unfortunately too bitter for that."

That's weird. The look he gave me when he entered the carriage, before he realized it was me, was quite powerful. "I thought you liked Sayanne."

His lips form a line. "Perhaps I'm a fickle drunk."

That doesn't make any sense. "Two days ago, you were looking forward to traveling with her. You *risked your life* to spend time with her."

He pauses, then says, "Have you ever..." He chuckles. "Felt like someone understood you? Felt a connection?"

With Marlak, tonight.

Wrong answer, Astra. That was a stupid dream. And I'm obviously never going to confess it even to my shadow. "With Tarlia and Sayanne. Sometimes." Have they ever understood me? Tarlia, maybe.

He looks down, his eyelashes covering his eyes like curtains, and inhales. "That vulnerability, openness, it's rare." He stares at me. "Except none of it was real." His voice is harsh with anger, contempt. "What she told me about you, it wasn't true."

"What did she say?"

"Oh, that you two humiliate her, mistreat her. It's not that she complained, more that she related her quiet steadfastness in face of horrors." He rolls his eyes. "The thing with deceit is that in reality, we see it. We have that feeling that something is off, and yet choose to close our eyes, choose to ignore that voice warning us."

His words stir something in my chest. I'm not sure why. But I'm not going to turn against my sister because of someone I barely know. "Maybe you're trying to smear her."

His hazel eyes are kind but sad. "Feel free to ignore my words, Astra. In time, everyone reveals who they are, and you're right that you shouldn't base your judgment of your friends on other people's opinions. Trust your heart."

"My heart's crazy." I don't know why I let that truth slip.

He shakes his head. "Whose heart isn't?"

We laugh and exchange a look. At that moment, I realize I can count on him as a friend. But it also feels like I'm betraying Sayanne—again.

"I'd better go," he says, "I'll stop by if I have news about the attack. We'll figure it out."

I smile. "Thanks."

He gets up, steps out the window and leaves the room. I look outside to see what path he takes, but I don't see him walking on the ledge, and assume he must have climbed down right from beneath my window. Not the easiest place to do that. Then again, maybe he's extremely good at climbing. Extremely good at everything. And yet pretending he's useless.

I get dressed quickly, even though it's still so early. I might not be allowed to check Tiurian dictionaries or language guides, but I can look at maps.

I'll figure out what this *Pit of Death* is, and what Marlak wants. Who knows? Perhaps predicting the disgraced fae prince's moves could save lives.

※

I NEED to be quick before the bell rings for breakfast.

Alone in our study room, I sit at one of its four long tables, with two books I took from the bookshelves. We can come here to prepare for exams, do assignments, or simply study, and I guess that's what I'm doing, as I have one of the books open on a map of our continent, trying to find some kind of clue, some kind of answer.

Pit of Death. It could be in the Endless Mountains. A pit, right? But that area is close to us, and not dangerous, as far as I know. It could be further south, beyond the Wild Fae lands, perhaps in the Spider Court, or even the Icy Lands. Or north of the Crystal Court, in the hodgepodge of small fae courts, the Fae Territory. Maybe it's in the Shadow Lands, where there are no kingdoms and no courts.

In truth, I'm lost. To start with, I don't have much information about the Fae Lands, so what am I even hoping to accomplish looking at an incomplete map? And it could be on another continent.

The tower he's looking for can't be on any map, or he wouldn't be searching for it, unless he didn't know which tower. But in the dream, he knew what the Pit of Death was —and so did I.

Unfortunately, all I recall is my fear of that place, and the even greater dread of what lies beyond it. But where is it? And how much of the dream was true? It's not like he's my husband.

With a deep breath, I shut the book closed, annoyed to realize I have nothing to work with, and the information I glimpsed in my dream is no more than gibberish.

I then open a book about the Crystal Court. I've studied their history, but maybe there's something I'm missing. I stumble upon a painting of the royal family before their king died, and see the two brothers, both with black hair, but only one of them with round ears. Beside them is Isabel, the king's daughter, a girl who was a little younger than the brothers. They're all dead now—except for Marlak and Renel.

Their mother married the previous king, who adopted the boys and made them heirs. Unfortunately, Marlak killed his step-father, mother, and sister.

The thought brings me chills.

I was kidnapped and restrained by someone who's cold-blooded enough to kill his own family, and it has to be true, if that's what his brother says, considering he's fae and can't lie.

The sound of footsteps catch my attention and I look up to see who's coming. Oh, no. I set my eyes on the book again, hoping he'll think I didn't notice him.

Why is Quin here? Why does his presence annoy me? I should be happy, right?

He pulls a chair beside me. "I heard you faced some troubles on your trip." There's something a little flat about his tone.

I keep staring at the book. "Indeed, I wouldn't call it enjoyable." I get up to put the books back on the shelf, but he follows me.

"Did you enjoy your company, at least?"

"I thought *you* were going on the trip. What happened?"

He stares at me, then rests a hand against the bookshelf. "I wish I had gone. I wish I had been there with you." His stare moves to my lips. "We never get a chance to talk."

I'm feeling cornered against the bookshelf, and the words I heard from Otavio's study are now ruining everything because all I can think is that Quin has been ordered to seduce me. Why else would he be singling me out like that?

He then says, "You're so beautiful, Astra." He moves closer and whispers in my ear. "Let me come to your room tonight. I can convince the guards to let me through."

I crouch and escape from under his arms, horrified that he's truly intent on giving me some practice. Can it be that my masters think I'm lacking? That I might be the one they'll send to get married? I could ask him if someone ordered him to do that, but I don't know if it makes sense or if it's pure paranoia.

With a fake smile, without any effort in making it look real, I say, "I have to hurry for breakfast."

"We still have some time. I'll walk with you."

There's no way to say *no*. I mean, perhaps there is, but it's true that we're both going to the same dining hall.

Why is it that I kept wishing he'd say these words to me, and when it happens, it's at the worst possible moment, when my mind's so muddled that it has no space for flirting or even lust? Perhaps I'm lucky and the timing is right to save me from heartbreak. Not really. I don't feel that I have a heart.

I tell him about the trip and the fake uneventful encounter with Marlak just like I told my masters. Everything so fake. Fake, fake, fake, which makes sense, as I'm a fake princess, talking to a fake prince.

At least we can't sit at the same table, and it's a relief when I'm alone again.

Tarlia and Sayanne soon join me, and we have a silent, awkward breakfast of grapes, porridge, and tea. Tarlia gives me a quizzical look, as if she wants to ask me something, but I guess she doesn't want to talk in front of Sayanne.

What have we come to?

A CLIMBING STRUCTURE has been set up on the roof where we train, but it's in the sun. If we were to practice in the evening, I'd have no problem, but I guess I'll stay under the canopy today. I'm wearing a heavy dress, with pockets for daggers.

Otavio rarely supervises our physical training, but he's here, and hands me a short rope to jump.

Leaning close, he whispers, "Actions have consequences. You'll jump until noon."

"Thanks." I smile at him.

It's not like I'm going to complain—or that I'm even allowed to complain. And in truth, I'm grateful this is the type of punishment I'm getting, instead of being expelled from the guard.

He smirks, then adds, "To protect your skin."

As if it wasn't burned already. I nod and start.

Is it possible to keep jumping for four hours? Is he hoping I'm going to beg for some rest? I turn the rope and make it go over me, then jump slowly. In reality, he never said how fast I had to go, and he's already heading to the door leading to the stairs.

Outside the canopy, Tarlia and Sayanne are climbing a wall made of wood with some rope hanging from the top of it. On the ground, there's an area with a feathered quilt. They're going to train jumping from the top of it, and I really wish I was out there, enjoying the thrill of the fall, imagining one day having to escape from a window after a daring adventure. Instead, I'm here, hiding from the sun.

The male substitutes aren't training with us today, and I'm glad I don't have to see Quin. I guess I'm not looking forward to some *practice*. Ugh. That conversation ruined everything.

Lord Stratson's daughter then comes to mind, with her rigid posture. Dead? And was it Marlak's fault? I agree with Ziven that attacking that manor doesn't make much sense, but is there anything in Marlak's actions that makes sense?

The dream comes to mind, with the mysterious tower beyond the Pit of Death. It could be anywhere. No, somewhere where there are monsters. Perhaps far north? And what is it he wants? He was interested in the chalice, at least for a while. Why would anyone who owns all the Crystal Court relics care about a stupid, worthless trinket?

Unless... It was not the chalice he wanted, but the beacon stone. He has loads of those, though. It could be a specific stone, perhaps connected to one of his relics. I'll need to get back to our study room and read about them. If our books are correct, he owns at least three swords, a few daggers, a bunch of rings, some chalices, and the crown, which is supposed to be a simple circlet, and can only be worn by the true king of the Crystal Court.

Now, King Renel can't wear it, since Marlak took it, and Marlak obviously can't wear it, or he'd put it on and challenge the throne. I still don't see how beacon stones or a tower can relate to that.

What I wonder then is how he was able to kill his family and escape the palace with all the treasure. Did he put it in sacs? Did he carry a trunk? Perhaps he used air magic and blew it all away. Didn't anyone notice it? I need to check the books more closely, or perhaps ask Andrezza.

Even jumping slowly, I'm getting tired. There are only two guards up here and one of Otavio's assistant. What happens if I stop and sit? What happens if I don't? And if Tarlia or Sayanne get married, will it make a difference whether I can jump, prepare poisons, or defend myself?

Perhaps I always thought we'd be chosen for an assassination mission. I never doubted that I was the most qualified for that. But to seduce a king?

I jump and jump, my mind circling like the rope. And then perhaps I should realize that my skills *are* useful. How many people know poisons like I do? How many people can unlock doors? They wouldn't squander all our training. I have to believe that Otavio truly intends to protect me. After all, he never told anyone what I was, he's been coloring my hair since I was little. That takes effort, time, commitment. He wouldn't throw all that work away and simply get rid of me. At least I hope not.

With that thought, I walk to the bench and sit, taking deep breaths. I've never disobeyed a direct order before, and I'm wondering what's happening to me. Well, I'm tired, that's what's happening.

But sitting doesn't stop the enigmatic questions from circling in my head. Would Marlak have attacked Stratson's manor? It's so illogical. But if not him, then who?

So far, nobody has mentioned the attack. I thought I was going to be interrogated again, but I heard nothing. Hey, I'd gladly sit indoors and answer a bunch of questions instead of jumping a stupid rope for hours. Maybe that's why they haven't called me yet. Maybe Otavio wants to make sure I'm sufficiently punished first. Or maybe they don't think I'm hiding anything. Why question me again, when they already have all the information they need? And yet I have a queasy feeling in my stomach, as if something's amiss.

Right as I think that, Otavio storms through the door, glaring at me, five guards at his heels.

Oh, shoot. I almost pick up the rope again, but it's too late to pretend I was following his orders. I notice then that three of the guards are royal guards, wearing their typical black sash. They answer directly to the king and rarely come to this tower. The way Otavio's glaring at me, I'm certain I'm going to be put in a cell or sentenced to death. Did they find out about Ziven's magic? About my lies?

Andrezza also appears at the door, her eyes wide, and I exhale in relief. For some reason, I always feel safer when she's around, but then the fact that both masters are here can't mean anything good.

Otavio turns to a royal guard. "*We* will talk to her." He then turns to me. "Follow us."

Tarlia jumps down from the structure and approaches us. "What's happening?"

"None of your business." Otavio doesn't even look at her.

I wave at her, and mouth, "Later."

She nods.

I also wave at Sayanne, who's on top of the climbing wall, looking at me and frowning as if worried.

Well, I'm worried too.

Not worried, terrified. This is not like when my master was threatening to get me expelled from the guard, get thrown away from the castle. I think even then I knew he didn't mean it. This is different, and much more serious. Scary.

Which of my lies got me in so much trouble?

# 6

The spiral stairs to the common area are a blur as I descend them with a heaviness in my chest, with absolutely no idea what's happening, flanked by Otavio and Andrezza, followed by more royal guards than I've ever seen in this tower.

When we reach the door of Otavio's study, he yells, "Give me an hour. I need to get her ready."

I flinch, then realize he was yelling at the royal guards, not me.

"She's supposed to come right away," a guard says. Not just a guard, I think he's the captain of the king's forces.

I'm so screwed.

Otavio glares at the man. "Tell your king that I'm protecting *his* daughter by changing Astra's hair color."

Now I'm very, very confused.

When the door of the study closes and I find myself alone with Otavio and Andrezza, I'm so terrified that I want to collapse and cry, and yet I hold myself together.

"The fae prince," Otavio says. "You didn't tell him you were Princess Driziely?"

I freeze, a cold chill grating my skin. He knew I was a

substitute and even my name, and I have no idea how. I'm wondering what he did with the information. This is the time to bury my feelings, keep calm, and lie on.

"It was fast. He realized we were from Krastel and left." This is very much in line with what I've been telling everyone.

"You said Prince Ziven introduced himself, and yet *did you* introduce yourself?"

"No. He didn't ask." I can't imagine where this conversation is going, and I don't hide my puzzlement.

Otavio paces back and forth.

Andrezza looks at me with concern, then turns to Otavio. "I think the bigger crisis is averted."

He places both hands on his forehead. "I guess."

"What's happening?" I finally dare ask, because I'm going to choke on my worry if I have to keep guessing for one more second.

Andrezza glances at Otavio and then, perhaps sensing he's too nervous, decides to answer. "Prince Marlak is in the castle."

My heart punches the cavity of my chest. Marlak? Here? How?

"Was he caught?" That's the only possible explanation, except that it's impossible. Human guards would never be able to subdue him.

She shakes her head. "None of that. He came for a marriage alliance."

Marriage? He wants to marry Driziely? I see now how him thinking I'm the princess could be problematic. But if he doesn't know... My head almost explodes imagining Sayanne with him. No. Wait. It makes no sense. And he's a disgraced prince with no power.

"The king wouldn't accept it, would he?" I ask. "I mean, what does he have to offer?"

Andrezza's look is laced with pity. "We don't know what the king agreed to. Or why." She swallows. "Apparently the prince had no idea who you were, and yet wanted to marry *you*."

I PINCH my arm until I'm about to yell, and yet it doesn't wake me from this strange dream. "Marry? Me? Why?"

Otavio sighs and looks away. "Gods know why."

I find it odd that he mentions gods and not the Almighty Mother, but it's true he's nervous, and that's definitely not the biggest issue here.

Andrezza then adds, "We have to get you ready. You're leaving with him right away."

Nothing makes sense. "Now?"

"Otavio asked for an hour, like you heard."

I'm trembling and speechless.

Andrezza gives me a kind look. "It will be fine. You were trained for this. It will be an alliance, and if you find out his secrets, we'll be able to use them to our advantage." The worry in her voice contradicts her calming words. She continues, as if trying to convince herself, "It's even better that you won't have to pretend to be the princess. I know it's sudden, but I think you'll do fine."

Otavio then turns to Andrezza. "Can you keep the commander busy? Go out there, explain I'm getting her ready? I need to change her hair color."

She looks at both of us, then nods and leaves.

"Sit." He points to a chair, his voice the gruffiest I've ever heard.

"Here?" Usually I color my own hair, but when he does it, which is about once a month, it's in a room with special chairs and basins.

"We'll have to be fast."

He pulls a cloth from a cupboard, ties it around my neck, then picks a bottle with a black liquid, puts on gloves, and applies it to my hair. "This won't last, but it's good for now."

Before I even realize what he's doing, he removes the cloth and says, "Follow me."

I pull a strand of hair to check, and it's indeed black, but not like the usual liquid we put on, but something that stains my fingers.

He pulls part of a bookshelf, revealing a hidden door. I thought I knew this study so well, and yet I never considered it could have a secret passage. We cross it and I find myself following him, descending narrow steps.

No. Wait. This doesn't make sense.

I stop. "Where are you taking me?"

"Where? You have to run, Astra."

"Run where?" He's always told me I'd find no shelter, no respite, that if I were to run away, there would be nowhere to go. "And why?"

He points back, in the direction of the study. "I did not raise you for this."

Technically, he did. The thought has always terrified me, and yet running away terrifies me more. "You raised me for what, then?"

"For something better." There's a mad glint in his eyes. "Now it's all ruined. All because you had to go out and... I don't even know what you did, Astra. You learned seduction, but it was not to bring a disgraced prince here, willing to have you at any cost."

"I... Didn't do anything. You can ask Ziven." I don't know why I'm trusting him so much, but what else can I say?

"It's over now. We can't undo what happened, but I'm not giving you to that monster."

I appreciate the feeling, and yet... "But then what am I going to do with my life? Wasn't I raised to protect Krastel? To use my talents in a marriage alliance? I secured an alliance! Let me prove what I can do!"

"Not like that. Not with a prince who has nothing," he roars. "I'll find a place for you to hide. We'll improvise. We'll find a way."

And yet none of that feels comforting. I don't want this strange marriage to Marlak, and yet I don't want to be a fugitive, to be nothing. And if the prince wants me even though he knows I'm a substitute, this is my chance to stop pretending, to be someone, to be myself.

It takes all my courage, and yet I manage to speak my mind. "No. I'm not a coward, and I have honor."

I turn and run up three steps, but then he catches me and holds my waist—not tight enough, though. I was expecting it, so I pull a dagger, turn, and point it at his throat. Otavio is a master beautician, a brilliant apothecary, but he's no fighter.

"Don't get in the way of my duty," I say.

He raises his hands and laughs. "*That* is not your duty."

"It *is* now. Are you going to help me or hinder me? I can tell them what you're trying to do."

"Go." He still chuckles. "Go then. Marry the freak. You know what's going to happen? You won't have color for your hair and they'll find out what you are. Do you know what the fae does to your kind?"

Oh, he wants to play this game? I can play it, too. "Then they'll find out you've been harboring me, lying about me. I won't go down alone. Unless you help me. Give me hair coloring. Let me do my duty to the kingdom."

He closes his eyes. "Astra. This is not what I wanted for you. You were meant for so much more."

"More what? Because I never heard anything." I never even heard any compliment, not that it matters now.

Otavio sighs. "Fine, then. I'll give you hair coloring and other supplies. Whatever happens, don't let him get you pregnant. Find his secrets, as many as you can. Find where he keeps his crown, and how to get it back to King Renel." He stops, eyes distant. "Yes, the crown could be our key." He turns to me again. "You're right that this might work out in our favor, since you insist so much. When he hurts you, remember it was your choice, Astra. Remember you shunned your escape."

I don't want to think about Marlak hurting me, about what he wants to do. And yet I don't want to be a traitor. "Escaping is dishonorable."

"Honor is a lie! It's a lie to make people stupid and submissive. It's a lie to manipulate those who get nothing for their loyalty."

I don't know what to say. I've worked so hard to have honor, to show that I could be more than I was born to be. But then, Otavio's upset. Words lose their meaning when we're like that.

I'm worried and upset too. How can I even judge him?

"Thank you," I say. "For trying to save me." It's true, I appreciate his effort. "But you trained me well, and I think I can save myself."

"You can still escape, Astra."

His voice is soft now, and it could be so tempting to trust him. To run.

And yet he has some strange plan that I know nothing of,

he speaks of murder as if it were something normal, he treats us as if we were animals to be trained and mated. I don't fully trust him, and I don't want to depend on him to keep me safe while defying a royal command, while shunning everything I've trained for. It's too risky.

Marrying Marlak is worse than dreadful, but I won't be betraying anyone. I'll still be fulfilling my duty. Why is Otavio putting the burden on me for making the only sensible choice?

"You know I can't."

He sighs. "Perhaps you're right." His shoulders are hunched, his posture defeated. Perhaps I've judged him wrong, and he does care about me.

We return to his study, where he prepares a small bag with beauty supplies, mostly hair coloring and some small bottles with poisons, gives it to me, then leads me upstairs.

When I get to my room, there's a small suitcase on the bed. Andrezza is standing in a corner, and gives me a forced smile. "You're getting new clothes, Astra. They said your dresses should befit your station. But you can gather small personal items, except books."

Almost nothing, then. But I do take some things from my vanity table, then sit on the bed and discreetly grab the pouch with the silver ducks. I put them all in the bag with the beauty supplies.

A maid comes in, carrying a simple dress in thin, red wool. "For your wedding, my lady."

It's a peasant's dress. Why are they making me wear that to marry a prince?

Andrezza turns to the others. "Leave. I'll help her get ready."

I remove my practice dress with the pockets for daggers,

and then put on that red thing. It's so easy to tie that I don't even need any help. "Why red?"

"I think it's a fae color for weddings. I..." She looks down. "Apparently, Marlak thinks you're a maid who was accompanying Prince Ziven, so they think you should wear a maid's clothes, to make it more believable. In the same way you'd take elaborate, rich clothes if you were pretending to be—"

"I understand." Really, the clothes don't even matter that much. I smile at her. "It makes sense."

She nods. "And the kingdom is providing no dowry, so you're not taking anything valuable. I guess that also explains the dresses."

"I'm glad I'm not going naked." I manage a laugh. No. What odd sound was that?

Andrezza smiles and yet it doesn't reach her eyes. "Don't worry. Your husband will provide for you."

Husband. Right. As if he wasn't a fugitive, disgraced prince. As if he wasn't the maniac who torched his family and burned Lord Stratson's manor. As if he wasn't the villain who kidnapped me.

It was my choice not to tell anyone about it.

I feel cold all over. Oh, he could literally cover me with ice.

"Also..." Andrezza pauses and swallows. Whatever is coming, I'm not going to like it. "I don't know all the details of the marriage contract, but they told me it has no virginity clause, so you don't need to worry if he finds out you're experienced."

Ugh? Can anyone call that experienced? It's like calling someone who played a few times with a wooden sword an experienced fighter. And how does she even know?

She continues, "Still, my suggestion is for you to relax but pretend it hurts, just so he thinks he's the first. Make him feel big, powerful, as if he's conquering you."

I think I might throw up.

The reality of what I'm about to do finally hits me, and hits me hard. *Relax.* I'll have to relax, during... Would he want to...?

True, I've been having dreams about it, but dreams and reality are completely different. My knees almost buckle, but what's the point of falling face down on the floor?

Andrezza approaches me and pats my face gently, as if the gesture was encouraging and not a soft version of slaps to the face. "Be strong. You're prepared for this."

I'm dizzy. Why didn't I run with Otavio? I know why, and yet... And then perhaps I simply didn't think this through.

She looks me up and down. "You're still beautiful, Astra. Remember to be enchanting, and you'll command him."

Command Marlak? Hilarious. I don't think she's seen him. My heart is going to explode.

"Ready?" Otavio asks from behind the door.

"Yes. Come in," Andrezza replies.

I lost my voice. Lost my courage. Even my honor is leaving me, as I regret not having chosen the coward's way.

Marlak, the real Marlak, is terrifying. The idea of being given to him... What a strange idea. I have to keep my wits or I'll faint. Well, what difference does it make if I faint or not?

Otavio is standing in front of me, and puts both his hands around my face. They're too hot even though they are cold, there's too much pressure even though there's none, and I'm feeling too strange.

He says, "Find out where he hides the Crystal Court treasure, especially the crown. The shadow ring, too." It's odd that he's repeating it, but I guess he's afraid I'll forget it. "That information is valuable. Find out his secrets, his vulnerabilities. We'll help you come back, and we'll try to contact you. Remember to answer to me." He looks straight into my eyes. "*I* can guarantee your safety."

Andrezza has a dry chuckle. "Don't you love how he leaves me out?"

I try to smile, but I think I'm making a dreadful grimace. Otavio often leaves her out, and much more than she realizes, if she doesn't know my secret. His words were for me, and they mean that I should trust him and answer to *him* only, not to him and her, not to him and the king.

He's the bearer of my secret, the protector of my identity, and this was a reminder. But she doesn't know about it, of course, and thinks he's just being careless with his words.

"I'm ready," I squeak. That sounded ridiculous.

And no. I'm not ready.

MANY TIMES I imagined getting married as part of my duty, but it was always in a distant kingdom, in a glamorous party, dressed as Princess Driziely.

I never could have guessed that my wedding would happen in the chapel of the Elite Tower, the chapel where I found my connection with the Almighty Mother. I was ready to lie and pretend in front of representatives from other kingdoms, but to lie and pretend in front of the priestess is a blasphemy that makes me sick.

And yet, I was the one who squandered the alternative and refused to run away. Will regret follow me for the rest of my days?

Otavio and Andrezza walk beside me and a few guards follow us as I enter the chapel. The king and queen themselves, surrounded by many guards, are sitting at the front.

Wow, I kept the king waiting. I don't know if it's an honor or a disgrace.

There's also a hunched figure in the front, with curly black hair to his shoulder, wearing a long-sleeved black shirt. He gets up, turns, and his eyebrows shoot up when he sees me, perhaps surprised with the new hair color or disappointed with the dress. Who knows what he wants? He's wearing earrings with crescents—just like in the dream.

My entire body trembles as I walk to him. I try not to look at his face, but from what I glimpse, it's set in an unreadable mask.

"Make it fast," someone says. The king. He definitely didn't appreciate the wait.

The priestess's eyes are wide, but otherwise, she looks composed.

This is the priestess who taught me about the Almighty Mother and my inner strength, who told me about the tricks of faith, who told me how to see my kindred soul...

It's shameful that she has to preside over this mockery of the holy wedding traditions. Why did they have to do the wedding here?

"Let us trust the Almighty Mother," the priestess says, looking at me. I give her a smile, feeling guilty for my inner grumbling. I have to trust. She continues, "Both of you, look at each other and repeat after me. I promise to honor and protect you, love and appreciate you, cherish and respect you."

I can't look into his eyes. I'll get too nervous, so I stare at his forehead while repeating the words. My hands are sweaty, but I don't want to wipe them on my dress. His voice and mine echo in the chapel, a dissonant harmony that crawls into my ears.

She continues, "From now until forever, we're bonded in light."

It's so final, so wrong. Words have power, and I wish I could mouth the words and make no sound, but it's just the two of us, and they would notice if a voice was missing. His own voice is the harsh baritone I've heard before. At least it cloaks my forced squeaks.

I still don't understand why he's here, and can't believe this is real.

"You can kiss," the priestess says.

Oh, dear. I suppose the time to panic starts now. I still don't dare face him.

He puts his hands on my shoulders and his lips close to my ear. That's a creative way to kiss at a wedding.

Instead of kissing me, he whispers, "Don't worry, I won't touch you." Then he kisses me briefly on the temple.

My breath hitches. *Now* I'm trembling from head to toe.

His tone, his voice, when he whispered, was the exact low, comforting rumble I've heard so many times in my dreams.

7

My suitcase and bag feel heavy in my hands as I follow Marlak, still unable to digest the insanity of what's happening.

I'm leaving.

Without even saying goodbye.

Tarlia's face flashes through my mind. There will be no *later* for us. Will we ever talk again? I'll miss her, miss Sayanne, even with her flaws. I'll miss Ziven, even if I barely got to know him. I'll miss my training, my room, my library, my classes. There's an empty road ahead of me, and I don't know where it leads. All I see is an abyss separating me from everything I know.

Some ten guards follow us down the stairs. This time, I feel that they're not watching me, but watching *him*. Fearing *him*. They've obviously never seen his magic, since even thirty of them would be no match for it. I pause just to catch a breath, and he looks back and frowns, annoyed.

"Give me that." He points to the suitcase.

I realize I don't even have an attendant. But it's fine. "I can handle it."

I'm not going to let a prince carry my luggage, and it's

not that heavy. My new ugly dresses are the things weighing the least right now.

He nods and continues, without insisting. Was I expecting him to insist? Marlak looks so out of place on these stairs, impossibly broad and large and alien. His scars are visible behind his left ear, and it's odd how the tattoos don't really disguise, but rather emphasize them. *Monster,* Otavio said. He had a good point. And good intentions—which I squandered.

At least I'm not afraid Marlak will hurt me, not in the worst way, at least.

I won't touch you.

I can still hear his soft, comforting words. I can still feel his quick, gentle kiss. At least he did something to assuage my fears. Perhaps it won't be that terrible. And yet I can still barely breathe.

In the courtyard, I have no trouble recognizing Marlak's carriage. It's a shiny white thing with golden engravings, with a moon and a star on the door. That's the symbol of the Crystal Court, and I assume this is, or should be, one of the carriages of the fae palace. I wonder if he also stole it after killing his family. That would explain how he hauled the fae relics. And yes, my mind is veering completely off topic. Perhaps that's what I need to do, in order to face what's coming. Whatever's coming.

The inside of the carriage has two seats facing each other, luxuriously cushioned in burgundy velvet.

He sits in front of me, and then we're on the move. I look down at my dress, the red so much lighter than the seat. A cheerful color. A strange color and a strange dress that, to be fair, doesn't even fit me properly, the fabric stretched over my chest.

"Happy?" He asks. At least it's his normal, grating voice, not the soothing one.

He's staring at me, really staring, as if examining my face.

A nervous laugh escapes my lips. "I should be, right? My wedding day." I don't hide the sarcasm in my words.

He runs a ringed hand through his curls. "Oh, yes. What a happy day. I'm also thrilled." His voice is flat.

"Why, then?" I dare ask. "What's the point of this?"

He glares at me. "What did you honestly expect? Did you think you could steal into my dreams, rip my secrets, and life would go on as usual? Did you think you could humiliate me, and there would be no consequences?"

Dreams? The dream about the Pit of Death? It can't be. If he's seen that, then he's seen... No. I feel all cold inside, and tell myself he must be talking about the incident in the cave, which is already humiliating enough for a few lifetimes.

"Oh." I manage to sound surprised, and then I chuckle. "Now I'm responsible for your dreams? Funny." I know it's wild to provoke him when I don't know what he'll do, but I don't see any other way out of this.

"You know what's hilarious? They had no qualms giving you away for *nothing* to be raped on your wedding night." I see a sheen of fury in his eyes—but it isn't a threat.

I don't think it is, at least. Or maybe that's my pointless, crazy hope. "You wouldn't do that." I can still recall his promise, still remember his soft, whispered words.

He smirks. "But they don't know that, do they?"

"It wouldn't cross their mind." Wouldn't it? I recall Andrezza's words... *He'll expect it to hurt. It makes him feel powerful.* Ugh.

"Come on, you can't be that naïve, *wife*." The word is laced in mockery, turned into some odd insult. "What do you think I told them? What was my reason to want you so badly?" He chuckles. "Political alliance? It was more like *oh, she's so pretty, I can't stop thinking about her.*" His voice is mocking and high and extremely irritating.

I feel shaken to my bones, and decide to throw all my inexistent caution to the wind. "So you think they expect you to be a brute who doesn't know how to seduce a woman?"

He cocks his head. "What else would they expect? Unless... Fair. They might think I'll rape you gently tonight."

That's not true. At all. "They did ask me—just so you know. And I chose to do my duty."

"Oh, I have no doubt they asked. Right after you had already been sold like a cow." As if his words didn't hurt enough, he adds, "For a couple cheap trinkets and some pointless promises."

Cheap trinkets. I'm not going to show him how deep his words cut, so I smile instead. "Congratulations, you got a bargain."

"I know. Impressive, right? That's the value of power, and why it's so coveted." He snaps his fingers. "You can just do what you want. Take what you want."

Like the fae relics. "Are you proud of that?"

"That's not how you should treat people. But this time it came in handy." He stares at me again. "A *forced* hand. I can't let you tatter my secrets to my brother. I just can't, wife." The word carries less bite this time. "You gave me no choice."

There's no point trying to be nice to him. I don't think he even likes me, so I decide to be honest—in part, at least.

"That makes no sense. Even if I *could* see your secrets, and let's not forget you're the one with the mind magic, how does that relate to King Renel?"

"*Prince* Renel. He's never been crowned."

I raise an eyebrow. "Oh. Have you?"

He laughs and looks away. "I must admit, wife, your

power is quite impressive. Quite impressive. Doesn't impress me, but explains what they were raising you for."

He knows too much about me, and yet, I'm not sure what he's referring to. "Really? Enlighten me."

There's still a smug smile on his face, but it softens as he looks at me, speaking slowly. "With your powers, you could bring my brother to his knees. You could make him your slave. It would be a beautiful thing to see, except for the part where he would get access to my mind. Now, I can't have that, can I?"

Right. Marlak's insane. "Wow, you concocted quite a story. What do you think the Crystal Court king would do with a human wife?"

"It's obvious, isn't it?" He shrugs. "Rape her. I doubt he'd do it gently."

"You're obsessed with that word."

"Shouldn't I be? I don't see why *you* are not concerned."

This talk makes me uncomfortable. "I'm not... I'm not the one they'd send for a wedding like that. And to wed the Crystal Court king... they might send the princess herself. It's a dream alliance." Maybe not, if I recall what I overheard, but there was no guarantee Otavio would succeed.

"An alliance that was carefully planned. Fair, maybe they'll send the princess. And they might send her *maids* with her. Same problem."

I'm rattled by how much he knows about me, and yet I don't want to ask how he learned it and reveal that he's right, in case he's bluffing. Also, I still don't think King Renel was the alliance Otavio and Andrezza meant. "The odds that your brother will want to marry Princess Driziely are zero."

"Then you're not paying attention. The Krastel King has spread far and wide the myth that his daughter is the most beautiful woman in the world, the most enchanting, that men who catch a mere glimpse of her go wild with desire."

"That's nonsense."

"Obviously." He gestures towards me. "I'm here looking at you and know that it's a ridiculous farce."

Wow, thanks! I mean, not that I think me and the other substitutes can drive anyone mad with desire, but the way he says it... I keep my face flat, though.

He continues, "You know why your king is doing it? To make her a coveted prize. The man who marries her will attain a symbol of power, a symbol of prestige. Yes, my brother would eat that up."

"Because you obviously think he's stupid."

"Not at all." His forehead has a slight frown. "He's brilliant. And he knows that symbols matter."

None of this makes sense. "He can have a beautiful fae wife."

"He can have *hundreds* of fae lovers. That's a different issue. He won't pass up this opportunity."

I roll my eyes. "I guess you have it all figured out, then."

"Oh, I do." I can see the scheming, the evil in his words, his poorly contained anger. "It's about predicting your opponent's moves. I won't lie." He leans forward, his face close to me. "There is a satisfaction in owning something that would be his."

As if he didn't have a whole bunch of stuff stolen from his brother. "I'm not a thing."

"For him, you'd be." He's still close, his smell fresh and citrusy.

Perhaps this is not the best time to realize I haven't even bathed before coming, so I stick to the topic, and I'm honest. "And I wouldn't be the one sent to marry him, if that ever came to pass."

"Well, that's not a risk I'm willing to take. Happy now? That you know why I married you? So you won't be wondering if I'm planning to feed you to the fish."

His logic is based on some bold assumptions, but I understand that he doesn't want me spilling his secrets, which means... It hits me then, and I meet his eyes. "You'll keep me as a prisoner."

"Right. Such a pity, you were so free before that. And prisoner, wife, is that really different?"

"A wife can come and go as she pleases."

"Not all of them, no." He points a finger at me. "That said, at least you won't be—"

"Raped. I know. Can you stop?"

"I was going to say *mistreated*, but it's true that your point is a lot more valid. And I'll protect you."

Still, this is a punishment, but I can't be the only one who's unhappy. I smile at him. "Congratulations. You just married a measly..." I was going to say substitute, but I don't want to reveal that. What should I say? Maid? Attendant? "Guard."

"You are the legitimate Crystal Court Queen."

Am I supposed to laugh? Maybe not. "I meant before."

He smirks. "You were the *future* legitimate Crystal Court Queen."

"Of course. I suppose this was written in the stars." My voice is full of sarcasm, but then I recall the threads of destiny. No, whatever this is, it has nothing to do with my visions, with my kindred soul.

"Things are only written once we write them. Then there's no choice but to accept what is." His voice is slow, solemn, perhaps pained?

I don't suppose he's trying to evoke pity, is he? He who

has committed horrific atrocities, such as… "Did you attack Lord Stratson's estate?" I blurt.

He looks at me and frowns. "I don't keep track of human lords, and much less attack them."

It sounds convincing, but it could be a lie. Wait a minute. Can he even lie? He looks human but he's a full-blooded fae.

I know the question is stupid, but it leaves my mouth before I call it back. "Can you lie?"

"That's a question without a satisfactory answer, wife." His mocking tone is back.

"You could say *yes*. That would be an answer."

"Well, my answer's *no*."

He stares at me with a mocking smirk, knowing I don't have an answer to my question, then extends his arms on the back of the seat behind him. My heart flutters for a moment, as I'm reminded of my dreams, when I'm nested in the space between his arm and his chest, enveloped in a wonderful feeling of love and safety.

Not *his* arms. It's not the same person. I need to remember that, so those visions don't muddle my mind.

Marlak's observing me, eyes narrowed, visibly displeased with something. I notice that his eyes look like they have a thin layer of black ink, but it's not ink. It's his dark, thick eyelashes that give that impression. For some reason they look beautiful and menacing at the same time. And I shouldn't be noticing his eyes.

"Wife," he says slowly. "You will be free—within certain constraints, of course." Like being a prisoner. I know. He continues, "And I'll do my best to provide and protect you, but do not play with me. Do not mock me. Are your powers impressive? Absolutely. Do they affect me? Not at all. So don't waste them."

Powers? Oh, right. He thinks I'm some kind of seductress.

I try to imagine myself in a dress with a low cut, and it just looks ridiculous. Then again, that strategy doesn't work for everyone. What would work for Marlak? Probably nothing. Covering myself in treasure, maybe, as if he didn't have more than enough.

"I don't have any powers."

"I know you don't. Not any that will affect me, at least, and I'd really rather you didn't make a fool of yourself." He leans over again, and the only reason his face is not close to me anymore is because I lean as far back as I can, even if it's a position that conveys fear. I don't care.

"Understand, Astra." His voice is slow and careful. "I don't think you're alluring, I don't think you're charming, I don't think you're attractive. Your pathetic attempts at seducing me are laughable. Your crude attempts at trying to elicit a physical response are not only pitiful, they're vulgar and tasteless. I suggest you stop them."

Great. Now I'm feeling angry and humiliated, and it's so hard to hold back my tears when I'm feeling like that. My only chance to keep them in check is by fighting back, even if nothing comes to mind but immature words.

"Oh, look who's talking. One would think you're prince charming. You're overcooked, *husband*." I can also make a mockery of that. "They forgot to turn you on the spit."

He laughs. "Oh, wife, you're so creative with your insults. You must think I don't have a mirror, but I do. I know very well that I'm ugly, disfigured, scarred." Those words are utterly ridiculous, but I'm not going to tell him that.

He leans forward even more. "I know very well that I'm repulsive. I know what I am. I know what I look like. What you don't know is that I can be a monster both on the outside and on the inside."

For a second, I don't have a reply. I don't know what to

say. Angry tears are threatening to burst through, but I won't let them. I won't let them.

"Oh, look at him. So manly and so threatening. Are you trying to compensate for something? Is it your itsy-bitsy weenie?" I know. I know I'm arguing like a ten-year-old, but it's either that or crying, and I'm not going to let him see me cry.

He leans back and laughs. "But you know exactly how tiny it is, don't you? You pretended to like it just enough."

Oh. He means... Oh. I can still recall holding it. No, no, no. It was a dream. *My* dream—and I have to erase it from my mind.

Keeping my face blank and even a little surprised, I say, "You're insane."

"Yes. I'm the one who's insane. I'm the one who plants dreams in other people's heads."

"You have your ring." I glance at his hand, but don't spot the Shadow Ring. "Usually. No magic can reach you. If that magic even existed. You're making excuses for your depraved fantasies."

He nods. "I'm glad you're aware they're depraved. And I don't think you understand how the Shadow Ring works."

"Perhaps you'd like to enlighten me?"

"Maybe. Once you stop it, Astra. Stop trying. It's useless and bothersome." His voice is sharp like a dagger, while his black eyes hide a storm behind them.

"You're delusional. Who in their right mind would want to seduce *you*?"

"Nobody. We both know that." He raises an eyebrow and smirks.

I don't know what he's smirking at, frankly, and yet there's a harshness in his eyes... I look down. He's pretty much telling me to stop the visions and dreams, but how am

I going to stop something I can't control? Can I confess I can't control them? I don't even know if he'd believe me.

"There's something else," he says.

Bracing myself for another round of humiliation, I stare at him. "Yes?"

"They'll try to hurt you to hurt me."

"I see. I'm your shield now."

"No. You're my weakness. Or at least it's how they'll see it. It's why you need to be hidden."

I scoff. "Just say I'm your prisoner."

"You know you are." He throws his hands up. "But you'll need to be careful, wife. You'll be a target. For what it's worth, I'm truly sorry for that." He manages to say that softly.

Not softly like in the dreams, thankfully, but he still sounds kind, as if he hadn't just called me a pathetic, unattractive, failed seductress.

"Yes. Poor you. So sorry."

He shrugs. "Well, if you can't handle the game, don't play it."

"I heard a different one. Don't play with fire if you don't want to get burned." I narrow my eyes. "But I guess you know that already."

His smile doesn't leave him, but he turns and looks out the window. I'm partly relieved to be spared of his digs, partly worried that perhaps I pushed him too far.

Pointless tears are still threatening to leave my eyes. Part of me is furious at myself, in disbelief at the ridiculous, immature words I uttered. Part of me is furious at him, thinking he deserved every cruel insult.

At least both parts agree that none of this bodes well.

I dare look out the window, don't see Mount Eye in front of us, and assume we're going south. But where? There are fields around us, a fresh smell of leaves—and something citrusy as well. That's *his* smell, I realize, and I have to control my head not to turn to him.

He's been silent for a long time, and I fear that if I break that silence, he'll surround me in a block of ice until we get to our destination. It does feel like there's ice around me, ice between us, so maybe there *is* some magic at work, something dreadful that chills my insides.

But then, this is what my life's going to be. The fae prince didn't wed me so we could become friends and have a lovely time together. I'm his prisoner, paying for what I've done, paying for the danger he thinks I could pose. None of it was my fault, but he doesn't know it, and I sure hope he never finds out.

When I look back at our interaction, I definitely want to disappear—again. Congratulations, Astra! Truly impressive. I mean, maybe I'm not an expert in seduction, but even a nitwit knows that telling someone he's *half-cooked* is not the way into their heart. And while I have no intention of *enchanting* him, pissing him off is a terrible survival strategy.

How do I fix what I've done? If I'm too compliant, he'll be suspicious—or worse, he'll think I'm trying to seduce him. If I keep defying him, I'll just aggravate him to a point of no return—assuming we haven't reached it yet. Haha. I mean, I have to be optimistic here, right? My best bet is to wait for him to calm down, observe him, then start over and find a way to gain his trust.

I try not to look at him as he runs a ringed hand through his black curls. Duh. I guess I just did, but I look away and swallow. He's so ridiculously good looking. I know, I know. It's not what I thought before. He's like the kind of food that tastes strange the first time you try it, but then, after a while, you realize you like it and even crave it. I'm not saying I like him, obviously, much less that I crave him. I mean the way he looks.

He might be able to lie, if he stared at me in the face and claimed he was ugly *and* owns a mirror. Only one of those statements can be true. I glance at him again, notice his eyes on me, and look away quickly. Oh, no. He's going to think I'm playing games, and I'm not. I hope my tan is saving me and hiding the warmth on my cheeks.

What I do know is that my mind will explode if I keep second guessing and trying to control my face, my body, my expressions, my thoughts.

"Astra." There's no anger or irritation in his voice and it surprises me—or perhaps scares me. I turn to him, and he sighs. "I'm sorry. I mean, I don't think I removed you from a decent life, but you obviously hold a different opinion. This won't be forever." He's gentle again. Oh, he loves to make me confused. "Once my brother's defeated, we'll annul the marriage, and you'll be free to do whatever you wish. I have no intention to keep you forever."

His words sting, and I'm not sure if it's because he used the verb *keep*, as if I was an animal, or if I'm smart enough to see the well-concealed reminder that he loathes me. I chuckle. "Cause I'm obviously pathetic and despicable."

"I didn't say that." He throws his hands in the air. "Wife. By the gods. I'm trying to comfort you. I already said I won't touch you. You should have seen yourself; you were pale. I mean, I should be offended, but I wasn't. Now I'm saying I'll set you free, and you're upset?" He takes a deep breath and covers his face with his hands.

"You're reminding me I'm your prisoner." There's no bite in my words. I'm tired of fighting and dreading going too far again. "And you know you might never defeat your brother."

"I will. I'll defeat him." There's no hesitation in his voice, and it's not like a wish, but as if he was stating something obvious. "If it takes long, I don't know..." He runs a hand over his curls, then stares at me. "After seven years, we can try to find another solution. It's a promise. So don't despair."

Seven tiny years. All my youth tied to someone who hates me. Why despair? But the truth is that he's trying to be nice, and maybe I should show some appreciation.

"Thank you." I smile, and add, "For your words. For trying to put me at ease."

The key word here is *trying*, right? I can't say I'm looking forward to seven years of this, but at least if he's cordial, it's not going to be the most horrific thing in the world.

He nods. At the end of the day, he *does* have power over me. There's no hope that I'll ever charm him, but it would be stupid to keep opposing him. And then, I also need to uncover his secrets, figure out where he hides his treasure. I need to remain true to who I am, and to everything I strive for, and use this opportunity to fulfill my duty.

The carriage stops, and a thin layer of ice covers the windows before I have time to look. I shudder, still recalling my first encounter with him. "What's happening?"

"I'll have to blindfold you."

"What if I say no?" It was just curiosity, but I realize it came out like a challenge.

Holding a strip of cloth, he blinks slowly and shrugs. "I could make you faint."

I turn around. "Fine. Use the blindfold."

Without touching me, he ties a soft velvety cloth around my eyes. I sense something different, something...

"Is it magic?" I ask.

"Indeed. You won't be able to peek."

I wonder if this is one of the stolen fae relics, but I don't ask.

The door of the carriage then opens and closes, and I realize I'm alone and can't see anything. Perhaps I should be glad he explained his motivations, so I don't think he plans to leave me here. Well, he said he wasn't going to feed me to the fish, but didn't mention anything about setting fire to a carriage with me in it.

He's talking outside, but I can't hear what he's saying, only that there's someone else—a young man, it seems—and they are laughing. It's probably the coachman, unless I somehow missed enchanted horses or something even stranger.

Unable to see anything, unsure what he's planning, I feel suffocated and anxious, so I take a slow, deep breath. Nerves just make everything worse. Of course, if he plans to do something to me, being calm while magically blindfolded won't help me much. Better than having a blurred mind.

The door near me then clicks open.

"Here," he says. "Take my hand."

I'm about to mention that I have no idea where it is, when I feel his fingers, gloved in some soft suede, touching mine.

"Wife, you're trembling." There's mockery but also surprise in his tone. "What were you thinking? That I was going to throw you into a pit or something?"

I almost ask him if he means the Pit of Death, but hold my tongue just in time. I'll never tell him about my dreams. Outside, I can hear the sound of rustling leaves and running water, so I know we're near a forest and a river or stream.

"What's with the gloves?" I ask, just because I found it odd.

I'm wondering if he's wearing them under the rings or over them, or maybe if he took them all off. What an incredibly useful line of thought.

He has a warm chuckle. "You're going to start telling me what to wear? A little early for that, wife."

"I was just curious," I mumble while getting out of the carriage. "I didn't see the shadow ring."

"You seem quite interested in fae jewelry."

"Who wouldn't be?"

He doesn't reply, just makes me walk a few more steps, then, swiftly and firmly enough that it doesn't even tickle, he holds my waist, lifts me, and sits me on a saddle with a backrest. I can smell the horse beneath me and feel it shifting, but I don't like it that there's nowhere to hold, that I can't see anything, so I place my hands in the rest behind me.

Right as I do that, I feel something against my hand. His leg—no. Oh, no. This is a double saddle, and he's taking the seat behind me. I can't believe what I just grazed.

I pull my hands quickly. "There was nowhere to hold."

He leans over and guides my arms to a strap in front of the saddle. "There." He then takes the reins, holding me in a loose embrace.

"I couldn't see." I feel that I have to explain myself. "It affects my balance." I know it sounds stupid, but it's true. This saddle is odd, and I don't even know what horse this is, and if it's a horse, and then not seeing anything...

"Huh. You've never done anything blindfolded?"

"No."

"Hmm."

I'm not sure what he means with that.

The horse then takes off, and a cool wind hits my face. Too fast. Also, although the gallops sound normal, at least to me, who's not in any way an expert in horses, the movements are too smooth, too... Different, and I'm not even sure why. There's an animal beneath me, for sure, but I don't know what it is. And then there's Marlak behind me, thankfully separated by part of the saddle, or I would recall...

Well, too late, the image just came to my mind, that strange vision I had in the cave, when he was behind me, when I felt him biting my ear, cupping my breasts, when I felt him...

I need to find a way to scrub that from my mind, especially when we're in a similar position, with his arms around me. And with a blindfold on, I can't even focus on my surroundings. No images in my mind but his arms holding me, and a feeling of peace, safety, love.

Not now, Astra! You're being taken by an exiled, fugitive prince to his hideout. And he thinks you're pathetic. There's nothing loving about this. Nothing romantic.

I focus on vomit-tasting passion fruit custard in all its disgustingness, and yet it tastes like the sweet, innocent hope I had, when all I wanted was some time with Quin's smile. Now I don't even care about Quin and I don't know where my life is taking me. Hopefully not the Pit of Death. Or maybe yes, if it's a super secret place, the very reason I'm here.

Maybe I'm going to the pit of despair. At least I'm good at climbing, and I'll find a way out of it.

8

The smooth gallop and the fresh, leaf-scented wind drive me into a pleasant lull, and despite myself, I can't shake off the feeling of being loved and protected, a stupid feeling just because somehow I keep thinking the arms around me are the ones from my dreams.

Despite my hunger, I could go on like this forever, in this pleasant limbo where I still don't know what my life is going to look like, where there's still no harsh reality to face. Nothing to face.

Nobody can go on like this forever.

Indeed, we finally stop. He dismounts behind me, and this time, my hands are safely clutching the strap in front of me. When he lifts me, I'm again surprised that his touch is firm enough that it doesn't tickle, which is for the best. I think he'd be pissed if I started laughing.

He whistles, and then the horse or whatever gallops away, the sound of its hooves on grass fading into the distance. I feel Marlak's hands on the back of my head, untying the blindfold, and then light assaults my senses. Too much. Too bright.

Slowly, as my eyes adjust, I realize that the sun is up in

the sky among fluffy clouds—and the scenery around me is wondrous.

We stand on a rocky river shore, encircled by mountains draped in lush green forests, appearing gray in the distance. The river is wide and blue, dotted with small islands. On the other side, there's a soft slope inclining into the base of a mountain. I look behind me, and see a cliff not far behind us, and more dark green mountains.

That many tall mountains, a narrow valley housing a deep blue river with islands, this has to be far south, right between the Crystal Court territory and the Wild Fae lands. I think I know where we are.

I turn to Marlak. "This is the Queen's Valley, amidst the Endless Mountains. And this is the Queen's River. Why the blindfold?"

He stares at me as if searching for something with his dark eyes. I can sense that he's still measuring me, still trying to figure out what kind of person I am. "Perhaps you know where we are, wife. Now, do you by any chance know how we got here?"

I glance back—and realize there was no way a horse would have galloped in that steep and rocky surface. Moreover, we traveled for only thirty minutes or so, and the journey here should have taken many, many hours. I try to glimpse a portal, some kind of fae shortcut, but there's nothing for my human eyes.

Somehow, this is when it hits me that I'm deep down in fae territory, with a fae prince. Despite his human appearance, his magic is not human at all. It's unpredictable, untethered to stones. Not only that, there's something wild and untamed even in the air.

I've always dreamed of traveling, and now I'm standing in this place where the power of nature humbles me. I might dislike the reason that brought me here, but I appreciate standing on this shore and seeing this part of the world.

"Impressive." I can't even hold back my smile.

He chuckles, a fast dry chuckle that I don't really understand. He's not laughing at me. It could be a chuckle of relief, except that it doesn't make any sense in this context.

I look around some more, still in disbelief that we are here. Only this morning, I was jumping rope in the shade of the canopy on the roof of my tower, and now there are no barriers around me.

"Ready?" he asks.

I'm startled out of my wondrous stupor. "For what?"

He points to one of the islands. "I'll have to hold you."

I'm still unsure what he means.

"To cross the river," he adds.

It's only then I realize something's missing. "Where's my luggage?"

Shit, shit, shit, if I don't have my hair color, I can't imagine what's going to happen.

"Nelsin's bringing it. One of my knights."

I hold back a relieved exhale and smile. "Oh. Right."

He still eyes me, searching. What is it that he's trying to find? I'm not the one hiding any fae treasure.

With his hands up, he asks, "Can I?"

There are no gloves now and he's wearing a bunch of rings, except for the Shadow Ring. I will never know how he was wearing gloves.

"Wife?" he insists.

Right. He wants to hold me to cross the river. What a gentleman, after ripping me out of my tower. I smile. "Sure."

Like that, he wraps his arms around me. My eyes are at his chest level, and I realize the height difference in my dream, when he rested his chin on top of my head, was correct. For a second, it's as if I'm in a dream again, and he's pulling me close in a loving embrace, but just a second.

In reality I sense wind under my feet, then we're floating above the rocks and the water, and finally landing on one of the islands. He lets me go as soon as we set foot on the ground, as if I were made of hot coal. Now that we're here, I can see a square, one-story building made of stones in the only clearing on the tiny island.

He points to the building. "It's simple, but it's safe."

For a runaway, disgraced prince, this is not bad, actually. "I wasn't exactly expecting a castle."

"Well, you should." He smiles. "I happen to own one."

"Right." I'm not going to argue with him or tell him that the crown of the Crystal Court will never sit on the head of the murderer of the previous king. He likely knows that much better than I do, which only means he's delusional.

It was quite bold of him to walk into the Krastel castle and not expect to be arrested and given to his brother as a prize. Why wasn't he arrested? I consider all his magic, and can only assume that they feared him, and maybe thought this would be a better long-term strategy than trying to deliver him to the king of the Crystal Court.

Indeed it *is* a better strategy, except that Otavio's behavior makes no sense. No, he was trying to protect me, and protecting people can be illogical. I feel a pang of pain when thinking of his desperation trying to get me away from the castle, away from Marlak. Love makes people stupid. Did he ever love me like a daughter?

"Come." Marlak gestures with his head, motioning towards the main door, an ugly thing made of bronze or some other metal.

I follow him. Inside, there's a spacious kitchen with three long, rustic wooden tables and a counter, followed by a hallway with a window at the end, and small rooms on either side. Rough stone makes up the walls, while the floor is polished wood. Each room has a wooden bed and a small chest with drawers. Everything is simple and basic, as if this was a place for traveling soldiers, not for royalty.

He turns to me. "Choose which room you want, and let me know what you need."

I pick one near the end of the hallway. It doesn't have a mirror or a dressing table, which is a problem if I'm going to color my hair. There's something else missing too. "Where do we..." Should I be ashamed to confess I need to pee?

"Outside. Usually." He points to a door on the other side. "But I converted this room into a bathing chamber." I follow him and see that it has a wooden tub, a pot, and even a mirror. "Let me know if it needs anything else."

There's something off about this. If this bathing chamber is for me, and he's brought me because of my dream, which was last night, then how... "Did you set it all up this morning?"

He eyes me and smirks. Eyes me too much. Oh, damn it. This was as good as a confession that I'm well aware of the dream I had. And then again, was it because of the dream? At least I keep my face neutral, showing no reaction.

He still considers me, then says, "I can be quite efficient."

"Good to know." I have to change the subject, fast. "If it's not too much work, is it possible to get me a dressing table, so I can—"

"Of course! I can't believe I forgot it. I'll get one in your room and one in this bathing chamber. If there's anything else you need, just tell me."

Yes, the location of the Crystal Court relics. No, I don't think that would go down well. Instead, I nod. "I will."

He looks away and fiddles with his rings, as if he's unsure

what to say. If he didn't even plan for this, and instead rushed into the Krastel castle this morning, then he's improvising. I still don't understand why he brought me here. The explanation about his secrets makes sense, but it can't be the whole truth. And yet, what is the truth?

He sighs. "I... suppose you're tired and hungry. Do you want to bathe, eat, rest?"

Well, he's smelling citrusy while I probably still stink from jumping rope, so the choice is quite obvious. "I'm hungry, but I think I'd like a bath before eating."

"Of course." He enters the bathing room, opens the window, and a jet of water comes through it, filling the tub in a matter of seconds. He does it so casually, like magic is nothing special at all. I guess for him, it isn't.

He then stares at me and pauses, as if remembering something. "Wait." He leaves the room and soon returns holding a soft bed cover in cotton. "I don't have towels yet, but you can use this for now." He points at the door. "It can be barred from the inside, but..." He bites his lip. "Sure, you can bar it. And close the curtain. I'll have lunch ready when you're done."

With that, he closes the door. It has a wooden latch that I turn. Only then do I take a deep breath. I'm alone and undisturbed for the first time since being summoned from the training grounds. It's good to know that I can be alone, that I can have a moment of peace, perhaps even many moments. I'll be able to color my hair. I'll even be able to prepare some concoctions and poisons, if necessary. I know that the bag Otavio sent me doesn't have only beauty products.

Would I dare poison Marlak? Kill him? Well, wasn't that what I trained for?

I'm glad to get rid of that ugly red dress, then remove my breastband and underpants, relieved to be naked, until I realize I have nothing else to wear and will have to put my underwear back on.

Terrible.

I don't see any servants or maids and wonder how this is going to work. Did he really say that *he* was going to prepare lunch? At least I know how to take care of myself and don't need anyone doing my hair, and yet it's still strange, for a prince. Then again, it's not strange for a disgraced, fugitive prince. Perhaps I should be glad we aren't in a hole somewhere.

I put my foot into the bath, which looks more like a huge wooden barrel. The water's extremely cold. I wonder if I should ask Marlak to heat it. I'm sure he can do it, with his powerful magic, but I'm already naked and frankly, starving, so I go in, just to freshen up. It's funny because in the Elite Tower, baths were a luxury, and I usually washed with a basin and a cloth. But this chilly water doesn't feel luxurious.

There's no soap and I'm wondering about the futility of this as I leave the bath before freezing. At least I have something that resembles a towel and I guess I got rid of any sweat from the morning training. As I'm putting on my clothes, I hear voices outside. One of the knights? A visitor?

When I open the door, I find the hallway empty. "Marlak?"

"Here," he replies from what is now my room. He's crouched over something. My bags. I notice that there's a bar with some hangers beside the door, and two of my new ugly dresses are already there.

Marlak holds a small drawstring pouch and looks at me, an eyebrow raised. "Is the Krastel kingdom so poor that this is all they paid you? Thirty-two silver ducks?"

Blood rushes to my face as I hear a loud pounding in my ears. How dare he? How dare he touch my belongings? How dare he ask about that?

I snatch the pouch out of his hands. "This is none of your business."

His eyes widen. "I was just trying to help you unpack."

Like a servant? No, he wanted to see what I brought, and the bath was just an excuse.

"They sent no dowry, therefore no money." My voice is a furious hiss. "You knew that when you made this deranged choice."

He shows me the palms of his hands. "I have no intention of claiming anything from you, I just..."

"You just what?" I'm still so angry that he touched my things without permission, that he invaded my privacy, without asking first.

"I'm surprised at how little they paid you, that's all." What an idiot.

"I'm not *paid*. I'm an honorable member of the Elite Guard."

"Wait." He raises an eyebrow. "You were a *slave*?"

Does he want my head to explode in fury? "I can see you know nothing about honor, and how could you?"

"Oh yes, how could I?" He snorts. "That said, I do know about *lack* of honor, and it usually goes hand in hand with exploitation."

"Nobody was being exploited, *husband*." I spit the word at him. "Don't talk about things you know nothing about."

"I won't." He gestured toward the dresses. "Now, I see you didn't bring all your clothes. Are you expecting to murder me that fast, or are you under the impression you'll return to your castle to pick up the rest?"

"I'm not going to murder you."

"I didn't think so, at least not until you got something useful from me, but now..." He looks around. "It's clear that you packed for less than a week. That said, you don't have enough money to last even a day, and the return trip is long. I must confess I'm puzzled."

"You shouldn't have gone through my luggage!" I'm so frustrated.

"Well, I had to."

He lifts his shoulders, then points to the cosmetics bag, and I notice right away that some bottles are missing. At least the hair coloring lotion is still there.

I glare at him. "You threw away my medicine! You had no right."

He puts a hand on his chest and takes a deep breath, pretending to be relieved. "Wife, dear, I'm so glad I did. Imagine if you had a stomachache and decided to drink some red herb extract. It would kill you. You had poison there. I can obviously see you knew nothing about it, and I can only assume that, in your complete innocence, you'd end up consuming it by mistake. I might have just saved your life."

I sigh. "There was no poison."

He smiles. "Again, there *was* poison, but fear not, it's all been properly disposed of. Aren't you glad I'm here, caring for your safety?"

I don't have a reply to that, of course. Insisting that there was nothing will only make me look stupid, and he knows I'm lying. "If you're so certain I'm going to kill you, why bring me here? Aren't you afraid I'll stab you in the back? Suffocate you in your sleep?"

He laughs, and it's a genuine laugh. "Oh, do try. I'd love to see that."

"You think I can't best you."

"I'm sure you can't."

He has just tickled that part of me that loves a challenge, but then he's right that this is not the time to kill him—or try to. The poisons were just a precaution. "It was my master who prepared my cosmetics bag. He might have thought it was good to be prepared."

"I suppose. You have many bottles with a black liquid, is it..." He looks at me. "For your hair?"

I don't like that look, and I hate that question. "Yes. I like to color it black."

He narrows his eyes. "But it was red, when... And it's..." He's staring at me, searching for something. "This is not your real color, but it's not red either, is it?"

"My natural hair is brown and boring," I say quickly—too quickly. I smile and make an effort to speak slowly. "I like it black."

He still stares, and for a moment I fear he's trying to figure out my real hair color, except that he obviously can't. He shrugs. "Black also looks good."

"Didn't you say I was ugly?" I know I shouldn't provoke him, but I can't stop myself.

"I never said you were ugly. I said you're unattractive and unappealing. There's a difference."

Right. Now I want to strangle him, but I just chuckle. "I wonder what gives you the idea that I care about your opinion."

He shrugs. "If you are trying to seduce me, I suppose—"

"I'm not!" I can't stand this stupid lie anymore. "I never tried to do anything, and you'd be the last person in the world I'd want to seduce. You, you are the one with the magic to plant thoughts in people's heads. You should look at yourself, look at *your* magic, and stop accusing me of what I'm not doing."

He shakes his head. "I can see images, thoughts, if I touch

someone and have that intent. I cannot plant ideas." He then stares at me intently, an eyebrow raised. "Or dreams."

I shake my hands in the air. "I'm not responsible for your dreams! I'm not." Perhaps I shouldn't be yelling, but I'm so frustrated.

"Fair, then."

That's it? That's what he's going to say? It doesn't even mean he believes it.

He continues, "Come, let's eat. I can hear your stomach growling."

"It's not just my stomach," I snap.

"Oh, I know." He laughs, then turns and walks down the hall.

What am I going to do? Stay here and starve? Obviously no, so I follow him into the kitchen.

On a table, there's a plate with cheese, bread, grapes, and some cold meat cuts, already thinly sliced. He brings two more plates, then sits and serves himself. I also sit, watch him, and do the same. I had so many classes on how to act around nobility, how to wait to be served, and now I'm not using any of that. Still, the advice to watch what your host does and then do the same still stands, and I guess I'm using it.

He swallows a bite of bread, then says, "I was hungry too. That's the thing with human bodies: we need to eat all the time."

"Aren't you fae, though?"

"Look at me." He gestures at himself, clearly aware of his build and how non fae-like his broad chest is. "I'm quite human. Voraciously human."

"But how..." I want to understand why he looks the way he does, but I don't want to offend him, and I'm not sure how to ask it.

To my relief, he doesn't wait for me to finish. "Generations and generations of fae intermingled with humans to strengthen our blood." He smirks. "All that human *strength* is bound to show up one day. Or maybe I'm cursed. Not even half-fae look like me."

"Does that mean you can lie?"

There's a challenge in his smile. "I'll let you figure it out by yourself. What do you think?"

"I don't know." And it's true. "You have fae magic, without opus stones. You're certainly not fully human."

"Neither human nor fae. It does put me in my own special place, I guess, belonging nowhere."

I disagree. "It's up to you. We can choose where we belong."

He tilts his head and gives me an unnerving stare. "Do we?"

I'm still wondering how to think of him, perhaps still wondering if he can lie. "Sometimes you talk like a fae, answering questions with more questions and vague sentences." I've never met a fae before, but I learned what they sound like. His way of talking likely means he can only say the truth, and that's why he has to twist his words.

"Incredible, right?" He strokes his chin. "Where would I have learned that?"

"You know what you are, then."

He stares at his bread and shakes his head. "I really don't, wife. But I came to the conclusion it doesn't matter."

We are silent, then, and I finish eating. I wonder if I should ask him about his family, about what happened, then I fear I'll upset him if I do. I guess I just wanted to understand what kind of person he is, what kind of person I'm dealing with, but then again, if he's fae, he's very good at deceiving and hiding his true feelings, and I'll have to keep that in mind.

He's still wearing lots of rings, but not the Shadow Ring, and I can only assume that he keeps it for special occasions, and wonder why he had it the day he attacked our carriage.

He stares at me. "What do you like to do? During your free time?"

I'm so startled by the regular question that it takes me a while to find my voice. "Train. And study."

"Physical training?"

I nod.

"I'll ask my knights to train you. Do you read? Poetry, stories..."

This could be my chance to find out what *azalee* means. "I like geography and history, but recently I was enjoying learning rare, old languages. Dictionaries."

He raises an eyebrow. "So you read *dictionaries* in your free time."

Fine, when he puts it like that, it sounds ridiculous, but I'm not going to back down. "I like to study." I'm not sure I'm making any sense and I'm thinking my request was stupid.

"Fair." He stares at me. "Would you be offended if I brought a seamstress? So you have more things to wear?" He shows me the palms of his hands. "You can wear the dresses you brought, if you prefer, it's just... Your clothes need to suit your station."

Station. What station? Disgraced prince's prisoner? Still, getting new clothes is a good idea, even if slightly humiliating. I shrug. "Why would I mind it?"

He points to the hallway. "You were furious that I helped you unpack."

"You threw away my poison flasks!" There. A drop of honesty.

"Oh, so you knew what they were."

"Yes, I'm not dumb." I also know that pretending ignorance is not going to work here. "It was not meant to kill you, but it could be useful."

He stares at me, considering, thinking. "If you feel you need to have an array of poisons, and if you convince me there's a good reason for it, I'll get it for you." He sighs. "I understand why you'd thought you'd need it. I mean, you don't know me, don't know what's going to happen. I understand. But I mean it when I say I'll protect you, so you have nothing to fear, Astra."

I stare at him, unsure what to say that's not going to sound like I want to fight. Part of me wants to fight because he's the one forcing me to be here, but I can see that he's trying to put me at ease. And then again...

"Well, I think you forgot it, but since you did, let me remind you that you kidnaped me, restrained my hands and arms with ice, then invaded my mind."

"You know I didn't." He chuckles. "You never let me get anywhere even close to your mind."

Oh, I had forgotten he thinks it was some kind of mind shield, and definitely forgotten I should never reveal that he has indeed seen my thoughts. At least he didn't notice my slip. "You still kidnapped me, made me unconscious, attacked Prince Ziven—"

"Ziven?" He frowns, confused. "I thought that was one of the other princes, the ones with powers."

Oh, shit. Did I just reveal Ziven's secret? If I make a fuss out of it it's going to be worse, so I show no reaction. "I guess you don't know Krastel that well, then."

"I don't. Regardless, I didn't hurt you or him, nor did I plan to do that. You, on the other hand, wanted to kill me."

"You attacked me first."

He scoffs. "Did I restrain you? Yes. Did I try to peer into your thoughts? Yes. Perhaps it's time you learned something important about me: I'll do anything to achieve my goals, and if I have to capture a foreign guard, I will. I can even do worse. Much, much worse." His posture is threatening, his voice chilling, and yet I don't feel that he's threatening *me*.

"What are your goals?" I ask slowly.

"I can't tell."

"You want to take King Renel's throne, don't you?"

He raises a finger. "*Prince* Renel. And I don't want to take anyone's throne."

"I wouldn't doubt that you have the throne, with the rest of the relics. How did you even carry them?" I think caution has just flown out the window, kicked by curiosity.

He smirks. "A mystery, isn't it?"

"Did you really kill your family?" I know I shouldn't ask that, I know, and yet the question sprang out of my mouth of its own free will. Still, the moment the words were out, I regretted them, as a shadow covered his eyes.

"This is not a topic I can talk about." His voice is measured, careful, but then he gets up. "Your knights will arrive soon and see to your needs." With that, he walks out of the front door.

If I was wondering how to make him angry, I think I found the answer. And I'm definitely not anywhere close to getting friendly with him and learning his secrets. It sounds stupid now, in retrospect, that I wished I had read the *Book of Seduction*. I can't even be civil! And I know how to be civil, how to be friendly and put someone at ease—at least in theory. Perhaps only in theory.

I finish eating, then put the plates on the counter, unsure what to do with them, and if I'm even supposed to do anything. Not knowing if I have to stay indoors or if there's any magic keeping me here, I risk stepping outside.

Nothing stops me, so I approach the edge of the island and sit on a rock, under the shade of a tree with tiny yellow flowers, some of them fallen, flecking the ground. In front of me, the river flows slowly, the mountains extend into forever, and the clouds glide in a bright blue sky. There's movement of fish in the river, and maybe even something else, like some kind of faerie water creature. Quite a few live in rivers, but I don't think Marlak would hide among them.

At least this is an opportunity for me to gather my thoughts. Marlak has found my poisons and knows I could kill him. He's definitely insane by bringing me here—unless he thinks he's untouchable, and I think he does, since he laughed at the idea of getting stabbed by me. Arrogance and pride are easy weaknesses to exploit. But then, he's right that there's no point in killing him now.

How does he know so much about me? I haven't even tried to figure that out, and, by asking the wrong questions and saying the wrong words, I haven't improved my chances of learning anything. When he returns, I'll need to remember my duty and put on a mask, become a different person. The question is *which* mask. Which mask will make him trust me?

As these thoughts cross my mind, I notice a movement in the water, a huge fish—or something else. I stare, trying to figure out what it is, but then I glimpse something moving on my right.

Someone, actually. I freeze, but just for a second.

When I sense that the person is close, I turn quickly and kick their crotch, hoping it's a man. It seems to have worked, as he hunches, and I take the opportunity to run back to the house, where I can find something to use as a weapon.

Someone else is running after me, though, but I feign right when they're about to tackle me, and they stumble. I keep running, with no time to look back.

The house won't keep me safe for long, if I even reach it. I don't have any weapon on me, not even a single dagger.

I'm screwed.

9

With two assailants after me, alone on this strange island, my chances are quite slim, but giving up before trying is never the answer. I focus on the Almighty Mother, on the infinite light, then I turn, about to send a flash of light, but all I see is a young fae man with his arms raised, as if meaning no harm.

"Tell us your name," he yells. "We come in peace."

There are two of them. Could these be the *two knights*? Oops. But they aren't wearing any uniform. "You first. Who are you?"

"I'm Ferer, he's Nelsin. You?"

Nelsin. Marlak mentioned that name indeed. "Astra."

They are approaching slowly. The man close to me is a fae with pointy ears, dark brown skin, and black hair in a lovely puffy hairstyle, wearing a sleeveless tunic and leather pants. Truly fae, with an odd, inhuman grace and beauty.

He says slowly, "We need to confirm you are who you're saying you are. Why are you here?"

"Marlak brought me."

"Why?"

Am I to be privy to his reasons? "Because he's insane!"

The fae chuckles. His companion, a blond fae who's farther behind, asks, "What are you to him?"

He wants me to say I'm his wife? I grit my teeth. "I don't know if *you* are friendly or not."

The fae further from me exhales. "You're his wife, aren't you? I brought your suitcase. You left the Krastel castle in a Crystal Court carriage, then were blindfolded."

"You could have been following me."

The dark-skinned fae close to me tilts his head. "This is an awkward introduction, without Marlak here. And you're right to be cautious. But we can't lie. Your husband sent us here, to protect you."

Well, Marlak did mention he was sending his knights, and either way, it's not like I can fight two fae. "Apologies."

The other fae approaches me, grinning. "At least you're brave and fearless. I can see why he'd pick you."

An odd laugh escapes my throat. I then notice the other fae. He's wearing a long-sleeved white tunic, open down to his stomach. His hair is long, wavy, and blond, but what I thought at first was a strange hairstyle are actually two ears, like cat ears, on top of his head. He also has normal, or rather, fae, ears.

He chuckles, and points to his head. "Yes, the four of them work. No, I don't have a tail." He shows me his hand. "Yes, I do have claws, but they're temperamental. And no, I don't purr."

I'm still surprised. For a second I wonder if one of his parents is a lion or tiger, then realize that's impossible. I know that there are fae with animal traits in courts other than the Crystal Court. It's just that seeing one of them is so astonishing. "You must have amazing hearing."

He shrugs and gives me a lazy smile. "I guess."

"You're Nelsin, right?" I want to make sure I got the names right.

Nelsin bows. "At your service, my lady."

Then I point to the dark-skinned fae. "And Ferer?"

The graceful fae nods.

I'm feeling bad now for fighting them. "Did I hurt you?"

Nelsin chuckles and shakes his head.

Ferer shakes his head as well, but he's serious. "You shouldn't be at the edge of the water alone like that. You need to understand that from the moment you chose Marlak, you chose a life of incertitude and danger. There are more enemies who'd like to get ahold of him than is even possible to count, and they'll target you."

Does he really think I *chose* Marlak? An odd chuckle escapes me. "Awesome perk, right? But at least I have a pleasant prince to keep me company—sometimes."

Nelsin grins and gives me a sideways look. "Methinks you like danger."

I laugh. "Who doesn't?" Do they realize I'm being sarcastic? I'm not sure.

We all enter the house, then Nelsin cleans the plates using water magic, and leaves them on the counter. Since Marlak has referred to me as a *guard*, I tell them what I used to do, without revealing too many details. I just say I was supposed to protect Princess Driziely.

The knights are both from the Crystal Court, but they say it's not a good place for someone who doesn't look fully high fae, or rather, with only human traits, except for the ethereal beauty, grace, and pointy ears, I guess.

I point to Ferer. "But you are..." I was going to say *normal*, but realize it sounds distasteful. *Human* is not the right word either. "Purely high fae, aren't you?"

He laughs and shakes his head, then shows me his neck.

It takes me a few seconds to realize he has gills. "Can you breathe under water?"

"For only a short period, unfortunately."

"You could hide that easily, couldn't you?"

He raises his eyebrows. "Should I? Should I hide what I am and stand with people who'd hate me if they knew everything about me?"

A chill runs over my skin. He's just described *me*, hiding my identity, but it's not like I have a choice. "Sometimes it's a matter of survival."

"What if my survival means the death of my brothers? Is it just survival?"

"I don't know." Indeed I don't. And his words make me uncomfortable. I haven't caused the death of a single darksoul, nor am I responsible for anything that happened to my ancestors. I try to change the subject. "Are things that bad in the Crystal Court?"

Ferer says, "For us, yes. We could face death or imprisonment and have no means of hoping for any justice." He then adds, "For us, Marlak's our true king." He takes Nelsin's hand.

I find the idea puzzling. "But he's..."

"Human? Maybe," Ferer says.

"See? That's what doesn't make sense," Nelsin adds. "You are born with cat ears, you're no longer *high fae*." He rolls his eyes and grimaces. "So they want human traits. You're Marlak, born with *only* human traits, and now that's a problem, too."

"But he's..." Was I really going to say *a family murderer*? I need to smarten up. "Exiled, right?"

Nelsin sighs. "Only a king can exile someone, and the Crystal Court has no king, so *exiled* is not the right word.

Marlak's *unrecognized*. Now, there's a solution for every problem. You being here only complicates the problem, but who am I to judge matters of the heart?" He looks at Ferer.

Rather, they share a look, and it's everything; as if they were seeing each other as the best version of themselves and becoming even lovelier by sharing that look. I realize they're in love, and can't help but feel a small pang of envy, unsure if I'll ever look at someone like that and see the same feeling in their eyes.

I smile. "You're a beautiful couple." They are. Love might be illogical, but it can make people magnificent. It even turns gorgeous fae into even more wondrous creatures.

Nelsin chuckles. "The cat and the fish. Who could guess?"

I chuckle too.

He then adds, "You and Marlak are also beautiful."

I almost choke on my laugh, unsure if he truly thinks me and the prince are something special and if I should or shouldn't deny it. I mean, they might notice we have separate bedrooms, but I don't know what they were told.

Ferer elbows his companion and looks at me. "We know it's just an alliance, not a love match."

That's a relief to hear.

Nelsin shrugs, his cat ears moving backwards a little. "They're still beautiful."

"Alliance for what?" I ask, wondering what Marlak told them.

They look at each other, then Ferer says, "Ask your prince."

"Oh, yes, he's so helpful and talkative."

Nelsin laughs, while Ferer watches me.

When people stare at me like that, I always wonder what

they're trying to see. A part of me always fears that they know, that they sense who I am, that they can see through my deception. I have to hope that's not the case, and perhaps keep hoping. Or maybe he wants to know what's between me and Marlak. I do wonder what the prince told them, what they make of this.

I'm not sure what people in the Krastel court would say if Aramel or his brother one day came in with a foreign *guard* for a wife.

They'd probably assassinate her. The realization stuns me.

I stare at the fae knights, wondering if they think of me as a nuisance, wondering if they'd murder me. Then again, they obey Marlak, and that's different from the situation in Krastel, where a king can overrule a prince. Also, since they're fae, their words are binding, and at least in theory, true.

Regardless, I should never lower my guard.

I SPEND the afternoon training under the shade of trees. Nelsin and Ferer drill me on what I already know, like basic self-defense moves. Later, when they suggest sword fighting, I tell them I'm only used to fighting with a dagger, and they're curious to see how it works, so we improvise sticks.

The tricky thing with fae is that they're so much faster than us. In a way, it's good to see that, to know what I would be up against if I had to fight one of them. As I dodge one of Nelsin's moves, he stops.

"This is hardly fair. What's the point of using a dagger against a sword?"

"I could have to pretend to be Princess Driziely or a noble. Women don't carry swords."

He's grimacing as if he'd sucked a lemon. "But what's the point? You got no chance."

"You're too fast. But against a normal enemy, I could dodge, hurt them, and escape."

"Fast?" He widens his eyes, and his top ears perk up. "Here I am, going slow."

Ferer is sitting, watching us. "You'll need all the advantage you can, my lady. Sword fighting might be a good idea."

I sit on a thick fallen branch.

"He's right," a deep voice says behind me. Marlak's walking toward us.

Did I feel my heart flutter? No, it was just startled. Perhaps the prince makes me nervous.

I turn to him. "You think I should walk around with a sword?"

"You're my wife. You don't have to pretend to be something you're not."

"I'm not pretending."

He tilts his head. "It looks like a large part of your training was about hiding the fact that you're a competent fighter, so that you look like a helpless damsel. I can see the wisdom in that, and how it can be useful, but now... If people want to hurt you, pretending to be weak won't stop them, it will just encourage them."

"How do you know about my training?"

He snaps a finger. "Magic, wife."

The rest of the afternoon is calm enough. Nelsin and Ferer leave for some time, and return with two nice dressing tables. The three of them, including the prince, prepare a salad with some cold meat, and we have dinner. I'm wondering when they'll give me some decent, hot food, but prefer not to ask.

Later, I play cards with Ferer, while trying to overhear what Marlak says to Nelsin outside. Overall, this is far from terrible, but I must remember not to get too comfortable, not to open up too much. After all, if I want to be loyal to my kingdom, I'll have to betray Marlak—if I ever manage to gain his trust to begin with.

Yes, there's that. Not an insignificant hurdle.

When night falls, there are no lights in the house except for two lightstones, one in the kitchen, and one in Marlak's room, where he's reading. Nelsin and Ferer soon go to bed, and here I am, hearing crickets chirping outside, unsure what to do.

I touch the walls and find my way to the back of the corridor, near Marlak's room, which is right across from mine, and knock on the door.

When he opens it, he's bare-chested, and yet I can't see much of his scars considering he's silhouetted against the faint glimmer from the lightstone in the room, where I glimpse a desk and some papers. He looks at the hallway. "Did they go to sleep?"

"I think so. I..." I need to ask for a light, for something. "Do you have candles?"

He retreats into his room. "Come in."

I remain at the door. Isn't he the one saying I want to seduce him? Why then is he inviting me into his dimly lit bedroom when he's half naked? He turns around and notices I'm at the door, but doesn't say anything. Instead, he grabs his lightstone and brings it to me. "Take this. Then bring it back once you're done."

I don't want to owe him a favor like that. "I think I'll go to sleep. I don't want to leave you in the dark."

"Are you sure?"

"I'm fine, thanks. Good night."

He nods. "If you need anything, don't hesitate to ask. You can call me or your knights."

Oh, yes, I'll stumble in the dark hallway and call someone. "Thanks."

I'm at my door, when I hear him.

"Astra." Funny how he sometimes remembers my name.

I turn.

"Don't lock your door," he says. "You can, but if ever something happens..."

"I won't lock it."

With that, I turn and go to my room. It's with a lot of difficulty and some mild help from the moonlight seeping through the window that I change into another dress, this one just as tight on my chest. I don't have any nightgowns, and don't want to sleep naked.

Finally, I murmur the protection incantation as low as I can by the walls of the room.

"Only light here. Light shields us and protects us from evil. Light shields us, and nothing can pass through this wall."

Light. The only light here comes from the moon. I guess some nights I'll only have the stars. Or nothing, if it's cloudy. And yet I need to trust that there's a different kind of light protecting me—despite everything.

This is not terrible, and it's a great opportunity for me. I'll honor my kingdom, and if Marlak has killed the people in Stratson's state, I'll make sure he regrets it. Justice. That's always an honorable goal.

When I lie down, it feels strange to be on a different bed, after years and years in the same room. Still, there's something calming here. I can hear the river flowing outside and smell the leaves close by, and yet it's not a place where I belong.

The mattress is firmer and the pillow thinner than what I'm used to, while the sheets under and over me are so much softer.

I close my eyes, hoping I don't dream about Marlak tonight. Because if I do, how am I going to face him tomorrow?

"Why, Marlak?" My entire body is trembling. I'm so angry. Furious, actually, and scared, or rather, terrified. Terrified of what might happen to him.

He's leaning against the balcony railing, a starry sky behind him, smiling at me. "I had no choice." How can he look so calm?

"There's *always* a choice. You could have waited, found another way. Something."

He takes my hands in his and pulls me close, staring into my eyes, a playful glint in his. "You're crazy if you think there's anything I wouldn't do for you."

"You think it's funny. Very funny what you did."

He runs a hand over my hair, perhaps aware that he can dissolve my anger with a few sweet words and caresses. "I did what I had to do, azalee."

"You should have given something else. Anything."

I close my eyes, still in disbelief, still unable to grasp how much he's risking. I'm so furious. And terrified. And he's not even taking it seriously.

My eyes open and I realize I'm not in that castle anymore, but in the river hideout. River hideout? How come I know the name of this place? My heart's still beating fast, but it was a dream. At least I was angry this time.

Was I angry because he married me? No. I was angry that he gave something away. But then, I doubt the dream has anything to do with our current reality. It was more like a memory, a vision.

Or maybe it's just that I'm so angry at him that I dreamed about it. Will he have the same dream as me? I wish there was a way to find out if that's really true, a way that wouldn't reveal that I'm dreaming about him.

I'm still trembling with an odd anger whose reason I can't fathom. Unless it's because he ripped me away from my life, he's forcing me to be here, he made a mockery of sacred wedding vows and keeps mocking me every time he calls me *wife* in jest. I guess I do understand where the anger comes from.

There's another smell in the room, and I realize it comes from my pillow cover, a sweet, calming lavender scent, and my eyes close, the anger slowly disappearing as my thoughts fade into the nothingness of sleep.

When I open my eyes, slanted sunrays cross the thin curtains of the Amethyst Palace windows. Not the Amethyst Palace, the river hideout, with its calming sound of water and leaves outside, and a citrusy smell. I feel strong arms around me, and his body. His body? Part of me thinks this is right, part of me is alarmed.

"Marlak?" I dare whisper, hoping I'm imagining things.

"I don't want to fight anymore." He kisses my neck and wraps his arms tighter around me. "I missed you."

He keeps kissing my neck, and then he bites my ear softly, as if to remind me that he remembers the cave. I should stop him, I know, but I don't want to. I like those kisses, and I can still recall him looking at me, that playful glint in his eyes.

You're crazy if you think there's anything I wouldn't do for you.

For a moment, I want to believe it's true, I want to believe it's him, I want to believe love like that exists. His ragged breath, so close to my ear, undoes me. I want this, I want *him*.

His hands then move apart, one of them caressing my abdomen, then moving up, over my nightgown, while the other moves down, reaching my thighs, then up again, between my legs. I want more. I want his hands all over me, inside me.

It's as if he can understand my thoughts, and then suddenly, with a firm pull, he rips the nightgown and lowers my breastband, freeing my breasts, caressing one of them with his hand. His tongue caresses my ear, while I can feel him hardening behind me, so close.

So far. I want him inside me. His fingers between my thighs are also teasing me, perhaps waiting for the moment I finally cave in and beg. Cave in. A nice description of our first encounter.

I want to chuckle. Chuckle until I break down laughing, chuckle until I break down crying. I want to laugh at myself, laugh at the absurdity of avoiding my husband, laugh at my ruined nightgown.

Ruined nightgown.

But I slept wearing a dress.

My eyes snap open and I recognize my new room in this strange house on this tiny island. I look back and, to my relief, see nobody behind me. I am still wearing a tight, uncomfortable dress. Inside out. I guess I didn't notice it in the dark. Great.

This dream felt so real, so strange. I hope Marlak didn't dream about it too.

I try to close my eyes and get some more sleep, but then I hear three knocks on the door.

"Can I come in?" Marlak's deep voice could shake the foundations of the house.

"It's early." I was going to say I was sleeping, but I guess that's ruined now.

"Are you dressed?"

Would he enter if I said I was naked? Then he's going to wonder if I'm sleeping naked. Oh, whatever. I sit up. "Yes."

He comes in, closes the door behind him, leans against it, and crosses his arms. "What did I ask you?"

He means the dream. Of course he does. I want to disintegrate and disappear, but I manage to pretend I'm not mortified and instead, feign confusion. "To leave the door unlocked? I did, as you can see."

He closes his eyes and takes a deep breath, then stares at me. "Yes, I asked you to do that, and I appreciate the trust. But I also asked you to stop the mind magic, stop trying to get into my dreams." He glances at me, as if realizing I'm wearing a crumpled dress, and not a nightgown. "Stop it."

I have to pretend I know nothing about it. "Why? Did you dream I uncovered your secrets?" I laugh. "Oooh. Watch out, husband. I know where you're keeping the crown."

He blinks. "You did something, and you know it."

I get up and stand in front of him. "I did nothing. Maybe if you tell me what happened, we can find a solution. Is that how it's going to be? You're going to wake me up every time you have a nightmare?"

He snorts and rolls his eyes. "Nightmare."

"You're saying I give you bad dreams."

He stares at me. "Astra, don't lie to me. Just stop doing

whatever you're doing. I'm asking you. It's *not* going to work. It annoys me. It's pathetic."

He must think I love it or something. Well, to be fair, when I'm dreaming, I do like it. Yikes.

I ignore those bizarre thoughts and shake my head. "I can't stop something I'm not doing. If you're having trouble falling asleep, find someone who can cure you. Drink a sleeping draught, I don't know. What do I have to do with it?"

He huffs. "If I find out you're lying, there will be consequences." His voice is a low, threatening rumble.

Still, I roll my eyes, then smirk. "Oh, really? What are you going to do, kidnap me, then keep me as a prisoner on an island?"

He leans over, so that his nose is almost touching mine. "Oh, no, not on an island. There are much, much worse places than here."

His proximity, his deep voice, his presence, and perhaps the memory of the dream almost makes me want to ask him to take me wherever he wants, do whatever he wants, as if it had been an invitation, not a threat. Perhaps it's his insanely compelling eyes.

I am losing my mind.

I keep my face flat. "I'm not doing anything, *husband*." I shrug. "But if you want help figuring out what's going on, maybe I can help."

Haha. Would he confess what he's been seeing in his dreams? That would be cute.

"Mark my words, and don't play with me." He points a finger at me.

It takes a mighty effort to shut down the memory of what that finger was doing just now, but I manage it.

"I have no intention of ever *playing* with you, so there's

no reason to worry." I hope he understands the double meaning of *playing*, and I hope he takes the hint.

He stares at me, his breath somewhat ragged—just like in the dream. I wonder what would happen if he kissed me. I wonder if he would like to kiss me.

I wonder if I got hit in the head.

Surprised at my own thoughts, I step back, crossing my arms so as not to show any signs of trembling. Did I just want him? While wide awake? This is terrible. But then, I realize what he's wearing, or rather, not wearing.

I scoff. "And it's quite rich of you to accuse me of trying to seduce you, when you come in here half naked." He's only wearing some kind of sleep trousers, and they hang low, so low on his hips that I can see a trail of dark hair leading down there. Not only that, his nipples look stiff and purplish, as if he'd just taken a very cold shower, or perhaps involved himself in ice.

He stares at himself. "So what? I'm half roasted, right?"

I shrug. "Imagine if *I* got into your room bare chested when you were half asleep."

His eyes look down at my breasts, constricted under the tight dress, then move up quickly, as if he's catching himself, as if he just imagined it.

Oh, no. It wasn't my intention.

I hope he hasn't just conjured a sexy version of me walking into his room, tits exposed, but I think he did. But there is something satisfying about it, satisfying in knowing that despite all his talk that I'm undesirable, he can still feel something.

He smiles, a cold, calculated smile. "It would be pathetic, wife. Desperate, useless, and sad."

"Then you're being pathetic right now." I get angry and

my ability to come up with decent replies disappears. I know, it's sad.

"I really don't think so." He chuckles and leaves.

I want to go out there and strangle him, but then he's going to say I'm doing it just to touch him, and I'll get even angrier.

I can't murder the disgraced fae prince. Not yet, at least.

10

I stare at myself and my crumpled, ugly, inside-out dress. It's so tight and uncomfortable I'm not sure how I managed to sleep in this. Perhaps that's where the part about ripping my nightgown came from.

Still, I refuse to change my dress, just so I don't give him the deranged idea that I somehow want to look pretty—or even decent. Like that, and barefoot, I head to the kitchen, stepping on the polished wood planks. Nelsin is preparing something, cheerily humming a tune.

He turns and smiles at me. "My lady! What do you usually eat in the morning?"

"Anything. I usually had porridge, fruit, tea, bread, things like that."

"We don't have tea or porridge, but I was preparing a fruit salad with nuts and seeds."

I approach him and see that he's mixing peaches, oranges, bananas, and strawberries with pumpkin seeds and almonds. I smile at him. "It looks wonderful."

The smile he returns is broad and genuine.

I decide to ask something I'm curious about. "When you want to cook, really cook, like a stew, soup, or even tea, where do you do it? I don't see a stove or any place for a fire here."

He looks back at his fruit salad. "We don't light any fire on the island."

"Oh."

I hear steps and see Marlak walking in, this time decently dressed with a sleeveless tunic. "Smoke could attract enemies."

Why is his voice like that? When he talks slowly, not annoyed, I can feel it reverberating through my entire body. Oh, I need to stick to the topic. "But you can heat water with your magic, can't you?"

Marlak shakes his head. "Unfortunately, no."

That doesn't make sense. Water magic usually allows the wielder to manipulate its state, turning it into vapor, ice, liquid. And then again, his magic is different.

He walks to Nelsin. "Not fae food, is it?"

"Oh, no." He has a satisfied smile. "This could feed a cow."

Marlak frowns. "And that's the problem. Cows eat grass."

The fae knight shrugs. "Bad comparison, then." He points at me. "She thought it looked good."

I nod. "It does." I'm not sure how long it will sustain me, but it looks absolutely wonderful.

"Fine." Marlak shrugs, then opens a metal cupboard, and I realize it has blocks of ice and some jugs with a white liquid in it. "We'll also drink milk." He looks at me. "Is it all right?"

"Yes." It feels weird to have this conversation, as if he didn't just storm into my room telling me to stop dreaming about him.

The prince sits in front of me, two cups on one hand, the jug in another. Those are big hands. No, no, Astra. Not the time to recall the dream—but I guess I just did. How am I going to survive like that?

He pours milk into a cup and passes it to me. "I'll need you to go somewhere with me today."

At least it's the grating, annoying voice.

I smirk. "Blindfolded?"

"No. But you'll get wet."

I can feel my cheeks getting hot, until I realize that he means going into the water, not... Oh.

Nelsin then puts the fruit salad on the table by us. "You two and your human appetites. Doesn't it get annoying?" I feel that the question is addressed to me, rather than to Marlak.

I shrug. "Well, I like to eat, so I don't mind having to do it often."

"Makes sense." Nelsin nods. "I'll leave you two alone, then."

"Stay," I blurt. "Keep us company."

The fae knight looks at Marlak, then at me. "Another time."

Was Nelsin ordered to leave? Great. Who's the one trying to make sure to spend time alone with me?

"Where are we going?" I ask, my voice flat, as I put some fruit salad on my plate.

"This requires a lot of trust on my part, but I want the river nymphs to protect you, so I'll have to introduce you to their queen."

Queen. As in Queen's River? But as far as I know, nymphs are a kind of fae. "Aren't they part of the Crystal Court?" I take a spoon of the fruit salad, and enjoy the contrast of the soft pieces of fruit with the crunchy nuts.

He shakes his head. "They're independent, and not fae, despite what fae royalty believe. But they're good at hiding, and much more powerful and numerous than most people think." He taps his fingers on the table, then stares at me. "If you let this secret into the wrong hands, you'll lose their protection, and might lose your life."

The sweet taste of peaches turns bitter for a moment. "What if someone were to imprison me, interrogate me, invade my mind?"

"They wouldn't be looking for something they have no idea exists, and nobody can invade minds."

"You can."

"I'm the only one." He takes a sip of his milk. "You'll meet their queen, and I'll present you as my wife."

"Will she know..." I'm not sure how to ask this. "Should I pretend..."

"She'll know everything. But let her see you, mark you with her protection. It could make a difference."

I take a sip of my milk too, then I decide to ask a question. "Why the effort? Isn't it easier to let me die?"

He raises an eyebrow. "Oh, definitely."

Asshole.

He shrugs. "But what if instead of killing, they decide to interrogate you, or maybe you decide to help them and reveal my secrets? I can't have that, can I?"

I roll my eyes. "What secrets? What secrets of yours do I even know?"

He leans back in his chair, running a hand over his black curls, no rings on his hands. "You tell me."

Why does he have to look so good? I close my eyes and shake my head.

MARLAK TAKES me to a rocky edge of the island. I'm still wearing my ugly dress, and he's wearing pants and a sleeveless leather top, displaying his muscled arms, scars, and tattoos.

"Can you swim?"

"Yes." I still recall being taken to a lake as a child, still recall the cold water, my difficulty to float, and Otavio there, yelling at me to relax—as if it was easy. Eventually, I think I learned some of it, or at least enough not to drown too easily. "I mean, a little."

"Hold my hand and trust me down there, all right? I will kneel to the queen, but you can just bow."

He sits on a rock, jumps into the water, without taking off any of his clothes, then reaches out a hand to me. I lean over and jump, but the water is cold, and I can't feel the bottom. For a second it scares me, and I find myself wrapping my arms around him, but then we're underwater, sinking, and I sense something changing around my head.

"An air bubble," he says. "It won't last long, but it's enough for now."

I'm still holding my breath, and he laughs.

"You can breathe."

I finally gasp for air, surprised that it's really air. There's so much water above me, and yet still so much below. This is nothing like the Sommet Lake, and I don't want to let go of him, but at least he hasn't said anything, and keeps going down. Down, down we go. How can a river be so deep? Or is my idea of depth completely wrong?

At least we finally reach the bottom, its sandy texture a soft caress on the soles of my feet.

He looks down, then looks at me. "I think I'll have to hold you."

I nod. Poor Marlak, having to do the great sacrifice of

holding me. And yet, when he wraps his arms around my waist, I just want to lean over and be embraced. It's as if my body doesn't understand the difference between dream and reality—or maybe it's just that this river is scary and I want to feel safer.

"Hold tight, and don't panic."

I'm about to say that I'm not panicking, when a swirl makes us spin and keep spinning faster and faster. At this point, whatever he thinks of me is the last thing on my mind, and I hold him as tight as I can.

His lips are close to my ear. "It's safe," he whispers.

That is the voice I know so well, the voice that often lulls me into a sense of peace, safety, love. I could swear that he holds me tighter, but I'm not sure about my senses anymore.

We stop spinning, but my eyes are still closed, my heart still accelerated. There's firm, sandy ground beneath me, but I'm dizzy and disoriented. Through my closed eyelids, I can see that there's a lot more light than before, as if we were closer to the surface.

When I open my eyes, I'm surprised.

We're in an underwater cave with rock walls, and there's white light coming from jutting crystals—so much light. Around us, some twenty strange creatures hold golden spears. They're guards, but their hair and skin are green and their eyes are black and huge, with no eyelids.

I hold Marlak tight.

"Nobody will hurt you here," he whispers, that soft, soothing whisper that's a balm to my heart, a promise of love and safety to my soul.

My heart throbs so loud that I can hear it, I can feel it knocking on my chest, as if to remind me of its existence, remind me what it truly thinks of the fae prince.

His arms let go of me slowly, and he takes both my hands

gently, then finally turns me, so that I'm looking in the same direction he is, where a tall woman stands. Her skin is bluish, like her hair, and she has those same odd eyes. Everyone here has pointy ears like the fae, but they're definitely not a type of fae, like I've always thought.

Still holding my hand, Marlak kneels, and I decide to do the same.

When he gets up, he says, "This is Astra Goldenstar, my wife and the legitimate queen of the Crystal Court."

Queen? He has said that before, but it sounds so serious now, so official. And to give me his name? I don't even have time to mull it over, as the woman smiles at us, an odd smile full of pointed teeth. I'd swim away if I knew how to do it, and if I thought it would help. But Marlak still holds my hand, and that helps me calm down. It's not fear that I'm feeling, it's a strange mix of awe and a certain apprehension. I don't know what it is.

The queen of the Nymphs bows slightly. "Impeccable choice, your majesty."

And then I hear her inside my head. *I know what you are. I know what you hide.*

I pull my hand from Marlak's touch, fearing he could hear those words, feeling exposed.

Have no fear, child. The queen says, with a soft voice. *I know what it's like to hide, to fear. I know what it's like to be hunted. I'll let you choose when your husband learns the truth about you. However, If I were you, I'd choose it to be soon.*

Can she hear my thoughts? *Please, don't say anything.* I look at her, waiting for a reaction, but she's looking at Marlak.

Still, her voice again sounds in my head. *You know what he is to you, don't you? I understand running from danger, running from foes, but why do you run from yourself?*

I'm not running, I'm sure I'm not running. Her words make me feel odd and queazy, but at least he holds my hand again.

He pulls me close and when we spin, I don't have any self control not to hold tight to him. We spin and spin, then he's swimming up, bringing me with him, and I feel rough stone beside me. The edge of the island.

I'm so dizzy, I barely feel when he pulls me up, when we walk back in the direction of the house, but then he stops, and gestures for me to sit on a fallen trunk. He moves a hand over me and I feel my body and my dress getting dry.

He sits beside me. "What happened?" His eyebrows are creased, as if worried.

I shake my head. "Swimming, spinning. It was strange."

He nods. "I know. I forget I'm used to it. But it's important because now you can count on their protection."

Right. If I ever fall into a river, I guess I'll be safe—if I don't drown first.

He stares at me again, that searching stare. "She spoke into your mind, didn't she?"

"Yes." I don't see the point in denying.

His stare unnerves me. "It disconcerted you. What did she say?"

The fact that he noticed how shaken I was is enough to wake me up from this stupor and remind me to stay alert. I smile at him. "If it had been meant for us both, she would have said it out loud, right?"

He tilts his head. "Maybe."

"Why did you present me as the queen of the Crystal Court?"

"Some people don't recognize my brother as the king."

I find it strange that he would refer to the nymphs as people. They felt like something else.

"For them," he continues, "I'm the king. You'll be the queen as long as you're my wife."

As long as... So it's not forever. It makes sense now. "Meaning until you defeat Renel, or in seven years, right?"

"That's when you can choose to leave, yes."

Choose. As if the decision was mine, and I know it isn't. "You mean I can choose to stay and then you'll be stuck with a pathetic failed seductress for a wife? And queen?"

"Exactly." His voice is so flat that I don't even know if he's joking or serious.

"One day you'll want to fall in love, you'll want a real marriage."

He looks away and shakes his head. "It's too dangerous. Anyone who's attached to me will have a target on their forehead, will have enemies at every corner."

I get up. "Oh, so *I* can be a target, and you don't mind?"

He gets up and towers over me. "I told you I was sorry for that, but it's *your* doing. You have nobody but yourself to blame, wife."

I clench my fists. "*Nothing* is my doing. Why don't we just stop this farce, and you take me back to my kingdom? I can even promise never, ever, ever, to tell anyone about any of those secrets of yours, of which I know nothing!"

"They won't take you back. It's done. You're stuck here, stuck with me, and yes, your life is in danger, but as you can see, I'm doing the best I can to protect you."

"Safe, but without freedom." *Without love.* Perhaps that's what's bothering me the most, the fact that I can't even hope, can't even make up love stories in my head. "What's the point?"

"Were you free before? Were you? You were raised in a tower, a prisoner just like..." He pauses, a shadow crossing his eyes.

"Just like whom?"

"A prisoner. In a tower. That's what you were."

"Yay. Now I'm a prisoner *on an island*. With my life in danger. Sounds so much better."

"We won't stay here long. I never spend longer than a month in a single place."

This is something I can work with, something I came here to find: information. I try to keep my voice level, even gentle. "So there are other hideouts?"

"Obviously. You'll soon get to know them all."

"Then you'll let me walk away with that knowledge?"

"When you walk away, that information won't matter anymore."

"You're not afraid I'll betray you?"

He stares at me, his voice flat. "No."

I'm not sure if he's implying he trusts me or that I have no chance of betraying him. I scoff. "You're quite sure of yourself."

"No." He smiles, perhaps realizing he can just repeat the answer and annoy me.

For some reason, I want to ask what happened in his past, what happened when he killed his family twelve years ago. "Marlak, how old are you?"

"A little late to get to know your husband's age, don't you think?"

I put a hand on my head. "How thoughtless of me, not to ask it during our long courting period, when I considered your proposal..."

He laughs, a relaxed laugh. "Twenty-four."

It's only then I realize it. "You were a child!"

"Yes. That's how humans and fae come to be. We're born really small, as babies, then become children—"

I don't know why he's trying to deviate from the topic,

but I stop him. "I mean when you... left the Crystal Court. You were twelve."

He raises an eyebrow. "Impressive. Not only are you an expert on poisons and fighting while pretending to be a defenseless damsel, your math skills are exceptional."

I shake my head and scoff.

"Truly, wife. You just made a calculation that few are capable of."

With that, he turns and walks to the house. Wait. *I* was going there, and he stopped me, now he's walking away? Still, I sit. He was a child, a child with a dead mother and stepfather, running away from the palace where he grew up... How did he have the presence of spirit to steal the treasure?

Marlak sometimes can seem like an impenetrable fortress, but he has clear weaknesses. If I learn to exploit them, if I identify what they are... I don't know if all I want is to find a way to make him free me, or maybe find a way to defeat him. A way to get his secrets and take them back to Master Otavio. Well, if Marlak isn't afraid I'll betray him, perhaps I shouldn't be afraid of betraying him either.

And yet, I can't shake the thought of a child running away from his palace, chased by his own brother—a child who's now a grown man, intent on killing this same brother.

Marlak is dangerous, and I have to remember that. Under his soft whispered words, his guarantees that he'll keep me safe, there's someone who'll do anything to get what he wants. He has admitted that himself.

What I don't understand is where I fit into all that.

Also, why do I have to keep dreaming about him? He can't be my kindred soul. Even if we were to ignore all that he's done, he hates me. The man in my dream loves me. Then why?

I don't know why I'm surprised that the seamstress looks so... fae. She's a pixie. With light blue shimmery skin, silver brilliant hair, and translucid, also shimmery wings, she might be the most beautiful creature I've ever seen. She's not young, though, and I can sense something ancient in her eyes, her manners, but other than that, I would think she was no older than thirty or so.

Her name is Irene, and apparently she's a renowned seamstress in the fae territory north of the Crystal Court. She measures me carefully, while I wear just my underslip. Nelsin brought her here blindfolded, so that all she's seeing is my bedroom, but I fear she could figure out where we are. Then again, I assume this is someone Marlak trusts.

He disappeared after our incursion into the river, not before telling me that I should get some trousers. His point about comfort is valid, but I think he wants me to look even more unattractive than I already am. Well, not a problem!

Irene is taking all kinds of measurements of my head. I guess she's going to make hats? I've never been measured like that before.

She steps back and looks me up and down. "So beautiful. Young love is magical, did you know that?"

Does she think I feel something for Marlak? Regardless, I disagree with her. "I think old love is better, love that survives the passage of time, survives tribulations. It's the kind of love I want."

I find my confession surprising. But it's true, and might be the reason being here bothers me, since I'm being robbed of the opportunity of chasing that dream. But then, the Elite Tower didn't give me that opportunity either.

The seamstress smiles. "Like an ancient tree, numerous

rings marking all the eras it's been through." She nods. "Wise choice, my queen." The title doesn't grate me for some reason. "But young love is like a blooming flower. They're both beautiful."

Flowers shrivel and die in days, so she does have a point. I smile.

She then chuckles. "It's surprising, you know?"

After many seconds of silence, I realize she's waiting for me to reply. I'd better reply, right? I don't want her to get upset and give me some prickly fabric. "What's surprising?"

"You. You are the surprise. Marlak always said he'd never get married."

Interesting. "Did he?"

"Oh, yes. I guess you don't know anything, right? Coming from a human kingdom."

She's dying to tell me more, I can feel it, but she wants me to ask. Well, I want information more than anything, so I don't waste the opportunity. "What is it I don't know?" I sense my heart beating faster, dreading whatever I'm about to hear.

"For years he courted the daughter of the Spider Court Queen."

Spider Court. That is a large court down south, beyond the Wild Fae lands. Not far from here. Quite close, in fact. I feel as if I'd just consumed some calapher powder, and now it's burbling in my stomach, about to expel its contents. Would he still be seeing her?

"What happened?" I ask, my voice thinner than I'd like it to be.

"He broke up with the princess. In his words, to allow her to find a husband, someone who could love her."

Yes, the contents in my stomach are definitely making a

racket. There's also an odd, ugly anger there, and I don't know why.

The woman continues, "Her mother, the Spider Fae Queen, never forgave him."

"But we're not far from her lands." Oh, no. I shouldn't have mentioned that.

"Far enough, I'd guess. But my point is that he was adamant that he'd never get married, that it would be too dangerous. And now you see, he found you, and you changed his mind."

"Because he doesn't care if *I* face any danger," I say, and then regret my words right away.

The fae stares at me, her eyes deep and black. "It's because you both decided your love was worth facing any dangers together. Love makes you strong, not weak."

Does she honestly think I'm in love?

She continues, "And perhaps whatever he said about the Spider Court Princess was just an excuse."

Spider Queen and Princess make me think of arachnids, and I wonder if he was kissing a hairy creature with eight legs.

"Is she beautiful, this Spider Princess?" I ask, even though I'm dreading the answer.

"She's lovely, for sure. Might be the loveliest young fae alive. But with my clothes, you'll look even lovelier than her."

Oh, so that's what it's about. Irene is a shrewd businesswoman, not a busybody, and she's hoping I'll ask her to make me prettier than the *loveliest young fae alive*. As if I cared about a stupid princess that he might have loved so much that he let her go.

I smile. "Actually, I want plain things. Basic. Bulky. And trousers. Clothes that will allow me to move comfortably. With pockets for daggers."

She blinks, staring at me.

I point at my chest. "And he chose *me*. I don't think he'll care what I wear, so nothing needs to be pretty."

"Absolutely. I'm sure he prefers it when you're naked, but you still need to be dressed when you leave your marital chambers or when it's cold. And you're a queen now."

Queen of the delusional fae. The thought makes me guilty. They're persecuted, not as much as darksouls, but still persecuted, and I shouldn't think they are delusional. And yet, I can't think of myself as a queen. My job here is to get information that will eventually go to Renel and strengthen *his* kingdom.

"A warrior queen," I say, even though it sounds strange in my lips. "Marlak himself told me I should get trousers."

"Yes, yes. With pockets for daggers." She's again measuring my arm. "I know that. And I see you're upset, my lady."

"I'm not upset." My voice comes out higher than I intended and I feel stupid.

"I mentioned the princess just for you to know how much he loves you. How exciting it is to know he's finally found his queen. There's no balance when a king is alone, you know?"

"But Renel is single, isn't he?"

She scoffs. "Like I said, no balance. And he's no king."

"Did Marlak, did he ever wear the crown?"

"If he did or did not, it makes no difference."

So he probably didn't, and its rightful owner is indeed Renel.

I wish I wasn't so angry at this seamstress, wish I could make some conversation, get to learn more about Marlak. No, I need to focus and pretend.

Smiling, I say, "I admire your loyalty so much. And appreciate it."

She is measuring my shoulders now. "It's a matter of survival. We protect our own. Protect ourselves."

"Right. And was Marlak involved with anyone else?"

"Perhaps." She's measuring my head again, and I sure hope it's not for a crown. "I'm not privy to his secrets."

Great. Now she decides to shut her mouth. Still, I need to learn as much as I can. "And this spider princess, did *she* forgive him?"

"Was it forgiveness, or was it hope? Perhaps now she'll be free to move on."

I grit my teeth. "Let's hope she does."

For some reason I want to squash that spider, when in reality I should be hoping that she could convince Marlak to let me go and marry her instead.

No, but then I can't uncover his secrets, can't finish my mission. That makes sense, and explains why I'm feeling this odd anger. I guess it's just that I don't want to miss this opportunity to prove my value.

The truth is that I can't figure out what goes on in my own head. No wonder even the seamstress is having trouble measuring it.

11

Nelsin takes Irene away, and I'm left alone with Ferer. He's chopping vegetables for lunch, and I realize I should offer to help, so he gives me a tomato. When I try to cut it, it flies from the board all the way to the other side of the kitchen. Mortified, I chase it, but the fae is faster.

Ferer takes the tomato and stares at me. "You've never cooked before?"

"No." I feel stupid, and add, "We had a dining hall."

"Huh. What did you eat when you took time off?"

"I... lived in the castle. Ate there." I don't want to tell him I never had any time off.

He goes back to the counter and washes the tomato in a basin. "You don't need to help."

"But then I'll never learn. Is there anything less slippery?"

He passes me some carrots. "Try these."

They are easier, but I think I'm chopping them at one tenth of Ferer's speed. Well, he *is* fae. I hear steps coming into the kitchen, and for some reason I know it's not Marlak.

Indeed it's Nelsin, who stands beside me. "Let me do this."

"She's trying to learn," Ferer says.

"Oh. All right." The cat-eared fae crosses his arms and observes me.

I wonder if they think I'm spoiled or something, but really, it's not my fault they never taught us how to cook.

"I was wondering something," I say, glad that my voice sounds casual and disinterested enough. "I don't know much about the other fae courts, but do the court names relate to the way you look?"

Ferer, who's cutting mushrooms, tilts his head, as if considering. "I... don't think—"

"Let me guess," Nelsin cuts in. "That old blabbermouth told you all about the Spider Princess, and now you're wondering if Marlak's into insects."

"Arachnids," I say, and a second too late realize how terrible it sounds. "I mean, spiders are arachnids, but I was wondering—"

"Yeah, yeah," Nelsin waves a hand. "I can see you are imagining young Marlak in bed with a spider, wondering how it works with the eight legs and all."

I stare at my carrot. "Spiders can sometimes climb onto beds. I'm not sure what this has to do with Marlak and the Spider Court."

Nelsin laughs. "You lie so pretty. Of course you're wondering what the Spider Court Princess looks like."

I continue cutting my carrot. "Well, that is a court with an animal name, so yes, I guess I'm curious."

The blond fae is beside me. "I can tell, but you have to tell me what the blabbermouth said." His cat ears move slightly forward, as if ready to hear me.

I let go of the knife and turn to him. "Fine. She did say

Marlak loved the Spider Court Princess so much that he spared her from a dreadful and dangerous marriage."

Nelsin scrunches his face. "She said that?"

Ferer puts his knife down and approaches me. "It was a long time ago. He was young. You know youth, how everything is eternal love."

I actually don't, but sure.

Ferer continues, "They were friends. And lovers, yes. I don't think they've seen each other in over a year."

"No!" Nelsin whines, clenching his fists in a dramatic gesture. "You're giving her all this information for free. Why?"

"If we don't tell her, she'll eventually ask Marlak, and I don't want to get Irene in trouble."

Nelsin shrugs. "It would be well deserved."

I agree with the blond fae for once.

"No matter." Ferer is still serious, then looks at me. "You'll hear all kinds of outrageous stories, and should give them no mind."

"I thought fae couldn't lie."

He takes a tomato. "You can. If you believe you're saying the truth, you obviously can, and if you interpret a story with a little more drama or color, of course you can enhance the tale in the way you perceived it. Now, there are other ways to lie, too rare, complex, and costly."

I'm stunned. "Really?"

"There's magic for everything, but some magic is not worth it. You'll probably never come across a fae who has struck a truth-bending deal, so it's not something you should worry about. Just be aware that not every word a fae utters is necessarily true."

I'm glad he's telling me that, and decide it's better to be more honest with them. "Thanks. This is all good to know.

Also yes, I was curious about the princess of the Spider Court and should have been honest."

Nelsin points at me. "Knew it."

His tone is playful, so I chuckle, even though I'm not finding any of that funny. And I want to know more. "She said the Spider Queen has become Marlak's enemy. Is that true?"

Ferer eyes me carefully. "I think she was hoping for an alliance there indeed." There's something careful, cautious about his tone. "I wouldn't say she's his enemy, though."

"But she hates his guts," Nelsin adds, still amused. "And I still can't believe we didn't bargain for all this information."

"There's no need to bargain," I say. "What do you want to know?"

I like these two, and in truth, it would be helpful to have them as allies, or at least gain some of their trust—only later to betray them. The thought knots my stomach. Well, what can I do?

"Nothing," Ferer says, then turns to his companion. "Marlak doesn't want us bothering her."

Laughing, Nelsin waves a hand. "Oh, I'm sure he'll be thrilled that you told her all about the Spider Court Princess."

"Irene's the one who told her."

Nelsin sits at one of the tables and rests his elbows on it. "Sad." He looks at me. "You were so cute, all jealous."

"Jealous?" What kind of folly is that? I can't help but laugh. "Oh yes, I wish I were in her place, meaning away from him."

The blond fae stares at me. "You don't like to be here?"

Perhaps I shouldn't be telling them that, but it's not like Marlak forbade me to be honest. I sit at the table. "I wasn't given a choice, that's all. I was traded like a cow. His words, not mine."

Nelsin narrows his eyes. "Traded for what?"

It sounds like a true question, and I'm surprised *he* doesn't know the answer. "Support? I don't know. Something with the Krastel King."

Ferer sits with us and glares at the other fae knight. "Leave it."

"I'm just curious!" Nelsin shrugs.

"So am I," I agree.

Then again, Marlak has told me his reasons, which I assume these two fae don't know. My presence here must be bewildering for them, unless they think the prince is in love with me.

That would be the only explanation.

I need to keep that in mind when dealing with them. If they believe Marlak's interested in me, they won't be happy thinking I hate their prince. No, I need to make it seem like he has a chance.

I relax my face to get rid of all my previous annoyance. "But... your prince has been kind to me. And having you two here shows how much he cares for my safety. So it's not bad."

Ferer just stares at me, as if sensing my lies.

Nelsin, for his turn, nods. "We're at your service, my lady."

We don't trade any other secrets, and they finish lunch, a salad with cold rice and pieces of roasted chicken, delicious, of course, except that I'm desperate for some hot food. Maybe I'll dream about it instead of dreaming about Marlak. That will be helpful.

I could have some sexy dreams about a beef roast with hot sauce, some pumpkin soup, mint tea, hot milk... I love hot milk. Oh, well.

In the afternoon, we go outside, in front of the house, under the shade of trees, and Nelsin drills me on some basic sword movements. I'm holding a wooden stick, but his instruction is helpful. I can't imagine myself with a sword though, and can't imagine that I'll be allowed to continue this type of training when I return to the castle.

When I return. Will I return? Is my life ever going to be the same again? Do I want it to be the same?

Want. It's an odd thing, a luxury we don't always have. What *can* I want?

Sweat drips from my forehead as I try to find an opening and hit Nelsin with my stick, but he keeps blocking me, and I don't want to stop and admit defeat. We're still in the clearing in front of the house, Ferer watching us.

When I finally touch his ribs, I realize he isn't focused on what I'm doing, but staring at something behind me. I turn and follow his line of sight, and see Marlak walking into the clearing, carrying a slim box in his hands and a bag across his shoulders.

"We'll prepare dinner," Nelsin says, before disappearing into the house with Ferer.

I bet they left because they think Marlak is courting me, and all I can think is that they must be the most oblivious fae in the world.

"How's everything?" Marlak asks. He's wearing a beige tunic, open at his chest, displaying part of his star-shaped scar.

For a second, I want to reach out and touch it. Crazy second.

I guess he's in the mood to pretend we're civil acquaintances, and I can deal with that.

I smile. "Good."

"I brought you a gift." His dark eyes have an odd warmth. "Belated wedding gift, but I needed to know what you wanted."

"And you do?" It's an odd coincidence, since I was just now thinking that wanting is a luxury.

He chuckles and drops his bag on the ground. "Not everything. Obviously." He shows me the thin, long box, which is actually a leather-covered case. "But you need a sword. A good one."

I take the case, surprised that it's lighter than I expected. When I open it, I see a sword in it, its blade covered in a black scabbard, its pommel encrusted with three amethysts on each side, its crossguard decorated with black onyx.

It's absolutely stunning—and familiar. I know that sword. I've seen it in drawings. No, the gems are different, but their location and shape are the same.

The sword is fascinating, and I can't take my eyes off it, but I do, to stare at Marlak. "It looks just like Dawnshadow. The legendary sword that saved the fae three hundred and fifty-four years ago."

His eyes widen, as if surprised, then he smirks. "Thinking of impressing a perfumed royal with your knowledge of fae weapons?"

"I could impress a stinky royal, too."

He rolls his eyes. "Wife. I bathe every day."

I narrow mine. "Why would I want to impress you?"

Marlak sighs. "Do you like the sword?"

"It's beautiful. An impressive replica, except that Dawnshadow has rubies, and these are amethysts."

He raises an eyebrow, that odd facial expression I've seen a few times, and then leans closer to stare at the sword. And stare he does, open-mouthed, then he stares at me, and back at the sword, until he steps back and smiles. "Right."

Did he bring the wrong weapon? Perhaps he thought he'd picked a cheap trinket instead of this impressive replica. "Is this what you meant to give me?"

He crosses his arms. "I want you to have a good sword. Do you know the story of Dawnshadow?"

Didn't I just tell him some of it? Regardless, I don't mind sharing more of what I know. I love getting answers right. "Nestex, the fae hero and first king of the Crystal Court, used it in battle and defeated the witch-king."

Marlak smirks. "I knew you would have heard that version, but it's not the true one. It was his wife, Rideia, who wielded it and killed the sorcerer. The sword is so good because Nestex went to the most renowned smiths to make the best possible sword for his wife, one that would be light enough that wouldn't tire her arms. The result is an incredible weapon—which saved his life. A woman's weapon."

I don't know if what he's saying is true or not. "Why would anyone change the story?"

"Too mellow? Sentimental? I don't know. But it's a sword that was not made to conquer or kill, but to protect someone he cared about."

Marlak doesn't care about me, so I'm not sure why he's telling this story.

I unsheathe the weapon and see inscriptions on the blade in fae runes. This is likely worth a fortune. "Really? You want me to have this?"

"Wife. Don't be difficult. It's the sword I had. My wedding gift."

So it's not going to be mine forever. "Are you going to take it back when you decide to get married?"

Marlak sighs and covers his face with his hands. "I *am*

married. And the sword is yours."

Mine. Just like... Oh, why did I have to remember that dream? I hope he didn't dream it too—but I doubt I'd be so lucky.

I focus on the sword. This is the first thing I'll own in my entire life, not counting the forty ducks. It almost feels like too much, until I realize something.

"Wait. You have the real Dawnshadow, don't you?"

His eyes have an amused glint and he shrugs. "Maybe."

Of course he does. He has all the Crystal Court treasure.

Perhaps one day he'll give the woman he loves *that* sword. I can imagine him kneeling before her, presenting it as a sign of his devotion.

This is not the real thing. It's fake, just like me.

It's a great reminder of what we're not, of what I'll never be to him, and it can help me focus on my duty. "I think this sword suits me perfectly."

"Glad you like it. What do you want to call it?"

"Is it a no-name sword? That insignificant?"

He chuckles. "Regardless of what it was called before, it's yours now, so *you* should name it."

I smirk. "Dusklight."

He nods. "Brilliant name. I'll let Nelsin help you adjust the scabbard. You should always carry it, and practice using it. I mean, I don't want you to chop your hands off, so be careful, but train with it."

I put it back in its scabbard and box, still feeling a little strange that I have something that's mine.

He takes the bag from the ground. "I also brought some books for you. You could read them at night."

"When it's all dark?"

He chuckles and shakes his head. "There's a lightstone here too."

I take the bag, and, unlike the sword, it's quite heavy. There is a blue crystal inside it, which I take.

He continues, "You'll need to call me or your knights to act—"

The crystal emits a blazing blue light when I hold it. "Activate it?" I ask.

He stares at me and the stone, an eyebrow raised. "I think you'll be fine."

I put the crystal back in the bag. The light dims, but not so much.

Marlak stares at me, that odd, searching stare. "What is your magic, Astra? What is it?"

"Magic?"

"That light. You used it when... we met."

What a creative way to describe our first encounter.

He continues, "And you just activated a lightstone. Humans can't do it—usually."

"It's not magic, I just trust the Almighty Mother."

He snorts. "The goddess from the fake religion your people made up as a justification for their bloodshed?"

I don't know what he's talking about, but one thing I'm certain of is that the Almighty Mother is real. "If she's fake, then explain my magic."

"I obviously can't. Come, let's go inside." He looks at the bag with the books and takes it. "Let me carry this."

I don't like it when he's nice like that.

Shouldn't I complain that he's trying to seduce me? But I guess he does it out of a sense of guilt—which only makes me think he's not a bad person, and that again complicates my plans.

My plans. He's been to his treasure vault or whatever today, so he has access to it. I need to learn more about it, but first, I need to gain his trust.

Not an easy thing to do when he keeps complaining I'm some pathetic failed seductress.

※

I'M ACTUALLY THRILLED with my gifts, especially the lightstone. It allowed me to bathe and color my hair in the evening, and now I have some peace of mind and moments alone to look at the books.

But first I stare at the sword. It's indeed the most beautiful thing I've ever owned. Fine, it's the first thing I've ever owned, but it's still so fascinating, so well built. The gems are of a high quality, a type of amethyst I've never seen before, in a bright purple, and expertly cut. We learned about weapons and jewelry and how to estimate their value, since it's such a useful skill, so I know it costs a fortune. I just never imagined I'd have something like that.

I sheathe the sword, annoyed at myself. What a sad little creature I am, to be so impressed with a simple sword, a simple replica. It was probably lying among Marlak's stolen treasure, and giving it to me was easier than commissioning a new one.

It's still a fascinating sword, but shouldn't change my opinion of Marlak, who's set on killing his brother and will do anything to achieve his goals. Marlak, who told me to my face that he bought me like a cow. Marlak, who's given me a stolen sword, as if he had any right to do that.

Oh, no.

In reality, Dusklight is not mine, and will never be.

I feel deflated, but can't summon any anger, and perhaps it's for the best. I need to think about my mission in a rational way, think about what's best for me, what's best for my kingdom, and not let my personal feelings about the disgraced, murderous fae prince get in the way.

Despite wanting to spend more time looking at the sword, I take the books. *Really, get a grip, Astra, it's just a sword.* There are five books in the bag, all bound in thick leather. These are also luxurious editions—perhaps also stolen.

The smell of paper, mixed with my own hair color chemicals, takes me back to Otavio's study. The feeling I get is strangely bitter, considering I miss the tower. Do I miss it? I'd better check the books, instead of asking myself asinine questions.

There's a book about the history of the Crystal Court, which should be interesting to compare to what I learned. There's one with old fae runes, and it's also incredible, since we don't learn about them in Krastel.

I'm excited again. One book is about the history of the Shadow War, the one where the sword Dawnshadow was used. I'm curious to see how its account is different. A large book is a Tiurian language guide, much larger than any book about that language I've seen, and this is probably where I'm going to start. There's also a book with a faded title. I open it and see: *Tiuris, the Fallen Kingdom.* I'm not sure what my heart does, but it feels like a somersault.

My people. No, not my people. I'm a Krastel citizen now.

Am I?

I have studied some history of the darksouls, but all it brought me was pain and shame. Perhaps I should eventually read this, and see if it differs from what I studied, but I decide to focus on the language guide first.

Soon I find *azalee*, which is indeed a Tiurian word. Odd for me to remember it, when I studied so little of this language.

I can't believe the meaning I read. *Wife.* But it says it's *wife* used as an endearing word, a loving word.

Great, so that's what I've been hearing in my dreams: *wife.* Perhaps the foreign word made me miss the sarcasm in it, the mockery. Way to ruin what once was my only comfort. The new question in my mind, however, is why he's using a Tiurian endearment in my dreams. Why that language?

I don't know what to think, but at least I have something to read to shut away my thoughts. I pick up the Shadow War book and lie in bed, starting from the first page.

Soon I realize that it's detailed in a way that's boring. The writer was not a historian but a general, and this is a dry account that includes numbers, materials, movements of troops. I'm reading the way they figured out how to make tents that could be used in the rain, when I find my eyes closing and set the book aside.

I'm tired of having my boobs squeezed in a dress, so I take it off and lie down only in my undergarments. Focusing on hot milk, delicious hot milk, I tell myself that's what I'm going to dream about. See? Sometimes I know what I want.

I REALIZE I'm in that strange palace, from where I can see the top of a forest and the night sky. For a moment, I'm aware I'm dreaming, sitting in a strange, empty kitchen with dusty counters. The Amethyst Palace is abandoned, and yet I'm here with Marlak, sitting at a mahogany table by a tall window. There's no moon tonight, only bright stars and darkness.

He takes two cups, holding them with one hand, and a jug of milk, and puts them on the table.

"Trouble sleeping?" His voice is rough and low and reverberates through my entire body. *Entire* body.

"You're going to wake me up if you keep talking like that."

"Like what?" His warm chuckle doesn't help. There's just something so comforting about it, so... I don't even know how to explain it.

He holds my cup and stirs the milk with a spoon, warming it slowly so as not to form a layer on top.

I watch his beautiful arms, covered with a long-sleeved shirt, and dare speak my mind. "It feels like an invitation to tear your clothes off."

He chuckles again. "Well... I wasn't exactly thinking about it, but if you're seeing such an invitation, you're not wrong." His dark eyes focus on me. "It always stands."

I look down at the table, less pleasant thoughts crossing my mind. "We have a rough day tomorrow."

"It doesn't need to be rough." He passes me the cup. "What if it all goes smoothly?"

"Let's hope so." I take a sip—and it's the best hot milk I've had in my life. There's something entrancing, magical about it, and it dissolves all my fears, my anxiety. It enters my body like a balm, calming me.

I smile and glance at the cup. "This is amazing."

His magnificent eyes are sparkling, and he nods. "Glad you like it."

He looks so beautiful under the light of the stars, his black curls silhouetted against the lightstone in the kitchen's corner, that light lining his shoulders, his arms. He's my beloved husband, my king. I want him now.

"Is it true?" I ask.

"What?"

"That the offer always stands?"

"Not only the offer, azalee." His voice now is even rougher and lower, his breath ragged. He eyes my transparent nightgown, my taut nipples inviting the touch of his tongue, then looks at my face again.

His eyes are always magnificent, but on a night like this, when they are even darker with desire, they're bottomless ponds that I want to jump into and never return.

I crawl under the table, caress his thighs, then lift his tunic and kiss his abdomen, tasting his soft skin under my tongue. I love to hear his breath hitching, to feel that I have him under my control. I move my tongue down, then unlace his trousers, and now he's all mine.

All I hear are his soft moans as my tongue swirls over the tip of his cock. Indeed it's standing—and throbbing inside my mouth. Slowly, I move up and down, as much as I can, caressing the rest of it with my hands. It's as if I'm holding him between my teeth, owning him, undoing him. I adore his cock, love what it does to me, relish the feel of it inside me.

The table above me then moves, and I feel a gust of air moving me backwards, then up until my back is against the wood.

"Hey, that wasn't fair!" I pretend to complain. "I wanted that other milk."

"Later." He's ditching his clothes, which is a lovely sight, then undoing the laces of my nightgown.

I stare at him. "Not gonna rip it today?"

"I'm in a gentle mood."

"Teasing mood, you mean."

He smirks. "If that's how you see it, so be it."

I want to reply, want to tease him, but my words are gone. I don't know where I am, what I am. All I know is what I feel. Unbound, uncoiled, free.

12

When I wake up, I remember some parts of the dream, but not others.

Everything after he laid me on that table is quite blurry. I just remember the milk. Oh. *That other milk?* I can't believe there's some strange version of me that would say that. Now he thinks I'm corny on top of everything.

From what I remember, at some point we broke that table and he held me up with air magic, but it's not really making much sense. Dreams don't make sense, of course.

I put on my dress quickly, dreading his knocks on the door, dreading having to confront him about something I can't control.

Because really, if I could control it, would I dream about that? Would I dream about *him*? Obviously not. I'd pick someone better looking. Strangely, my mind goes blank when trying to come up with someone else to dream about.

It doesn't matter. I sit and wait for him, my heart getting louder and louder in my chest. But minutes and minutes go by, and since Marlak doesn't knock, and since I'm hungry, I leave my bedroom and go to the kitchen—where he's sitting, as if waiting for me.

"Hey." I smile, making sure my face looks neutral and a little sleepy. "Where are Nelsin and Ferer?"

"Busy, but they prepared some breakfast."

I think he has an intense stare, but I try not to look at him and head to the counter, where I see some fruit, bread, and jam. Without waiting for an invitation, I pick a plate and serve myself. Marlak gets up and stands right beside me, doing the same, but I ignore him and sit with my plate, while he places his on the table and goes to that box where he keeps cold things, probably using his water magic to form the ice.

"Do you want some *milk*?" he asks, and I sense a slight edge in that last word.

Right. He wants to play a game, but he has no idea I'm a master at it. I keep my voice neutral. "Sure."

He takes two cups in one hand and the jug with the other, then sits and looks at me.

"Trouble sleeping?" His voice is low, quiet, soothing.

Asshole. *That*'s the voice. Perhaps he's using some air magic to caress me down there. It can't be possible that a voice does that.

And yet I show no reaction. "No. Why?"

He stares at me. "Nightmares."

"You should really see someone about that."

He keeps staring. Is he trying to figure out if I had the same dream as him?

Haha. Good luck with that. It also means his strategy is shifting, and maybe he's not as convinced that I'm behind the dreams. That's great.

"Who knows?" He shrugs. "What if my next night goes smoothly?"

I pretend to be concerned. "You've been complaining about this for a while."

He watches me as I take a sip of my milk. "You prefer it hot."

"I do, but it's fine. If we ever go somewhere with a stove, I'll drink all the hot milk in the world."

He looks thoughtful. "Is there any other kind of milk you like?" He asks it with a straight face, though.

"Yes." I let the word hang for a second while he looks at me, an indecipherable look in his eyes. "I had goat milk a few times in the castle, and it was wonderful."

He sighs. "I'll ask Nelsin to bring some."

"No, it's fine. This is amazing." I know, I know, I shouldn't have used this exact word, but I didn't want to miss the opportunity to mess with his head.

He rolls his eyes. "Wife. It's just milk."

"I mean all the food. Your knights are talented cooks. Or food preparers. What do you call someone who doesn't actually cook?"

He's tapping his fingers on the table, likely mulling over our conversation, noticing I didn't blush, didn't show any reaction. He's probably thinking he's the one with the corny dreams where I wear transparent nightgowns.

"I think it's *cook*." He chugs his milk in one long sip, then parts his bread. "They bring a lot of stuff from outside, like bread, sometimes some roasted meat."

He takes a bite and leans back in his chair, his eyes lost. Definitely thinking about the dream. Hopefully coming to the conclusion that it was *his* depraved fantasy, and I had nothing to do with it.

Meanwhile, I'm here wondering if he can have floating sex while using his air magic and if it's even possible, but I'll die with this curiosity rather than ask.

One part of the dream was clearly wrong: Marlak can't heat liquids. Then again, that was *my* fantasy. I take full responsibility for dreaming about a cup of hot milk.

The rest... I don't know where the rest came from, but as long as Marlak doesn't know either, I can live with it.

※

Nelsin and Ferer show up with two large suitcases, and then Marlak leaves.

He's doing something during the day, and yet I'm stuck here, with no idea of what he's planning. The truth is that this island is just a pretty prison.

And then, he never claimed I would be anything other than his prisoner. Perhaps trying to gain his trust is a useless endeavor. What information have I gained since I got here? What did I learn with this incredible power of dreams that he thinks I have?

Nothing.

No. I think back to the dreams, think back to that palace.

Amethyst Palace. That can't be the Crystal Court castle, can it? No. It's not a place I've ever heard about. Why is it abandoned? What were we going to do the next day? Something that made me worried, something difficult, but what?

I need to pay more attention to what I see, to what he says. Details could matter.

Details.

If I close my eyes, I can still feel the texture of his skin, the heat of his body against mine, the softness of his tongue, the firmness of his... hand. That was what I was thinking.

Why do these dreams have to be so realistic?

Those are *not* the details I want.

"Astra!" Nelsin calls me from my bedroom, taking me out of my reverie.

I go there and see that they are taking clothes out of the suitcases. My new wardrobe. I'm happy and relieved that I'm finally going to have decent, comfortable things to wear.

A quick glance at a white, shimmery thing crushes my hope, though. It's a nightgown, not anywhere close to decent. Not only is it see-through, it's so similar to the one I wore in my dream last night that chills run down my spine.

"You don't like it?" Nelsin asks.

"How am I going to wear this?"

"Like a dress? But it's for sleeping."

I don't think he gets it. "If I need to get up, I'll be half naked."

He frowns, confused. "No. You'll still be dressed."

I nod, unwilling to debate modesty standards with a fae.

The seamstress sent four nightgowns, and while they look comfortable, they are all lacy, translucent, and quite indecent. Great.

Other than those atrocities, there are trousers, tops, underpants, socks, breastbands. I'm not sure anything here looks bulky and practical, though. The few glimpses of the leather reveal some delicate engravings, the linen has fine embroidery, and there are some items in colorful, but very expensive-looking silk. At least there are no dresses, so the seamstress listened to *one thing* I asked. Other than that, there are flat shoes, boots, and sandals that look comfortable.

I pick a blouse, a breastband, underpants, and a pair of trousers, and go to my washing room, so glad to get rid of that wool dress, get rid of the humiliation the Krastel royalty made me go through.

And yet it's them I'm loyal to.

I take a deep breath. It's not their fault. They were just trying to ensure I could convince Marlak I was a lowly maid. The excuse sounds flimsy even in my head. A castle attendant working so close to royalty doesn't dress in rough, cheap wool.

Perhaps I'm overthinking. If I keep doing that, I'll question everything I've striven for. I'll even question who I am.

I put on a new breastband that can be tied in the front, and it's so comfortable, with tight straps, providing good support. The trousers are made in thin, malleable leather and while they seem uncomfortable at first, the truth is that I feel like I'm wearing nothing, except... I feel that there's something in the pockets; two small daggers. I'm not surprised they're arming me, since Marlak thinks he's untouchable, I'm just surprised it's so discreet. Well, better than nothing. The only issue is that I can see the shape of my hips and thighs—and everyone else will be able to see it.

I try a gray, sleeveless blouse, likely made to match, and it's comfortable and cool as well. The blouse has a deep neckline, which shows a lot more of my chest than I would like it to. All right. *Now* I'm dressed like a seductress.

I sigh. The clothes are comfortable, though—and beautiful. Still, the lack of a skirt or at least a long, loose tunic feels strange. Am I really going to go around exposing my butt? It's either this or the ugly red dresses, and the material of these clothes is so soft.

Marlak might complain, but it's not my fault. He should have given Irene better instructions. And then, he was raised as a fae, and none of these clothes would be even remotely scandalous for them. So I'm good.

The woman who stares at me from the mirror is so different. With her tan skin and black hair, it's almost like another person. And yet I feel the same. Perhaps it's just another mask, a mask to look like I'm adapting to this new life. I like this mask, though. I look like a warrior, and can't wait to see what I'll look like with my sword strapped on.

Not *my* sword, the stolen sword Marlak thinks he has the right to give me. Still. It's a nice fantasy about the person I could become if only...

I don't know.

Not once in my life did I have the right to choose what to wear. In a way, I'm not really choosing now either, but it's all made for me, and I see a powerful woman in the mirror, someone who'll fight for what she believes.

Yes, I'll adapt.

I leave the bathing room and see Nelsin, who raises his eyebrows, lifting his top ears as well. It's funny how I find them normal now.

"You look radiant, my lady."

"More comfortable." I don't need any effort to smile.

Well, I can move, I can breathe, and it's incredible to realize how important those things are.

The training in the afternoon goes much better, and I even get to use my sword. I'm still not sparring with it, but learning some basic movements. Nelsin says that it's important to make it feel like an extension of my body and also strengthen my arms so that I don't get tired when wielding it.

Tired is the last thing I'll feel. I know it's wrong, and it's a stolen sword, but I can't help it, I love it. I love the feeling that I can be in control, that I can attack, that I can be dangerous and powerful and not need to hide any of that. I mean, of course I'm still far from dangerous, but the thought that I *can* be any of that is freeing.

Exercising here, with the earth touching the soles of my feet, birds singing above me, the river and the enormity of the mountains around me, makes my heart swell. I know that this is not forever, this is not my life, but I can enjoy this moment, pretend that this is who I am.

I close my eyes and feel the sword, its weight, its balance. The sound of the river water and the wind relax me and remind me to let my body flow. I can definitely feel the sword, and the movements I just learned slowly become my own, become natural.

I can even sense Nelsin approaching me. No, not Nelsin.

I open my eyes and realize it's Marlak—much farther than I thought, staring at me. I don't know if he's puzzled, surprised, or what. I could think perhaps fascinated, but that's my creative mind seeing things for no reason.

Either way, I barely get a glimpse of his expression, because as soon as he notices I see him, he looks away and walks inside. I'm guessing he's too royal for a simple *hello*.

At night, I read the history of the Crystal Court. So far, nothing's majorly different from what I learned. I do eye the book with the Tiurian history, but that topic always hurts too much.

I don't know if I'm prepared to open that wound, that odd wound that never heals and yet hides itself so well. I like it like that, where I can't feel it.

WHEN I OPEN my eyes this time, there are no awkward or embarrassing memories of strange, food-fueled dreams. There are also no empty palaces or mentions of lost towers.

All I remember is him, on top of me, inside me, rolling slowly like the water in the river. Slowly, as if we had all the time in the world. Slowly, just because we wanted to extend that time as much as we could.

That was how I felt, and if I close my eyes I can still feel Marlak inside me, as if he didn't belong anywhere else, as if two parts kept apart had been joined at last.

None of that is true, none of that is reality, and yet in these early hours of the morning when even the light is not quite up yet, it's easy to get confused, it's easy to even wish it was real.

No knocks on my door, no censure, and perhaps I can enjoy the dreams for what they are, for those moments of sweet illusion.

I get dressed and leave my room and almost stumble into Marlak, who's leaving his as well.

Will he confront me?

His eyes travel down and up quickly in a disinterested stare. "Are you happy with your new clothes?" At least his voice is kind.

"They're comfortable." I don't want to seem too grateful. After all, it was his choice to bring me here. And then again, he could have left me with the rough, tight dresses. "Thank you," I add, and no piece of me falls out because I said that.

I know I need to gain his trust, but the trick is doing it without making him think I'm trying to seduce him.

He's awfully quiet, though. Did he dream it too? Did he feel how close we were?

I'm starting to think that even if we share the same dreams, I'm the only one who *feels* them.

They must be dreadful if they are just some random sexy oddness without that deep connection. Then again, connection or not, I'm sure I would like to stop this craziness a lot more than even he does, but what can I do?

It's just us in the kitchen this morning, and I can hear my steps on the floor in that silence. There's bread, jelly, and fruit on the counter. I serve my plate while Marlak serves his, then I rush to the cabinet where he keeps the ice and the milk, meaning to take it, just to break our routine, but the door doesn't move when I pull.

"The ice locks it," he says, standing behind me.

Why do I notice how close he is? Why does it feel so intimate even if we aren't touching? Those stupid dreams have definitely polluted my mind.

I step away, and he opens it without difficulty, then passes me the jug. I take it to the table by the window, and he's right behind me, holding two cups.

"Where's Nelsin and Ferer?" I ask as I sit down.

"Busy. Don't worry, they'll be back before I leave." His tone is reassuring, his voice calm, that soothing baritone that's not quite like in the dreams, but too dangerously close.

I wonder why he's being nice and if he's just going to pretend that the dream didn't happen. Perhaps he doesn't remember it. Or didn't dream it.

He sets his dark eyes on me. "Happy with the reading?"

"Yes. Interesting books." I decide to take the opportunity and ask a question that has been bugging me. "Why did you bring the Tiurian history?"

He eyes me for a second longer than I'm comfortable, then takes a deep breath. "You said you wanted dictionaries. Tiurian is the only language that has one—other than the runes. I assumed you were interested in that civilization."

Civilization. An odd word to describe a group of people who were far from civilized. I nod. "Everything is learning, right? What about you? Any interest in languages?" More specifically, in certain Tiurian words, but I'm not bold enough to ask that.

"Aramids uses some Tiurian words."

Panic hits me as I realize I don't know what he's talking

about, as if this was a question in a test, and I was about to fail it. No. I know it.

"The poet! Died fifty-three years ago." Only after I say it, I realize I shouted it.

His eyebrows raise. "You like poetry too?"

"I..." Again I feel like I'm about to fail, like I won't be worthy of my position, my title, but then, I need to tell the truth. "I've studied *about* him, and read a few of his pieces, but Aramids wrote popular poetry and I didn't study that." It feels like a deficiency, in retrospect.

The corners of his eyes strain and he gives me a look that feels like an odd mix of pity and puzzlement. "Did you ever read for fun?"

I don't like the way he's looking at me. "I didn't have free time." Why is it that something that always gave me pride is now tainted with a hint of shame? There's no shame in working hard.

That look again. I hate that look.

"But it's fine," I add. "I love history..."

"Yes, I know. You had a blast reading dictionaries and history books." He has that neutral tone that I can't quite figure out, even though I'm sure he's being sarcastic.

I smile. "I did."

He looks at our empty cups, apparently only then realizing he hasn't filled them, and then proceeds to pour milk, like usual. His expression is focused, thoughtful.

At least that pitying look is no longer on his face when he looks at me again. "I'll have Nelsin bring you Aramid's *Song of Despair*. I think you'll like it."

I try to recall what I learned about that poem. "It's... about a war, right?"

He chuckles. "Wife. You don't have to know everything. Did you know that?"

I don't want to argue and I keep my tone light. "I'm saying I haven't read it. It means I obviously don't know it."

He sighs. "Well, it's a story. A made-up story. I read it once and thought it was fun."

"I didn't know you had time for fun."

"I know, right? Kind of hard to squeeze it in between all the evil scheming."

He chuckles but I don't, even though I realize I should be laughing at his jokes, but then if I laughed too late, it would be strange.

I decide to ask a genuine question. "What's the point in a story that's not real?"

He leans back in his chair and brings a ringless finger to his chin. "The feelings are real. There's something about feeling them while knowing you can't truly get hurt."

"Feelings? Like despair? What's the fun in it?"

"Well, if you're depressed, you look at your own life and say, 'nevermind. This could be so much worse.'" He chuckles again. "No. It's about getting out of that dark place, and reading sometimes makes you believe you can do it too."

"What's your dark place?" I blurt. It's a genuine curiosity, even if I realize I'll probably never get that answer.

He seems unfazed and smirks. "Tell me yours, first."

I shrug. "I don't have a dark place."

"As I suspected." He stares at me with an eyebrow raised. "Perfect life, with no free time and all that. Lots of history books and some dictionaries. Plenty of space in your tower."

I don't know what he's trying to get at, but I smirk. "Exactly."

He nods and eats a piece of bread. When he finishes, he says, "Is there anything else you need? Anything you didn't mention, or that I forgot?" He tilts his head. "Don't say freedom, as I can't give you that yet."

"Do you really think I know your secrets?"

He stares at me. "There's something odd going on. Of that I'm sure. Now, I don't even understand the extent of it, since you're not going to admit what you're doing, right? Would you like to change that? Maybe we can find a solution together."

His face is open, earnest, and more than anything, I'd love to trust him, but I know I can't.

I shake my head. "I'm not doing anything."

He has a mocking smirk. "Of course. So it must be something on my end. I need to be cautious and see if someone can help me. That said, is there anything at all you'd like?"

There is, but I'm not sure it's possible. "A letter. Can I write to my sisters?"

His expression softens. "I'm so sorry, Astra. I can't go into Krastel now. It could be dangerous."

"But you went to pick me up."

He shrugs. "I had no choice."

If we don't go to Krastel, how am I going to contact Otavio? Suddenly, I'm drowning in panic. "My hair coloring. I only have a supply for three months..." I realize I forgot to hide the fear in my voice. What a stupid mistake.

"Three months is a long time."

"But I can't—"

He chuckles. "Calm down, wife. Give me one of the bottles and I'll find something similar for you. I won't let you die of sadness because your hair is not black."

I laugh as well. Haha, so hilarious being afraid of running out of hair coloring.

He continues, "We're going to attend a coronation in a week."

"Yours?"

His laughter is warm and rich. "Ours, you mean. No. Not

yet. It's the Court of Bees." That's a tiny fae court, in that area where there are some thirty of them. "It's best if you come with me. Bring your sword, and practice with it as much as you can. And maybe... Maybe write your letters. I'll read them, just to make sure there's nothing compromising, but write them. Maybe there will be a human emissary who could bring them to your kingdom. How's that?"

I smile. "Helpful." I doubt any human kingdom would step foot so far in fae territory, and the idea of having my letters read is dreadful, but I guess he's trying to be nice.

He gets up. "I'll be away for three days and—"

I feel punched in the gut. "Going to the Court of Spiders?" I blurt. Oh, how dreadfully I'm forgetting all my training.

He pauses and stares at me with a curious and amused smirk. "Jealous?"

A bitter taste sets in my mouth. To be very honest, I hate the idea that he could still be courting someone while naming me his wife. He could certainly have kept me as a prisoner, right? Without this mockery. "Curious."

He shakes his head. "I haven't been there in over a year, and I have no plans of returning anytime soon."

"Where are you going, then?"

"*That* is a secret."

I feign confusion. "I don't understand. Didn't you say I knew all your secrets? What's the matter?"

He chuckles. "Lots of matters. Maybe one day I'll trust you, wife."

With that, he goes to his room. I notice then that there's someone at the door. Nelsin is watching me. "Don't worry. The day will come," he says.

He thinks I'm upset that Marlak doesn't trust me? Odd.

I smile and nod, as if I was grateful for the reassurance.

I don't like the idea of spending so many days away from

Marlak, with no chance of finding out any of his secrets, but on the other hand, going to a fae court with him will be a trove of information. And I'll get off of this island. And get to know more of the fae territories, something I've always dreamed of.

It's such an amazing opportunity! I need to ignore the sting of his planned absence and focus on this coronation and everything that it will bring. Everything and everyone I'll get to know.

13

I know the sound of his breathing when he's asleep. It's the sound of calm, peace.

I also notice when the cadence changes, and know that he's awake. This time, there's also a soft, almost imperceptible moan.

Something's wrong.

I'm resting against his chest, but his star is hidden under a thin tunic. I try to place my hand under his tunic to see what's there, but he holds it in place.

"It's nothing." His voice is slurred with sleep and exhaustion.

It's definitely not nothing, and I notice then that he has some cuts on his left forearm and a scary gash on the back of his hand.

I look at him. "What happened?"

He kisses my forehead. "You worry too much."

I wasn't even worried, not until he said that, at least. I point to his hand. "Who did this?"

He tries to chuckle, but it sounds all wrong. Of course. While he might think it's hilarious, his body disagrees. "Me, obviously, while fighting back."

I push his hand away and lift his tunic. He has some cuts and scratches, but nothing deep, and I exhale in relief.

Still, something's wrong.

"Look at me." My voice is trembling.

"I'm always looking at you."

His lips look normal, his coloring has no change.

I just have this feeling... Something's wrong, wrong, wrong, and yet I don't know what it is.

It's when I remember Otavio's voice. *Few can recognize the symptoms of acrilantis. When they do, it's too late.*

I look at his hands again, and indeed, under the nails, it's redder than usual. A subtle sign that most people miss. Shit, shit, shit.

I can barely breathe. "You're going to die."

"Indeed. It's what usually happens. You're born really small, then you become a child—"

"Listen to me." I don't have time for his sass. "Listen to me." My voice reverberates through the room, and only now I realize we're in a gigantic chamber with high columns and a tall, domed ceiling. Everything is ancient and odd, and made of some gray stone. But that's not what matters. I need him to listen. "Now. Now, Marlak, not in one hour, not in ten minutes. You're going to find some root of alastacia and eat as much as you can."

He frowns. "Root of what? You think I'm an apothecary? Or a gardener? An herbalist?"

"I don't care. Find it. Eat it. Or you'll die." I don't understand why I don't simply go and get it for him. Why I don't let him rest while I find the root. My words don't make sense. "Now. Find it."

He stares at me, eyes wide. I hope he's truly listening.

I continue, "If you can't find an herbalist, go somewhere near a swamp. The plant has small red flowers."

"That's poison!"

"Yes, the flowers and the plant could kill you. The root will save you."

Marlak sits up, still holding me. "And if I don't find it?"

"You'll die!" My yell is a squeak, my throat constricted with desperation.

"I'll find it, azalee. You're not getting rid of me that soon." He kisses my temple, just like he did at our wedding. "I trust you."

"Tell me you're going to get it, then."

He holds my face with both hands and plants a brief kiss on my lips. "Of course I am."

My eyes open suddenly, wet with tears, and I can barely breathe.

I'm in the river hideout, no light coming in through the curtains. It's the middle of the night. Was the dream real? Was Marlak poisoned? My heart is throbbing in desperation. But there's nothing I can do.

Isn't there?

I could wake up Nelsin and Ferer. They might have a way to contact him. But then, if I say I dreamed about Marlak, and if he also had this dream, he'll know I've been dreaming about him. And maybe the dreams are not related to what's truly happening. They could be memories or predictions. They could even be nothing.

I mean, some of the dreams were definitely *not real*, considering we couldn't be doing what we were doing when each of us were in our own room. And yet. What if this is a warning?

Sure, I might regret this, but regret might come anyway, so the only thing I can do is choose the milder regret, and that's why I head to Nelsin and Ferer's room and knock softly. I should be banging on that door, given the urgency of the situation, and then again, I don't know if there's any urgency.

There's something tapping softly, but it's not me. I open my eyes and find my room inundated with sunlight. No. No. It can't be. Didn't I go to Nelsin and Ferer's room? I want to scream, but how can I make any sound when I can't even breathe? Marlak could be dead now.

That tapping again, and I dare look. There's an odd creature there, with green skin and large black eyes—a nymph. My heart wants to jump out of my chest as I walk to the window and open it. I'm not afraid of the nymph. I'm afraid for Marlak, feeling guilty that I didn't warn anyone, didn't try to do anything.

"Y-yes?"

The creature blinks, then I hear a feminine, soft voice. *Your husband is safe. Don't fret, child.*

"Are you sure?" I whisper, then add, "Can you see my dreams?" That would be so awkward.

I hear a chuckle. *We sense your feelings, child. But don't worry. Your husband is safe.*

"Thank you," I mouth.

The creature turns around and walks away, truly walks, graceful like a fae. She's wearing a long tunic whose edges float slowly as if it was still in water. I had no idea nymphs could come to land, and no idea they could sense feelings, or whatever it is they did.

I don't think the nymph was lying. Now, of course I could be wrong. And then again, why would she come here to deceive me about something so personal? And Marlak trusts them.

I sag back on the bed, exhaling more air than I ever thought I could hold. So my dream *was* real? And I *did* indeed warn him?

What if I had never had that dream?

Marlak would be dead now.

The thought chills me. I don't even know where all this terror is coming from.

Well, if the disgraced prince dies, I'll no longer have a purpose, so I suppose I'm afraid of the uncertainty that would come with that. That's a logical fear.

Yet I'm still wondering who poisoned him, if they'll try to kill him again, if he'll ever make it back home. Is this what my life is going to be like? Agonizing for a prince with more enemies than I can imagine?

I DECIDE to trust the nymph and end up not telling my knights about the dream or my suspicion of poisoning. I spend the morning training with Ferer. While he's quieter, he has better tips about hand and foot position than Nelsin. It's like he observes me better, something that can still be somewhat disconcerting.

Later I climb some trees. In truth, it was something I always dreamed of doing. Dreams can be so silly and simple. From the top of a rosewood tree I look at the river, dotted with islands. No signs that there's any life down there, that they could be watching us. The idea should bother me, but it doesn't. Being surrounded by nymphs gives me an odd sense of safety, protection. I then stare at the mountains surrounding us.

Would I be able to see Marlak returning? Where is he? What is he doing? I still hope he isn't visiting some lover, putting into action all those things he'll do to me only in dreams.

My thoughts are weird today. I obviously don't want

those dreams to become reality—but I don't want him to be with someone else either. It would complicate my life, I think, and maybe my mission here would be ruined. I think that's why the thought bothers me so much. And then there's that small fear that he is indeed dying, that no dream could prevent it, that the nymph lied...

At night I get to the *Song of Despair*. The Tiurian History book still sits on a corner, and I get the sense that it's staring at me in disapproval. A normal person would be curious to learn more about their past, learn if the history of their people is being told differently.

There's nothing normal about me or my situation, though. I was raised to be Krastelian through and through, loyal and honorable. All I learned about Tiurians—or dark-souls—were their awful crimes and barbarities, and I don't know if I can handle any more of that.

Looking away won't save me, won't change me, but at least it won't hurt me.

And I need to read the epic poem that Marlak was so excited about. I open the *Song of Despair*, and soon the rhymes and meters disappear, and I find myself caring for Sefel, the main character, whose beloved was kidnapped, and now he's willing to go down to the depths of the world to get her back.

That kind of love is the love I wanted. I used to still have hope that I would find it, but now... Is it possible that I'll find it after seven years? Or maybe that I'll find a way to be free before that? I certainly won't find love while tied to Marlak.

At least I can leave these questions for another day. For now I want to see if Sefel finds his beloved or not. It's agonizing, in a way, because when I think he's getting close to victory, he encounters more and more tribulations.

At least he now has a traveling companion, the witch

Herafes, who wants to avenge her family. It's funny how she's at ease with her magic even though she's not fae and doesn't have an opus stone. Only a darksoul would have magic like that in real life. Well, this is a completely fabricated story, and here, magic like that is not something to be feared. I wish... I don't know what I wish, but I keep reading.

The poem is getting more and more complicated, and every time I want to sleep, Sefel and Herafes get into deeper trouble, so I keep reading a little more, until I force myself to put the book away. I don't dare glance at the Tiurian History tome, lying at the bottom of the pile, buried under books that cannot harm me.

In truth, I try to sleep because I hope my dreams will tell me if Marlak survived, if everything is fine with him.

***

ALL I REMEMBER IS his hand, his hand with that dreadful gash, now a craggy line, no longer bleeding. I can still feel it cupping my breast, caressing my thighs. The hand is healing —and he's alive. Quite alive, taking me with the urgency and fervor of someone who's seen death crossing his path, as if it was our first and last time, as if there was no tomorrow.

Of course, none of it was real.

I put on a pair of leather trousers and a silk top and leave my room. The kitchen is empty, I guess because it's still early. I grab a piece of bread and sit at a table, when I see Nelsin coming from the hallway.

He eyes my plate, then frowns. "You should have called me."

"This is fine. Tell me something—if you can. Are you able to contact Marlak, or check if he's all right?" I know, I know, I'm asking this one day too late, but I trusted the nymph.

Nelsin pulls a chair, the chair where Marlak usually sits, which makes it look even emptier. He rests his elbows on the table. "I'm not allowed to answer that."

These words shouldn't surprise me. "What if I sensed he was in danger or something?" This is uncomfortably close to the truth, but I need to know.

The fae shakes his head, his cat ears flapping slightly with the movement. "Our task here is to protect *you*, not him."

"I'm not the one out there facing dangers."

Nelsin eyes me. "It makes no sense, right?"

"Does your prince ever make any sense?"

His eyes sparkle with mischief. "You know what? We're going out today. Would you like that? Off of this island."

"Is it safe?"

"Oh, yes. We won't step into enemy territory or go anywhere where we could be spotted. And I'm sure you're tired of being in the same small space for so long."

The same small space. He hasn't seen the tower where I grew up. Then again, the island isn't much bigger.

He leans forward. "You like to climb, right? We'll find a rock wall for you."

I think he's trying to do something nice for me, but there's something odd about his invitation. "Are you allowed to do that? Get me out of here?"

He leans back and shrugs. "If I think it's important, yes."

This is some interesting information. "Let's go, then."

I hope I don't regret this.

I KNOW there's something Nelsin's not telling me. Why would he choose to take me out of the island right when Marlak is away? When, coincidentally, Ferer is also away?

My best guess is that he's doing something he isn't allowed to do, but it can't be just because he wants to take me for a walk, can it? Of course not. There's more. I know it, but I want to find out what it is.

At least the curiosity about where Nelsin is taking me replaced my worry about Marlak, and perhaps seeing him in a dream last night was enough to quiet that nagging anxiety.

Nelsin told me not to bring my sword. Thankfully, he said nothing about daggers. Still, as I stand at the edge of the island, I decide it's better to offend him than to risk my life.

"You're not tricking me, right? You mean no harm?" I chuckle, and it sounds right, but I had to put an effort to fake it.

He raises a hand and shows me his palm. "No harm. I have sworn an oath to protect you, my lady, and even if I hadn't, I'd never do anything to hurt you."

"I didn't think that, I just—"

"I know."

A disk of ice forms in front of us. He steps on it, then reaches out for me to step on it as well, which I do. Soon we're gliding gently over the river, towards the other side. Nelsin's water magic is quite impressive, and it's something I'll have to remember.

Ha. Remember when? I don't think I have any chance against him. Perhaps that's what I need to keep in mind: how utterly powerless I am in this place.

On the river bank, he winks. "Don't tell anyone about this."

"It will be our secret." Had I been just a little prudent, I guess I'd be asking him to take me back to the island right now.

But that island is my prison. Should an inmate ask their jailer to put them back in their cell?

There are pebbles and mud under my feet, but he leads me inland, towards the small cliff. Among some rocks, I see a circle of white mushrooms. A faerie portal? I always learned that they exist only in human stories, created by people with little understanding of magic.

Nelsin steps in the middle of the circle, a mischievous grin on his face, his top ears pointed forward. "Yes, yes. We do travel through those."

I step in. "Are you going to tell me where you're taking me?"

"Why? If I can *show* you?"

It feels like he's working some air magic, blowing a powerful circular current around us. As far as I know, Nelsin wields only water, though.

When I look around us again, we're in a plateau, near a tall rock cliff, some two times the height of any climbing structure I ever trained on, surrounded by mountains and more mountains.

Oh. So we are indeed climbing, and that's what this is about. I don't know why I feel deflated. Maybe because I thought I was about to find out some juicy secret? We didn't even need to come here, as we could have climbed the cliff by the Queen's River.

There are only tall, green mountains around this valley. So many, so tall... It means we're still somewhere among the Endless Mountains, so not far from home.

Home.

Not home, the island. Do I even have a home? Is the castle tower my home?

I stare at the rock wall, and can easily see nooks and fissures, making it as easy as a ladder. Without wasting any time, I run to it and move up as fast as I can. There is a certain satisfaction in knowing that I can depend on my body to pull me up, trusting it to vanquish a wall that would otherwise look insurmountable.

And yet every rock has cracks.

This is much more freeing than training on the roof of the Elite Tower. There, all I could see was the city and farms surrounding the castle, while here I get to see wild, untamed mountains, covered with ancient trees. It's peaceful. Powerful.

I look down and see Nelsin laughing. "You're fast!" His voice echoes in the emptiness around him.

"What did you expect?" I shout back.

I shouldn't feel giddy that I can do something well, but I can't help it. I love beating a challenge.

The fae uses a disk of ice to float up to me. I'm not sure how he can like that. There's no place to hold, and a stronger wind current could push him from the surface. I think it's scary and a thousand times worse than moving up while holding onto the firm rock.

Still, I mock a frown. "That's cheating."

"No." His top ears move back and forth. "I never said *I* wanted to climb."

I just laugh and shake my head. In truth, I'm enjoying being here. "Thank you. This place is beautiful. Where are we?"

I see a microsecond of a smirk—or maybe imagine it—then he's pointing to the area beneath the cliff. "Look."

My stomach suddenly feels empty and floaty. Marlak is there, looking up, his expression neutral, wearing a light tunic and brown leather pants and boots, no rings or gloves.

The first thing I check is his left hand. No recent scar or any visible wound. No sign of that ragged cut.

It was a dream, Astra.

A dream. Not reality. And it might mean he wasn't even poisoned. Or can it be that it's faded and hidden among his older scars? I don't want to look too much, but there's something strange about him. He's looking in my direction but it's as if he can't really see me. He lacks that intense stare he usually has, and my stomach drops for some reason. I want to climb down and check on him, but at the same time, he seems so cold, so distant.

I turn to Nelsin, and find him watching me intently. Too intently, his top ears pointing forward.

"What's he doing here?" I ask.

He lifts one shoulder. "What do I know?"

Can't he see that there's something wrong with Marlak? Doesn't he care?

"Well, I'm climbing down." Then I add, in a lighter tone, "To keep practicing." I don't want him to start thinking that I *care* for his prince.

I approach the edge and turn to grab onto the rocks for my descent, but then I hear an inhuman scream behind me, and look down. Four figures are approaching Marlak. They're wearing black cloaks and hoods, and I can't see their faces, but they are all pointing swords at him. He should use his magic, but all he does is take out his own sword. I had never seen him carrying a weapon, but I'm glad he's doing it.

Something's wrong, and this is not going to end up well. We need to help him, fast. My hand is trembling as I turn back and search for a place to put my foot, when something pulls me. Someone. Nelsin. He's pulling me away from the edge.

"What's wrong with you?" I want to punch him.

Nelsin turns me and holds me in place, pinning down my arms. From this position, I can look at the valley, but can't move, can't do anything.

"Our goal is to protect *you*, not him," Nelsin says from behind me, his breath close to my ear.

Marlak is surrounded, and even though he's keeping the assailants at bay with his sword, I doubt he'll be able to hold on much longer.

"Then at least *you* should go! Use your magic. Do something!" I'm screaming. I'm so angry.

"I've sworn an oath." He sounds apologetic, but it's a feeble excuse. And his voice is too calm. Why is he so calm? Can't he see what's going on?

"Something's wrong with Marlak!" I yell, because it seems that I truly need to state the obvious.

Behind me, Nelsin doesn't react.

Right then, I see a sword hitting my husband's shoulder. He's still defending himself, but he won't last. My breath stops.

I STOP WIGGLING and trying to free myself, as if I had given up. Nelsin still holds me firmly, his two arms circling me. I lift my hands, then put one leg behind one of his, and throw myself back toward the ground. As we fall back, I pull the sword from his belt and knee his groin.

"Don't stop me," I say as I get up.

There's no time to think. I throw the sword down the cliff, then jump, aiming for an area with soft grass. I've never jumped from such a height, but I have to trust the Almighty Mother. It's that trust that guides me to a soft, undisturbed patch of grass, that guides me into a perfect roll, absorbing my fall.

Nelsin's sword glints on the ground, near a rock, and I run to grab it, but then I glance beside me—and stop. There is nobody attacking Marlak anymore.

And no Marlak. I stop breathing.

No sounds of any conflict or assailants. I rush towards the place where he was, while Nelsin's voice mixes with the wind.

There's nothing. Nothing. Just grass and rocks and emptiness. Infinite emptiness.

"Astra!" Nelsin shouts from behind me.

And then it hits me. Why he didn't help. Perhaps even why he brought me here. I feel anger stinging my eyes and turn to him. "Traitor!"

He has his hands raised, top ears flopping down. "It was an illusion."

What? The words don't make sense, but they're enough to stop me. Only then I realize I was rushing in his direction, sword in hand. I don't even recall picking up the weapon. I don't even know what I planned to do with it.

"An illusion, Astra," he repeats, then the four hooded figures appear behind him, except that they have their hands up and move their hips as if following the rhythm of a happy song. "Are you hurt?"

My pride is, and it gets even more wounded as I watch the figures disappear behind the conniving fae.

I'm such an idiot. The realization of my foolishness hurts the most. From the moment I saw Marlak, I knew he wasn't himself. Well, of course. It *wasn't* him. And Nelsin thinks this is funny?

I throw his sword on the ground, hoping it gets badly

damaged in the fall, then approach him and push him. "You're an asshole!"

He falls back, way back, and hits the ground hard. I can't have pushed him that hard, can I? I almost feel sorry for that. Almost.

Sitting up slowly, he stares at me. "Astra, did you get hurt in the fall?"

"I jumped. Didn't fall. And your joke is atrocious." Then I add, "Are *you* hurt?"

He rubs his hands over his face. "Listen, I'm sorry. I never thought you'd jump."

"What did you expect? What was the point of this?" My voice is high, my eyes are blurry, and I'm pointing a finger at him with trembling arms.

"First, I wanted proof that you can be trusted. That you care."

That's ridiculous. "I do *not* care!"

He blinks slowly. His top ears are folded down. "If you were to see Marlak getting hurt, it would bother you."

"*Anyone* getting hurt would bother me."

Nelsin rubs his face some more. "Yes. Including Marlak. But... the thing is, what I did today, staying there with you, that's exactly what I would have to do in case something like this happened. My order is to protect you, not him. And I wanted your help. To convince him to change his orders."

This cat fae is definitely crazy. "Right. Let's trick and humiliate her, that will definitely get her to collaborate with me."

"No, no. Nobody was humiliated. I just wanted you to see. I'd never guess you'd free yourself from my grip, or that you have some magical jumping abilities. I'm glad you do, and that you're not hurt. But if this had been real, would you really try to take on four enemies on your own?"

In truth, I wasn't thinking at all. Had I been thinking, I would have realized that it wasn't Marlak in less than a second, but I have a good explanation as to why I jumped. "If your oath is to protect me, and if I got myself in the heat of the action, you'd have to intervene, right?"

There's something new in the way he looks at me, like a spark of admiration. "Yes. But it's not a good solution. It would be dangerous."

His point is ridiculous. I can see that it makes sense for him, but why did he have to do that? "Next time, talk to me. If something bothers you, tell me. Don't trick me. Don't deceive me."

It just feels so awful to be caught in such a crude trick. And it was my fault for not paying attention, or rather, paying attention and yet ignoring what I noticed.

He's still sitting. "I didn't mean to upset you."

I'm getting worried that he still hasn't gotten up, and I crouch by the fae. "Are *you* hurt?"

He stares at me, opens his mouth, as if to say something, closes it, then looks away. "I'm sorry."

If he weren't hurt, he would have denied it by now. "I didn't know I was going to push you like that. I didn't mean it."

"It's not too bad, my lady." He grins. "I'll be up in one minute."

That's a relief to hear, especially because then I won't feel guilty for still being furious. "I'll climb again, then. While you rest." I need to get rid of this anger, this shame.

"No." He's getting up slowly. "Stay close. Just in case. Outside the island, I can't let you out of my sight."

I'm about to tell him he can see me on the rock wall, but perhaps it's better to remain with him and check if he's all right. And running from what just happened won't erase it. I do need his trust, after all.

Nelsin's standing in front of me, a hand behind his back, a subtle grimace on his face.

"Truly. I'm sorry for pushing you," I insist. The truth is that I *am* feeling guilty.

His grimace disappears, replaced by a crooked smile. "It's nothing!"

"I still shouldn't push people. But you shouldn't have tricked me."

He stares at me, still with that glint in his eyes. "Fae sometimes need to test others, especially people who can lie."

Test. What was he even testing?

My heart then jumps, aware of the answer a second before me. Of course. He and Ferer think their prince is in love with me, and I guess Nelsin would like to know if the feeling is mutual.

I can picture the cat-eared fae babbling to Marlak about how I jumped from the top of a rock wall for him. Oh, so much love! So touching! I have to stop this insanity before I even try to picture Marlak's reaction.

"You can't tell anyone about this." My voice sounds shaky. I'm still trembling in anger and now I'm consumed by this new worry. "What happened here has to stay between us. Can you promise—"

"My lady, a promise is—"

"Oh, tell him, then. I'll also tell *my* version. And it won't be flattering."

His head is tilted, examining me, his ears perked up. "Why wouldn't you want him to know that you're brave and reckless and wild? People often do acts of bravery just to impress others."

"Impressing Marlak is the last thing on my mind."

Then again, no, Astra. If you want to gain his trust, it's a good thing. On the other hand, I can imagine Marlak laughing at my stupidity, at how easily I was tricked, laughing at my feeble attempt to rescue him, laughing because he's getting the deranged idea that I somehow care for him. But gaining Nelsin's trust *is* a good thing.

I add, "Let him find out who I am. Without tricks. And I'll ask him to change your oath so that you can protect both of us. You have a good point."

Nelsin nods, then I hear a vibration, like...

I stare at him. "I thought you didn't purr?"

"So did I." His eyes are wide, staring down at his chest, spreading his arms, as if to see if he can find the source of the sound.

Then I hear something whooshing beside me, and too late, turn to see a dart embedded on Nelsin's shoulder.

Is he really going to trick me with another illusion?

But then he pushes me behind him and forms a wall of ice in front of us. It's a small, thin barrier, which collapses into thousands of pieces in one second.

I can't see anyone or anything around us, but Nelsin's body is taut, his ears folded back, almost hidden amidst his blond hair. There's no way he would be faking all that: he's afraid.

14

I might have trained using daggers, but the goal was mainly to run, to escape. How and where am I going to escape if I'm in the middle of a valley? And how can I fight an enemy I can't see? *When you're overpowered, the only solution is to escape.* But escape where?

There won't be any running here, but I can do the only thing I know how to do, which is to cast light. I don't know what difference it can make when the day is already bright, but I don't know what else to do.

Light, light, light. I keep the thought firm in my head and heart, and then emit a burst around us. At that moment, I see two fae, each of them at some twenty feet from us, both of them with tangled dark hair, dressed in rags.

One of them shoots something, but I'm fast enough to dodge the projectile. It's a dart, like the one that hit Nelsin. My light's gone, and I can no longer see them, as they have some kind of invisibility glamour that my light seems to break.

If they're shooting, it means they're going to keep a distance, at least for some time. I take the two daggers from my pockets and hold one in each hand. If they come close, I'll try to keep them away.

More light. I need more light. I focus, and another burst comes from me. I see the fae now, much closer, and this time, when the light is gone, I can see that they are not completely invisible, but look like ripples in the water. I aim—and throw a dagger. The fae who was shooting darts falls to the ground. That was a clear shot. His companion is running towards us, sword in hand.

I grab Nelsin's sword from the ground, as if I was about to fight the assailant, but hold the weapon with my left hand. The fae is coming towards me, and I raise the sword, as if to parry him, but I throw my dagger with the right hand. I can barely believe that it hits his throat. The fae emits a gurgly scream, but keeps running, so that I need to parry indeed. His blow is weak, though, and he soon falls. I'm afraid he's dead.

That's when I dare look at Nelsin.

He's pale, his eyes cloudy and wide. "I'm paralyzed, Astra. And have no magic." He motions to the fallen fae with his head. "Kill them. Fast."

Kill. Kill? Am I ready to do that, when they're already defeated?

"Fast," Nelsin insists, his voice piercing me with its desperation.

I shove down my horror and approach the first fae I hit. He's lying down, eyes closed, and yet I don't dare touch him to see if there's still a pulse. My dagger, now bloody and murderous, is lying beside him. This is wrong. You don't kill an enemy who's already fallen. And we should ask them who they are and why they were attacking us.

"Kill him!" Nelsin yells. "He's something else, Astra. Not a fae."

Is it right to kill someone because they're neither fae nor human?

And yet they were attacking us. I decide to listen to Nelsin, so I pick that dreadful dagger and slash the main artery on his neck. It's bloody and messy and horrific. He was so pale already, and now he opens his eyes and stares at me, stares at me before those eyes become glassy and lifeless. An accusing stare. A life I took away—as if I had the right. And it wasn't in self defense. There was no excuse.

"The other," Nelsin pleads.

This is wrong. I turn to him. "I think he's dead already."

"They are not alive, Astra. They're bloodpuppets."

Bloodpuppet. I've heard that before. Some kind of monstrous creature. I approach the other man. This one has a smirk as he eyes me, even though blood is pouring down his throat. I'm about to kneel to stab him, when Nelsin screams, "Back off! Don't touch him. Don't touch him."

I take some steps back and look at the cat-eared fae, wondering what's the meaning of this.

He's still sitting down, his eyes even wider. "Run. Go in the direction opposite the cliff, and you'll cross a stream. Keep walking and you'll find a village. There, find a tavern called Summer Dusk. Say you work for Marlak and they'll help you. Run."

I'm not sure why he's saying that. "We defeated them, didn't we?"

"Run!" His yell is a terrifying shriek. "Please. Survive this."

That scream is enough to power my legs into action towards a desperate escape, but I don't let them. "Why?"

"He's turning into leech roaches." His breath is so ragged that the words are clipped. "You can outrun them now. You won't be able to outrun them later."

"What about you?"

"It was a pleasure serving you. I'm sorry for this. Truly sorry." He then smiles. "I had a good life. Now run!"

I'm no coward. "I'm not leaving you. How do we defeat these roaches?"

"Fire, Astra. Run. Please. I'm begging you. They won't reach you across the river."

"Can't I just squash them?"

I sense that he'd be shaking his arms in the air if he wasn't paralyzed. "They fly. And they'll kill you."

I try to see where these creatures are coming from, what they are, and then I see the body of the second fae, the one Nelsin told me not to touch. There's no body anymore. It's a mass of... What is that? It's breaking up in pieces, and getting darker and darker. I'm guessing these are the leech roaches.

"Run!" Nelsin shrieks.

I do, but in his direction. "I'm not leaving you."

He laughs in disbelief. "I don't need company in death, Astra."

"Shush. Let me focus."

I don't know if he indeed falls silent or if I'm just blocking whatever he's saying. I don't know if I'm crazy or if this is the right thing to do. It feels right, and I choose to trust this feeling.

More than ever, I can't let my trust falter, I can't doubt myself. No, I don't need to trust myself. All I need to do is trust the Almighty Mother, trust her light.

Only light here. Light shields us and protects us from evil. Light shields us, and nothing can pass through this wall. I imagine a bright circle around me and Nelsin, a bright circle stronger than anything.

I see then some of those creatures flying towards the

A CURSED SON

other fallen fae. It makes no sense since they're so small, but they're devouring his body.

I shut my eyes and ignore that gruesome spectacle, making an effort to keep just light in my mind. Just light. Light. Nothing but light. It surrounds us. I can hold it, I know I can hold it, but I'm also realizing we'll need help.

There's one person I'm connected to, one person whose mind I can peer into. Still surrounded by that light, I call my kindred soul.

He'll come to help us—when he can. All I need to do is not falter for even a second, keep that protection standing, and trust the threads connecting souls. He'll come.

Time. We often think about it as something measurable, precise. One hour is one hour, one minute is one minute. But it isn't like that, is it? It's malleable and flexible and changes as we change.

I've been holding a wall of light for an eternity. For days. For hours. I don't know how long. All I know is that mine and someone else's life depend on it. I've been trusting and holding, giving everything I can as if all I need to do is hold on for one more second. Just one more second. And one more. And one more.

I think about my kindred soul, my real kindred soul, the one who holds me in my dreams. I feel that connection, and feel that my call has been heard. Still, I don't know when he'll arrive, and I refuse to entertain any doubt whether he'll come. All I need to do is hold this light for just one more second. A second containing infinity, life, hope. And love.

So much love surrounding me. I can feel embraced and protected. This is...

Real?

There might be new sounds around me, but I don't want to pay attention, don't want to lose my focus. Until I feel something touching my shoulder. Two hands. I know those hands.

Marlak is in front of me. "Astra? Are you all right?"

I could hug him, kiss him, love him until the end of all eras, and yet this is my grumpy husband, the one who hates me. It doesn't matter how I feel, though. All I can do is nod and force myself not to collapse. I'm not even sure I nodded. It feels odd to be pulled back to reality after being in that light for so long, after almost becoming one with it. My knees want to buckle, but I don't let them.

His jaw relaxes as he takes a deep breath and stares at me. It's a new kind of stare, but I'm not in any condition to try to understand what it means. Around me, I see a layer of ice trapping those creatures. Insistent creatures, who'd been trying to reach us for hours—now all dead.

I might not be able to stand straight anymore. I don't know how I stood for so long, and yet the hands around my shoulders let me go. That's when my knees finally buckle.

Beside me, I hear, "What's the meaning of this?" He sounds like thunder when it cracks at the same time as lightning.

I don't know the meaning of anything. I don't want to know anything. No. I can't collapse. I see then that Marlak is talking to Nelsin, who is standing, so that's one good sign. The knight's shoulders are hunched, his head down, top ears hidden by his hair.

"Apologies," Nelsin mutters.

I feel I need to intervene. "He was trying to help."

Marlak glares at me. "I wasn't talking to you."

The words sting like a lash. Well, he *is* an asshole. At least the sting wakes me.

Marlak turns back to Nelsin. "Explain everything. It's an order."

The blond fae faces the prince. "I brought Astra here to see how she'd react if you were attacked, and cast an illusion." He glances at me quickly. I sure hope he doesn't tell Marlak everything. "It seems she wouldn't want to see you harmed."

I exhale, relieved that he didn't mention my foolish jump.

I see a vein popping in Marlak's neck. "Did I ask you to test her? Did I ask anyone to doubt her?"

"I didn't feel it was right that I couldn't protect you as well." Nelsin looks down and shakes his head. "It was foolish and wrong."

Marlak touches the blond fae's chin and lifts his face. "Listen to me." His words are slow, measured, his voice low. "You are sworn to protect her, not me. *Her*. If you see her with a knife trying to kill me, you protect *her*. If I'm about to die, you protect *her*."

That's the stupidest thing I've ever heard, but if he's that suicidal, so be it. I'm not going to point out that he's dumb, especially if he'll yell at me.

Nelsin nods quickly. "Understood. Then, as we stood here, two bloodpuppets appeared out of nowhere. They had invisibility glamour and magic-sucking darts."

"From which court?"

Nelsin's lips form a line. "I don't know. One of the darts hit me and impaired my magic. Astra killed the puppets, though."

Marlak turns to me, his mouth open. Was he doubting I could kill anyone? He turns back to Nelsin, who continues, "But they had some dark magic, and one of them turned into leech roaches. I told Astra to run. I begged her, but she didn't."

The prince huffs. "Yes, it would be so great for her to run alone, right at the edge of the Wild Fae Lands. I can't see how it would be dangerous."

Nelsin swallows. "Better than being devoured by leech roaches. But she cast this light shield and asked me to be quiet. That was what I did, as I waited for my magic to return."

Marlak rests his face in his hands and closes his eyes, then takes a deep breath. "I flew all the way from the Eerie Court when I... I saw it. It took me over three hours."

"Indeed," Nelsin says. "It felt like much longer. My magic got back to me, but it wouldn't work outside her shield, and I was afraid to disturb it, so I waited. I'm glad you came, and I'm ready to face the consequences of my actions." He then kneels and looks down.

I fear that Marlak is going to behead him, and say, "Don't hurt him!"

All I get is a glare in response.

The prince turns to Nelsin. "You're henceforth dismissed from your duties as a royal knight."

Nelsin looks up. "That's it? What I did is unforgivable."

Is he really complaining that he didn't get a strong enough punishment?

"Rest assured you won't be forgiven." Marlak's deep cutting voice sounds terrifying.

Nelsin then turns to me. "Whenever you need me—"

Marlak steps between me and the fae. "No. I don't want you anywhere close to her."

"I have a life debt to her," Nelsin says.

"A life debt to me too," Marlak roars. "Because had you served anyone else, you'd be killed for your insubordination.

And yet you'll be able to walk away, unharmed and free. Don't get close to Astra."

Nelsin bows. "Noted."

Marlak then turns to me. "Let's go. We lingered too long."

"What about him?" I point to Nelsin.

The fae smiles. "I can run, my lady."

"Not *your lady*," Marlak yells. "Go before I change my mind."

Nelsin glances at me, nods, and then runs in the direction opposite of the cliff, just like he told me to do. I hope he'll be safe.

Marlak then whistles and turns to me. "If unusual steeds scare you, I suggest you close your eyes."

"Do I look like a wimp?"

He tilts his head, considering me. "Fearing strange things is normal. It doesn't make anyone a coward." He raises an eyebrow. "Or wimp."

"The answer's yes, then."

"Obviously. But looks can be deceiving. Whatever you did today, that was... I'm just glad you're alive."

He says it as if he cared, as if I wasn't a threat to him, capable of spilling his secrets. Sometimes I think he cares, but it's a strange way of caring.

I see then what he's talking about. It looks like a horse, but it's coming from the air. Its body is black and leathery, but cracked, like cracked skin, with red gashes that look like raw flesh underneath. The horse has a long, sharp silver horn and lands beside us.

"That's Cherry Cake." Marlak pats his head. "He's a dark unicorn. You've met him."

So that was what we rode after leaving the carriage. At the time, I thought it was too fast and smooth, but I could never have guessed it was a flying steed. I'm entranced by the creature's horrific beauty, when I realize something. "How does it fly with no wings?"

Marlak snaps his fingers. "Magic." I can sense that he's still angry, still grumpy, as he approaches the unicorn. He turns to me. "I'm glad he still has the double saddle."

He lifts me and puts me in my place, then mounts the creature. I can see that it's docile, and indeed smells like a horse.

Marlak's arms are soon around me and we're soaring in the air. For a moment, I wonder what would happen if someone saw us, but then I realize we're in fae territory and this is probably not unusual.

I want to look down and appreciate the view, but the idea that I'm flying on a creature with no wings is quite frightening, and in truth, I'm weak from whatever I did this morning.

The loud sound of wind at least is a respite from any harsh words from Marlak. Marlak. It's when it hits me that he came. I called him and he came, from wherever he was. And yet, I didn't call *him*, I called the one who holds me in my dreams.

The realization is dreadful, but I can no longer run from it: they're the same person. I feel a flutter and emptiness in my stomach, and a chill down my spine.

It means I'm riding with the man who's been my solace, my comfort for a long time. And yet there's such a huge difference between the dreams and the reality. Such a huge gap. It's as if we're completely different people when dreaming and awake. I'm most definitely sure I wouldn't dream about a man who tells me to shut up and says he wasn't talking to me.

And yet he came.

This time, there are no sounds of hooves on the ground,

and I can only assume it was a glamour. Marlak has so much magic that I can't even keep track of what he can and can't do.

The memories of the strange fae and those horrific roaches then return and I shudder. I could have died. Died, if it wasn't for my trust in the Almighty Mother. Or I could have run, but then Nelsin would be dead, and he didn't deserve it. His idea was childish, but he couldn't have guessed we'd be attacked. And who attacked us? These are all questions I'll have to ask Marlak—if he's ever in a decent enough mood to talk to me.

I think about Nelsin again, and remember the day when I thought I was going to be expelled from the Elite Guard, when I thought my life would have no more meaning. I don't think it's fair to do that to him, despite his mistake. Yes, I almost died, but so did he, and sometimes a negative experience is the best teacher. I'll need to talk to Marlak—if he ever wants to listen to me.

The unicorn, Cherry Cake, lands on the island, and Marlak helps me dismount.

Marlak—my kindred soul. Why, why why?

I'M SO glad to be back on the island. Perhaps I'm starting to consider this place my home. It's a problematic thought, but I'm too tired to scrutinize it right now.

Marlak takes me to the kitchen and I collapse on a chair.

He's doing something at the counter, then brings a plate with a sandwich on it and sets it before me. "I bet you're starving."

Oh, it's for me? It's only then that my stomach growls, as

if it had been in a slumber and was now awakened by the smell of food. Cold food, but food, nonetheless.

I waste no time before taking a big bite. Too big, I realize, once it's all in my mouth and I can barely chew it.

Marlak shows no signs that he noticed I'm eating like a starved animal. He's looking away, thoughtful, then his eyes settle on me. How can they settle and yet be so unsettling? And yet I can sense that his mind is not completely here, as if consumed by other thoughts. "So you're not afraid of Cherry Cake?"

To be fair, the fact that it flies with no wings is quite spooky, but my mouth is too full to say any of that, so I just shake my head.

His eyes are distant again, while he nods. "I should have known." He looks at me and smirks. It's the first smile I see on his face today. "But the blindfold is more dramatic, isn't it?"

I'm about to laugh, when I notice his left hand resting on the table. On its back, there's a fresh ragged scar—just like in the dream. So it *was* real. It's only then I notice he's looking at me. That's the searching stare, smart black eyes seeing who I am. He noticed I noticed.

"You got hurt?" I ask with what I hope is the most natural voice ever.

He brings up his hand, as if to examine it. "A little, yes." He then looks at me. "Were you... expecting me to be hurt?"

A careful question. I lean back in the chair. "Why would I expect something like that?" Then I take another big bite of the sandwich, first, because I'm hungry, second, because it gives me time to think before talking.

He stares at his hand again. "Sometimes..." He's measuring his words. "People can see things far away, things in the future. It can happen."

I'm still chewing that big bite, so I nod.

He's mulling over something. "I saw you. In danger."

I swallow, then snap my finger. "By magic?" I don't know why I'm making fun of that now. I know I called him, I know I trusted our connection. Maybe now that I'm here, safe, I would like to pretend it never happened, that it was some strange coincidence.

He rests his face on the palm of his hands. "No idea what that was, wife. I'm glad I found you."

"But if you're so worried that I'll reveal your secrets, you should be happy if I died." Perhaps I want to see his reaction.

He frowns. "Don't say nonsense, wife."

It's not nonsense, but I'm not going to argue like a ten-year-old. I just take another bite. I'm not sure how he expects me to eat when he's staring at me like that.

"You were shimmery."

"What?" I ask, still with my mouth full.

"When I got there. What magic is that, Astra?" He glances at my arms, as if looking for a bracelet. "Is it some kind of opus stone? You need to tell me, just so I know what it is and how to better protect you. Maybe you could even develop your magic more."

"I just trust the Almighty Mother and her light. That's it. I'm not supposed to ever try to do any magic."

"Why not?"

Oh, no. I can't believe what I let slip. I can't do any magic because it could turn dark and dangerous and people would soon know what I am. I decide to give a stupid excuse. "I'm not royal family."

He tilts his head. "You're my wife now, Astra. There isn't anything you can't do."

Oh, I'm pretty sure I can't use people's blood to feed my

magic. Of course, I don't say any of that. Instead, I smile and take another bite.

At least he's talking for the both of us. "Your magic, or whatever you want to call it, was incredible. You're quite powerful."

I just shake my head, my mouth too full, the idea too strange.

He continues, "And you truly use no stones?"

I show him my unadorned hands. "Where?"

"You tell me." He raises an eyebrow, that odd, curious expression.

Does he think I have an opus stone stuck in any of my cavities? As if he hadn't poked around them many, many times—in dreams. And this is not the time to think about that. "No stones. And it's not really magic."

He bites his lip. "You had to kill two men."

"Yes." I don't know what he's getting at.

"Don't let their deaths haunt you. You did what you had to do. And if they were bloodpuppets, they were already too far gone for any help."

"I killed only one." It's true that I can still see his accusatory stare. "I should have killed the other faster, but—"

"You can never know what magic is controlling them." Marlak's looking away, thoughtful. "I can't imagine who would have sent them. And to attack you?" He closes his eyes, as if in pain.

"What exactly are bloodpuppets? I've heard the term, but never studied it."

Marlak taps his fingers on the table, a crease forming in his forehead. "A type of dark magic that hasn't been seen in over a century. Their life force is sucked, and then they become instruments serving a powerful magic wielder."

"How come they aren't common?"

"The magic's too difficult, I assume." He looks up, takes a deep breath, and shakes his head. "I still can't imagine who would create them, send them. It's so strange."

"Your brother?"

"No. Not Renel, no." He sounds certain, and I wonder if he's defending his brother. "Someone else in the Crystal Court... They'd need to be too powerful. Someone in another court? Why?" He rubs his eyes, then looks at me. "The only right thing Nelsin did was identify them quickly for what they were, but he should be the one fighting, protecting you, never the other way around. I'm truly sorry for my poor judgment, for placing my trust in the wrong person."

"He couldn't have known we'd be attacked."

"He shouldn't have taken you off the island on his own!" His voice is higher pitched than usual, then goes back to normal. "At least if it had been him and Ferer, it wouldn't have been as bad. Even then." He clenches his fists over the table and stares at me with those deep, black eyes. "You could have died, Astra."

And yet I look back and all I remember is that light. It's as if I shut my eyes and refused to stare at death right in front of me. "I'm glad you came."

His chuckle is bitter and wrong. "So am I."

A warm feeling settles in my stomach. *He cares*, a strange voice tells me. *He cares about you.* As if the fact that he doesn't want me to die was something to be giddy about. As if I never imagined things to mean more than they do.

He continues, "And you should be safe here. How can I even do anything if I can't trust my knights to keep you safe? And what foolishness was that about *testing* you? I never asked anyone to test you."

"You trust me that much?"

"I do *not* trust you at all, wife. I know that if you have the chance, you'll turn around and tell all my secrets to your king, who in turn will sell them to my brother. There's nothing to test you about. We both know who we are and where we stand." He runs a finger through his black curls, as if to remind me of what I cannot touch.

Nelsin comes to my mind then, believing he was living the last moments of his life, pleading for me to run. He would be someone who would trust me.

"Nelsin almost died. He was willing to stay behind."

Marlak fists the table and my plate shakes. "How would that help? Just try to think how many things could have gone wrong if you had run."

"We survived."

He huffs. "I know what you want. You want me to forgive him, right?"

Indeed. That's true. "Yes. People learn from their mistakes, and become better."

"People who disobey once might disobey twice. I'm fair, but when trust is lost, it's lost. There's no gaining it back."

"I trust him."

Marlak leans forward on the table. "Astra, the day you become my wife in earnest, you might tell me what to do. Right now, I don't care about your opinion."

The day... what? Become his wife in earnest? My mouth hangs open, and I'm almost stunned into silence, except that I need to ask a question. "Since when is that an option?"

He blinks, confused. "What option?"

Is he pretending or testing me? I don't want to repeat his words, but I'll have to. "Becoming your wife in earnest. Since when is that an option?"

His eyebrows crease. "Since never."

"You mentioned it." Yes, I have to point that out, or he'll start claiming I'm delusional.

"I traveled back south in a hurry and found you surrounded by murderous, blood-sucking insects. I was poisoned last night and almost died. I don't know what I'm saying." He looks at my empty plate, then at me. "You should rest, azalee."

"What did you say?"

"Wife, you need to rest." His chair screeches in agony as he pulls it back suddenly.

The floor then tilts—and the ceiling. My vision blurs.

I'm falling from the chair, falling into a precipice.

No, someone's holding me. I feel as if I'm being carried, but I don't know what's happening anymore. The veil between life and dreams and death has thinned, and I'm at the edge of it, conscious and unconscious, fallen and standing.

I'm in my bed in the river hideout, while at the same time standing on the balcony in the Amethyst Palace. I'm flying on a wingless unicorn and yet lying on my bed. There's light. And darkness. And blood. So much blood.

15

I am again in the Amethyst Palace, that empty, abandoned palace, and we're standing on that balcony. The moonlight caresses treetops and some mountains in the distance.

"You know the truth now." His deep voice draws my attention.

For some reason, I was trying to look at that mountain, memorize it, but why should it matter more than him?

I reach out and touch his hair. "Do you?"

He kisses the palm of my hand. "I've always known it." His soft chuckle is so comforting.

We walk inside, then dance among abandoned, dusty furniture, dance when no song is playing, except in our hearts.

The next moment I'm in my bed on the island, and my husband's hand is touching mine. Then someone is giving me hot soup, and I'm sitting up, half awake. It's not Marlak, though, but I don't know who that is.

Before I have time to find out where that soup is coming from, I'm by the cliff, surrounded by leech roaches, and watch them as they devour that fae's body. Once they're done, when they are about to attack me, they form a face in the air, a face with accusing eyes, reminding me I'm a murderer.

Marlak puts a hand in front of my eyes and pulls me in his arms, and we spin and spin towards the Nymph court. So much spinning.

When my eyes open and I recognize my room in the river hideout, I'm relieved to be awake again, relieved to be rid of those restless dreams.

There are no sunrays entering through the window. Instead, there's only dim, diffused sunlight filtered by clouds, and I don't know if it's early or late.

I'm alone, and it's strange. I could swear there was somebody by my side. Marlak? No, he wouldn't... I stop myself before I even finish the thought. He wouldn't care? Wouldn't he? He came to save me.

Before, I could pretend it wasn't him in my dreams, I could tell myself it was a strange coincidence, someone who looked just like my kindred soul. I could tell myself I was projecting my dreams onto him for some mysterious, odd reason.

But now, I know it's not true. It was Marlak who came to save me, who showed up with a ragged gash on the back of his hand. There's no more pretending that they are two different people, except that they *act* differently. Real-life Marlak is not at all like dream Marlak.

Isn't he? I remember his kiss at our wedding, his whisper in my ear. Then again, his soft words were his assurance that he wouldn't touch me. It's a nice version of his constant reminders that he finds me unattractive.

Perhaps there's no point in wondering why he's in my dreams. Some things have no reason. I can't start thinking Marlak's my kindred soul or I'll make foolish decisions.

With that thought, I get up. I'm not wearing a nightgown, but a tunic and leggings. I don't even remember getting dressed, bathing, or lying down.

I hear some happy humming coming from the kitchen. That is most definitely not Marlak. When I enter it, I see the back of a blond fae with cat ears doing something by the counter, and can't believe my eyes.

"Nelsin?"

He turns and puts a hand over his chest. "I didn't see you. My lady! You're back!"

"I never left. But you..." I look around, searching for a sign that something's amiss, but it's just the kitchen in the island house. "Is this real?"

He bows. "I'm honored to be back at your service. You saved my life."

I don't think I did anything special, but I don't want to say that and dismiss his gratitude. What I don't understand is how Nelsin is here. "Did Marlak change his mind?"

Nelsin sighs. "Yes, even if what I did is unforgivable."

"Everyone makes mistakes."

He looks at me. "And we learn from them. I want to do my job right this time, and I think our prince understood that."

So Marlak *can* be persuaded. Interesting. And now I have someone who trusts me working for him. These are incredible developments, not to mention that I'm happy that Nelsin is here. And I have another question.

"I... was someone giving me hot soup, or was I dreaming?"

Nelsin chuckles. "I brought it. Rushed here with the hot container. I knew it would help you heal. Seems like it did!"

"Thanks!" I am so relieved to see him, to know that he's

alive, that he's here. I approach him and wrap my arms around him.

Nelsin returns the gesture in a warm, friendly hug, perhaps the kind of hug I've been missing since I left the tower.

"Incredible." Marlak's voice cuts like a blade, and I let go of the knight and turn to my husband. He's glaring at us. "You thank not the person who saved you, but the one who put you in danger."

I open my arms. "Do you want a hug?"

"I want *nothing* from you," he snaps.

If there was any doubt, now I'm sure this is *not* a dream. "Then what's your problem?"

He pulls a chair, making it screech against the ground as if it's screaming, then sits. "You slept for more than a day. You could have died." He spits those last words with so much anger he almost growls.

I barely see Nelsin walking away, and I'm not sure I like the way Marlak treats his knights, who have to scurry away like mice.

Still, I sit across from my husband. "You sure sound happy I'm alive."

"Then you misunderstand me. I'm not happy at all that you were in danger. I'm not happy at all that my orders were defied. But hey, go ahead." He waves a hand. "Embrace *him*."

Oh, it's all about pride, then. "Do you have friends, husband? People to hug you?" I don't know why I'm unwilling to measure my words, and why I'm saying that. It's not like I have a ton of friends either.

He leans over. "Hugs are for children."

I'm not sure if he expects a reply to that, and I don't know what to say.

The truth is that I didn't get hugs from loving parents as

a child, and for some reason the thought stings, but then I had my sisters. Marlak probably had a happy childhood, which only makes all that happened even more horrific.

I wish I had brought a cup, a plate, an apple, something to occupy my hands, rather than having just this empty table between us.

He points at the hallway where Nelsin went. "He's back because you saved his life, and he'll be loyal to *you*, and that's useful to *me*. Not because you asked. But he shouldn't—" He pauses, his chest moving up and down in a deep breath, then he looks at me. "How are you feeling?"

"Good. Normal. Hungry." As if replying to this last point, my stomach growls.

Marlak gets up and walks to his cupboard, speaking while giving his back to me. "This should never have happened." He points to the rooms again. "I still don't trust him." He then takes the jug of milk and the two cups and brings them to the table.

I look at him, so good looking, so intimidating, and yet so normal in our daily routine. *When you become my wife in earnest.* His words echo in my mind.

Would I want to become his wife for real? Would I want to kiss him on a morning like this? Spend the nights together, making those dreams come true? There's air in my stomach, air as if he was working some magic in it, making it spin and spin and spin. My head spins too, and I don't understand what I feel, if it's fear, yearning, horror, shame.

Could I turn my back to Otavio, to Krastel, to my sisters? Would I be happy with Marlak? Would he eventually hurt me? Would he mock me if I showed any feelings for him?

I take the cup he gives me and drink it.

He blinks slowly. "You're quiet."

"Better than saying nonsense."

He's staring at me, thinking, observing. "Are you feeling well? Recovered?"

"I think so."

"You're coming with me." He says it fast, as if it was a decision he's just made. "I mean, there's no hurry. Eat, change, and bathe if you want, and then we'll leave."

Has a week gone by already? "For the wedding?"

"Later, yes. Now..." He stares at the edge of the table. "I'm heading north again." He looks at me. "And bringing you with me."

I almost choke on the milk. Really? He's going on his super secret mission and taking me?

Well, this is fantastic.

I want to ask why he changed his mind, if he's not afraid that I'll find out all his secrets, but I have the presence of mind to keep quiet. After all, I don't want to give him any reason to reconsider his odd decision.

"I'll get ready." I set my cup on the table and get up.

Oh, I so want this!

This is my chance to figure out what he's looking for, to unveil his secrets, to peer into his heart.

My chance to find out who he is—and then use all of that to betray him.

My heart stops beating for a second.

Well, it will depend on what I find out.

I'M STILL in disbelief that Marlak wants me to travel with him, still waiting to hear he changed his mind, that he decided to take me to a dungeon. Well, he never said *where* he would take me or what he's going to do to me. And yet I have that odd certainty that he'll never hurt me. Not physically, at least. And sharp words cause nothing but scratches.

After a cold meal and a chilly bath, I put on leather leggings and a linen tunic, and go to my room, where Ferer is waiting for me. I'm so glad to see him! Weird that I'm starting to find my situation here normal and bond with my jailors.

He's sitting on a chair by my bed and smiles when he sees me, but there's something about the tightness of his jaw or perhaps his posture.

"Are you all right?" I ask.

He forces a bigger smile. "*I* am. How are you?" His voice is tight, though, and there's a strange coldness in his eyes.

"Perfect. Are you…" I'm having trouble figuring out what's wrong with him, when it hits me. "Did something happen to Nelsin?"

He huffs. "Something. He lost his honor, that's all." He clenches his fists and looks down.

I can only assume that they're no longer together, and can't imagine what it must be like to break up with someone you love. "Everyone makes mistakes."

Ferer huffs again. "Most people don't *survive* such egregious mistakes."

I approach him and touch his shoulder. "But we did. We're here. And you're glad Nelsin survived, aren't you?"

He clicks his tongue and points to an extravagant suitcase on my bed. "I'm here to help you pack. Put everything you'll need there, enough for four days."

The suitcase is an ostentatious enormity, in old, hardened brown leather with golden details and encrusted clear stones. They don't look like opus or beacon stones to me, but I could be mistaken. I think they're some kind of crystal. What's odd about it is its size.

"It's heavy and cumbersome," I say. "Who's going to carry it?"

"Your prince will take care of it. Make sure you leave room for his clothes as well."

I try not to make a face, but I don't know if I manage it. We're *sharing* a suitcase? I picture my underwear entangled with his. Well, we've done much worse in dreams. And yet, this is real, it's different.

Regardless, who am I to question Marlak and his travel arrangements? I pick up what I think is enough, including underwear, since I don't plan on stopping wearing it, and put it carefully on one side of that monstrosity. My most comfortable trousers and blouse are there as well, for sleeping. I'm still wondering how he's planning on carrying this, unless...

"Are you joining us?" I ask Ferer. I still don't think it's fair to make him carry this thing, but it's the only idea that makes sense.

"Not in principle, no. But I'll be here, waiting for your return." His face then hardens. "Nelsin will be here as well."

I don't like to hear the anger and distaste in his tone, and I can see that being upset at Nelsin is eating him from the inside. "He survived this time. You don't know about the future. You don't know what's going to happen. Enjoy the time you have, the moments you have. Resentment hurts you as much as it hurts him."

"Wise words, my lady." He bows slightly. I don't know if he's mocking me. "One thing I know about advice: usually the one who gives it is the one who needs it most."

I don't know if he thinks his words will annoy me, but they don't. I smile. "Indeed. If I ever get upset with someone I love, I'll heed my own advice and not squander our relationship because of one mistake."

He's closing the suitcase, then pauses and looks at me. "Let's hope so."

There's something eerie in that stare, as if it was a warning.

In truth, there's few people I love. I'd say Tarlia and Sayanne, I guess. Until some time ago, I might have included Otavio and Andrezza on that list, but I'm wiser now. It's weird to think that wisdom means loving less, but I guess it does.

I can't count dream Marlak because he doesn't exist. Dream love doesn't exist.

The thought drowns me in infinite emptiness.

I STEP out of the house and see Marlak sitting on a log, resting his chin on his hand, his black curls covering part of his face like a curtain, shielding his eyes from me. Like that, he doesn't look dangerous. I'd say he looks weary and perhaps tired, almost vulnerable. And yet it's just an illusion, or perhaps what my mind wants my eyes to see.

His left hand still has that recent wound, the wound he got in his travels. And now he's taking me with him on his dangerous journey. I don't feel scared, though. I feel relieved. I think the worst is always not knowing, and more than ever, I need to learn everything I can about him.

I'm wearing a leather surcoat like I was told to, and it's making me feel hot and stuffy. The day is cloudy, but it's warm and humid, and I can only assume we're going to do some magic traveling somewhere cold, except that Marlak's wearing only a thin tunic. Perhaps he's going to ditch *me* in some magic ice prison. I'm about to find out.

There's no sign of the suitcase anywhere, and I'm still

wondering if Nelsin will bring it or maybe if it was all a prank and I won't have anything to wear. At least my trousers and tunic are comfortable, in case I have to keep them on for eternity—or for a week. I don't want to imagine attending a wedding wearing stinky clothes, but maybe it's not as bad as attending my own wedding in a rough wool dress.

When he finally turns and looks at me, he raises his eyebrows, seeming surprised or startled. I can never quite decipher his expression.

"Ready?" he asks.

All I manage is a nod, and then he gets up and approaches me. Now that he's this close, I feel even warmer, with some difficulty to breathe. I am drawn to those eyes so dark and deep, and I still want to run my fingers through his black curls. There's no shame in wanting foolish things, as long as we're aware they're foolish.

And yet it's hard to be aware of anything when he's standing so close, his scent enveloping me. I shut my eyes when he wraps his arms around me, trying to focus and telling myself that this is daytime Marlak, not the man from my dreams, but a huge part of me doesn't trust that story anymore.

It feels like he's doing some air magic inside my stomach, giving it a fluttering, chilly feeling as we drift over the magical waters housing the nymphs, towards the riverbank.

There's something so elegant, so controlled about his magic. Perhaps the ease, naturality of it. It's beautiful, fascinating even.

He's looking up and I follow his line of sight and see a black form emerging through the gray clouds. Soon I recognize Cherry Cake, Marlak's wondrous magical unicorn. The creature lands beside us, and Marlak taps his flank, then pats his head in a caring gesture.

Perhaps this is the answer as to who Marlak hugs: his steed. Better than nobody, I guess.

I notice then the double-seat saddle. It's made in brown leather with some details in gold and even some decorative gems along its seams. It can't be a saddle improvised the day he picked me up. No, it's old and worn, even though it's well-made and expensive. I wonder if it's one of the Crystal Court relics and who it was made for.

My thoughts stop as he approaches me and puts his hands on my waist. I still don't know how he does it without tickling, but then I'm on the saddle, and soon he's behind me, his arms around me.

"Hold tight."

Why does Marlak have to use that soft, warm voice sometimes? I wish it was always grating and hating and annoying, so at least it would be consistent.

My heart wants to do something in my chest, but I tell it to behave.

And then we're soaring up in the sky.

Last time I flew on Cherry Cake, I was exhausted from hanging on for so long and still traumatized from the attack, so flying on a wingless creature was the least of my worries.

But now?

Now that I'm awake and alert, I'm wondering how in the world this creature flies, and holding that strap in front of me so tight that my knuckles are turning white. At least Marlak has his arms around me, touching the sides of the saddle, but then I realize there are no reigns and I don't even know how this unicorn flies. In fact, I don't even know where I'm going and if someone will shoot a poisoned dart or arrow or throw some flying, murderous cockroaches at me.

And then it hits me that this is being alive. Alive, unsure about what's coming next. I look up and see that we're about to reach the clouds. Of course I've always wanted to touch them. Who hasn't? Watching them float softly in the sky, they're a thing of wonder. These are gray and don't look as fluffy, but still... I'm about to reach the clouds.

We pierce them, and for a moment I'm surprised that they're not like soft wool. I know they're just water, and yet it feels strange that inside it is like being in a thick mist; everything light gray, almost white around me. And then we burst through—and I'm stunned.

The sun is shining. Of course it's shining. It's not as if it would disappear when it's cloudy. And yet knowing and seeing are different things.

Up here is a sunny day, perfect blue sky above us, with endless fluffy clouds below. I don't even fear falling anymore, as that silly part of my mind thinks that I would land on some fluffy wool, like a thick pillow.

I know it's not fluffy, and I'd fall right through it, but at least the illusion quiets my fear, and that's good. Fear is based on perception, after all.

And then there's Marlak behind and around me. Strangely, he's not a source of fear, but of comfort, which I shouldn't be feeling. I should be alert at each and every second, a quiet, astute observer, and yet I have to spend my mental alertness reminding me this is not a dream, something completely obvious.

But if I look around me, flying so high on this magnificent creature feels like dreaming. Cool wind hits my face, refreshing, renewing. I feel none of the stuffiness from down below and the overcoat is quite perfect for the weather.

Life is duty, honor, but it's also a series of moments. The truth is that I don't even mind his arms surrounding me. When the wind forces us into silence, I can almost think that he's indeed the person from my dreams. And being near him is wonderful. I'll remind myself of the reality when we land. Why ruin perfection?

And yet I'm already anticipating the landing, wondering about where he's taking me, wondering what I'll find out, and hoping there are no assassins waiting for us.

16

We've been flying for about an hour, the sun right above us, so I don't have much sense of direction. My skin is tanned, so at least it won't burn anymore, and I can enjoy the sunshine.

Below me, the clouds start to get thinner, and I see patches of a dark green forest and a wide, lazy river, and then soon we're descending.

Cherry Cake lands with a thud on the riverbank. I wish I could dismount on my own, but the unicorn is much taller than a horse. I wonder how come I didn't notice it when I first rode on him.

Marlak holds me and dismounts me as if I were a child, then pats his unicorn, who flies away. This is a thick, wild forest, quite hot and humid with so many trees I can't count, vegetation in the soil, covering trunks, everywhere, with running water close to us. We're in the north, in one of the small fae courts, but I'm obviously unsure which one.

He glances at me. "We're going to walk now."

I don't know if he expects a protest or something, but I just nod while I remove my overcoat.

He points down. "Careful with the ground, not to step on anything or stick your foot in a puddle. We're going to the Misty Court."

That's... not a small court. They used to be big in the past, until about a hundred years ago, when smaller courts started eating away their territory.

"No assassins there?"

He tilts his head and raises a shoulder. "The queen has little to gain from presenting my head to my brother. Obviously, other fae in her court might not see it the same way, so it's good to remain alert." Then he adds, "But it's safe. Nobody murders anyone on an official visit. They'll do it in the dark of night, when deeds like those can go on in secret."

I mull it over. "But if they want to present your head, they'll want their deed to be known, won't they?"

"Known by the right people only." He then chuckles. "Don't worry, *wife*. Queen Benda is an ally, and her entourage is sworn to her."

There's something mocking in his tone, as if I was being silly, and I was just curious.

"I'm not afraid," I correct him.

He blinks. "I didn't say you were." He then glances at me again, and notices that I'm holding my overcoat. "Give me that."

"I can carry it."

"I'd much rather you had your hands free. Give me that."

Well, it's not like I want to keep carrying it all the way to who knows where, so I give it to him. He then points somewhere among the trees, to a high, rocky hill.

"Her castle's up there. It's quite majestic, actually. Can you spot the windows from here?"

I can only see a thin strip of the hill from between trees, and there are no obvious windows. If it's fae glamour or some trick, I don't know. "I can barely see any castle, husband."

"True, we'll see it better once we get close. You're going to love this. She has one of the oldest libraries on the continent."

For a moment, I see myself uncovering hidden truths, finding out more about the Tiurians, perhaps finding out something that Krastel doesn't know. What a silly thought. And I'm surprised that this is what this visit is about. "You're going there to check some books?"

"If she lets me, yes."

I look back at him, and see no more overcoat in his hands. Did he just throw it away? I could have done that as well. I wonder what I'll wear when the weather is cool, but I'll just trust that he'll have something.

We keep walking, and I decide to ask a question. "What's the etiquette?"

"Didn't you study the Misty Court?"

Is this a test? "I did. They were once as big and important as the Crystal Court, except that they shrunk as the latter grew. A lot of it happened after the River of Tears Treaty, when the human territories were separated."

"Indeed. How do you think they feel about the Crystal Court?" I don't know why he's asking me that.

"I don't think there's any enmity, but I could be wrong." Then I add, "I don't know much about the fae, Marlak."

He stops walking and stares at me, eyes wide, as if stunned.

I chuckle. "Yes, make fun of me. I don't know everything, husband. And I want to learn how I'm supposed to behave. I was never prepared to pretend to be the wife of an exiled prince."

A huff of air comes out of his mouth, almost as if amused,

but not quite. "Disgraced prince. Technically, my brother cannot exile me. Uncrowned king, if you want to be more precise. And you're not pretending, as I believe you know."

Uncrowned. So indeed he has never put on that crown—and yet he has it. He must know it doesn't belong on his head and would kill him.

"Marlak, just tell me what you expect of me during this visit."

His chuckle is warm and deep and does something to me. "You don't realize what you just did, do you?"

I don't know what he means, so I decide to joke about it. "Tons of things. Talked, walked, breathed. My heart's beating. I'm not aware of everything going on in my body, no."

"Yes. Too much going on." He laughs again, a relaxed laugh. "Fae here are not formal. You don't need to bow or anything." Interesting. He certainly had no qualms kneeling to the Nymph queen, and yet that wasn't such a huge secret, or he wouldn't have revealed it to me. He continues, "Just be yourself, and you'll be fine."

Myself? As if I didn't have at least some ten different versions of it. "Oh, yes, I'll just act like I usually do when I visit fae courts."

"Pretend it's a human kingdom. You trained for it, didn't you?"

"How do you even know that?" Yes, I could pretend he's imagining it, but I don't think it will work. And this question has been gnawing at me since I first met him.

He watches me, then raises a shoulder. "I told you I have magic."

Magic. Mind magic? By the Almighty Mother. I freeze. Can he read my thoughts? I know what he has seen is quite embarrassing, but the idea that he knows what I'm thinking has never crossed my mind.

He stops and stares at me. "Why are you so pale?" The tone is both mocking and concerned, which only makes it confusing.

"Are you reading... Can you..." I realize the question is stupid. He's not going to tell me the answer.

I decide then to picture vividly something from my dreams, and imagine myself unbuttoning his trousers.

His light chuckle interrupts the image. "You're afraid I can see your thoughts? I can only do it when I touch someone, if I have that intention, and I never do it without warning. With you, you're well aware I couldn't see a thing. And what is it you're hiding, anyway?"

"Would you like it? If someone invaded the privacy of your mind? A place you don't even reveal to your friends? Sometimes not even to yourself?"

He looks down and shakes his head. "I can't do that, Astra. I can only do it with focused intent, and touching someone."

"Then how do you know what I trained for? That it was me, not the princess, when you met me?" I know I'm being vulnerable asking this, I'm even giving him information, in case he wasn't sure. But he *was* sure, and he shouldn't have known any of that.

He fiddles with his earring. "That is *my* secret. One day perhaps I'll tell you."

"You don't trust me." Well, why would he? And yet somehow I felt like stating the obvious.

"I do trust you, wife." The words take me by surprise. "I trust that you're still serving your murderous kingdom, and will bring them anything you learn about me if I give you the opportunity."

True, but then... "If you really thought that, you wouldn't have shown me the Nymphs."

"I'm clinging to the hope that your own sense of self-preservation will keep you quiet about them. Also, I have no plans to give you the opportunity to turn around and betray me."

True. Keeping me on an island or by his side at all times should be enough deterrent to treason. And yet nobody can control someone else forever, nobody can keep from making mistakes. He has to know that, and yet I guess he does, and that's why he won't tell me anything. Still, I get glimpses here and there. I know about his unicorn, I have some grasp of the extent of his magic, I know he's looking for old books... I'm getting there. It's all a matter of patience.

But I still don't know how he learned about me, my name, my training. I'll have to grab some more patience and wait for the right opportunity. Eventually, I'll find out. I still wonder if he can see my thoughts, if I'm letting some of my mask slip.

He's looking at me as if trying to pierce my mind, then says, "We'd better be quiet from now on. Quiet and alert. We're getting close." He smirks. "Ready to climb a ton of steps?"

"Couldn't you just use your air magic to bring us up?"

"*Could* is not the same as *should*. You don't visit another court flaunting your magic. In fact, flaunting my magic is the opposite of what I ever do."

"I'm guessing you'd need to cause a hurricane in order to flaunt anything." It's a joke but also a test. I want to know the extent of his magic.

His chuckle is dry, and his eyes are somber. "Or worse. Come on, silent and alert, wife. That's the etiquette from now until the palace."

This is a golden opportunity. I'll get to know a fae court,

see a queen, see how she reacts to Marlak. I might even visit an old library. What a trove of information!

In the end, Nelsin's disobedience came out in my favor, if this is the reason Marlak's bringing me. I still feel bad about the cat-eared fae, as I recall his regretful tone, and the coldness with which Ferer mentioned him. I hope they'll get together again. And I hope I find out many, many secrets.

We keep walking until we edge a steep, rocky hill. It's the only hill in the area, and perhaps artificially or magically built. The stairs at its edge are thin and have no railing. Marlak pushes me ahead of him, so I go first.

"I want to keep an eye on you," he mutters.

"Afraid I'll push you?" I whisper.

"Afraid you'll lose your balance. You seem to forget I made an oath to protect you."

I don't need protection from easy-to-climb stairs, but if I tell him that, it will sound like I'm quarreling. I just nod and begin my ascent, Marlak right behind me.

I have to give it to him that the steps are indeed narrow. They're just a little wider than the ledge outside my window, the ledge nobody goes to, but the steps are winding and rough. I can't imagine who climbs them, or how they bring supplies to the palace, unless they use air magic or have flying creatures. That's what I have to assume, and maybe these steps are made just to humble foreign visitors and hinder humans. As we move up, I see no signs of any windows, but I do look back at the valley and the wide river again, trying to get a glimpse of where we are.

"Eyes on the steps, wife," Marlak chides me.

"I'm not going to fall."

"Still, eyes on the steps. Let's go."

I take a deep breath and continue the ascent, aware of my breath getting ragged. I guess two days of sleeping ruined my fitness, or maybe the steps are indeed steep. Marlak's breath behind me is steady, not the least affected by the effort. Well, he's fae. A weird fae, but fae, nonetheless. I guess his breath only gets ragged in my dreams. Great, why did I bring that up?

When I think we still have a few turns, as I can still see much of the hill above me, the stairs end, and I come face to face with a huge wooden door with delicate engraved flourishes. The step right below it is larger and wider, and Marlak stands beside me. For a second I think he's going to take my arm, but he doesn't. I'm not sure if he changed his mind or if it was just my impression, and I don't know if I'm disappointed or relieved.

The thick door swings open to reveal a single guard, with a spear in hand. He's a fae with very pointy ears, straight brown hair, and medium skin, and looks purely high fae to me. For some reason, that makes me uneasy. I had in my mind that the lower fae were the ones supporting Marlak, and then again, that might be the case in the Crystal Court, but not elsewhere.

I need to become more friendly with my dear husband and learn more about fae politics—or else try to pry more from Nelsin and Ferer, as all these small courts confuse me.

Beside me, it's as if Marlak has become taller, bigger, more powerful. A true prince.

He puts a hand on his chest, and inclines his head. That looks a lot like bowing to me, but what do I know?

"I'm King Marlak, of the Crystal Court, and seek an audience with your queen."

King... I want to scoff, but I'm used to his preposterousness by now. I'm a little ticked that he didn't introduce me, and then again, what do I know about fae decorum?

The guard looks us up and down. "She's expecting you."

Right. Another advantage of a long staircase is giving hosts plenty of forewarning about visitors—or attackers. Unless they can fly or float, of course.

If she sent a single guard, she's not afraid of Marlak, and he must be right that she's an ally. Then again, power is a flimsy thing and can shift hands easily. It makes sense to be amicable to someone who could be a future king, unless she plans on bringing Marlak's head to his brother. I truly hope that's not the case, but then, I trust his magic and his willingness to keep me safe.

We enter a large, tall hall, simple like the exterior, its walls made of rough rock, with moss growing among some crevices, and a set of wooden stairs leading to a kind of mezzanine. This place looks even more unfinished than the house on the island, and I'm wondering at the fae standards of living.

The guard climbs the wooden steps and we follow. Upstairs, I understand why this is a palace. It's still made of rock, but with many glass windows. There are tapestries on the walls and many types of fur rugs on the floor. A woman is lounging on a chaise, two fae servants massaging her feet, while another massages her back.

Some ten guards stand at some distance from her. There's a table on a corner with fruit, cheese, meat cuts, and drinks. Although the space is simple, everything in it is luxurious.

The woman—I can't believe it. Her chest is not exactly bare, but all she's wearing is a necklace with thin silver chains, as if decorating her rosy, taut nipples. Her hair is black, but it's so shiny that it looks almost silver. Her skin is light and perfect, as well as her sculptured features and piercing gray eyes.

I glance at Marlak, just to see his reaction. I never took him for the gawking type, but in front of this queen, even I want to gawk, and I'm not even into women. He doesn't look impressed or surprised, and maybe that's not an unusual fae attire. The idea of me suggesting walking into his room, tits out, sounds a lot less alluring if it's something fae can do so nonchalantly. Suddenly my transparent nightgowns make even more sense.

I don't like it, though. I don't like to understand so clearly why Marlak can stare at me in the face and tell me I'm unattractive. Compared to this queen, I am.

He approaches her and kneels. Kneels! Then he takes her hand and kisses it. "Queen Berta. Your beauty is as astonishing as always, more dazzling than the sun."

Great. I want to puke. But I don't want to feel like an idiot, so I decide to act like an idiot and follow suit, kneeling by her after he gets up. She frowns, but I ignore it, and take her hand. "Your tits are incredible, as appetizing as ripe mangoes."

She widens her eyes, and I feel Marlak pulling me back to a fur rug, where he sits cross-legged. I do the same beside him.

The queen has her eyes on him. "Oh, princeling, what a scare you gave me, when I heard you saying the Crystal Court King was here. You made me think of your odious brother."

Marlak's eyes twitch, but it's the only sign he didn't appreciate what she said. He smiles. "It's me. Your devoted ally."

The queen gets up, and I notice that her long skirt is

partly transparent. She kneels in front of Marlak, then puts her hands in front of her, so that she's on all fours, her necklaces dangling in front of her. Her voice is husky and seductive as she says, "I want more, though. You're of age now."

Something bitter is stirring in my stomach. The position she's in, I wouldn't doubt she'd ask him to go behind her and get into the action, and I don't know if he's the type of man who would refuse such an opportunity.

I want to look away, afraid of what I'll see, and yet I want to keep looking, to make sure I'm wrong. I know I'm not supposed to care about him, but he's still my husband, and I don't want to go through the humiliation of witnessing him make love to another woman right in front of me.

"Indeed I am," he says, his tone neutral.

Queen Berta leans back and sits on her heels. The necklaces settle between her breasts now. "Then my proposal is the same, princeling."

He lowers his head. "A very generous proposal. It would be quite tempting, but I'm already married."

Her eyes finally set on me, and she sneers. "To this one, I suppose."

"Indeed." His voice is level except for a subtle, sharp edge, like a splinter in an otherwise smooth piece of wood.

The queen pouts. "I'm not the jealous type. As long as there are no bastards, you can keep her as your bed servan—"

She doesn't get the chance to finish the word as her eyes go wide, and she moves her hands to her throat, as if suffocating. I look around to see if the guards are going to move, but they're all surrounded by ice. The temperature in the room plummets. Ice covers the windows and then the glass blasts into thousands of pieces.

Marlak gets up and extends a hand to help me do the same, then points at one of the broken windows. "That's our way out."

So we'll... jump? I can hear steps down below, and don't need to be a genius to guess that there are more guards coming. Marlak walks to the window. There's a precipice below us, much unlike the side of the hill from where we came. I assume we're on the edge of a plateau.

He opens his arms, and I don't need to wait or ask. I lean in and let him hold me, then close my eyes as he embraces me—and jumps.

I THOUGHT he had air magic. Or that we were about to land on Cherry Cake or something.

No. We're falling.

This is not how I'd like to die. Dying in my kindred soul's arms, though. Not exactly a tragedy.

My kindred soul. I love him—in my dreams. And I'm about to die because he's an idiot in real life. I think about the Almighty Mother, think about light, but I can't come up with a way to save us.

The ground is about to squash us, when a powerful gust of wind finally slows us down. Not slow enough, as I soon reach the earth beneath me, hitting my feet with a thud. My balance is all wrong, and I fall—on top of Marlak.

My chest touches his, and he stares at me and chuckles, his eyes a mix of relief and amusement. "You thought we were dying."

In less than a second, I release my grip on him and get back on my feet. "Oh, yes. That's hilarious."

Slowly, he rises and stands beside me. "I didn't mean that." His voice is soft, but he chuckles again. "I... for a moment I feared I'd fail. My magic slipped, but then..." He pauses, and smirks. "It came back."

"How great to hear you almost killed us."

He places a hand over his heart. "You mistrust my magic that much?"

Nuts. He's the one who said his magic failed! But I focus on something useful—and a thousand times more urgent—and point to the top of the hill. "How long until they send someone to kill us?"

He narrows his eyes, as if calculating. "Three, four minutes, I'd guess. Quite enough."

"Enough to escape?" He must indeed be crazy, or else he has a plan I don't understand.

"We just have to reach the river." His voice is calm, and he points in the direction opposite the hill.

"And they'll magically leave us alone?"

"Exactly." He snaps his fingers. "Let's go."

He tugs my arm before I register what he wants me to do: run.

As we dash through uneven terrain, leaping over tree roots and prickly bushes, I thank Otavio and all his grumpy assistants who kept me in shape. There's no sound of footsteps behind us, but a bell rings in the castle, now getting farther and farther behind us. Despite running the fastest I can, I struggle to keep up.

Relief comes when I spot the banks of a river. This is not a wide, lazy river, but one with a fast current and a foaming white surface.

I trust Marlak as he pulls me, thinking he's going to glide us to the other side, but instead, we fall into cold waters.

Soon I feel that strange air bubble around me, Marlak holds me, and we spin.

When we stop, I open my eyes, wondering if we're in the Nymph Court, but we're just in another river. It's not the Queen's River amidst the Eternal Mountains, but there are too many trees by the banks for me to know where we are.

Marlak pulls me onto firm land.

While thankful we escaped, I'm wet, tired, and dizzy. His mood is definitely different, as he sits on the muddy bank and bursts out laughing.

I want to punch him. "What's so funny?"

"I'm just relieved, wife."

I decide to voice the question that has been bugging me. "Did you have to do that?"

His laugh stops. "Yes. Fae respect oaths, but they also respect power. And they'll test your boundaries. What do you think she was doing?"

I shrug. "Trying to seduce you, I suppose."

He wrinkles his nose, as if smelling something putrid. "She's delusional."

"She's gorgeous."

He huffs, rolls his eyes, and stares at me.

I don't know what all that meant, so I ask, "What?"

"If beauty swayed me, I'd be on my knees for you."

Oh yes, I'm so beautiful, completely drenched here. And I don't know why he keeps saying he or his brother would be on his knees. *I* would be the one on my knees if we ever... I'm pretty sure I'm going gaga.

"I thought I was unattractive," I remind him.

"You are." He shrugs. "Like I said, beauty doesn't sway me."

"Fine." I get back to the point I was trying to make. "Did you have to almost kill her?"

He frowns. "She just passed out. Astra, she suggested I should keep you as my bed servant. That's a royal prostitute, in case you don't understand. If I let her insult you like that, I'd be letting her insult the Crystal Court Crown, insult *me*." So that was what it was all about. Of course. "It was a test."

"Now you passed it, and made a lifelong enemy."

"Doubt it. She'll laugh about it tomorrow." He pauses, then rubs the back of his left hand, over the new, jagged scar. "I might have to pay for her windows, though. I..." He closes his eyes, takes a deep breath, then looks at me. "It was the right thing, considering her insult."

"We could be in an old library now, instead of drenched here." I'm still wondering what I could discover in ancient books, still carrying a sliver of hope that there's something about my people I was never told. Stupid hope.

"There are more libraries." He waves a hand, then stares at me with his impossibly dark eyes. "You don't care about what she said? What she did? The way she ignored you?"

What I hate was the way *he* was ignoring me when we first came into her presence, but I don't want to say that. I snort, as if the idea was ridiculous. "Should I be jealous?"

He fiddles with his rings. "Not jealous. Insulted."

"When someone's beneath me, I don't care about their opinion." This sentence was part of my training to act like a princess, but it's a good reminder for myself. I often forget it, but not always.

"True." He tilts his head, considering. "They still shouldn't say it like that." He then stares at the river, as if looking for something, then back at me. "The coronation is tomorrow."

I'm surprised at the change of subject, and not only that. "Already?" In my mind, we still had some two or three days before it.

He nods. "We can set up camp now, so we don't need to travel again."

Camp? "Can't we travel in the river, or with Cherry Cake? Or a fae portal?" Then I add, "I'm just curious." And it's true.

His eyes are unfocused as he shakes his head lightly. "Not really. And camping is safer."

Camping without supplies, near a castle where they want us dead, in an area where someone might try to kill him—that sounds fantastic. I keep the thought to myself, though, and smile. "All right."

He points further down the river. "There are small islands there."

We walk by the margin until we approach the "islands". They're more like sandbanks with some sparse ground vegetation.

He holds me, then we float gracefully across the river to an island smaller than our kitchen in the hideout. Now that I've experienced the clumsy way he stopped our fall, I'm not so sure his magic is that controlled.

"Couldn't we have escaped like this?" I ask. He blinks, and I add, "From the castle. Floated to the river?"

He walks around the island, as if to double check that it's indeed tiny. "Air is not my primary magic."

It makes sense. "It's water, right? Or rather, ice?"

His steps falter and his eyes widen for half a second, but then he raises a shoulder. "I suppose."

"I mean ice because you can only chill water, not heat it, so your magic is different. It's not really water magic."

It's as if he's not even listening to me, his eyes far away, and yet he says, "Indeed."

At least I learned something about his magic, but it didn't feel like a win.

I shiver in my drenched clothes, not looking forward to beg him to dry me or to spend an entire night like this.

He notices me, and says, "You're cold."

"A little."

"Hang on. It will get worse before it gets better."

So many things are like that. I sense some air around me, and it indeed makes me feel colder, until it doesn't, and my clothes are dry.

"Thanks." I manage a sincere smile. He's still wet, his thin tunic sticking to his body. I wonder if he knows how stunning he looks, or if he truly thinks he's ugly. "You should dry yourself."

He glances at his clothes. "I'm not cold. I rarely feel it. Perhaps you're right that my magic is ice, not water."

His chuckle sounds wrong and bitter and pained.

Does his limited water magic bother him? He's so powerful, though. I can't imagine him upset about any magical shortcoming.

I take a deep breath and try to change the subject. "So we'll stay here until tomorrow?"

He nods. "Night will fall soon, and I'd rather not travel during that time. Tomorrow, the Court of Bees will be secured. There's a peace treaty that prevents anyone who visits a coronation from harming another guest. We'll be safe there."

Meaning that we aren't safe here. And it looks like we'll spend hours and hours without anything to do, anything to eat. I try to look at the bright side. At least here, I don't suppose he'll storm away if I approach a touchy subject.

"Will the Nymphs keep us safe?" It's a guess, and something I want to confirm.

"Yes, obviously."

"You really trust them."

"I don't trust anyone." He shakes his head and laughs, then raises an eyebrow. "But I have alliances."

Interesting, interesting, interesting.

"Queen Berta was your ally."

"And as you saw, she wanted to reinforce that alliance. Had she not offended me, we might have come to some profitable agreement." He sits on the sand and plucks some of the thin grass barely covering it. "At least I know where she stands."

The wind pushes a strand of my hair onto my face and I notice how opaque it looks compared to the beautiful fae queen. "Will there be more queens like her?"

"Like what?"

"Wanting to marry you."

He exhales in what almost sounds like a chuckle. "Most definitely. If not for the advantage of the Crystal Court, for strong heirs, because of my magic. They'll want me to be their breeding stallion."

I sit beside him, over a fallen branch, thinner and more uncomfortable than I expected. "Is the idea so despicable?"

He eyes me and snorts. "To be wanted for my power? Obviously."

True, but still. I want to understand why he married me. "You could forge a strategic alliance. That could help you."

He rubs his face with his hands, as if tired. "No. I don't need an army or funds or soldiers. I don't need another kingdom."

That must mean that he's not planning on waging war against his brother, or he would delight in an alliance with a powerful queen. "What is it you need?"

He runs his hand through his hair. "You've snatched a lot of secrets from me today." That means I won't be getting an answer. How surprising. With eyes set on me, he asks,

"What about you? Aren't you going to tell me about your magic?"

I exhale, partly annoyed, partly tired. His question poked that constant, buried fear deep within my chest. "I worship the Almighty Mother and she gives me strength when I need it."

"Is that true, or what they trained you to say?"

"You saw it. She gives us light."

He blinks slowly. "I did. You were glowing. I had never seen anything like that."

"You had never seen anyone who had faith."

He grunts. "Fair. What about... your mind magic?"

I shake my hands in frustration. "I don't have any mind magic, unlike you. Ask *yourself* what happened, not me."

He takes a deep breath. "So you know nothing about dreams?"

I shrug. "A little, yes." I'm going to give him a completely useless, generic answer. "Dreams can sometimes have meanings. It can be something you're worried about, something you fear. It can also be something you want, like a repressed desire." I keep my face straight, even though deep down I'm snickering. "But what does it have to do with mind magic?"

His gaze is piercing. "Sometimes I wonder, dear wife, if you take me for a fool. You did something and you know it."

If he thinks he'll make me confess, he's delusional. I feign confusion. "When? Tell me. Tell me what I did. Maybe I can help you understand it. I don't do well with riddles."

He looks away and strokes his chin. "Me neither." He pauses, then looks back at me. "Maybe your magic came about because of faith. I'll accept that. Have you ever wondered what you could do if you had more control over it? Yes, it's great to connect with some power when you're desperate, but perhaps you could do more."

This change in subject catches me by surprise. "I should call upon the Almighty Mother more often?"

"Yes. Understand that presence within you. Some people say that magic has a cost, but for people like us, with power coursing through our veins, magic as part of our nature, it's the opposite. The cost is in not using it, repressing it. Magic is life and energy, and it needs to flow—like water. You keep it stagnant, and it spoils. Your magic is your energy, Astra. You need to control it and allow it to flow."

Magic. Cursed, deadly, horrific darksoul magic? I'll never use that. His words snake around my neck like a too tight cord. Through my constricted throat I manage a whisper, "It's not magic."

His gaze softens and he brushes a strand of hair away from my face, obviously unaware that the gesture brings shivers down my spine.

To make everything worse, he speaks in a low, rumbling voice. "Your connection with the Almighty Mother, then. Because I never see you using it. Or practicing it. Imagine how incredible you could become if you used at least part of your potential. Not that you're not incredible."

Incredible? His words send a gust of air to my stomach. Crazy, dumb stomach. I'm not incredible, just incredulous that he's calling me that. Sometimes I wonder if *he's* trying to seduce me.

I can't tell him how dangerous it would be to attempt any magic. I can't tell him how it would reveal my identity, how it would put me at risk. I can't tell him how it would put *others* at risk.

He's staring at me, though, reading too much, and asks, "Are you... afraid?" His tone is concerned or perhaps... pitying?

"No!" I snap. I shouldn't have snapped. I soften my

features, relax my body, and aim for a calm voice. "I'm happy the way I am, Marlak."

His eyes are searching and kind. "Apologies for the misguided advice, Astra."

Perhaps he doesn't mean what he said, but his tone is earnest, disarming.

It would be so easy to reach out and touch his hair, so easy to kiss him. Would he kiss me back? Or would he be offended at my *pathetic* attempt at seduction?

I recall Queen Berta and think that he must indeed be made of ice if not even bare tits impress him. Would he react differently if he saw *my*—

Horrified at my deranged thoughts, I get up. "Are we going to endure hours here without any food? Any supplies?" I don't hide the annoyance in my voice.

He puts a hand over his heart. "Oh, how cruel it is to be underestimated by my own wife."

"I'm not your wife. Not in earnest." His words, not mine.

"Oh." He moans as if in pain, but his tone is mocking. "And then reminded that I'm not loved. You salt my wounds, wife."

"Your nonexistent wounds, husband. It's not like you want to be loved."

"Oh, no. I want to be hated." He chuckles and gets up. "I'll get our stuff, you fussy little thing."

I'm not a thing is at the tip of my tongue, but I suspect he's baiting me, so I smile. "Great."

He nods, glides above the water to the river bank, then walks into the forest—and leaves me here alone.

So it turns out that, unlike me, he *can* walk away. And I'm the one who's trapped and abandoned, unsure where I am, at the mercy of a dart from the river banks, or a kidnapping fae, not to mention those flying cockroaches.

I take a deep breath. *Trust the Almighty Mother.* The Priestess's words come to my mind, clear as if she was standing right beside me, and I can feel the comforting presence of the powerful goddess. I'll be safe. I still wish Marlak was here.

And hate myself for wishing that.

17

I don't even have time to dwell in my loneliness, as soon Marlak is back, suitcase in hand, gliding gracefully over the river to our little island. His magic *is* impressive, when we're not jumping from a window above a cliff.

I point to the suitcase. "I suppose it was lying in the woods, coincidentally near where we ended up."

"Exactly." He gives me a smug smirk.

And then again, how did he get the suitcase? Cherry Cake? Ferer? Nelsin? Can Marlak communicate with one of them? Can he summon objects?

Hang on. I was just spitting random ideas, but this last one has a lot of merit.

Summoning.

It's the only thing that can explain the suitcase in his hand. It can also explain how he stole the relics, and there goes my mental image of a 12-year-old running away with a huge sack on his back. It's a sad image regardless.

There are no signs of sadness in the grown man in front of me as he sets the eccentric suitcase on the sand and opens it. He takes out a rough, huge burlap bag, and a silk package, which he opens, revealing bread, cheese, and two canteens.

His eyes have a playful glint. "Happy now?"

I'm still thinking of the young kid running from his home, the young kid who might or might not have murdered his family, the young kid with part of his body burned.

He stares at me and his hands, the glint in his eyes gone. "I guess cheese isn't your favorite food."

I smile and take a piece of bread. "I like it. And I was starving. I get grumpy when I'm starving." I wink. "Thankfully your super discreet suitcase was close by."

I grab some cheese, put it on the bread, and take a bite, realizing too late that I should have washed my hands, but I suppose the sand from the river bank is clean. At least it's crunchy.

Marlak sets the food over a rock, then opens the burlap bag and reveals a huge stretch of leather. I remember the history book with the description of camping tents, and realize that's what it's for.

First, he places some dented stakes on the ground, then he extends a thin piece of leather that has hooks in it. The hooks get nested in a dent in the stakes, so that the leather is slightly suspended.

I suppose it can become a decent bed. Marlak then sets up some thin branches and places the cover. Other than that, there's only a thin blanket, and no pillows. And it's small. Horrifically small.

I can't imagine what's going to happen when we fall asleep and start dreaming. Actually, I *can* imagine it—in vivid details.

His voice disrupts my dread. Dread? Or yearning? No, no. I refuse to consider that possibility.

"What?" I ask, realizing my stupor made me deaf for a moment.

"I have a sleeping bag. The tent is for you only." He wiggles his fingers in the air. "No need to get all pale imagining the horror of having me near."

"Why would I imagine that?"

"If you didn't know I had a bag, where else would I sleep?"

I shake my head. "I was thinking about that history book. They mention when they invented this method of setting camp."

"Odd." He scratches his chin, his expression thoughtful. "I don't recall that book being that terrifying."

Obviously not, it's boring history. Its subject, though... "War is scary."

"That *is* true." He approaches the edge of the tent and gestures to it. "Come. Sit. I'll fill the canteens."

I do as he asks, and it's like sitting on a taut hammock.

Meanwhile, Marlak approaches the edge of the island. For some stupid reason I was thinking he'd kneel by the river, but he just opens the canteens and brings water flying into them. Water magic. Of course.

I recall his feat in the Misty Court's palace, those walls of ice, when there was no water around, and decide to ask about it. "When you confronted Queen Berta, you created ice, and yet there was no water around us."

He sits beside me, perhaps taking the mundane question for an invitation. "The day's humid."

"So you can conjure water from air."

"If it's humid, yes. Air from water, too. When a river flows fast, it has tons of bubbles." He makes a gesture with his hands.

"It must be nice to have elemental magic."

He smirks. "It must be nice to have light magic."

"It's not the same."

He brings the package with the bread and cheese. "You have a beautiful power, Astra. You should develop it."

I try to suppress any signs of discomfort from my face. "If I say I'll develop it, will you be quiet about it?"

"No. I'll want to help you."

I take more pieces of bread and some cheese, keeping my eyes steady on my hands. Could Marlak ever guess what I am? It's not a risk I'd be willing to take. "I was under the impression you thought eventually I'd betray you. Why would you want me to be more powerful?"

The intensity of his stare squeezes my chest. "I also swore to protect you. How easily you forget that. The best way to do it is by ensuring you can defend yourself."

I decide to say something dangerously close to the truth, just for this conversation to stop. "In Krastel, anyone who wields magic without beacon stones raises suspicion. Having magic there, as a human, is not safe."

His posture stiffens. "Yes, yes. Silly me, to forget that."

I gaze at him, hoping to understand his reaction, but his face is as expressive as a piece of wood.

He says, "Eat, wife. I don't want you to die from starvation. We'll have decent meals tomorrow." His voice is so cold that for a moment I wonder if he summoned a wall of ice between us.

Bizarre reaction. Is he offended that I refused his help? Does he think I have an issue with magic? I don't want to ask, though, so I eat in silence, and he does the same. All I hear are the chirping of the birds, howling of the wind, and flowing of the river.

I recall Marlak's words: magic is like water, it needs to flow. But aren't placid lakes perfect the way they are? I don't want to ponder which powers I lack or which powers I could wield, if I tried. Is it a waste, or just caution? I don't think I'll ever meet anyone who'll be able to answer my questions, to guide me. Is there another one of my kind anywhere?

Why are these long-buried questions surfacing now?

I get up and stare at the ocean of clouds covering us. "No stars tonight."

"There goes our opportunity to stargaze together," he drawls.

I turn to him. "Is everything a mockery for you?"

He runs his hand through his stunning curls. "Most definitely not, wife."

"Stop calling me wife. You've said it. I'm not your wife for real. I'm your prisoner."

"It's your choice. Why are you blaming me?"

Right. My deranged choice to dream about him and discover his secret. Only once, of course. Since we got married, I never saw anything compromising enough that would give me bargaining power. But I don't say any of that. Instead, I sit beside him.

"Just call me Astra."

He eyes me, then looks at his jagged scar and rubs his index finger on it. "Is it that despicable? Being my wife?"

"Well, I'm not. How can I ever know what it's like?"

He spreads his hands, his mocking tone returning in full force. "Such a mystery."

Yes, it *is* a mystery, because I'm never sure why he gets upset at certain things. I try to change the subject, and point at his recent scar. "How did you get this?"

He raises his hand to his eye level and examines it. "I got unlucky." He turns to me. "Then lucky."

"That's not vague at all."

He chuckles. "Fine, I'll tell you. I got hit by an arrow and didn't think much of it, but I had a dream about this woman, who told me I was poisoned and convinced me to get an antidote. She's stunning. Dazzling like the sun if it didn't blind you, her voice more soothing than a harp's song. She's wise, kind, caring. A true queen. The most fascinating—"

"You're married," I interrupt him, heat rising to my cheeks. He's mocking me, even though he's saying it with a straight face. It was *me* in the dream. Me, not the person he's describing. "You shouldn't be dreaming about beautiful women."

The edge of his lips hint at a smirk. "How am I supposed to control my dreams?"

"Don't tell me about them. I don't want to hear them."

He frowns. "Are you... jealous?"

"I'm tired of the mockery, that's all."

"Astra, it was *you* in the dream. *You* told me about the antidote. You saved me."

"Then thank the dream version of me. Don't make up a story about a mysterious woman saving you."

He shrugs. "I *did* thank her. Quite profusely. Ardently." I remember those dreams, remember his fervor. "She's quite... lovely." He looks at me. "Not you?"

For a split second I wonder what will happen if I say it's me, if I confess I remember saving him, remember the way his body moved when he "thanked" me. I wonder if he'll thank me some more. I wonder what his skin will feel like against mine, knowing it's real, knowing it's true.

But it's not true, is it? And he's testing me to see if I confess I'm aware of the dreams.

I roll my eyes. "Obviously not. That's coming from your mind, Marlak. But I'm glad your dreams about me saved you."

"Yes. My dreams about you saved me from a poison I wasn't aware existed. You studied poisons, didn't you?"

I give up. "Tell me how you know that, and I'll tell you what I studied."

He rubs his chin, thinking. "That's not a good deal. Give me something more."

"A kiss." Where did this demented idea come from? All I hear is my heart throbbing in anticipation while I wish I could swallow back the words.

He shakes his head. "I told you I wouldn't touch you, wife, and I'm not going to force you to do it to get the information you want."

Well, that's humiliating, but at least it means no kiss. I chuckle, pretending it's nothing. "I was joking."

"See? Look who's mocking now." He sighs. "Let's do this: I'll tell you how I know about you, and you'll tell me what you studied, what you prepared for. Is that a deal?"

"Yes, but you can't tell anyone about the substitutes."

"I won't." He pauses, runs his finger over his curls, and takes a deep breath. "One of the relics, it's a seeing ring. It's not... I can't look at it and ask to see something. It doesn't work like that. It's confusing most of the time. But I can get glimpses of things. And I saw this place, like a classroom, where three girls studied. There was this older man, with long, brown hair. It happened only some five, six times, and I could hear them calling you Astra, hear you studying about other kingdoms, anatomy, how to assassinate someone, how to pretend to be the princess. It took me a while to figure out I was seeing Krastel, and it was the princess decoys, especially you."

"Substitutes."

"Yes, substitutes. So I saw you a few times. With magic, like I always said. My understanding is that you'll replace the princess. If the king strikes a dangerous marriage alliance, he's not going to sacrifice his daughter, but one of you. You could also act as assassins, thieves. I suppose... pretend to be the princess, infiltrate somewhere, then steal something. Is that right?"

"Yes." There's no point in contradicting him. "We're elite guards, but I guess you knew that already."

He shakes his head. "I want to understand what kind of mind training you got. To resist me."

Oh, no. He's going there, and I doubt he'll accept my usual excuses. I try to give him some part of the truth. "We train how to lie, pretend, keep secrets, so maybe my fortitude of mind played a role."

"You are trained to seduce as well." That's not a question.

"Not... trained. It's true that they teach us that—or try to. But I'm horrible at it."

"Astra." He tilts his head. "You know what you did to me. You know it. Give me just a little bit of honesty, just a little. Maybe then I can stop with the mockery, as you call it."

"I do *not* know how to seduce anyone." This conversation churns old acid in my stomach and I want it to stop. "I never even had a proper lover. The only person who ever looked at me was a foreign captain who told me I was too low for him."

"He... what?" His voice cracks like thunder, and I fear there's a storm coming.

I also realize I spoke too much.

The twirling seams at the edge of my tunic catch my attention. So much work to sew them in that shape.

Words struggle to traverse my closed throat and an

ocean of contained tears, but I manage a murmur. "It was nothing."

I can't believe I just laid out my most vulnerable moment.

"It was *not* nothing." His voice explodes in an earth-shattering roar. "Who was it? I want the name."

Struggling to contain my tears, I force myself to keep my voice level. "It *was* nothing. A meaningless dalliance."

Marlak's hand touches the back of mine, and I don't have the strength to push it away. I don't want his pity, though. I don't want anyone's pity.

But then the anger vanishes.

I'm with Tarlia and we're laughing, walking up the stairs to our quarters. She's been pretending to be Princess Driziely, and spending time with the Tirenzy prince.

Although that kingdom is a prosperous island, Otavio warned us that it was too small, not powerful enough for a marriage alliance. Tarlia has to be polite, to avoid offending the prince, but she also needs to make sure he never proposes.

Her solution was a diet with lots of eggs, cabbage, broccoli, and beans. Her walk in the garden with the prince was punctuated by many, many flatulent sounds. Meanwhile, I was pretending to be her handmaid, my hair brown, standing at a distance, talking to Rowe, the captain of Tirenzy's guard.

The scenery changes and it's night. I'm lying on cool, soft grass, stargazing with Captain Rowe, dizzy from wine, and yet drinking more and more, my senses muddled, the stars turning double. He's older than me and blond with hair cropped close to his scalp, not the best-looking man I've ever seen, but he's kind and funny, and when he looks at me and the corners of his eyes crinkle, I believe I'm the most beautiful girl in the world.

I know we don't have any future, I know I'm not supposed to dream about love, and yet when his lips are on mine, all my fears dissipate. There's only soft grass beneath me, his body above me, and that dizzying feeling. I'm dazed, relaxed, free. Tonight I can dare, I can be someone else, I can surrender.

I'm not sure I feel everything, but there's no pain. It's like we are discovering a secret, doing something magical that only we can do. We spend the entire night together, and when I climb to my bedroom, it's already time to get ready for breakfast.

The following night, I return to the gardens, seeking that magic, that glimpse of something more, that feeling that everything could be different. But without the wine, nothing is as magical as the first time. I'm not sure I like being called *tasty* or the way the first thing he does is turn me around, raise my skirt and move aside my underwear.

Before I even realize what we're doing, he's inside me, moving franticly, his hot, ragged breath on my ear. It's true that we have to be quick, as a guard can pass by at any moment and catch us. And quick he is, moving away from me and buttoning his pants before I have any time to enjoy our activity.

My thighs are wet when I turn to look into his eyes. We're doing it all wrong tonight, as only now he kisses me, his mouth tasting of strong liquor. I'm not sure if I like any of this, but I'm still clinging to the magic of the previous night.

He pinches my cheek. "Tasty, I'm leaving tomorrow and I'll miss you."

"You can write." I don't know why I suggest that. What is

he going to write? *Dear Tasty, oh, it's so good. Yes, good. Yes, that's it. Oh, so tasty.*

His eyebrows move up, an amused expression on his face. "Write? To you?"

I don't see why he thinks the idea is so ridiculous. "As friends." Then I add, realizing my mistake. "But you don't have to."

"Mara," he says. At least I'm using a fake name. "You're a *maid*. Pretend you never spoke to me."

His words pierce my skin like thousands of needles. My own voice is gone, lost along with my dignity.

At least he doesn't notice my reaction. Instead, he turns and leaves. I don't know why it hurts. I wasn't hoping to marry him. I don't think so, at least. I don't know what I was hoping. It was nothing. I knew it was nothing.

It's morning, and the Tirenzy prince summons me and Tarlia, who's still pretending to be a flatulent Driziely. While the prince speaks to my friend, Rowe takes me aside. There's no way to avoid him, to refuse his summons. Today he's clean-shaved, well dressed, and doesn't smell of alcohol. I can see why I was attracted to him.

He's the one who starts speaking. "I want to apologize."

I stare at the wall. "For what?"

"I was rude, Mara. I don't want you to think I'm ungrateful."

"It doesn't matter." I still can't face him.

"Here." He offers me a pouch. "For you."

Perhaps by curiosity or some stupid hope that an apology can come in a pouch, I take it.

He smiles. "To compensate you. My appreciation for your services."

I open it, and I guess I'm still too speechless to say

anything, when I realize it has forty silver ducks in it. Not even enough to pay for a dress.

The foreign visitor is taking me for a whore—and a very cheap one.

I never tell anyone what happened, never confess my shame. It should have been obvious it was all he wanted. For a wine-filled moment, it was what I thought *I* wanted. But I never expected to see my worth in a pouch. *You're just a maid.*

No, asshole, I'm an elite guard. But the words sound hollow, words that never leave my mouth. At least the coins are a great reminder of my foolishness.

Perhaps the pain is not about a stupid captain, or getting poorly paid for lousy sexual services. What hurts is the very real possibility that there's no love for me in this life where I might have to pretend to be the princess, where I cannot be myself, where I can't even correct an asshole who thinks I'm a maid.

"You're brokenhearted," the priestess says.

I fix my features quickly. "No. Just tired."

She stares at me. "I might have something for you. Would you like to see—"

I have to stop this. This is not happening. I have to stop this.

I push Marlak's hand from over mine. His eyes are wide with shock.

My vision gets blurry and a loud buzz masks any sounds around me other than my blood pumping furiously in my veins.

How dare he take this memory from me? How dare he invade my thoughts?

A CURSED SON

AMIDST THE BUZZ in my head and the pounding in my chest, I can barely recognize the figure in front of me.

It's Marlak, the disgraced prince who has stolen my most shameful memory, but it's also Commander Rowe paying me forty ducks, Otavio claiming that if not for him, I would be dead, Andrezza distilling her hatred of my kind, Sayanne staring me down with judgmental eyes.

And then I see blood. Just blood. A strange memory that never made any sense, the only memory I have when I reach for any recollection of my parents. In a second everything turns to blood and then they're no longer there. Blood, and I'm alone in the world.

In front of me is the prince who peered into my mind, the man who mocks my dreams about love, who tells me over and over how pathetic I am, as if I had to be reminded of that. He has his hands in front of him, perhaps aware of what's coming.

I grab my dagger, and in one swift movement, I cut his palm. A tiny cut—but large enough.

Before he retreats, I pull his hand towards me for a taste. Just a taste. A taste of his life, his magic, his power. All that power he uses to make me cower. Magic flows indeed, and it can flow in one's blood.

He doesn't pull his hand, doesn't fight me, while the pounding in my head gets stronger. An inferno rages inside me. So much fire. Fury is becoming fire—horrifying, destructive fire. But I can also sense the air around me and the water in the river.

I step away from him and launch a barrage of ice pebbles.

He blocks them. Of course he does. I sense the air around him and make it push his body, but he blocks it again. Then I feel a gust of wind involving me as we both glide over the river. I throw an ice spear at him, but it breaks and falls in the water.

We land on another island, and he stands in front of me, his arms relaxed, as if he didn't consider me a threat. I throw more ice pebbles at him, try to imprison him in an ice wall, then try to push him with air. He manages to block everything.

"So *that's* the real you," he says with an infuriating smirk. "I was wondering when you'd remove that mask of the well-behaved princess."

I try to take the air from around him, remove his ability to speak, but instead, air is removed from my lungs. The asshole is fighting back.

Not only that, he's chuckling. "What are you going to do about it? I stole your secrets, wife. Aren't you angry?"

I focus on the river water, and throw a surge of sharp icicles in his direction, but he pushes them away before they reach him.

And the worst is that he goads me even more. "Come on, wife. Show me."

Air. I focus on air. All the air around him, air inside him, and pull it towards me. Marlak falls to his knees, a hand to his throat, but he's smiling.

"What's so funny?" I roar, and as I do that, I lose touch of my magic.

Not *my* magic. His.

What have I done?

I've just shown him exactly what I am, exactly what a darksoul can do with blood magic. And for some reason, he thinks it's hilarious.

"I want to see you," he says. "The real you."

I close my eyes. If I don't calm down, I might kill him, and the idea horrifies me.

My knees feel as brittle as the ice I was throwing at him.

Marlak *has* seen the real me, and it's not this furious creature gone berserk with anger.

The real me is the one who would never want to see him hurt, the one who'll jump from an unreasonable height straight into danger to save him. I try to take a deep breath, but my chest is shaky and my vision blurry.

He's in front of me now, all traces of mockery gone from his face.

"I'm truly sorry, Astra. I swear I didn't mean to do that."

I glance at the palm of his hand, terrified to find a wound, but, to my relief, there's only a minuscule cut. I sigh. "Why did you provoke me?"

"Because you hide what you are. You hide your power. You hide your anger. Don't you think it has a price?"

What I am. He knows what I am. The words sink in slowly, sink in and lodge into my stomach like a boulder. I'm shaking and it's no longer anger. "What are you going to do?"

"Now that you've spent your fury and might hear me? Apologize."

Blood rushes from my face, my legs wobble, and a new buzz fills my head.

He continues, "It's fine to have magic, Astra. You're no longer in Krastel. Nobody cares about it here."

I'm not sure I understand what he's saying, but at least I get my voice back. "You shouldn't have done that."

"I know. It was wrong. I didn't mean it. I just heard someone hurt you and wanted to know who it was. I just wanted the name, wife. And then I was in that memory and somehow couldn't get out. Trust me, I didn't want to see any of that."

My greatest shame.

Such a stupid little incident. Such a little scratch in my deeply wounded heart, and yet it doesn't make it hurt any less. "And yet you did."

"I'm truly sorry, wife. And you're right to be upset at him. People's value should never be their social standing. You're right to be upset that a man turned something beautiful into a commercial transaction. Two people together, even if it's a fleeting moment, if it's not deep, is a beautiful connection, not something that can be bought."

The more he speaks, the worse I feel. "I don't want to hear your opinion about it, Marlak." My voice is a rough, unpolished hiss. "Use your magic to wipe it from your mind."

He shifts, a shadow covering his face. "That's the magic I most wish I had, Astra." There's so much sadness in his voice. "It doesn't work like that. But you have nothing to be ashamed of. Do you want me to kill him?"

"No!" Does he think he's being helpful? "I could have slipped into his room and slashed his throat, I could have poisoned his food, I could have strangled him. If I wanted him dead, he'd be dead already, but I'm not going to sully my soul for such an insignificant worm."

"My soul's already filthy, I could—"

"I can take care of my problems!" I don't want to hear his apologies, his offer to kill the stupid commander. I don't need his pity. "And he wasn't even a problem." I hate, hate, hate bringing this up, discussing this, admitting the truth. "*I* was stupid, and the mistake is mine."

"Frankly, I disagree. All you expected was some respect." I want to interrupt him, make him stop speaking, stop bringing this up, but it seems every time I open my mouth it gets worse, so I let him continue. "Everyone deserves respect. You couldn't have known he was so vile. Sometimes we need to smell people's stench to realize how rotten they are. The issue is we only notice it from up close." Marlak takes a deep breath. "And I'm sorry. For breeching your privacy. Truly sorry."

"What about goading me? Won't you apologize for that?"

His eyes have an odd sparkle. "Astra, you should have seen you. Seen the magic you can wield, seen how strong you are. Why do you hide yourself? Why do you bury your powers?"

I'm not sure if I chuckle or choke. "Isn't the answer obvious?"

"Because humans don't allow magic except with beacon stones? Because they don't want anyone who's not royal having it? You don't live in Krastel anymore. You're my wife, and you can be as strong as you want. You don't need to pretend you're small anymore. You don't need to hide."

I'm still trembling, still wondering what he's going to do with the rest of the information he just got. "You think the fae won't mind?"

"Do you think they notice who has and who doesn't have beacon stones? Do you think they tally which humans have magic?"

Does he understand it? Or is he pretending to be obtuse on purpose? "You think they won't mind what I am?"

"A human with magic? Why would they mind it?"

I stare at him. He hasn't mentioned *darksoul* or *Tiurian*. "You know why," I whisper.

"Astra, somehow they made you afraid of your strength. It's a smart strategy, for sure. But the stronger you are, the less you'll have to fear, the less you'll be in danger. You should never fear your magic, never fear yourself. Your light magic, it's beautiful. Magnificent. I bet you truly believe it's only faith, and not your own magic, but it has to be a combination of both. The more you know yourself, the less vulnerable you'll be."

I try to be more direct. "The Tiurian Kingdom has fought the fae."

He blinks, then frowns, as if confused. "What do the Tiurians have to do with this? And if you look far enough in the past, everyone has fought everyone."

Do I have to spell out everything? I suppose I do, even though I can feel a bitter taste in my mouth. "In Krastel, they kill humans with magic, thinking they're darksouls."

"They're ignorant."

Ignorant. Has he truly not noticed what I did? Has he not realized why I hide my magic? I swallow and stare at the river, taking notice of my surroundings. "Why did you bring us to this other island?"

"Why?" He has a light chuckle. "Tonight, when you sleep safe from the elements, you'll be glad I didn't let you destroy your tent."

I don't have any smart reply. *How thoughtful* crosses my mind, but the truth is that it *was* thoughtful, and indeed, in my rage, I don't think I would have noticed a tent—or anything else.

He adds, "It's good to let go of your anger, Astra, instead of letting it poison you."

"No. I could have destroyed the tent—and hurt you." In truth, I'm ashamed of my outburst, ashamed to think I could have wounded someone during my lunatic lapse of consciousness.

"You didn't attempt anything I couldn't block." He shakes his head and chuckles. "It was good practice. We should do it more often."

Of course I couldn't beat him. I was using *his* magic. A small fraction of it, but still his magic. Didn't he recognize it? Didn't he notice me cutting his hand? Drinking his blood?

I can still taste it, its sweet, metallic tang. I wish I could drown in it, drown and stop feeling, stop hurting for things that shouldn't even hurt. I wish I could drink it all and deprive him of his evil magic that lets him snatch my most private secrets. There's no more blood coming out of his thin cut, though.

His lips tighten, I suppose from noticing my face. He shrugs. "Or maybe not."

"I'm tired, Marlak." Tired of everything. Tired of my strange magic, tired of hiding, tired of lying to myself.

"You barely got started." He steps closer to me. "Can I hold you, or are you going to use your air magic to bring you back to the other island?"

"You want me to beg for your help?"

"Not beg. I was just checking if you wanted to do it on your own."

"I can't."

He tilts his head and smiles. "Perhaps you could."

"I don't want to talk about it. In fact, I don't want to talk—at all. I need some time to rest."

I should use this moment to try to gain his trust, but I'm still upset, and I don't want to ruin everything. I'm uncertain if he hasn't realized what I am, and wondering if he's playing some cruel game pretending he's oblivious. I need silence, need to get my thoughts together. And I need to stop wanting to strangle him.

I say, "But please, oh magnanimous husband, please use your mighty magic and float me back to the tiny island where we're supposed to spend the night."

He nods, then whispers, "I'm sorry." His arms surround me and we float back to our island.

I wonder why he can't just float me the way he did when I was attacking him, but I don't want to ask, and it's true that it looks harder and less precise.

His embrace is pleasant, though. Too pleasant.

I wish I could just lean on his chest and feel his hand caressing my hair. The thought unsettles me. I'm horrified by my feelings, afraid of how vulnerable they make me.

And now that he knows my secrets, I'm more vulnerable than ever.

18

Alone in the tent, I lie awake, stirring through restless thoughts. I still can't believe what happened. Can't believe I used magic. Can't believe I tasted blood.

I often wondered if the story about blood was a fanciful lie, a way to claim darksouls were monstrous.

And yet it's true.

Not only that, a part of me knew exactly how to access this magic. Perhaps it was indeed a part that had been repressed, a part that slipped through in my outburst. My mask fell. And Marlak delighted in seeing the creature beneath it.

Marlak. His magic is incredibly dangerous, if he can rip secrets from people like that. It's what he tried to do in that cave all those days ago. But he doesn't even care about the human kingdoms. I can't imagine what he was trying to find in my mind. Whatever it was, he didn't try again. But why? Or did he find it?

Does he know I'm Tiurian? Is that what he wanted to find out? Is he pretending he didn't notice it? I'll need to watch him and figure it out—once my mind isn't twirling and I know my mask will stay put. If I can quiet down the thrumming of my heart, perhaps I'll hear the secrets lingering between words.

A new sound then catches my attention, a soft tap on the canvas covering me. For a moment I wonder if a bird landed there, or if it's a branch that the wind carried, but it continues. Tap, tap, tap, like... rain?

I push the flaps aside and see Marlak still dry, sitting on a log, holding his sleeping bag, while drops of water fall all around him. I bet he has some kind of air shield or else he's manipulating the water not to reach him. Eventually he'll have to sleep, though, and this is the kind of quiet rain that will last the night.

Lying on a wet sleeping bag might be a suitable punishment for invading my mind, but he also made sure this tent didn't get damaged, knowing it was for me. I can't let his thoughtful action soften my heart, but I can act like a decent person.

"Husband," I say. My throat is hoarse.

He turns to me, still managing to look sorry. I have to remember that he wasn't sorry when he was seeping through my memories or goading me into using magic.

"Yes?"

I despise what I'm about to say. "Come inside."

He blinks fast, his eyes widening, but then he shakes his head. "Not a wise idea."

"You think you can sustain that magic and stay dry all night?"

"Oh, no." He smiles. "I know I'll get wet. But it's fine."

"The tent is dry. Come in." Why is he being so stubborn? Actually, I know why he prefers to stay in the rain. "I have no plans to attack you or attempt to seduce you, and I can promise I won't grab you while you're asleep."

"Good for you. I can't make that promise. Depending on

what I dream, I'll most definitely grab you." He raises an eyebrow. "We don't want that, do we?"

What I don't want is to hear him explaining why grabbing me would be dreadful. I take the suitcase that's lying on a corner. "We can put this between us. It's big, bulky, and hard. You're welcome to cuddle it if you have a nightmare."

He sighs. "Are you sure? Aren't you still upset?"

"Marlak, I'm furious." I don't see the need to lie. "I thought some time alone would wash away the anger, but it didn't." My tone then changes. "I still don't want to see you sleeping in the rain." I feel I spoke too softly, so I shrug, and aim for a flippant tone. "And this tent is still standing thanks to you, so it's only fair."

He looks at me, at the suitcase, then at his bag. "I thought we'd be sleeping in the Misty Palace, Astra."

"I'm sure she has some room in her bed for you."

He rolls his eyes and huffs, picks up his bag and brings it inside, then takes off his shoes and lies beside the suitcase.

Now that we're both here, I realize that the tent is tiny, and with the suitcase, we'll both be squeezed against the edges, but at least we'll remain dry. With a barrier between us, there's no risk of dreams and reality getting mixed.

The air in the tent gets warmer, while the rain keeps its steady, lulling rhythm.

A new fear is settling in my heart, though.

Despite everything, despite my anger, part of me wishes that suitcase was gone. Part of me wishes I could hug him. I can tell myself they are silly wishes, but the fact that they exist is alarming. Marlak might already know what I am, and I don't know what he wants to do with that information.

Imagine how much more power he'll have over me if I fall for him.

The rain keeps falling outside.

Inside, I can no longer deny I'm falling.

"You need to tell him." The Nymph Queen's voice is in my ears, and I'm awake in the River Hideout.

No. I'm in the Amethyst Palace, walking amidst broken furniture and glass shards, trying to find him. I want to yell, but my voice doesn't come.

And then I'm safe in his arms, his ringed hands caressing my hair as I lie on his chest with that beautiful star.

All I feel is peace.

I hear birds chirping, water flowing close by, leaves rustling in the wind, and his low, steady breath telling me he's asleep. I open my eyes—and realize I'm leaning on Marlak's chest.

Startled, I jolt upward, my sudden movement waking him up as well.

"What's—" He sits up fast and bumps his elbow on my head. "Sorry."

"Where's the suitcase?" I ask, panic rising to my chest.

He looks around, then covers his face with his hands. "I can't believe it."

Right. If he can summon an object, he can make it vanish as well. How come I didn't predict it would happen? I'm just glad this was one of the milder dreams.

I shrug and smile. "It's fine. See? Nothing happened. Now, I know you can summon that suitcase, so there's no need to do it in the woods."

He stares at me. "There are other things you know I do, and I still don't do them in front of you, Astra."

"I had no idea that summoning an object was so intimate."

"I'll go get it." He crawls out of the tent without waiting for a reply.

I look outside and see him gliding over the river, and take the opportunity to exhale slowly.

I can't believe what happened, or perhaps, what didn't happen. I can't believe we were so lucky tonight.

The dream with the Nymph Queen comes to mind. "Tell him," she said.

Is she right? Does it mean he doesn't know?

And then I recall the destroyed Amethyst Palace. There's a knot in my chest, a tremor in my hands. Was it a prediction? Is something bad happening? The morning air is colder than yesterday and I shiver and return to the warmth of the tent. Even though it's not properly insulated, it still has Marlak's warmth. I can sense it's his.

Odd that someone with icy magic would create so much heat, but maybe there's no correlation. I can still taste his blood, still feel a fiery sensation all over my body. Well, it was Marlak. Of course I'd feel his magic as something hot. Not only hot, there's something else, an odd warmth in my chest when I think about him.

Something changed.

Was it really just his thoughtfulness in making sure the tent stayed intact? His fury at Commander Rowe? His words, telling me to embrace my magic? But I hated those words. Or was it his face staring at me, admiring my power, instead of fearing it?

And then maybe I'm making up all that in my mind. Maybe he has a plan that involves uncovering my identity, and here I am, catching feelings for the man who has told me more than once that I'm pathetic. Right now, I can see his point.

He opens the flaps of the tent and puts the suitcase there with a smirk on his face.

"See? I got it. Nothing was lost or taken."

I stare at that thing that should have been a barrier between us.

The real barrier between us is our secrets. I don't think either of us can wish them away.

THERE ARE no clouds hiding the sun today. I changed my clothes in the tent, we ate dried bread and cheese, and now Marlak's packing everything.

I can't forget the feeling of holding him, feeling his skin, his warmth, making part of the dreams real, and yet I can't shake the awkwardness of it.

"Your magic, Astra," he says as he's folding the canvas. "It might have attracted the bloodpuppets. They tend to track a magical signature. Until now, I was thinking they were searching for Nelsin. That perhaps someone found out he was working for me, or he got into some trouble. But now..." He stares at me. "I'm thinking they might have been searching for you. I can't help you, Astra, if you're not honest with me. I can't figure out who tried to attack you."

His words make sense, except for one huge detail. "I didn't use any magic that day, before they found us. How could they have been tracking me?"

Marlak throws the folded canvas into a pouch bag, his expression thoughtful. "And why would they be tracking you? Because you're my wife, sure." He looks up, thinking. "But how would they know?" He shakes his head. "You need to be honest with me. I made a vow to protect you, but I can only do so much when you keep so many secrets."

"As if you didn't keep any."

He throws his hands in the air. "It's different. You might turn around and tell your kingdom everything, and they'll tell my brother. What am I going to do with your secrets, Astra?"

He could do a lot if he wanted to destroy me, destroy Otavio, even put my sisters at risk. Even then, a part of me wants to open my heart to him, a part that thinks he'd never harm me, but that's the same part whose heart is already more than open, who's completely dazzled by him.

"Give me some time," I say. "To trust you. And trust goes both ways."

Strangely, I don't feel that there's any deception in my words, that I'm trying to gain his trust and snatch his secrets. It's more that I need to think about it, I need time to breathe and mull it over. The truth is that I want to trust him, and that's a terrifying truth.

He sighs and looks at me. "Don't put yourself in danger, Astra, because of some misplaced fear that they instilled in you. We don't know if there's something after you, and we don't know how long we have."

I still can't believe anyone would chase me. It doesn't make sense. I decide to change the subject. "The Court of Bees will be safe, won't it?"

"We won't stay there forever, wife." He clicks his tongue. "I'm not mocking you. Or me. As a matter of fact, in the coronation, we'll need to look like a genuine couple. Using an endearment helps. I don't want any more queens with proposals, and I want word to reach the Spider Court, to prevent them from thinking I'm available or lying about my marriage."

I don't want queens proposing to him either, so there's no reason to say no. But there's another problem. "Won't they try to make you a widower?"

"Not in the coronation. But that's not the greatest danger. The greatest danger is my brother. That's why we're always hiding."

"It could have been a queen trying to kill me, a queen who knew how to target Nelsin's magic."

"They'd need to know too much. Nobody knows who works for me. I'd say nobody knew who was my wife, but your king and some people in your castle know, and they might have let that truth slip..." He scratches his chin. "Maybe. Maybe they had another way to track you and it was someone hoping to kill or kidnap you." Setting his eyes on me, he takes a deep breath. "And why Nelsin was incredibly irresponsible. Speaking of Nelsin, we're going to meet Ferer's sister. Pretend you don't know her brother. She'll make your dress for the coronation, and..." He bites his lip. "Yes. We'll be safe for a while."

"You're worried." I don't know why I'm voicing my observation out loud. Perhaps it's just that I feel a chill down my spine, or just that it's the first time I sense hesitation coming from him.

"Danger always follows me, wi—Astra." He blinks. "Why do you hate the endearment?"

"Oh, such a sweet, genuine—"

"It *is* genuine. I made an oath to protect you and I take it seriously. I made a mistake, and trusted someone I shouldn't, but—"

"Call me wife, then, if it makes you happy. It doesn't make a difference."

"True, Astra. It doesn't."

Great. Now he's making fun of my name.

He turns and whistles, and to my surprise I see Cherry Cake emerging from amidst the trees in the river bank.

"We'll fly low," Marlak says. "It's the only way."

He then carries me across the river, so that we land beside the unicorn, and lifts me onto the saddle. This time I look back to see what he's doing, and notice that he has to use some air magic, since the creature is so huge. Our eyes meet and I turn away fast, before he can make anything out of it.

By low I guess he means flying right above tree level, where we can go fast, but not be spotted from a distance. Trees and trees flash by beneath us, and then, after about half an hour, we dip into the forest again, where Cherry Cake gallops on the ground, stops, and we dismount.

"We're getting to Serenade," he says. "Close enough to the Court of Bees, on the border of the Misty Court and Crystal Court."

"Where you're not welcome."

He chuckles. "It depends. But yes, many people there would love to kill me and try to get a boon from my brother or the Court Council." Those last words are spat in anger.

That anger puzzles me. The Crystal Court has a council that helps govern it, made up of merchants and other important representatives of their society. I always thought it was a brilliant idea, but it seems that Marlak doesn't agree. "You don't like the council?"

"I was too young when I..." He swallows, then lowers his voice. "Left. Too young to like or dislike them. The thing is, there's nothing keeping them from getting rid of me, and I know they've sent assassins before."

"Unlike your brother. He can't kill you." At least that's what I got from his words, and I want to see if I'm right.

Marlak snorts. "Oh, don't worry. He can do plenty of other things to me and the people I care about."

"Has he ever tried to do anything to the Spider Court Princess?"

"That court is powerful and well protected, and I don't think anyone knew about me and the princess." He gives me an odd look. "You're quite interested in it."

"Not *interested*. Cautious," I say quickly, before any unhinged ideas invade his mind. "You claimed that being near you was dangerous. I want to know what I'm up against."

He exhales and shakes his head slightly. "Crisine and you, there's no comparison."

I hate the sweet way he says her name, the flippant way he says the rest. *No comparison*. I shouldn't feel anything, but it's not my fault if there's a rock in my stomach.

Thankfully he's too lost in his thoughts to notice any reaction and continues, "And yes, your life is in danger, which is why I insist on you taking control of your magic."

I can't stop myself from rolling my eyes. "I bet *Crisine* is good with magic."

He's still lost in thoughts, his mind far away. "She's fae born and never had anyone telling her that magic is dangerous. You can't compare."

Compare. Asshole. "I have no intention to compare myself to a fae princess."

He stops walking and stares at me, his eyes wide. "Astra. *You* brought her up."

"For a valid question." Not for him to say that she's so much better than me.

He opens his mouth, but says nothing. Instead, he pauses, then asks, "Are you jealous?"

I don't want to consider this possibility, so I pretend to

misunderstand the question. "Of her magic? I don't know what it is."

He runs a finger over his hair, then sighs and extends his hand. "Touch me. It won't make it right in relation to what happened yesterday, but I can show you what happened between me and the princess."

I want to say that I have no intention to intrude in his thoughts, that it won't give me back my secrets, that I don't care.

Instead, I feel myself stepping forward and clasping his wrist, eager to see everything he wants to show me.

I'M IN A RICH BEDROOM, all white, with translucent curtains and an enormous four-poster bed. Breathing is almost impossible, as if my chest was being squeezed. So much pain.

And then I see the cause of my pain, when I stare at those eyes and the ocean of sadness in them. Crisine is beautiful. Stunning, and it's not only because of her silver hair, tan, almost golden skin, or warm, golden-brown eyes. It's the familiar comfort in looking at her. And now she's hurt and yet I'm the one overcome with pain.

"No, Marlak." Her voice is soft, pleading. "Why stop something that brings us joy?"

I shut my eyes. Why indeed? Why create pain when there's no need? But I know this is the right choice. I just never imagined it would be so hard.

"You need a husband," I say, trying to make sure my words don't hurt her. "Your mother wants you to make an alliance, strengthen her kingdom. Find that husband. It's not me."

In truth, I'm well aware that her mother wants me to

marry her daughter, wants to have an excuse to declare war against the Crystal Court, and I don't want anything to do with it. I don't want to be a pawn in her bid for power. But Crisine isn't aware of any of that, so I don't want to blame her.

She fists her hands. "I'm *not* my mother. I never said we had to get married. Things are great the way they are. Why change them?"

Herein lies the other problem. How long are we going to keep lying to each other, pretending we can live day by day, ignoring the future? I reach out a hand and touch her face. Too late, I realize it's a mistake, as she closes her eyes. I want to kiss her and ignore all the other problems. Kiss her and stay in this bedroom until forever, but I can't forget my—

I realize I'm in Marlak's mind, in the past, and for a moment I can't hear his thoughts anymore, until I'm back in.

"I have to go," Marlak says, then pulls his hand. My hand. "I want you to be free to find the love you deserve, to start a family. The longer we keep pretending this doesn't mean anything, the longer I prevent you from finding your true love."

Her laughter is bitter. "I don't need *true love*." She mocks those words. "I just want *you*. We could be amazing together."

I step back, realizing there's no easy way to do this, no way I can walk away and not hurt her. "I can't. For too many reasons. Goodbye, Crisine. Don't make this worse than it has to be. You'll always have a special place in my heart." I know because it's in agonizing pain.

I turn around to leave, one of the hardest things I've ever done, but she's fast and steps in front of me, blocking my passage. "Don't you dare go away. Step out of this door and I'll never want to see your face again."

Her anger relieves some of the pain in my chest. "If that makes it easier for you, I understand."

"Screw you," she yells. "Screw you and your sweet, meaningless words. You think you'll have a chance like this again? A chance to have a kingdom backing you? You think you have the slightest odds of getting back that throne? You have none. You're nothing. Nobody will support you. Nobody wants you as a king. Are you going to refuse the help of the Spider Court? Are you that much of a fool?"

The angrier she gets, the easier it is for me, even though it hurts for a different reason now. "I guess I am."

She still stands between me and the door. "Don't be ridiculous. Don't squander this chance. We'll retake the Crystal Court. Together." So she agrees with her mother's plan. Interesting. What a fool I was. Her eyes have a mad glint now. "We'll be great. Together. Without me, you'll never achieve anything. You're nothing but a dishonorable, disgraced prince."

"I know." And somehow I feel no shame.

"You think anyone will look at you? You're disfigured, Marlak, with human ears to make it worse. Nobody will want you. For your magic, maybe, like a breeding bull, but that's it."

Her words don't hurt, they don't hurt half as much as leaving her was hurting me. They're a strange balm, wiping the pricking sensation I had before. I smirk. "I'm glad to hear what you think of me. I just don't understand why you're blocking the door."

There's a sudden change in her face. I can see the regret in it, but I don't know if it's because she thinks she hurt me or because she realized she let her mask slip. "I didn't mean it." Her voice is soft now.

"Cris." I don't know if I laugh or sigh. "You meant every word. And you can't lie. But it's good to—"

"I meant that *other fae* think that. That's why I always tell you to use glamour, get your ears fixed. It's a simple operation."

I'm tired of it. She doesn't move away from the door so I cross the room and go to the window. I don't even look back at her as I say, "Goodbye."

Then I jump, hoping my air magic will be enough to save me. At least all I'm risking now is physical pain, and that's the gentlest type of pain.

I move my hand and stare at Marlak in front of me, glad to be away from that agonizing scene, glad to be away from his mind, and yet surprised he felt so much.

His eyes are wide. "I didn't expect it to be so..." He blinks. "Vivid."

What I remember the most was his pain. His regret. "You loved her."

He looks down, his forehead creased in thought. "At some point, I thought I did. But I had to leave her. Our goals were different."

"Why did you want me to see this?"

"To make up for yesterday. And to assure you that I don't have anything to do with her anymore, despite what you'll hear. And you might hear a lot of stories." He swallows. "Her mother hasn't given up on an alliance. I need her to know that it's over."

"Is that why you married me?"

He laughs. "No. It was mostly to prevent you from marrying my brother. Letting the Spider Queen know her daughter has no more chance is just a bonus."

"I see." I try to keep walking, but I'm dizzy.

That scene can't get out of my head. All I feel is his pain, a pain that spreads through my chest.

Did he think I was jealous? It's confusing. I know he saw my past with Rowe, but I don't think I wanted to see this. But if it's true, at least I know it's indeed over. *If* it's true.

I turn to him. "How do I know that vision wasn't an illusion?"

He shrugs. "You'll have to trust me. First, I can't create illusions. Second, even if I could, I don't think I could have concocted something like that, with that much detail, that much feeling, then send to you as a thought. That said, I didn't know it would be so realistic. I didn't know it would feel as if I was there again. I'm sorry. It was horrible."

It was. "I thought you had left her to protect her. Because you loved her too much."

He raises a shoulder. "What else would I tell anyone? What else would she say?"

His explanation makes sense, but only in part.

I remember something then, after we visited the Nymph Queen. I remember his words as if he had said them a moment ago. "But you told me that you can't get married because it's too dangerous. That anyone who's attached to you will have a target on their forehead." Why do I remember it so clearly? Maybe because of an annoying detail. "Not me, of course. You don't care if *I'm* a big target."

"You know I care. You also know I had no choice. So it's different."

"I see."

And I can't stop seeing, can't stop that vision, can't forget that feeling that there was a rope around my heart. Marlak's heart. So he *can* love. Why does it bother me? I don't want to think about the answer.

He exhales. "At least you won't think I have a secret affair with Crisine. I hope it helps."

Helps with what? But I don't want to ask. And then again, he showed me some of his past to make up for his blunder, hoping I would see his heart, hoping I wouldn't believe in rumors. I decide I should offer at least some appreciation.

"Thanks for the honesty. And—" I shouldn't say this, but I don't agree with her words. "I don't think you're disfigured."

Marlak has a warm chuckle. "Oh, no. Just half roasted. I do appreciate the honesty from the start, though."

He doesn't sound upset, and I don't want to elaborate and tell him he's stunning. After all, he keeps repeating that I'm unattractive. I guess I did enough, and in truth, it changed his mood.

He stops, and says, "We're getting there. Pretend you don't know Ferer. Try to pretend you like me. I know the Spider Court won't be happy with it, but it's not the biggest danger hanging over you." He raises an eyebrow. "Unless you have your own plans."

"What plans could I have?"

"No idea."

19

Marlak and I walk silently through the thinning forest, and I can see signs of human—or rather, fae—intervention here and there. A few chopped trees, some carvings, an old broken trap. He often stops to listen, and I sure hope he has at least some fae hearing because I can't hear anything other than the wind caressing the leaves above us.

At some point, he stops, and then makes a sound like a bird hooting three times, pauses, then repeats it. He's calling someone.

Whoever that is, they must be busy, as minutes and minutes go by. I lean on a tree trunk, trying to get some rest, feeling the rough bark behind me. Wasn't I the one who wanted to step into a fae forest? Here I am—waiting.

Eventually, I hear steps approaching. Marlak stands in front of me, as if to shield me, but then steps away, and I see clearly that the newcomer is Ferer's sister. She has the same dark brown skin tone and puffy hair, the same ethereal fae elegance, and looks around fifteen, but fae might look younger than they are. I don't notice any gills, but then I realize her hands have webbed fingers.

She smiles at both of us. "There you are. I thought you weren't coming anymore."

"Here I am," Marlak says, then points at me. "And this is my wife, Astra."

"So I heard." She approaches me and extends a hand. "I'm Lidiane, and I assume you've met my brother."

"I... have heard of him."

Lidiane rolls her eyes. "Come. If you don't hurry, you'll have to go naked. I'm sure you'll look good. We could spread some glitter—"

"We need a glamour." Marlak interrupts her. I'm glad he's not on board with me going to this party naked. "Now." Right. That's what he means. "I don't want us recognized, not even her."

The fae tilts her head. "You know it can't do much." She stares at him. "But it can avoid gossip, at least."

The fae raises her hand, and I feel a ticklish sensation on my face and scalp, as if someone was caressing it with a feathery brush. I look at Marlak, and notice that his hair is turning brown, and he no longer has a bald side. His scars are faded too, not completely, but I suppose enough that he won't be recognized from a distance. I check a strand of my own hair and notice that it's dark blond.

"Let's hurry," Lidiane says. "This glamour will last five minutes at most."

"Really?" Marlak asks. "I thought... Well, it should be enough."

Lidiane is walking fast ahead of us. "Don't forget I'll need to save my skills for dressmaking—in record time."

"Fair," Marlak says. "And apologies for not coming earlier."

The fae waves a hand. "I know, I know. It's not easy to

stop by when you're running away like that." She turns to me briefly, her face playful. "You're one brave woman."

I don't know what to say to that, and thankfully I don't have to, as Marlak replies for me. "She is."

Lidiane winks at me, then turns.

Brave. I don't think I'd call myself that, but I'll take it. It's not as if Marlak was going to tell her that being here is not really my choice.

Would I want to be back in the Elite Tower? Training so that one day I could become an assassin? I don't want to examine such traitorous thoughts, and as I look around, at least I'm distracted enough that the tangled threads in my head won't disturb me.

We're still in the forest, but there's more distance between the trees. Among them, I can see a few houses made of wood planks, with clay tile roofs. There isn't any paved path connecting them, as if this was still part of the forest.

I bet this is a lovely place for families. I've always wondered what it would be like to grow up in a house, to play with neighbors, to go to the market with my parents. What it would be like to have a life outside the thick walls of the castle. And I guess I'm back to traitorous thoughts.

Marlak walks close beside me and whispers, "This is the edge of Serenade."

Serenade. I had never heard of this city before today, but we don't study much about the north of the Crystal Court and the small courts in this area, as if this part of the world didn't matter, or maybe because the borders change so often that Krastel scholars don't want to go through the trouble of updating and then re-updating books and maps.

We reach one of those houses and Lidiane opens a thick wooden door. Inside, it's not as cozy as I imagined. It's one room with a bed in a corner, a wood stove in the other, a door to a small washing room, and a table by a wall, with only one window providing light. By the bed, there are shelves with sewing materials, many patches of fabric, and a few rolls with silks and velvets.

Marlak looks around. "I thought... I thought we were going to your shop."

"I..." She looks down. "I had to close it."

"Close it?" His voice has an explosion of power that startles me. "Isn't Ferer helping you?"

Lidiane sits on a chair and fiddles with her hair. "He is, but... I was tired. I found stable employment elsewhere."

"Where?" He voices it like a demand.

"Leave me, Marlak. I can make my own choices."

"Where?" he insists.

"The kitchen at the Owl Inn. I'm missing work now. Happy?"

"Are *you* happy?" he asks.

Lidiane crosses her arms. "Things are tough."

"Ferer should be helping you."

"Marlak, leave me. I'll make a gorgeous dress for your wife, like I promised."

I can see him shifting, as if uncomfortable. "We can go elsewhere."

"No." She glances at me. "I want to do this. People still come here, and I make clothes at night. Maybe more fae will come."

Marlak sighs. "I'm sorry. Are you sure you don't need more help?"

"No!" Her posture is stiff in the chair. "It's good like this. Get that council and your brother out of the palace, and things will change. You need to do what you need to do, and you shouldn't worry about me. I'm fine."

I see then a shadow across his eyes, a flicker of pain. Is he unsure if he'll ever take the throne? Or is he upset he can't do more now?

What I'm starting to understand is that Marlak depends a lot on alliances and promises. I'm also realizing he *has* friends, like Ferer and his sister, and is capable of caring for people.

"Now go," Lidiane says. "Leave me alone with your wife."

He looks at her and me. "Absolutely not. I need to make sure you're both safe. I'll turn around, won't listen. Won't see anything."

And indeed Marlak takes a chair, turns it to the wall, and sits on it.

"Get a book, at least," Lidiane says.

He huffs. "I'm fine."

"So I guess you're all set." Her tone is sarcastic, then she turns to me and shakes her head. "Is he always that clingy?"

"Recently, yes. But I don't mind it."

If it wasn't for that attack, Marlak would happily travel and leave me on that island. So yes, I definitely prefer clingy Marlak.

She smiles, then looks at him and then at me. "Well, it makes sense. We'll have to be fast. I only have four rolls of fabric, and I hope you like one of them."

They're not full rolls, as there is very little fabric left in each of them. Two are velvet, blue and green, and two are silk, gray and red. I also see patches of many types of fabric by it. This house is very modest, and I imagine that those rolls are her only valuable possessions, waiting for the day a noble walks in asking for a dress.

Perhaps she could buy more fabric if she got paid, but I don't know if Marlak will pay her fairly. I almost offer to give her my thirty-two ducks. I'd be glad to get rid of the rest of my shame, after spending eight of them on the passion-fruit custard, but I fear offending her by paying too little.

"I…" I notice her voice shaking. "I can get something else at the market."

"No. I'm thinking." I'm not going to make her spend her hard-earned money. I take a look at the small patches of fabric. "What are those?"

"Leftovers. I get them to practice."

There are many of them. "What if you used those pieces? For something different. I assume you'd like me to wear something unique, right?"

She bites her lip, looking so young and uncertain, but slowly, I see a smile cropping up on her lips. "Are you sure?"

"Yes."

"We could make leaves," she suggests. "Make you look like the ground of a forest, all colorful." Her voice changes, and there's a new energy in it. "I'll have to hurry like crazy, but yes, it can work."

"I'll help," I offer. "As much as I can, of course."

Marlak pushes his chair and stands beside us. "I'll help, too. I can turn away when you measure her."

"Turn away?" Lidiane has a puzzled expression.

He shrugs. "It's good form, isn't it?"

It's her turn to shrug. Then she looks at us. "Are you sure about this?"

"Yes," I say, and notice Marlak and I spoke at the same time. My cheeks feel warm, and I keep my eyes on Lidiane.

"Let's get to work, then." With a giddy smile, she grabs a measuring tape from a corner, then gestures for me to come close. "You can keep your clothes. I know how to discount the difference." She stares at my top and wrinkles her nose, then turns to Marlak. "Irene, really? That gossipy old fool? I could have done much better."

"And you will," Marlak says. "You're the one I chose for a coronation. Irene is for clothes nobody will see."

Lidiane still has a grimace.

Marlak's right, though. It's funny how I'm starting to understand him. I bet Irene provides her services based on a promise of keeping working for him if he ever takes the throne, and I bet the materials and labor are nothing to her. Lidiane is clearly struggling, and to demand her to make clothes just for me to wear while secluded on an island would be untoward.

The girl still shakes her head. "I'm much, much better than Irene. Even though she's good. Anyway, let's get to work."

And work it is. I kept waiting for her to protest, to say we shouldn't help her, at least to tell Marlak not to bother, but it's not the case. She gives each of us a pair of scissors, a paper template, and tells us to cut leaves out of the fabric. Her tone is firm, not the least worried about ordering *her king*. Then again, I don't know if she thinks of him as her king. Marlak isn't upset. While he's clearly not skilled with scissors, he's doing his best. And so am I.

I never had any classes on cutting fabrics, but I try to do it carefully, aware that she only has so many leftover pieces. In fact, the truth is that I never had to work a day of my life, I never had to wonder if I'd have enough to eat. I don't know if Lidiane and even Marlak can say the same. Otavio always told me I was privileged, and I can see some truth in his words, even though I was also a prisoner.

Was. Have I escaped?

I don't want to think too much. All I do is cut, cut, cut. If I had to make a dress in a few hours, I'd simplify it as much as possible. When I suggested this, I was thinking the pieces would be much bigger, but then, she's the one trying to gain a reputation as a dressmaker.

Lidiane is sewing the pieces together. Her speed is impressive, perhaps magical. Even then, oh, there are so many leaves. The sound of her needle moving fast and mine and Marlak's scissors and their thisk, thisk, thisk is peaceful.

There's a satisfaction in working together for a single goal, in knowing that we're getting something done, and something magical about turning these leftover pieces of fabric into beautiful leaves, and then a beautiful dress.

As I'm focused on a yellow piece of silk, Lidiane touches my shoulder, startling me. I almost drop the scissors.

"Time for a break. I'm not going to let you starve."

Marlak is sitting, arms crossed, no longer cutting any pieces of fabric.

I glance at the stove, wondering if I'll finally have a soup or stew or anything hot. Instead, Lidiane pulls bread and dried meat from a cupboard, then a jug of water and some cups. And that's our lunch, for which I'm grateful.

"Thank you, Lidiane," I say. "For the food and the dress."

"This?" She grimaces, pointing at the bread. "This is horrible, but I don't have time to cook for you. And the dress... is my pleasure. My dream, really, to dress a queen. Of course, I wouldn't have guessed it would be an uncrowned queen, but..." She bites her lip.

I think I know what she's getting at, and give her a reassuring smile. "Dreams never come true the way we thought they would, but it's still great to see them realized."

Then the truth of my own words hits me with a chill. I glance at Marlak, wondering if he's indeed my dreams coming true. I have to look away quickly because his eyes meet mine.

I try to wash my feelings with tepid water, but it obviously doesn't work. I hope Marlak didn't make anything out of my mention of dreams.

"It's great," Lidiane says. "Regardless if you'll ever wear a crown or if I'll ever have my own shop."

"Of course you will." Marlak glares at her. "You can't give up on your dreams."

Lidiane shakes her head. "It's not *give up*, it's just… Adapt."

He waves a hand in the air, as if it could shake that idea out of her. "You shouldn't have to adapt to a cruel world. The world needs to change."

She shrinks her shoulders. "I can't change it, Marlak. But who knows, maybe this dress will get me a few clients." She looks at me and smiles. "I used to think that all I needed was one opportunity, one chance. But it's not that simple."

Meaning that she doesn't think this dress will change her life. But maybe it can help. And I don't want her to be so cynical, so I say, "The opportunities will come. One might not be enough, but as they pile up, you'll see a difference. I'll honor this dress and make sure it shines and shows your talent. You've achieved *one* dream, and it means that the rest can become true as well."

She chuckles. "I love optimistic words. Humans are great at saying them, since you can lie."

"I meant what I said!" I protest.

"I'm not complaining. I like those words. Have any of your dreams come true?" She stares at me.

I feel called out, but then I point to Marlak. "Right here. He's the man of my dreams," I deadpan.

The hilarious part is that it's true. I don't think he'll be upset I'm saying that, since we are supposed to pretend we're a real couple.

"More like nightmares," he adds, just because he has to

remind me he's an asshole. I look at him and he's smiling, though. I guess he thinks it's funny.

We finish eating, then get back to work. I admire Lidiane's patience, skill, and attention to detail. I learned how to differentiate cheaper and more expensive clothing, as it can be a crucial skill to identify important and less important members of royalty and even weed out impostors. It's all about the details, the care, the finish, and hers are all impeccable, even done in a hurry in a one-room house.

The day is getting darker when I get to put on the dress. Marlak turns away, like he promised, and Lidiane does her last adjustments. She arranged the green leaves on top, and slowly they turn darker and blue, with a mix of many colors if you look closely, and then purple at the bottom. I don't want to look down too much and mess up her measurements, but I'm curious to see the dress, and there's no full mirror in this house.

Lidiane then turns to Marlak. "You can look now. There's nothing indecent."

"Astra's never indecent," he says, then turns. He stares at me, and his jaw hardens, but it's swiftly replaced by a smile as he turns to Lidiane. "Beautiful work." He's still pale, though.

"Are you sure?" she asks. "If you didn't like it—"

"Astra, do you like it?" he asks.

"I love it," I say quickly. I'd hate for Lidiane to feel that her work is not appreciated. And it's a magnificent dress, better than anything I ever wore.

The girl nods. "Let me know what people think. When you can, of course. I'm sure you're both going to disappear again."

"The life of a fugitive." Marlak sighs, then messes the top of her hair. "Stay safe. And let Ferer know what you need."

He takes a pouch of coins and puts it into her hands. "If I could, I'd ask you to stop working in that kitchen, but the money is yours, so it's your decision."

She puts the pouch back in his hand. "I don't need it and don't want it. It's an honor to help you."

He puts it on the table. "Then throw it away."

Lidiane shakes her head. "Your carriage should arrive soon."

I realize that I don't have my cosmetics bag, and my shoes are far from fancy. It feels a little awkward to ask, but I have to. "What about makeup? And... shoes?"

The girl looks at me. "Right, humans like to change their face for special occasions. I could do a light glamour."

"No glamour," Marlak says. "If they notice it, it will look like she's trying to hide something." He turns to me. "Fae nobility don't tend to wear makeup. When they do, it's extravagant golds and glitters, but in your case, a clean face will be better. As for shoes, again, there's a difference in taste, and fae privilege comfort. Regardless, I'd rather you had something you can run with—just in case."

Lidiane's forehead creases as she turns to him. "You think there will be trouble?"

"Probably not, if the rules stand, but then again, what if? It doesn't matter how good you are with magic if you can't stand on your feet."

I *can* stand on my feet, no matter how high my heels are. I can even run, but if they think this is how I should go to the coronation, I'm not going to argue. The truth is that it *is* comfortable. "Makes sense."

The girl stares at me. "If you're uncomfortable, I could—"

"No, Lidiane," Marlak interrupts her. "She needs to look natural. It shows that she has nothing to hide. It's better."

What we're doing tonight has political implications

other than just letting the Spider Queen know her daughter lost her chance, and I can see that every little move is calculated.

"I'm fine," I assure her. "Used to being *unattractive* by now."

Marlak exhales. "You want a compliment, wife? You look stunning. Now let *me* get ready."

He retreats to the private washroom. Lidiane shakes her head and laughs. "You two are funny."

"Funny?" That's certainly not the word I would pick.

"Yes." She shrugs, and I realize she's not going to elaborate. She then lowers her voice. "My brother mentioned you."

"What did he say?"

She chuckles. "I feel like I'm becoming a blabbermouth, just like Irene."

"You don't have to say it." I think she's already saying too much in confessing her brother told her about me.

"I *want* to say it. He likes you, and that's a lot, coming from him."

"Why? He doesn't usually like people?"

"He doesn't *trust* people. You, he trusts."

I'm surprised, considering Ferer hasn't been that friendly to me. I take another look at her house. "What about you, do you trust your brother?"

"Obviously."

"Then tell him the truth. There's no shame in accepting help." I don't know what she's going through, but she's clearly hiding something from both her brother and Marlak.

She closes her eyes and shakes her head. "You don't add weight to an overloaded cart." There's a certainty in her features when she stares at me. "I know what I'm doing."

I gesture to the dress. "You sure do. Thank you so much."

"I'd do it even if you were awful. But you're not."

Marlak comes out of the washing room then. He's wearing leather trousers and a silk black shirt, with a deep, unbuttoned V in the front, and a necklace with a crescent pendant. It's very much like what he usually wears, except for the necklace, and I assume there's some strategy in it.

To me, he still looks like the prince who spent hours cutting pieces of fabric—and that, strangely, only makes him more beautiful.

He raises a hand. "Please do not make any comments on my looks."

I'm glad he's grumpy again and reminding me why I'm not supposed to admire him. "I wasn't going to say anything."

"I just wanted to be sure."

Lidiane covers her mouth with her hand. She's chuckling. So *that's* what she finds so funny. She stands in front of us. "I'll do a light glamour on you both, just for you to get to the carriage. It should arrive at any moment now."

With that, she passes her hands around my head and I get that ticklish feeling again.

"From where did you get the carriage?" Marlak asks.

She's now working on him, turning his hair brown, covering the side of his head. "Lost Pony Inn." She smirks.

"Oh." Marlak looks worried for a second, but then chuckles. "What a shame. They'll have to spend a few hours not licking Renel's boots."

She moves her hand away from him. "Exactly. I'm strategic."

Marlak turns to me. "Some merchants in this area are extremely loyal to my brother. Lidiane here, as a *loyal subject*, tends to work with them."

"Of course," she says in a mocking tone. "It would be *horrifying* to serve the disgraced king."

Marlak shakes his head. "I'm pretty sure if you say disgraced *king,* all of that effort will be in vain."

She punches him lightly on the arm. "You know what I mean."

"I do." His tone is serious again. "Stay safe. Please."

She nods. "I'm going to ask the same. Be careful out there. And I'll glamour the carriage. So you won't be overheard."

Night is already falling when we walk outside, and I can see the faint glimmer of a few lanterns at a distance, lighting other houses. We're enveloped in the darkness of the forest and dusk, covered in a sky turning purple, from where a few stars already glimmer.

I don't dare say anything, knowing we might be watched, knowing we're about to step into a carriage that serves Marlak's enemy. Not Krastel's enemy, though, not Otavio's enemy. I'm starting to fear that I'll falter when the time comes to return to my kingdom and turn my back to Marlak. Is it the dreams that are making me confused? Or our reality together?

Horse hooves at a distance bring me back to this moment. I'm reminded that all I can do is keep playing this role. What role? Potentially traitorous hostage-wife? That's literally what Marlak thinks I am, so it's not even a role. And yet little by little, I'm learning some of his secrets, but I don't think I'd ever put Lidiane in danger, for example, and somehow he knows that. There's a tenuous line of trust connecting us.

The carriage, a simple thing in dark polished wood, pulled by a single horse, stops in front of the house. The coachman is a fae with green skin that's thick like bark. My understanding had been that high fae were the ones supporting Renel, but I suppose it's more complicated than that.

"Hey, Sain!" Lidiane greets him in a friendly tone. "These are the two nobles going to the Court of Bees coronation."

He looks at us up and down. "From which court?"

"Don't be a busybody," she says.

I can't miss the fact that she's being quite informal with him, as if they were well-known acquaintances or even friends. She's good at pretending.

"I need to make sure they're guests," the coachman explains.

It's Marlak who replies, "Your dutifulness is appreciated, but unnecessary. Only guests will be allowed to enter." He turns to Lidiane. "Can you get us another carriage?"

"Oh. Sure!" She manages to look embarrassed.

"No," the coachman says. "Apologies. Come in. Always an honor to serve fae nobility. Apologies."

Marlak stares at him, an eyebrow raised in a condescending expression I had never seen him wearing before. "I'll accept it this time." He turns to me. "Come."

Lidiane herself opens the door and we step in. The interior has only one row of seats covered in dark brown leather, so we have to ride side by side.

"Thanks," Lidiane says while waving her hand.

I wonder if anyone else can notice what she's doing, if her magic is that obvious to anyone who looks. And then again, maybe it's normal to seal a carriage carrying nobles so that they won't be overheard.

The door closes, leaving me alone with Marlak, less than a palm separating us. I can sense that space between us bothering me like a loose pin pricking my skin. I just don't know if what bothers me is that we're too close or too far. I don't know what I think anymore, or what I feel.

I'm hoping this coronation will give me some answers.

We ride in silence for some time, as darkness sets in. Beside me, Marlak is silhouetted against some of the faint moonlight from outside, his glamour already fading.

After a long time, he asks, "Do you want some light?"

"No, it's fine."

"Oh. I forgot you don't really need it." A note of amusement colors his voice.

He means because sometimes I can produce light? "It doesn't work like that."

"We'll get there soon." His voice is soft, reassuring, and he places his hand on the seat, beside mine. Then he looks outside. "I don't sense any trouble."

That does *not* reassure me. "How long until we get there?"

"Half an hour or so. We should be safe."

Why is he saying that? I was perfectly convinced that our disguise was going to keep us safe in Crystal Court soil, and now his uncertainty is putting me on edge. But then, his magic is powerful enough that we should be safe from most attackers.

I decide to ask, "Is there anything I should worry about?"

"No." He turns and looks outside again. "Like I said, the road looks clear."

It's unsettling to realize I'm still rattled from my encounter with the bloodpuppets. That said, it was recent and horrible. I try to change the subject. "You really care for Lidiane."

A faint light comes from one of his rings, and I realize its gem is a lightstone. Neat. He stares at me. "She's Ferer's little sister. A friend."

Did he think I thought he was interested in her? Ugh. "I know. It looks like you like her like a sister."

His expression is distant, thoughtful. "Perhaps." He then closes his eyes, his expression pained. "There's nothing I wouldn't do for my sister." His face then relaxes. "At least I can do something for Ferer's."

His sister, the one he allegedly killed. There's something wrong with that story. He would never do that to Lidiane, let alone to his real sister. And then again, is this the real Marlak, or just a role he's playing?

No. There's a lot more to what happened, a lot that I don't know. I want to ask, to understand, but if I try to do it now, he'll only retreat even further into himself.

I look at the rings on his hand. The one that's shining has a clear stone. There's a new one, golden with a snake on it, and one with a moon and a star, matching the earring he's wearing. No sign of the most powerful ring in existence.

"No Shadow Ring today?" I ask casually.

He stares at his hand, as if only now noticing something's missing. "Not sure it would match my look. You're sure interested in fae jewelry."

"If it can protect you, it can protect me as well. Of course I'm interested." I truly need to understand why he had the ring when he met me, but has never worn it since. "And if you have it, it doesn't make sense not to wear it for a coronation." A new thought crosses my mind. "Or are you afraid it can be stolen?"

"The fae relics can't be stolen, wife."

I know that, and yet there's something that doesn't make sense. "If they can't be stolen, how did you steal them?"

He stares at me, then chuckles. "Why ask a question

when it contains the very answer you seek?" He raises an eyebrow. "Or is it that formulating the question is the answer in itself?"

He's trying to play me, but I'm not going to let him. "Oh, mighty, wise husband, why answer a question with a riddle, when you can just give me the answer?"

"Because you know the answer. You said it."

The answer. *They can't be stolen.* So he didn't steal them. Borrowed? Maybe he has the right to summon them because he's a member of the court? Maybe he summoned them and that doesn't count as stealing? I decide to insist. "The fact that you didn't steal them doesn't tell me how you took them."

"It makes no difference." He looks away and takes a deep breath. "And there are things I cannot say."

Obviously. I know he doesn't trust me, and it makes a lot of sense. "I understand."

"No, you don't." He stares at me with those fascinating dark eyes, the light from the ring turning his expression sharp and somewhat eerie. "I *cannot* say." He emphasizes it. "To anyone. I..." He shakes his head. "Cannot say."

"You can't talk about the relics, then?"

His chest moves up and down. "Of course I can. It depends. It's not like I can list what I can't talk about, or I'd be talking about it. I can tell you about the Shadow Ring, though, since you've been fascinated with it since you saw it."

"Who wouldn't be fascinated with the most powerful fae relic?"

"Not the most powerful." His chuckle is light, at least. "You shouldn't trust everything your human historians tell you, even if the exaggeration can come in handy sometimes.

That ring, it won't make anyone immune to magic, like you seem to think."

"What does it do, then?"

"It can block another fae's magic for a period of time. Since it can block only one person, its use is rather limited."

I decide to ask a direct question, even though I know I might not get the answer I want. "Why were you wearing it when you met me?"

He shrugs. "I just had it on me."

"Except that you've never worn it since."

"I guess not." He stares at his hand. "I don't always wear the same rings, wife."

And I suppose that's it, as far as the answer I'll get from him. But I'm starting to understand him better, and I know that he gives me direct answers when he wants to. He's vague when he's trying to hide something, or maybe when there's something he can't tell me. I don't know which is which, but I do know that the Shadow Ring is important. Whose magic would he like to disrupt? His brother's, of course. But why did he have it on him that day? I need to figure it out.

But then, if it's true that it can block just one person's magic, I can see how it's not a good weapon when you're going to a coronation where you could face many potential enemies.

We ride in silence for some time, until I hear other hooves behind and in front of us. I don't want to stick my head outside, but I try to look. It's useless because I don't have a good angle to see behind me.

"We're in the Court of Bees," he says. "And there are more fae coming. You didn't think we were the only guests, did you?"

"No, but you talk about enemies and all that, I wanted to check."

"True. Let's get out." He knocks on the roof three times, and then our carriage halts.

After opening the door, he extends an arm to me. I'm painfully aware he's not glamoured and is very obviously looking like Marlak, but at least he doesn't have the light anymore, so maybe the coachman won't notice.

I hold his forearm, and we descend. This is a pebbled road, with some carriages ahead and behind us. There's a castle down there, made of white marble, with steep silver spires. It's not big, but still quite majestic for what is considered a minor court.

Down there, in front of the castle, two small ponds reflect the reddish light from dozens of bonfires. I can smell a pleasant scent of smoked rosemary and roasted meat—and then terror seizes me.

Everything turns black around me, and all I can feel is fear, horror, dread. Then there's fire, so much fire, and all I want to do is run, disappear, all the while feeling that my heart might kill me at any moment, going faster and faster, about to explode.

20

I'm falling into a pit of nothingness and pain, surrounded by murderous fire, consumed with self-loathing. All I want is for this feeling to stop, but it never does. The pain goes on and on and on, something ripping me from the inside out, as if my soul was being cut into pieces. Not even any physical pain compares to that. I'm drowning in dread, suffocated in terror, while the flames of shame consume me.

Darkness. Nothing. And fire. So much fire. My only hope is for death to take me. But I need to undo this. I need to fix it. And yet I'm in so much pain.

I'm disgusted with myself, as if my body was a rotten corpse I had to wear. Disgusted, horrified, consumed by eternal, everlasting pain. If only it could stop.

"She'll light your way." The priestess's voice comes to me.

Light. How can I think about light when fire is so evil?

"This light is not evil," another voice says. "Trust it."

Light. I need light to come out of this. Light will protect me and guide me.

Instead of fire, I try to imagine light around me,

protecting me, surrounding me. Light healing those horrible feelings.

I open my eyes.

There's no fire around me, no magic, no danger. I'm at the edge of the road to the Court of Bees castle. Our carriage is moving away, and Marlak is in front of me, shaking, his hands covering his face.

I realize it then.

Those were *his* feelings.

"Come," I say softly, and pull his arm, careful not to touch his skin, afraid I'll slip into his thoughts.

I don't know if I'll be able to get out of that stupor if it happens again. Still, I guide him away from the road, so that we're alone among trees, where nobody will see us.

"Marlak. Husband," I say softly. "It's not real." It might be real for him—a memory. I add, "Right now. You're safe."

His breathing is ragged, and I don't know if this vision could harm him. It's the worst feeling I've ever had, but I don't know how to get him to come back from this.

"Marlak. We were going to the coronation at the Court of Bees. But we don't have to go." My words sound so pointless and silly.

I want to comfort him, caress his hair, but I don't know if it will pull me again into that despair. And yet I can't let him go on like this. It's too much pain for one person to bear.

Trust the light to guide you.

I'll have to trust. Imagining that light surrounding me, I wrap my hand around his left wrist, that wrist with the rough, scarred skin.

And then I'm in darkness, despair taking over my mind. It's either fire or darkness, and they're both horrific, all-consuming. I don't know if I should try to run or simply let it devour me.

No. Those are not my thoughts. Focusing on the light, I imagine that I'm holding a ball of light in my left hand, a ball so bright, powerful and brilliant that it can wash away all that despair.

I find myself in the hallway of a palace, my feet bare, stepping on polished wooden planks. The walls are made of a pink marble, everything illuminated by light sconces. There's a thick wooden door in front of me. Behind it, I can sense that there's only pain. I want to turn away and run, but I can't.

I open the door, and heavy, dark smoke greets me. I expand my ball of light to shield me from it. There's fire, so much fire, and so much pain. That sense of despair and dread settles over me again, but I brave it and step forward.

This is not real, and I *can* cross the fire, I *can* cross the smoke. It doesn't look like it, though, and as I approach the wall of flames, painful heat bites my skin.

No. This is not real. Even then, I focus on my light and imagine a shield strong enough to keep those flames and that noxious smoke away.

I have to cross it, and slowly, I do.

In a corner, I see him. It's Marlak, but not Marlak now, but when he was much younger. He's crying, calling his mother, the side of his body freshly burned. And yet it's not the physical pain that's disturbing him. It's his loss. Horrific loss consuming him like fire.

I kneel by him. "Marlak. You're no longer here. It's a memory. There's life and friendship and love for you out there."

His eyes are filled with tears, and all he can do is look at me and shake his head.

"You're brave," I say softly. "You can get up and leave."

"I did." His words come among sobs. "It changed nothing. I don't want to be brave."

What can I tell him? That there's fresh air outside? That he can leave? If he's feeling the despair I was feeling, there's no point.

A solution then comes to my mind. I need to shield him from those thoughts, from that pain, that despair. I sit beside him and embrace him, enveloping him in that healing light.

"It's over. You're no longer there, Marlak."

"I'm always there. Always there. It never goes away."

His voice is different, not the young teen voice I just heard. I look again, and we're kneeling in the forest by the Court of Bees Palace.

Marlak is staring at me, his eyes wide, while his fingers clutch the pendant in his necklace. "I'm always there," he repeats. "I'm..." Closing his eyes, he takes a deep breath. "I'm not afraid of fire. It's just..."

I almost tell him it's fine, that he doesn't have to explain, but it's as if he's ashamed and trying to justify himself, and I don't want to interrupt him.

He fiddles with his pendant. "That memory is always there, deep within my mind. I never left that moment, Astra. But I can push it away. Push it down, maybe. I feel like I'm always standing on a thin layer of ice, separating me from those thoughts. But it's so thin, it can break so easily... Sometimes, when I see fire..." He closes his eyes. "I know it's ridiculous."

"It's not ridiculous."

"It is. It's ridiculous, wife." He swallows. "And now you know it." He's pale, sweating, but at least his breathing has slowed down.

"You're not your trauma, you're the person who overcame it."

He releases a bitter chuckle and lets go of the pendant he was holding. "But I never did. I never did." His eyes are brilliant with unshed tears, and he's still trembling.

"You did, Marlak. You got out of that room, you're here. You're helping Lidiane. Protecting me. You saved my life."

He blinks and takes a deep breath. "I know."

The look he gives me feels so honest, so true.

I ask, "Do you want to go back home?"

He leans his forehead on his hand. "Like a coward?"

"You're not a coward."

"Oh. I am." He looks around him, as if only now realizing where he is. "I need to attend this ceremony. Show them I'm not afraid. Let them see you."

I try to think. The bonfires are bothering him, and yet they are just in front of the palace. "Is there a back entrance? We could go around—"

"It won't look right to sneak in like that." He looks at me. "I'm not afraid of fire. If I focus, I think I can walk through that, then we'll be inside. It will be fast."

"I'll hold your arm and make sure you don't feel that again."

He nods and gets up. "Let's do it. While we can."

I'm not sure he's ready, but I also know that the anxiety of facing a fear will only increase the longer we wait. I get up and take his arm, making sure to hold his wrist, from where I accidentally glimpsed his thoughts before. There's nothing there, not even any fear. He turns to me and gives me a tight, lip-only smile.

"Let's go, wife."

I keep touching his wrist, my arm entwined with his, which looks normal for a married couple. Like that, we're back to the road, where a few carriages approach the castle. Down there, the bonfires look much smaller than when I first saw them, just eight in total, surrounding the grass-covered front of the beautiful castle.

I can hear my heart as if it was beating behind my ear. Or is it *his* heart? The door is just there, a huge, open door, with a fae man receiving guests. We just have to make it to that door. My heart is so loud. There are no more sounds around me, no hooves, no chatter, no wind rustling leaves. Just two hearts.

The door is there. And so are the bonfires. So much fire. For a second, I'm in the Crystal Palace again. So much dreadful, fetid smoke.

No, it's an illusion. I focus on light. We're walking to the Bee Palace. My heart is so loud. And getting faster. Can we make it? It's such a long path, and so much fire. Fire then surrounds me, fire and dread and despair.

I focus on light. We're just walking to the palace. There's nothing to fear now. Yet my heart is loud and my breath is ragged, and I feel a strange type of cold covering all my skin from the inside, while fire roars in front of me. So much fire. And light. there's light protecting us. There's fire burning everyone I love.

There's light. Light. We're approaching the door. I focus on the door and light and nothing else, amidst the strange silence and emptiness surrounding us. It feels as if there's dark smoke in my stomach, dark smoke poisoning everything, turning everything into ice. I feel I'm going to be frozen to death and I embrace the thought.

No. We just have to get to the door. There's light protecting us. None of this is happening now. And yet there's smoke, so much smoke. Burned flesh and hair and I'm burning.

No, we're not burning. The door is there. This is just a path to the main door of the palace. The smoke here smells of lavender. And yet all I smell is hair burning. Everything is burning inside and out, and I'm about to collapse.

Three more steps, just three more steps.

The mouth of the fae by the door moves, but I hear no sound other than my heart. He gestures for us to enter, and then we're inside the palace—and I can hear again. Trembling, I take a deep breath, glad to fill my lungs with clean, refreshing air, and get rid of that dread weighing me down.

These were the most horrible steps I ever took. Still, I smile at him. "We made it."

Marlak is pale and slightly trembling, but he squeezes my hand and gives me a look. There's so much in that look. Gratitude, appreciation, admiration. My heart speeds up for a different reason now, but then the look is gone, and he lets go of my hand.

In a second, his expression is haughty, princely, and distant as he looks around the room. There's no trace of the prince who was panicking a few seconds before. If I hadn't felt it, I could easily believe he had pretended it all—but nobody can pretend horror like that.

At least I don't have to feel any... compassion for him anymore. He's quite capable of taking care of himself, as long as there's no fire around him. Perhaps I was wishing he'd show at least some appreciation for more than a fraction of a second, but this is Marlak we're talking about.

Marlak, the disgraced prince who burned his family. The boy I saw wouldn't have done that, at least not on purpose.

The man I know can't wield fire.

That story is all wrong. No doubt something tragic and traumatic happened, but not in the way his brother told the world. I don't even know Renel, and I hate him already.

WE'RE IN A MASSIVE BALLROOM, with windows from floor to ceiling on the sides, wide stairs at the end, and many round columns in the middle, sustaining its high ceiling. There are large, colorful cushions by the walls, where some fae are sitting. While most of them look high fae, I can spot some blue or green skin, scales here and there, and a couple horns.

Some men are shirtless, some women are wearing revealing dresses, and nobody has high heels or any kind of fancy shoes. My dress fits right in, even though my skirt picked some dirt in the hem, but at least it blends with the multicolored leaves.

"Come." Marlak takes my arm again, but he's still so cold, so distant.

Perhaps I was thinking that crossing the fire together would bring us close, but in truth, he must hate me for glimpsing his weakness. And yet he seems so much more human to me.

He brings me to a table behind a column with glass cups filled with colorful liquids and many bite-sized appetizers.

"Is it safe?" I whisper. I figure that as a human, newly wedded to a fae, it wouldn't be weird to ask.

"The food is. As for the drinks, it depends." He smirks and points to the red cups. "Those will make you want to have sex."

I grimace. "People need a *drink* for that?"

He laughs. "Incredible, right? I don't see the point either."

Meaning that he normally wants to have sex—or that he sees no point in sex. Why am I thinking about that?

He points to a yellow drink. "This one is piss."

"You're joking."

"I'm not. It's queen's piss, filtered and brewed to improve the taste."

"You've had it?"

His nose scrunches lightly. "It's a delicacy. Sometimes we can't refuse a toast."

Oh, yuck. "Is there anything I *can* drink?"

He looks up and bites his lip. "The purple one. It will make you dance more once you start."

"That's the *harmless* drink? What are the others?"

"The blue one will increase your senses. Your physical senses. The orange one will make you want to get rid of your clothes. That green... Helps with endurance."

I guess some of what I heard about the fae is true. "Is this party going to turn into one big orgy?"

He laughs. "No, no. Don't worry about it. There are alcoves upstairs, and many will seek the privacy of the woods. Not everyone is comfortable doing it here, and either way, they do it in small groups, like six at most, so it won't be everyone with everyone."

Is he serious? "Right. So a few small orgies then."

"Yes, a few. But I think most of them will wait for after the ceremony, and we can leave."

"Not interested in some fun?" I ask, half kidding.

He looks me up and down. "No."

Did he just think I was suggesting... I pull his hair so that he lowers his head enough for me to whisper in his hear, "I wasn't offering."

"I know." He snorts.

"I was joking," I insist.

I don't want him thinking I was suggesting we should go to an alcove upstairs and get down to business. For a brief second, I wonder what it would be like to drink the red liquid, blame the fae drink, and surrender to my desires without guilt, without shame.

My desires.

My thoughts tell me surprising things. Disturbing things.

He pinches the tip of my nose. "So hilarious, my sweet wife."

The touch feels intimate. I take a glass with the purple drink and chug it in one long sip, trying to wash away my thoughts. It tastes like thin, watered down grape juice.

Maybe everything is juice, and Marlak is messing with my head. It would mean that he can lie for sure. I'm still uncertain about that.

"You're not drinking?" I ask.

He points to another table, on the opposite end. "I'll get some wine."

"Why didn't you tell me?"

"I wanted to make sure you knew about the fae drinks first, so you don't drink something by mistake. And fae wine is stronger. I'm not sure you should—"

"You truly want me to drink piss, right?"

"I told you what it was made of. And there's water as well, wife." He pinches my nose again.

I don't know why he's doing that. Perhaps because we're in public. I feel heat rising to my face, heat going down my body, maybe because of all that talk of orgies and thoughts about drinking the red liquid and what could happen. What would never happen, considering he's very clear he doesn't want me.

As we walk to the other table, a dark-skinned fae woman in a long white dress, wearing a necklace made of huge pearls, stops us. With spotless skin, and wavy, long black hair, she's stunning, like all fae. No wonder they don't need to wear makeup.

She smiles at us. "Marlak. You graced us with your visit."

He bows slightly. "The invitation is an honor, your highness." He points to me. "This is Astra, my wife and queen."

I'm really silly because I get a buzz in my stomach when he says that. Of course, it's the stomach, not the brain, and it doesn't understand how shallow the words are.

The queen's smile is warm when she looks at me. "So you do exist."

In imperfect flesh and bone. I almost crack a joke, but then I hold my tongue and make the same gesture he just did. "It's an honor to be here."

"I'm queen Neliara, and you'll soon see my future king consort." She puts a hand on her chest, then narrows her eyes at me. "Have *you* been crowned?"

I smile. "A lot needs to happen before that." It's vague enough as an answer, and I'm glad Marlak didn't interrupt me or answer in my stead.

"Indeed." Her smile is still friendly, but there's something calculating about her stare. She then makes a gesture with her head, pointing to the door. "Come outside. You don't want to miss the roasted pork."

Outside.

To watch things getting roasted.

I don't think there's anything that could be worse for my husband, but I see no malice in her tone.

"Apologies, your highness," he says. "But my wife is allergic to smoke." His tone is smooth, and he sounds like he's saying the truth—and yet he isn't.

He can lie.

Marlak can lie, and now I'll have to revisit all our interactions and every little thing he's ever told me.

I don't have time to mull over that discovery, as the queen sets her eyes on me, a puzzled expression on her face. "Really? And you married the fire prince?"

Fire? I want to choke, but I laugh instead. "Hearts are illogical, your highness."

She laughs and walks away. I can't shake her calculating look, nor Marlak's lie, and also... *fire prince*? The only reason I don't ask him about it or tease him is because of what I just saw. The queen likely thinks he burned his family, and this is not the time to bring that up.

Marlak said she's a potential ally, but I suppose nothing's that simple.

"So. Wine?" he asks, as if nothing happened.

"Is everything all right?" I whisper.

"Everything's great. When you're surrounded by fae with superior hearing, everything is *always* great." He gives me a pointed look, and I get it.

I mean, I think he should have given me more instructions before we got here, but maybe the idea is that I'll act like his clueless human wife—which I am.

We get to the other table and he fills a silver cup with wine, then takes another cup. "Half water, half wine?"

I don't want to test if the fae wine is different. "All water."

He pours the liquid into the cup and gives it to me. When I hold it, the coldness in the metal bites my hand. The cup is foggy, and filled with ice, not water.

I turn it over, showing that nothing falls from it, and stare at Marlak. "Hilarious."

He flinches and his eyes widen, then takes the cup from me and puts it back on the table. "You'd better serve yourself." His voice is slightly raspy, and there's something uncertain about it.

It's when I realize he froze the water by accident, and all his haughtiness and confidence are just a mask. A mask made of ice.

I wish I knew what's beneath it other than all that terror and pain, and yet all I can do for now is pour water into my cup and hope eventually I'll glimpse enough through his cracks.

He places his own cup on the table, and a quick glance tells me he froze the wine too. I take another cup and pour some for him.

The corners of his eyes are tight, and yet they meet mine with a new depth. There's fear there, a fraction of what I saw in the vision, but it's buried beneath his thick veneer of pride. And there's some warmth too, something inviting. I could get lost in those eyes. I *will* get lost, called to the depths of an ocean I can't control, unless I escape while I can.

That's what I do, when I turn and look at the room again. Is it spinning, or is it my mind? Even the floor I step on no longer feels solid. There's nothing to ground me, when I no longer know what I feel.

It's not the drink that's doing that, it's my confusion. It's realizing that I had been believing in lies, that I had been guided by misconceptions.

Marlak is not a ruthless family murderer. But he can lie.

Has he lied to me? Not in these visions. But why does everyone think he's a brutal family murderer if it's not true?

"Astra." He holds my elbow. "Are you all right?" His tone is concerned, to make matters even worse.

"I'm..."

All of a sudden, his eyes widen as he sees something by the door. His posture shifts, and he steps away from me quickly. I see a hint of panic his eyes can't hide, some strong emotion stirring beneath the surface.

A chill takes over my stomach. I want to look and find out who came in and caused this sudden reaction, but I fear I'll see the Spider Court Princess. I know my fear's not logical, but I still dread that despite everything he told me, despite everything he showed me, deep down he still loves her, and now, seeing her, he realized he doesn't want her to think their story is over.

But dreading is worse than knowing. I'm about to turn and look at the door when he pushes me behind a column. I'm stunned. He didn't hurt me, but his movement was rough, almost aggressive.

Something's wrong. Or maybe everything is just the way it was always meant to be, and I'm the one who wasn't seeing things right.

※

Marlak's posture is still stiff while he presses me against the column, then whispers in my ear, "Whatever happens, my brother can't notice how much I care for you."

Care? There's a riot of fluttering wings in my stomach. I hate that his words do that to me. But still... He cares?

With a storm in his eyes, he steps away with a new, careless swagger. Fake swagger, but I don't think most people would notice it.

And here I am, left alone with my own storm of emotions. No, I need to breathe—and think. Marlak means that he cares for my safety. He has said that many times. It's not that he *cares*. And even if he did, what difference would it make?

The idea makes my torso feel like a hollow chamber from where my heart reverberates. Such a loud heart. Louder than my thoughts.

What difference would it make if he loved me?

All the difference, a traitorous voice replies.

No difference.

Why should I spend a second thinking about something that isn't true?

Perhaps because I was abandoned behind a column, holding a cup of water. I take a sip—and almost spit it. From the surprise, not the taste. It's wine. Stupid metal, hiding the color of our drink.

Marlak would certainly like me to remain hidden here, but I need to see Renel.

Would he look like someone who can lie about a tragic event in the past? Is it something that can be seen on one's face?

In fact, I need to place my cup on a table, and that's the perfect excuse to get out of here. I keep my eyes at my destination, trying to glimpse things from my peripheral vision, but I can't see anyone who could look like Marlak's brother.

I stop at the table and then turn. The first thing I see is not Renel, but Marlak himself, talking to a woman—a beautiful fae woman, obviously. They're laughing, as if nothing's happening, as if he didn't walk away from me, and he's touching her elbow.

A bitter taste settles in my mouth.

Fantastic, Astra, now I'm going to be overcome with pointless jealousy of someone who isn't even mine. And yet I do feel something, especially when he turns and his eyes pass right over me, as if I didn't exist.

Rude. And strange.

And it's odd to realize how unusual it is for him to ignore me. I don't want to dwell on that, or start wondering if the woman is a potential lover. Is she?

Elsewhere in the room, I still don't see anyone who could be Renel. I decide to take another sip of the wine. It's zesty, refreshing and fruity, and doesn't taste of alcohol. I could chug it all down in one sip, if it wasn't for Marlak's warning that it's strong, and I trust him.

I trust him.

My thoughts can shock me sometimes, but in this case, I don't see why he'd lie about a drink. But he *can lie*, and could be lying about so many little and big things that I never noticed. From the corner of my eye, I see that he has just touched her hair. Wonderful. Flirting right in front of me. I feel a bonfire in my stomach and heat stinging my eyes.

Even more wonderful is me here, furious. I stare at the inside of my cup and see my own bare face in its reflection when a man's voice startles me.

"A human here?"

I turn and see a blond fae with straight, long hair tied in a low ponytail. Wearing an elegant, embroidered green velvet suit, he would fit perfectly in a human court, if it wasn't for his pointy ears. He has to be a noble or someone in high standing, probably from the Crystal Court, and yet I know he's not King Renel. First, Renel has dark hair. Second, he wouldn't be sauntering around the palace all by himself.

"Why does it matter?" I ask. And it's true. Does anything matter?

He glances at Marlak, then back at me. "A traitorous monster recently kidnapped a guard from Krastel."

He's talking about me, and a few thoughts run through my mind in quick succession.

At first I want to mock him and say that it sounds terrifying. Part of me wants to correct him and tell him that nobody was kidnapped. I got married out of my free will, after all. Sure, the choice was either to become a disgraced fugitive or marry one, but it was still my choice.

His words, calling Marlak a traitorous monster, don't sit well with me. And yet, right now, all I remember is my husband's warning that his brother can't know how much he cares about me.

Renel can't know that I don't hate his brother. And this is likely his emissary or something.

I look down at the empty cup. "Where did you hear such a thing?"

"The wind carries words." He frowns, then looks at Marlak and back at me. "Don't worry. No horror lasts forever."

"Some scars never fade." I'm thinking about invisible scars, the ones that keep hurting. Marlak's scars.

"I'm truly sorry." His eyes then glance away quickly, and his posture stiffens.

It's when I notice Marlak beside me, ignoring me and staring at the blond fae. "Oh, look at that," he says. "My brother's pig. Is Renel too scared to show his face?"

The blond fae smiles with his lips and yet scowls with his eyes. "His Majesty is busy, taking care of an entire kingdom. Of course, you wouldn't know what it's like."

"No idea." Marlak then grips all my hair and pulls it softly, still barely looking at me. "Now, if you'll excuse me." He takes a step away while pulling me like that.

"Wait," the blond fae says. "I'd like a word."

"You've said more than twenty already," Marlak snaps.

"For your ears only. Let's go outside, and leave the lady with her refreshments."

Marlak yanks my head. I swear I'm going to yank his hair after all this is done. To make it worse, he sneers. "This? No lady. Are you going to refuse to talk in front of furniture as well?"

The blond fae glances at me, then focuses on Marlak. "Your brother has a proposal. I'd like to talk to you alone."

Marlak lets me go, then grunts, "Go fetch me a drink."

I guess I'm supposed to pretend this is all quite normal,

so I walk away. It's annoying because I wanted to hear what the fae had to say. Actually, I can still hear it.

I rush to the table with all the fae juices, get the green drink, and then rush back to the column near where they are standing. I can hear Marlak's voice from here.

"That's a shit proposal. I already come and go as I wish in the Crystal Court."

"You'll have *safe* passage." It's the blond fae's voice. "You and the people who support you."

"As long as I don't threaten Renel." Marlak scoffs. "I might look human, but I am a fae, Azur, and as such, I despise deals with ambiguous wording."

"But what Renel is asking is of little value." The fae, Azur, says.

"For me, there's value in depriving Renel of something pretty."

"Perhaps you've come to care for the human wench?" Even from here, I can hear the malice in the fae's voice. There's a threat there.

"I care for all my property. That should be obvious. I won't even part with a worthless earring for empty words. Now get Renel to come and negotiate, and give me proper terms, and perhaps we can have a deal."

"Show me some good will, then. Let me get a taste of your whore."

Suddenly it makes sense. Azur is testing Marlak, and what he does now will determine the opinion he gets.

21

I want to do something, but I don't know what. My heart is knocking on my chest, as if to remind me we might be in danger, as if I didn't know that already.

If Marlak does to him what he did to the Queen of the Misty Court, then they'll know I can be a target.

Marlak chuckles, though, then says, "Renel should let me use his castle while we're at it."

"You borrow his carriages from time to time, don't you? It's the same."

"The deal is between me and Renel." Marlak hisses. "A worthless pig like you isn't getting anything. Get him to find me and deal with me."

"Then make it easier for him to find you, Marlak. You're the one who's hiding."

A thin layer of ice is forming on the floor and the columns. I decide to intervene and approach them quickly.

"My husband, the drink you asked." It's the green juice, for endurance, and I had meant it as a joke, but now I fear it will only make things worse.

He takes the cup and turns it over. "I don't drink this crap."

Nothing falls on the floor. Of course. It's frozen.

Azur sneers. "Losing control of your magic again, Marlak? We wouldn't want that, would we?"

"Why not?" Marlak shrugs. "Maybe I could kill you by accident."

The blond fae holds his arms behind his back. "You know well that the truce magic laws—"

"Prevent any aggression." Marlak has an amused expression. "We'd need to see what happens when it's an accident."

"Consider my proposal," Azur says, then turns around and walks away.

There's ice forming on the floor, and I need to get Marlak to calm down. "You said there are alcoves upstairs, husband."

His face is puzzled when he looks at me.

I smile. "I want to see one." I hope he doesn't decide to be an asshole right now and tell me I'm being pathetic.

"Sure."

He takes my hand and we climb the marble steps. I don't get any thoughts or visions from him this time, but I sense he's troubled. The second floor is a mezzanine from where we can still look downstairs. We dodge a couple kissing, then he pushes me against a niche, makes an ice wall behind us, and lights his ring.

"What happened?" I ask.

Marlak closes his eyes and takes a deep breath. "I hate them." Then he looks at me. "Did you... did you by any chance...." He puts a hand on his head.

"What?"

He shakes his head. "I was wondering if you spoke to anyone, but I don't think you did. And it's stupid. Everyone knows I got married. It's obvious Renel also does. And now they want you." His voice is shaky.

"I think he was just testing you."

"Obviously. And it doesn't bode well."

"You didn't seem to give a crap for me, Marlak. They won't think you care what happens to me."

"But he wanted *you*. He had a proposal that I'm sure he believed was good enough. In exchange for *you*." His eyes are wide and wild. "Why would he propose that if it wasn't you he wanted?"

"As a test?"

Marlak shakes his head. "It doesn't work like that with fae. If they propose a deal and someone else agrees, then it's done. A fae's words are binding. Renel sent his henchman here for you. I just don't understand why."

"He must have known you'd say *no*."

He rubs his chin. "If that's the case, that's incredibly troubling." He looks at me. "I'm so sorry, Astra. The way I treated you, the words I let him say."

I shake my head. "You did what you had to do." I hated being told to fetch a drink, and having my hair pulled, even if gently, but in retrospect, I can understand why he did it. "He was goading you, Marlak. Who is he, anyway?"

"Azur. Renel's number one man. General, spy, bootlicker, I guess the job depends on the day." Marlak sighs. "People say that he can sense emotions."

"He won't know why you were agitated." At least I hope so.

His eyes meet mine. "You noticed it."

"You were already agitated before, with all the freezing. Does your magic usually do that?"

"Get out of control?" He chuckles and looks down. "Yes, Astra, my magic is renowned for going berserk."

What happened twelve years ago? The question is at the tip of my tongue, but I know this is not the time.

I try to say something that will comfort him instead. "It doesn't matter. He said it: you're always hidden. He can't find you, therefore can't find me. It makes no difference if they're looking for me or not."

He takes a deep breath. "I'll make sure he never finds you."

We're so close. He touches my face and runs his finger down to my chin.

The way he looks at me makes me believe that he cares. More than cares.

I feel his movement in my spine, lighting it with a strange feeling, like charged clouds in the sky. I feel it in my core, with a new warmth. I feel it in my chest, in a fluttering feeling. I need some air, and my legs are wobbling.

But then he snatches his hand away and turns to face the ice blocking our exit.

"We should go downstairs." His voice is clipped.

I'm still trembling, but part of it is shame for believing in something that isn't real. And there's a question I need to ask while we're alone. "Who was the fae woman you were talking to?"

He turns to me, an amused smirk on his face. "Why do you want to know?"

I wish I could shove his face down in some dirt and wipe that smirk. "What's so funny?" I snap. "I need to know your allies and your enemies."

"I wasn't laughing." He stares at me, but at least now he's serious. "She's an attendant in the Court of Bees. I was friendly to her so that Azur would think I was flirting. I wasn't really flirting, though. I wouldn't trick someone like that—or dishonor you."

"You pretend well."

He blinks. "I do, yes. You can pretend too, can't you?"

"I suppose."

The temperature here is getting colder, and I have to rub my hands on my arms.

He stares at the wall of ice again, then all of a sudden it shatters into pieces. Instinctively, I raise an arm to block my face, but there's nothing coming in our direction. An air shield, I realize.

"Azur's gone." His voice is distant. "We can go back downstairs and continue to pretend we tolerate each other."

Pretend. That's what it is for him. "Won't people tell Renel?"

"He'll trust Azur more than he trusts hearsay. And the damage might already be done anyway. Let's go," he says, walking away ahead of me.

It's a reminder that he can be rude even when there's nobody around to see it.

I could just stay here and wallow in my silliness, but I guess I'm going to be a good wife and dutifully follow my husband. It's what I'm here for, isn't it? I don't even know what I'm here for anymore and what I'm going to do if Otavio ever communicates with me. Will he ever find me?

I feel that there's an abyss dividing my past and my current life, and no bridge joining them. For now, all I can do is follow Marlak, watching his dark curls in front of me, until suddenly he stops, turns, and offers his arm. I guess he remembered he's supposed to pretend to be nice.

I avoid his eyes and look down at the ballroom. And then...

No, it can't be. I remember Nelsin's tricks, his stupid illusions. I don't want to believe my eyes, and yet I'm dashing down the stairs.

TARLIA. Here.

I can't believe it, and yet it's her, smiling at me.

I'm so glad to see a friendly face, someone I trust. All I know is that I'm wrapping my arms around her before even saying *hi*.

When we part, she's laughing. "Astra, you're all right!"

The relief in her voice stirs a chunk of guilt that had been revolving in my stomach for days. "They didn't let me say goodbye."

"We know."

Her use of the word *we* makes me look at who's beside her, and that's when I see her companion, so princely and handsome in a dark suit.

"Ziven!"

I'm about to hug him when I feel a gust of air between us, then a pair of arms pulling me back. Marlak, his body close behind mine.

"I'm Marlak, Astra's husband." He extends a ringed hand to Ziven.

"We've met before." Ziven ignores Marlak's gesture and crosses his arms.

Tarlia then curtsies. "A pleasure to meet you, your highness. I'm Princess Driziely."

Princess. Of course. And she looks the part, with a silver tiara framing her perfect auburn curls. Her makeup is subtle, but I notice that her lashes are longer and darker, her eyes brighter, and her cheeks rosy. Her dress is dark blue with embroidery on the chest and a straight cut, much simpler than the dresses used in Krastel ceremonies, and yet perfect for a fae coronation.

"And Astra's friend," Marlak says. I can feel his chest moving behind me. "I'm glad to meet you."

He doesn't extend his hand this time, but keeps holding

me tight in what could be a pleasant embrace if it didn't make me feel trapped. I'm also aware that he never holds me like that.

I brush all these thoughts aside and ask, "How's everything?"

"Good." Tarlia glances between me and Marlak, her tone cautious. "Big plans for my birthday party."

That's the party I heard Otavio mention. I have so many questions to ask her, so much to say, but it's hard to do that when she's pretending to be someone else.

I'm about to ask a vapid question, when Marlak says, "We could go upstairs. So you two can talk."

Tarlia nods. Marlak pulls my hand and we climb the stairs, then walk to an alcove. Tarlia and Ziven are right behind us.

Marlak turns to me and her. "You two go in, and I'll block the entrance so you aren't heard." He turns to Ziven. "I suppose you can keep me company."

Ziven glares at him. "Sounds delightful."

"It does," Tarlia says, as if to end any argument, then walks inside.

I'm about to follow her, when Marlak pulls my hand, then leans down, so that his lips are almost touching my ear.

"I trust you," he says, and kisses my temple like he did at our wedding.

The gesture feels tender, even if it might be a warning, or maybe part of his pretense. And yet he moves away and I can still feel his lips against my skin and his warm breath in my ear, bringing shivers down my spine.

I dread meeting his eyes, as I'm not sure what I'll see in them—or worse, what he'll see in mine, but I need to look at him, if only to let him know he can trust me, and that I'll never reveal his secret.

When I look at his face, I try to tell him that, but all I see is a turbulent darkness hiding something deep within. And yet it's a familiar darkness.

I don't know how I feel, just that I need to gasp for air.

Quickly, I turn and follow Tarlia inside the alcove. A single sconce with a lightstone illuminates delicate flowering plants climbing along the stone walls, two benches on the sides, and pillows on the floor on the back.

I hear a cracking sound, and turn to see a wall of ice enclosing us in that small space.

Tarlia approaches the ice wall and runs her hand over it, then turns to me. "Impressive magic."

"Yes, but—" I almost say that Ziven can also do it, when I realize he might not have told her about his powers. "I can't believe you're here. You and Ziven!"

She waves a hand. "We were worried about you. You think we wouldn't find you?"

Her words take a while to sink in. "You—came for me?"

"Of course! We wanted to see you." She chuckles. "Poor Ziven, I think he wanted to rescue you. I can see now that it's not necessary, but at least I know you're well." She then lowers her voice. "You love him, don't you?"

That's... a bizarre assessment. Extremely bizarre.

I always thought she was quite observant, but perhaps I was wrong. "Ziven? I barely—"

She punches my arm. "Don't be silly. Ziven! Why would you care about Ziven? I mean your fiery fae husband."

I feel like something hits me hard in the chest. It's strange to have someone I trust voice so clearly a thought that terrifies me. But she's wrong.

"He's not fiery. And I don't... I mean, I won't say he's terrible, but we don't get along well." I'm struggling to find the right words. "He's... I'm his prisoner, actually, and he doesn't like me. Humiliates me, tells me I'm pathetic and unattractive. And he's in love with a fae princess." I know that's not exactly true, but I need Tarlia to understand that there's nothing between me and Marlak. "She's too important for him to put her at risk. Me, he doesn't care."

There's concern in her face as she pinches the bottom of her lip, as if thinking, then stares at me. "Are you sure? The way he kissed you—"

She can't be serious. "His kiss? A kiss here?" I touch my temple. "That's the second kiss he ever gave me. The first one was at our wedding, because he was *forced* to kiss me. And now I think he's trying to pretend he cares for me. But he doesn't like me."

Tarlia frowns, then says, "I guess that sounds horrendous."

"It's not horrendous. I'm just saying there's nothing between us."

She stares at me, a long, searching stare, then says, "You look good, Astra. And by good, I don't mean just glowing and beautiful. You look happy."

Her words surprise me. *Happy?* Is that how I feel? "I'm not sure if *happy* is the right word, but I'm not being mistreated or anything." I need to change the subject before she keeps asking more and more. "And how are things going with you? With Sayanne? The Elite Tower?"

She leans against the wall. "The same. Different. It's just two of us now, and Driziely's birthday is coming soon. I'm here, so I assume I'm the one who'll be playing princess, now that you're gone—"

"They wouldn't pick me."

"Astra." She tilts her head and stares at me. "Please. Let's be honest. You always had preferential treatment."

"I was never sent on assignments."

She chuckles. "Which only means you were not disposable like us."

I hate the word she's using to describe herself. "You are not disposable."

"Replaceable, then." She rolls her eyes and shrugs. "They could use Sayanne, but now that I'm here, I suppose I'll be the one who'll have to seduce a certain fae king."

"Fae?"

She sits on the bench and takes a deep breath. "What other important alliance would they want? One too dangerous to send their own princess?"

"Renel?" Could Marlak have been right all along?

She raises an eyebrow. "Most likely."

Renel. I consider what he told everyone about his own brother, compared to Marlak's horrific memory. "Renel's cruel, Tarlia. You can't marry him."

"Astra, you found your way out. Let me find mine."

Her way out. It was what she always wanted, why she always wondered if we would survive being substitutes. But she doesn't need to marry Renel for that. "If you want to escape, maybe I could—"

"No." She sits straight. "I didn't choose to be in this game, no. But I'm going to play it to the end. And if that king decides to be cruel to me, he'll find himself missing a certain appendage."

Her focused expression turns into laughter, and I end up laughing with her, even though I know it's not something to be taken lightly. "You need to be careful, Tarlia."

"Well, I'm getting good at braving assassination

attempts." Her tone is light, but she doesn't sound like she's joking.

I freeze. "Did something happen?"

"No. I mean I'm getting good." She smiles. "Training."

"You meant something specific." It didn't sound like she was talking about training. "Tell me, Tarlia. Tell me everything. I need to know what's happening."

She holds one of her curls and stares at its tip, then caresses it as if it's a cute little pet. "I..." She looks at me. "You know life in the tower is hard. You know that. And the birthday celebration is coming, and—"

"What's happening?"

She looks away again, then back at me. "Fine. Sayanne pushed me from a window."

"What? How did you survive?"

"I grabbed a ledge and stopped my fall, then jumped into a lower window. But you don't have to believe me."

I don't know what to think. "You almost died?"

"I almost fell, but I didn't. I'm alive."

My head is spinning. "And Sayanne? She *pushed* you?"

She rolls her eyes. "Who knows? Maybe her hand slipped. And her legs too, when she came in and hid in my room. When I was coming back—" She shakes her head. "You don't have to believe me, Astra. I know she's your friend. And... life in the Elite Tower is hard. It's not that I forgive her, but... I understand desperation."

I swallow. I still can't believe Sayanne would do something like that, but it's not that I don't believe Tarlia, it's just that it's too hard to digest.

"I'm sorry. Are you safe now?"

"Yes. I'm locking and barring my doors and keeping a distance from her, except when we eat. And Ziven has been sleeping in my room."

"Ziven?" I'm partly surprised, but mostly happy for her. "That's nice."

"No, no." She shakes her hands in front of her. "Not like that. We had to work together to figure out a way to get here. We're also trying to find out what they're planning. So *that's* what we do."

"But you like him, don't you?" I recall the way she looked at him back then, before all of this happened.

"He's smart and a good friend, sure."

I eye her. "Tarlia, I mean *like* him. Don't try to fool me. And if you get along..."

She shrugs. "Oh, yes, it's so romantic when all his effort is in trying to find a way to see *you*. No. Erase that. It *is* romantic, actually, but not for me."

Does she think he's interested in me? "What do you mean?"

"He's intercepted messages, found this invitation, found a way to convince Otavio that coming here would be a good idea, all of that to see you. What do you make of it?"

"He said he was my friend, after we..." I was going to say *were attacked*, but I don't know how much he told her. "Traveled together."

"Oh, yes. Just a friend. You're definitely not on his mind when he's rubbing his sword."

"You said you wanted to come too. Because you're my friend."

She stares at me and raises an eyebrow. "Who knows? Maybe I do think about you when I'm—"

"I don't need to hear it."

She laughs. "We grew up together, silly. Of course we're friends. As to him... I mean, I understand love at first sight, but I've never heard of friendship at first sight, but who knows, maybe that's what it is."

"We're friends." And it's true. "But he doesn't even know me well. You two, on the other hand, seem to be pretty close."

"Super close. United with the goal of rescuing a poor damsel who doesn't get enough kisses from her fiery husband."

I punch her arm, and it's not lightly. "Stop it. I said I didn't want any kisses."

"You *didn't* say that, but I'm glad you clarified it. And no, Astra, I'm not going to be someone's third option, even though I'm far from even being an option right now."

"I see. How's Fachin?"

She leans back on the wall again. "No idea."

"I'm sorry."

She snorts. "Don't be. He got what he wanted, I got what I wanted, and at some point we stopped wanting it. It happens. Plus, it's not like he could fuck me with Ziven around."

I think it's more likely that she didn't want to see Fachin anymore once she got close to Ziven, but she'll probably be upset if I tell her that. I try to ask something else. "What did you and Ziven find out?"

"Not much. They want Renel to fall madly in love with fake Driziely, and I guess from there, gain power and influence over the Crystal Court."

I remember then the day I was by Otavio's window. "I heard Otavio and Andrezza once. It seems that this is *their* plan, not the king's."

"Obviously. They think they control us, so once we're in a position of power, they'll be powerful as well."

"It sounds too..." I'm not sure how to express it. "Simple. For me, it felt as if they, or perhaps Otavio only, had a specific goal. I mean, he could be rich without going through all this effort, and he already has influence in Krastel. What can he want with the Crystal Court?"

Tarlia crosses her arms. "I don't know. Powerful people crave more power. I guess we'll find out soon."

Soon. When she gets married. The idea is dreadful. "Renel is Marlak's enemy. It would put us on opposite sides, Tarlia."

She winks. "Or maybe we can work together and reunite the family. Who knows?" Her expression changes then, becoming serious. "I'm not going to step down or run, Astra. Especially now that I know how much Sayanne wants this and how far she'd go to get it."

"I understand. I wouldn't have run either." And in fact I didn't, even though Otavio gave me that chance, but for some reason I don't want to tell her that, at least not yet. "I'm not asking you to step down, it's just... It won't be easy, Tarlia."

She shakes her head. "Nothing's easy, but what's the alternative?"

"I don't know."

Tarlia pauses and takes a deep breath. "Also, Otavio asked me to deliver a message to you. He's saying that he's the only one who can keep you safe." She rolls her eyes. "So dramatic."

Of course she thinks he's dramatic. She doesn't know. "That's it?"

"No." She has her usual mocking face. "He wants you to know that he hasn't forgotten you, and for you not to despair. Your torment will end soon." She breaks down laughing. "The horrible torment of no kisses."

I don't find it funny. It's too similar to Azur's words. "Do you know if he's planning a rescue or something?"

"Ziven has been intercepting some messages, but we

haven't found anything mentioning you. So I don't know. Otavio didn't ask me to try to get any information from you, so I assume he'll eventually contact you." She creases her eyebrows. "I'm not sure how, though. And I can't see what he'd gain from removing you from your husband. It doesn't make any sense. But sure, if by torment he means your marriage..." She bites her lips and closes her eyes. "Unless he knows about a plan to kill him."

I feel a sudden emptiness in my stomach, but try to ignore it. "He's not easy to kill."

"Did you try it?" Her tone is curious, not playful or even accusatory.

"No. Even if I hated him, I would first learn where he keeps the crown."

Shit. I realize I don't need to know where he keeps it. Marlak can probably summon it any time he wants. All Renel needs to do is find a way to convince him to summon it.

Tarlia watches me, as if she can see the wheels in my head turning. "Astra, you'll need a plan. Otavio will eventually find you, and you'll need a better story than saying your husband is horrible because he never kisses you."

"I never said that!" I'm so annoyed that she keeps insisting on it. "And I'll tell Otavio the truth: that I don't know anything."

She pauses. "You think he'll buy it?"

A loud crack on the ice wall startles me, then I see it turning into water. That's not Marlak's magic.

Ziven's voice echoes from outside. "He's listening to everything! So am I. Not on purpose."

I'm out of air. I can't believe it. Can't believe we were so naïve. Can't believe everything they heard. I look at Tarlia, who pales, then we both head out of the alcove, except that Marlak steps in front of me and blocks my exit.

22

"I'm sorry," Marlak says. He's in front of me, arms spread apart, pushing me into the alcove.

Tarlia is walking away, pulling Ziven. "We'll wait for you downstairs." Her voice sounds far away. Gone.

I want to ask her to wait, but I don't think she'll even hear me.

Marlak is still blocking my exit, making me feel cornered—and angry, so angry.

I step back and glare at him. "You said you trusted me! You said we weren't going to be heard!"

"I didn't say by whom."

"You're an asshole, did you know that?"

"I've been called much worse, wife. And can you blame me for wanting to be cautious?"

"Yes! Wasn't it enough to steal my secrets once? You had to do it again?"

"Astra, I don't know who you are. Really, truly, who you are."

"Well, ask!"

I feel the stone wall behind me, and realize I'm stepping between pillows, on the back of the small alcove. I don't know why I'm retreating so much. I guess I just want some distance, and yet he's getting closer and closer.

Marlak puts a hand on the wall. "Do you really think I'm in love with Crisine? After everything you saw?"

"*That's* your problem? Not you overhearing me?"

"I *had* to overhear you. You think I don't care about you?"

"You said it. Many times." He's so close that I wish I could disappear on the stones and plants behind me.

"I never said I didn't care about you, Astra. Quite the opposite. Are you really upset I don't kiss you?"

"No. I—"

He then kisses my eye. My eye. I take a while to open it and see him staring at me, his eyes wild. "You want me to kiss you? I can kiss you."

He kisses my cheek. It's a quick, brief kiss. I'd say an angry kiss, but there's something sweet about it.

My heart is jumping while I'm trembling. He stares at me, and I don't know what he wants me to say. Do I want him to stop? Do I want him to continue?

"Is that what you want?" he asks, then kisses my chin. "See? I can kiss you."

I don't know why he's angry, why he's threatening me with kisses. This is all so silly and ridiculous—and wonderful. And then it all turns into laughter. Unbridled, joyous, silly laughter.

He's not amused. "You think it's funny."

"No." I can't stop laughing, though.

"Let's see if *this* is funny."

I feel his lips on mine. I feel the world dissolving around me. There's only us and this moment, us and our mingled breaths and caressing tongues. I reach out and touch his hair, his hair that's softer and more wonderful than anything I ever imagined, and pull him closer to me. I don't want this to ever end, this piece of eternity between us. My heart and lips are one.

His ringed fingers touch my face and shoulder. A delightful touch. I'm breathless, ecstatic—and aware of what I feel for him. The startling thought makes my breath hitch.

Our lips part, and yet our faces remain close. At least I can see his eyes now, see a thousand unsaid things in there.

"Astra," he rasps between short breaths.

I pull him towards me again. I want to kiss him fiercely, madly. I want to kiss him and show him a fraction of what I feel, and then let that feeling swallow me whole. The wall behind me spins and the world tilts, and I find my back against the pillows on the floor. His body is over mine, his hands trailing over my exposed skin. A thrill runs through me as his rings graze my thighs, as another hand cups my breast, all the while his lovely curls curtain my face and brush my neck. I realize how desperately I've been wanting him.

He parts our kiss, then brings both hands to my shoulders. His eyes are on mine, fiery, intense. "Do you truly want this?"

"What does it look like?"

He lowers my dress, then, gently, kisses one nipple, then the other. "Magnificent. You're magnificent, Astra. And you know what? I don't care how or why you're doing this. Make me your fool, seduce me, torture me." He runs a finger over my cheek, the gesture so gentle. "Just tell me you weren't coerced into doing this."

Erm... What? "Coerced?" I pull up my dress, covering my breasts, and sit. "You think what? That I'm pretending or something? Didn't you just listen to me? Did you hear about any evil plan to *fool you*?"

"I..."

I'm feeling foolish and all that wanting is turning into anger bubbling in my chest. "What about you? Didn't you say I was unattractive? Pathetic?"

His throat bobs. "Idiotic lies. What did you expect me to say? That I couldn't stop thinking about you? That I was doomed the moment you faced me without a hint of fear? Meanwhile, you were plaguing me with dreams and visions. You're still doing it, and I don't even understand what your goal is."

I can't believe what he just said. "You still think I'm influencing your dreams?"

"Are you going to keep denying it?" The pitch of his voice rises. "It gets impossible to talk to you when you won't admit the obvious."

I get up. "Oh, you think I like it. You think I *chose* to dream about the man who kidnapped me."

He gets up too, his eyes wide.

My fists are clenched and my throat dry. I'm so angry. "You think I created those visions? That day in the cave, when you tried to peer into my mind and then those visions came, that was the most shameful moment of my life! Do you think I wanted to have mental sex with my captor? Who would want that? You think I like to wake up and then find you mocking me because somehow, and I really don't know how, I was dreaming that I wanted *a different kind of milk*?" My voice doesn't come close to the derision I feel for what happened. "Who even says that? *I* don't say that. I—"

My trail of thought gets lost as I notice the horror in his expression. His face is red and his eyes are so wide they're almost bulging.

"What?" I whisper.

I close my eyes as he moves his arm, then I hear a crack. He just punched the wall beside me.

"What are you saying, Astra?" There's an odd desperation in his voice. "Is it true? You created none of that? You were subjected to it, just like I was? That first day, those visions, I always thought you wanted to make me feel like a savage, wanted to humiliate me, wanted to delight in giving me pleasure from imagining myself fucking you in the crudest possible way. It felt good, Astra, to take you from behind and enter you without even caring if you were wet enough. But I wouldn't do that. Not in our first time, at least, not without knowing what you like." He takes a deep breath. "I thought you were creating everything."

I still can't believe him. "You think I'm depraved."

"No, but you were raised to seduce, Astra. I figured I had fallen into your trap. What was I going to do? It's not like you ever told me you didn't create the dreams."

That has to be a joke. There's fire in my stomach and mist in my eyes. I ball my fists as if I could contain a sliver of my anger. "I did! So many times! I did! You wouldn't listen."

He has the gall to wave a finger in the air. "You pretended you didn't know what was happening, wife. You even mocked me, told me to seek treatment, when you knew damn well what was happening. Instead of talking to me, so we could figure out a solution together, you kept quiet."

"You would humiliate me! You would think I wanted you."

"Oh." He tilts his head. "And that would be despicable."

"When you kidnapped me, yes. After you forced me to marry you, then told me I was undesirable, what did you expect? Imagine me saying, *Oh, husband, by the way, I have sexy dreams about you almost every night and don't know why.* Would you really expect me to confess that?"

"Sexy." He huffs. "If you didn't want these visions, and if you felt them the way I did, there's nothing sexy about them. I'm horrified, Astra. You should have told me."

"Would you have believed me?"

"I'm believing you now." He places his hands on his head. "I... I didn't know what to think, Astra. I thought it was an elaborate plan to seduce me, but I didn't understand why. Our first meeting was strange, but then..." He sighs. "The dreams, they were like some dreams I had before, except that now I saw you clearly, and then I could think about nothing except you. Even though I was convinced I was being manipulated, convinced of some ulterior motive, I couldn't help it; I had to have you."

I'm confused, dizzy, and I don't know what to think anymore. "Wasn't it because you feared I'd find out your secrets and tell your brother?"

"That, too. Part of it. But I tried to learn everything I could about you, and then I found out they were probably going to try to marry you to Renel. I had to prevent that." He closes his eyes, takes a deep breath, then stares at me. "Astra, if you have the same dreams I have, you must be under constant torture."

This was not how I expected him to describe it. "Torture?"

"The torture of wanting someone so desperately that little else matters. Maybe... when I tried to look into your mind, I think it ignited some magic, something. A mind connection." He frowns. "We need to break it."

Break it. He doesn't want it. I can't imagine myself without those dreams, and he doesn't want them. "Why didn't you try to break this connection before?"

"I couldn't even figure what it was. But if our minds are bonded..." He scratches his chin. "And if both of us don't want it… There's someone… I think there's a way. And I can deal with torment. But you… no. You should not be subjected to that." He takes my hand and kisses it. "And those dreams create thoughts that might not be true. Feelings that might not be true."

He's gentle, and yet thinks that dreaming about me is a torment. For a long time, I wanted to be rid of those dreams, and yet now that he's suggesting it, it feels like losing a part of me. But perhaps he's right that the dreams create feelings that aren't true.

He clasps his hands around mine and looks at me. That look. I don't even know what he's saying with it, but it doesn't seem to be that he wants to get me out of his mind.

He then pulls his hands back quickly, I guess because he realized what he was doing. My hand is still up, and I don't know what to do with it.

I feel a bitter taste in my mouth and something constricting my chest. Are we just going to pretend our kisses didn't happen? Or are we going to blame them on our dreams?

He's giving me a questioning look, as if waiting for something. An answer maybe. Some words that could change everything. I wish I could understand what I feel, dive into the depths of my mind, but the idea of getting a glimpse of that is terrifying. Perhaps he's right.

I relax my face into a semblance of a natural smile. "Let's break this bond, then. And I'm sorry I didn't tell you before."

He shakes his head, his eyes unfocused. "You feared I would think you were interested in me."

"No. I…" I don't know what to say. "It was embarrassing."

"I understand."

"No, it wasn't…" Words fail me. What do I want to say? That the dreams weren't bad? A thick mist shrouds my mind.

Thankfully, he doesn't wait for an answer and offers his arm. "Come. We still have a coronation to attend."

This time, when I place my hand in that space between his elbow and ribs, the feeling is different. It's hard to delude myself that I'm pretending after those kisses, after what almost happened, and yet the kisses were as ephemeral as the dreams, an illusion to be forgotten.

But something changed. Now I know that he wants me. And then, is any of that wanting real? Or is it because of our mind connection?

We get to the top of the stairs, from where I can see most of the room. Tarlia is talking to some fae noble, Ziven beside her. Very few people are indoors, as they're probably enjoying the music and bonfires outside.

That's when I see *her*. Crisine.

Even though she's not looking at us, I can still recognize her profile and hair, as if it had been etched on my mind in that vision. She looks stunning in a silk white dress, and is accompanied by a small retinue of fae nobles wearing white cloaks. Marlak must have seen her, but I feel no reaction from him as we descend the stairs. His arm around mine feels so warm, our closeness so heavy.

Then I notice the fae by the door running outside, and another fae coming in, his eyes wide, looking around the room.

"Something wrong?" Marlak asks, his voice booming in the hall.

The fae guard approaches us. "Nothing to worry. The grounds and the castle are safe."

"Do you need any help?" Marlak asks.

The man hesitates. "There are... death bees down in the village, but they won't get here."

"I can help," Marlak says, then unlaces his arm from mine.

The fae bows. "That... will be appreciated."

Death bees. I don't know what they are, but I still remember the leech roaches. I can't imagine that this attack is a coincidence. "It might be a trap," I whisper.

Marlak takes my hand and kisses it. "I'll trap the trapper. Stay here with your friend. You'll be safe in the coronation grounds, and I'll be right back." He looks at me, as if about to say something else, but I guess he changes his mind and turns around.

With that, he descends the stairs, then follows the guard to the back of the room, from where he exits. I remain here, dreadful memories of him poisoned unable to leave my mind.

BELOW ME, the guests who remained act as if nothing happened, go on drinking and talking, or lying on pillows, sometimes exchanging drunk kisses. I reach for the handrail, my steps unsure.

Tarlia approaches me. "What's wrong?"

"There's a death bee attack in a village."

She frowns. "Death bees?"

"I don't know what they are, or how dangerous. Marlak is going to help."

She bites her lip. "It should be easy for him. I guess that's where the name of the court comes from."

"There's so much we don't know about the fae."

We get to the bottom of the stairs and Ziven joins us, standing beside it. "Astra," he says. "It's not true what Tarlia said, that I am interested in you. I'm your friend."

"I know." I point at her. "She has quite an imagination. I'm sure you just wanted to do the right thing."

Tarlia rolls her eyes. "Oh yes, I'm so confused. Apologies."

Ziven glares at her. "Maybe *you're* the one in love with Astra."

She chuckles. "If I liked girls, I would. Look at her and tell me she isn't the prettiest woman in this coronation."

Tarlia is baiting him, I know it. Is she hoping he'll say that *she* is the prettiest? Or thinking he'll agree with her?

Ziven raises one shoulder. "That will depend on one's taste."

He glances at me, and we exchange a smile. I think we both agree Tarlia's assessment is absurd.

"I'm glad you're both here," I say, trying to end that subject.

Then, from the corner of my eye, I notice Crisine looking at us. Crisine, her hair silver and brilliant, her skin and eyes light brown. I think her expression is mild curiosity, but I can't be sure from this distance.

"Oh, so that's the one." Tarlia is using a mocking tone, and I'm not sure why. "The reason you won't get kisses from your fiery husband."

"Stop it." I glare at her and discreetly point at Ziven.

She chuckles. "My dear *cousin* here heard everything, Astra. No need to be shy." In a lower voice, she asks, "You really think your prince loves *her*?" Her nose crinkles.

"I don't know."

Tarlia opens her mouth, closes it, and points behind me.

Crisine is standing there. "Apologies for disturbing you."

Her voice is soft and melodic, the kind of voice I'd love to hear reading for me, but I recall Marlak's vision and how her voice was different, harsher in it.

I blink. "It's fine. Do you need anything?"

She looks down at her hands clasped together, then back at me. "I only need a minute. To talk to you alone."

I don't trust her. Her meek, even nervous posture makes her seem harmless, but I have an awful feeling about this. That said, Marlak spent years in a relationship with her, so she can't be a monster.

Tarlia answers before I have time to say anything. "You can talk here."

"I wasn't talking to you," Crisine says, her tone flat.

Tarlia smirks, her posture and expression the perfect haughty noble. "I'm the Krastel princess and I'm talking to you."

Crisine turns to me. "I only need one minute. Please. It's important."

"Astra, don't," Tarlia says, and I wonder if she's worried about me or upset she's being ignored.

Shit. If I don't hear what Crisine has to say, I'll keep wondering forever, regretting I didn't take this opportunity to learn more about Marlak. But I don't trust this Spider Princess.

"One minute?" I ask.

"Are you afraid of me?" Crisine's lower lips tremble. "I won't harm you. This is a fae's word."

Simple promises can conceal many tricks, but what can she do in one minute?

Ziven is looking at Crisine intently, as if trying to see what she's hiding, while Tarlia crosses her arms, looks at me, and shakes her head.

"Fine," I say.

"As your princess, I forbid it!" Tarlia says.

How dare she? I turn to her. "I don't work for you anymore. And I'll be right back."

Tarlia's lips form a line. I feel bad for her, but I need to hear what this fae princess wants to tell me.

Crisine leads me to the back of the room, behind a column. "So it's true you were her maid?" she asks.

The word irks me. "Guard. I was Princess Driziely's guard. Now tell me what you want."

She stares at me up and down. "Guard. Humans are funny."

"Our minute is almost over."

She holds my arm. "Hardly. One minute in private."

In one second I feel something sticky covering my arm, then the room spins and Crisine and I are standing on a ledge on a high hill, from where I can see plains and more hills at a distance. My stomach sinks. Alone here, she could do anything to me.

I pull back my arm, but keep my voice firm. "Where are we?"

Her expression is calm, and she shows me the palms of her hands. "I just wanted some privacy, Astra. I'll take you back after I say what I have to say. I can't lie. Why are you so scared?"

"I'm not scared, just wondering about your intentions." I have a dagger on me, and for some strange reason, the thought comforts me, even though I have no idea what kind of magic this woman has.

"All I want is to warn you." Her voice is gentle, sweet even, just like when you want to disguise a poison. "A broken heart is a tough thing to heal."

"You think mine is going to be broken?"

She runs a hand through her brilliant hair. "How can I know? But what I can say is that Marlak is hiding secrets from you. He has his own plans, and you'll never be a priority for him."

"What plans?" There's cold air in my stomach, as I dread her reply.

"You think he shares his secrets?" Her mocking chuckle makes my hairs stand on end. "Oh, no. Never."

So she has nothing to tell me. Wonderful, just wonderful.

She continues, "If you stop and think, you'll realize that there's only one explanation why he would marry a simple maid." She clears her throat. "Apologies, a guard. He wants something from you. Once he gets it, he'll toss you."

This thought has crossed my mind before, but coming from her mouth, I want to believe it sounds ridiculous. I make sure to keep my body and face relaxed. "Then what? You think he'll run to you?"

Her laughter is loud, and she even inclines her head back. "Oh, no. I think he'll find another victim. Someone else who'll play a part in his evil plans."

"Did he break your heart?" The question is genuine. I know what I saw, but I don't know what she felt.

"No. I was relieved when he was gone. But I was young and naïve once, and while I believed his sweet words, he took shelter in my court, took advantage of our generosity. Only took. Without ever giving anything back. That's Marlak. He can make you believe he could freeze the ocean and quench the stars for you. But he can lie, and lie he will."

I feel a shiver down my spine. Her words hit a part of me that had been wondering all those things, and now they echo in my head. But I think that's exactly her goal: to make me doubt him.

I snort. "And you're worried about my wellbeing?"

"No." She shrugs. "But I thought you should know."

"Now I know. Can we go back?"

"Of course." Her smile looks genuine and friendly, and for some odd reason, that spooks me.

It's possible I'm misjudging her, though. She holds my arm, but suddenly jerks back, her eyes wide.

A second later, I see two men wearing white hooded cloaks, holding her back.

"Not her!" she screams, and the three of them disappear.

I'm not sure what happened. Was she kidnapped? Attacked?

The last thing I saw were the fae men taking her, but they wore the same clothes as the ones in her retinue. Could they be from the Spider Court? Was she attacked, or was she pretending?

Now I'm alone here, and don't even know where I am or how to get back. I look down at the scenery below. The moon rays illuminate a forest, a road, but there's no sign of the castle or the coronation bonfires. I'm either on the other side of the hill, or far from the castle.

Perhaps I could try to contact Marlak like when I was attacked with Nelsin, but if he's doing something dangerous, I don't want to disturb him.

I try to calm down and think. The wind is chilly and fresh with the scent of the forest. After so many years confined to my tower, I can appreciate the beauty and freedom of this place. Lonely, isolated freedom.

Was Crisine attacked? I recall her scream, her words. She said she would take me back, but never said when. What are the odds that someone tracked her here? Perhaps they tracked her magic.

Still, I have a feeling that it was an act, a way to leave me up here by myself. Maybe I'm imagining it because I don't like her. If she *was* kidnapped, I need to inform someone as soon as possible. But how? I still don't want to try to reach for Marlak. But this could be a trap, and perhaps the plan wasn't just to leave me up here on my own. Perhaps there's something coming.

The wind chills me, and I rub my arms. I wonder what Tarlia is thinking, wonder what will happen if Marlak returns to the castle and doesn't find me, wonder what's going to happen to me. I should try to reach out to whatever bond I have with Marlak, but now, when I'm not in danger for my life, not in a moment of supreme desperation, connecting with him feels like an impossible dream-fueled delusion. So much of my life lately feels like a dream-fueled delusion.

Meanwhile, Crisine might be in danger. Or maybe she's laughing at my expense. I can't do anything in either case.

Breathing slowly, I focus on the scent of trees and earth as I look at the expanse below. I pull my dagger from the enclosure in the dress and keep my ears perked. No. I need to make an effort and find my connection with Marlak.

My connection—which he wants to break. An odd chill fills my chest.

Then I see something; a dark shape approaching. I wonder if I should conjure some light or hope that darkness conceals me, and that whatever's coming never sees me.

23

I don't move, don't even breathe loudly.

If whatever is flying isn't after me, I hope I can remain unseen.

Otherwise, all I have is my light and my dagger. Such a remote location. A perfect place to get someone killed.

It's most definitely too late to regret ignoring Tarlia's advice. Ignoring it even though I know she's smart and observant. In my defense, I was curious. Stupid curiosity.

The dark figure then turns and I see its shape against the stars.

A flying horse. No, a unicorn.

All the tension and fear unfurl from my body, replaced by hope.

As he approaches me, I can see some of its red markings and the pointy, long horn, and I finally breathe again. It's Cherry Cake. Cherry Cake, come to save me.

He lands beside me, too large for this thin path. I'm so happy that I want to hug him, but I just pat his thick neck, caressing his rough, hairless, leathery skin. The double saddle is still on his back, and now it has a kind of rope ladder hanging from it. I wonder if it wasn't there before or if

Marlak wanted to hold me. Perhaps the first time, when I was blindfolded, he thought it would be easier.

Regardless, I should stop trying to figure out my husband's intentions. Instead, I climb on Cherry Cake, holding the strap in front of me as tight as I can as he takes flight. I'm not sure if I should shut my eyes to avoid looking below or keep them open to help with my balance. I fear I could fall at any moment.

Fear. Not always logical. I decide to look at the stars above and the forest below and recall all the times I walked outside my tower, dreaming of freedom. Still, I keep holding tight to the strap.

We circle the hill, and then I see, at a distance, the Court of Bees castle, its bonfires looking like tiny lamps from up here. I also glimpse small chunks of light among trees and wonder if they are villages, wonder if Marlak is unharmed, and even if flying here is safe for Cherry Cake—and me.

I don't know where this unicorn is taking me or how he found me, but I trust him, even if I'm still holding tight to the saddle strap. I just hope he's not putting himself in danger for me. Perhaps the darkness of the moonless night will provide cover for our flight.

We're still high above the forest when a scream reaches us from down below. And another, the sheer terror of it penetrating my skin and clawing at my bones. I don't know who's there, but I know they're in danger. I don't know if I can do anything, but I have to at least try.

I tap softly on Cherry Cake's neck, unsure if he'll understand me.

"Down," I whisper, because I don't know what else to do.

He jerks sideways, enough for me to shut my eyes and regret all the decisions that led me to this point. Then we descend. From up here, I see some kind of stone walls, like ruins, and some fire from beneath trees, as if someone is moving a torch. There's a lightstone too, its bluish soft glow contrasting with the orange of the fire.

Cherry Cake then floats close to the treetops. After a few seconds, I understand. He can't go down there—but he's brought me close enough. I can jump from here, but I hesitate. Then another scream pierces the stillness of night, and I decide to check if it's safe from above, and do what I can.

There may be a reason I heard the scream, a reason I could sense that fear in my own skin, and it's not right to ignore it.

I jump, cursing the noise I make as I crash over thin leaves, horrified that I'm actually falling between branches, until I'm able to hold on to one of them—then fall again, until my feet hit a solid branch. I slip, but I'm able to stop my fall by holding onto other branches, and then I steady myself to look below.

Two fae girls are down there. Teenagers, by human standards. One of them has blue skin and hair, and the other has wavy black hair and brown skin. The blue-skinned fae is the one creating blasts of fire, while a swarm of large flying creatures surround them.

Death bees. Shit. They're not attacking just the village. I see a few of them flying up towards me. Light. Light is the answer, but if I'm going to use it, I might as well help the fae girls below.

With that thought, I jump. My fall is not that graceful, but I land behind the fae with fire. Light. I focus on light and create a flash, and the creatures slow down, disoriented.

The black-haired fae stares at me as if I were a ghost, while the other fae is busy producing a blast of fire that burns a few of the insects.

"I'm here to help," I mutter.

I think about light again, considering a shield, but then I realize that the flash was more effective, and do it again.

The insects are disoriented, and the blue girl burns a few more of them. I see another flash of light then, much weaker than mine. An illusion. The other girl's magic.

That gives me time to concentrate, imagine nothing but light, bright and strong and powerful. So powerful.

"Close your eyes," I warn the girls, then close mine as well, as I create a blast so bright that I can see it through my eyelids.

And then it's dark, and the bees are fallen. The blue fae sends a blast of fire to the ground, and burns the insects easily. I exhale in relief, and the girls hug.

"Who are you?" the dark-haired fae asks.

"I was at the coronation. I'm Astra, Prince Marlak's wife."

"Prince?" The girl chuckles. "Fine. I'm Malena," she points at the blue girl. "And you never saw her with me. Promise you won't tell anyone."

I wasn't expecting lifetime servitude, but a thank-you could have been nice. Still, I shrug and say, "Sure. I was just trying to help you and your nonexistent friend."

The blue girl chuckles. "I'm happy you're here. But please forget you saw me."

"Who am I even going to tell?" That's when I notice Malena's dress. It's bright blue, with a deep v cut, and her pearl necklace reminds me... Reminds me of the queen of the Court of Bees. The girl is someone important in that court, and she might fear I'll tell the queen about this meeting. I try to assuage her. "I'll keep your secret, don't worry."

"Promise," Malena says. Demands, actually.

I don't like her tone, and I don't think she'll believe my word anyway, so I say, "In exchange for what?"

She bites her lip, then the blue girl says, "We won't tell anyone about your magic."

I almost shrug like it means nothing or as if people wouldn't believe them, but they are fae; their words are always believed. I can't see how this light would cause me problems, but it all depends on the intention of the person telling it. But they are just afraid I'll spill their secret.

I smile. "Deal. And I wasn't going to tell—"

Sensing a movement to my right, I pull my dagger, then I see a tall fae, wearing plain black pants and a vest, holding a sword. From the corner of my eye, I see more movement, then realize three newcomers are holding the fae girls and have daggers on their necks. My stomach drops.

"It's simple," the man beside me says, his voice grating my insides. "Come with us and they won't be harmed."

Me? Why me?

"They'll kill us!" the blue girl screams.

I see a flash of fire in her hand and realize she's going to fight, then I step away from the man and point my dagger at him, even though it looks ridiculous.

The blue fae's fire is quenched but I don't have time to see how exactly because the man near me advances with his sword. I dodge him. One of the girls screams and I think it's better to stop this before they get hurt.

"Promise you won't harm them!" I yell.

My heart's hammering in my chest. I don't understand why these strangers want me, but I don't think we can fight our way out of this.

Indeed, Malena is fallen to the ground, and a man holds her down with his booted foot. Two men are holding the blue girl's arms, even though she's struggling.

"Why?" the man asks. "We can take you without any promise."

They're going to kill the girls. I know it, but I don't know what to do or how to save them. If I could use some magic, the time would be now. An endless scream is lodged in my throat. A useless scream.

A fae man is about to stab the blue girl, but I don't have time to stop it or look at it, as the assailant close to me advances with his sword. I dodge it, trying to think of the Almighty Mother, trying to hope for something that could change this.

I'm berating my lack of magic when a strong gust of wind hits me to the point I lose my balance.

The men are no longer close to the fae girls, and my attacker falls. I step back, then feel more wind, loud on my ears, pushing my hair back from my face.

The assailants are on the ground, gasping, with a thick layer of ice around their hands, then they faint. Air and ice magic. That has to be Marlak.

From beneath the trees, I hear his deep voice, somewhat breathless. "Don't kill them."

He runs to me, but stops when he's close. I don't know if he was going to hug me and changed his mind or what. Instead, he turns to the girls, or rather, girl. The blue fae has disappeared. He asks, "Princess Malena?"

Princess. Makes sense. The girl sighs. "Yes. I was just taking a walk when I was attacked by death bees." She points at me. "She helped me."

Marlak glances at the scorch marks on the ground, and I wonder if he can sense the fire magic. But then, he must be thinking it's the princess's magic.

The girl continues, "Then these fae came. Wanted to kidnap your wife."

Marlak stares at me, shadows dancing in his eyes, then looks away and sighs. Malena puts a finger over her lips. I guess despite everything, she still doesn't want me to tell anyone about her friend.

He turns to me then. "What were you doing here?"

His voice is soft, calm, but I can sense the storm underneath it. I'm pretty sure I'm about to see the tornado when I tell him that his beloved has been kidnapped.

"Crisine." My voice cracks so much, I'm not sure how I manage to sound intelligible. "She asked me to talk to her, and brought me... around here." I don't want to say I was on a hill far away and mention Cherry Cake.

He frowns, and I continue, "But then two fae came. They took her, while she screamed."

Marlak is still frowning. "But you're not worried." His tone is flat.

"I..." How do I say it? For some reason I don't think that was real. "It felt... forced?"

"You thought she *pretended* it?" I hate his accusing tone, the anger in his words.

"Maybe not, I don't know. I could be mistaken. They took her, and I was left alone."

The princess stares at me with curiosity, while Marlak shakes his head.

Four horses then arrive, carrying Court of Bees guards. Two of them dismount and rush to the princess. "They saved me!" Malena yells, then tells them what happened, omitting her friend.

One guard comes to us, while another checks the fainted men.

Marlak repeats what he was told, strangely omitting Crisine, then says, "Apologies to your queen, but we'll have to leave now. We wouldn't want to cause any more trouble."

Tarlia and Ziven come to my mind then. They must be dying with worry in the Court of Bees castle. I turn to the guard. "The Krastel Prince and Princess will be worried about me. Can you let them know I'm well?"

The guard nods. "I'll tell them right away. It's a promise." He taps Marlak's shoulder, but looks at both of us. "We won't forget what you did today."

Marlak shakes his head. "It was nothing." He points at the fallen men. "Tell me what you find out about them. I'd appreciate that."

He then takes my hand. I don't know why it feels so comforting to feel his rough, scarred fingers entwined with mine, why it's so good to feel his touch. It's as if there's an energy connecting us, moving through our arms and hands, all the way to our hearts. Mine, at least. Dangerous feeling—and yet, I don't want to pull away my hand. And like that, Marlak and I are on our way to the forest.

I smile at the Court of Bees princess as we pass by her. "It was a pleasure to meet you."

She nods, but it looks like a small bow. "Same."

I'm still shaking from the attacks, from what I saw, and in this state, the darkness of trees looks looming and dangerous, a place that might harbor all kinds of enemies. I shouldn't feel like that, though. The attackers were defeated. There shouldn't be anyone else after me right here, right now.

"Are you all right?" Marlak whispers.

"Yes. Just... spooked."

"I know. We'll talk later."

He pulls my hand and gives it a quick kiss.

I'm stunned, since I thought we were back to no more kisses, but I don't want to say anything lest I attract some strange creature. I don't want to berate or tease him either, considering I'm not even sure how I feel.

Leaves ruffle above us, and I step closer to Marlak, but he whispers in my ear, "It's Cherry Cake."

His low voice and warm breath bring a pleasant shiver down my spine. I need to stop feeling like that or I won't be able to think anymore.

At least, the magnificent unicorn lands in front of us and I can stop thinking about Marlak's voice. No, I'm still thinking about it when he lets go of my hand and puts me in the saddle. Strangely, this time I don't see that little rope ladder I climbed up to escape from the hill.

Marlak climbs behind me, and then we take off, gaining altitude quickly, fresh wind on my face and shoulders.

"We're going north," he speaks close to my ear again, so I can hear him despite the wind.

I wonder if he's doing it on purpose to get a reaction. My body does react, but whose body wouldn't? I nod because I know he won't hear me with the wind. And the truth is that I'm stunned and tired, with too much to process, too much to think about, and yet now that there's no danger around me, all I can think about is his lips on my breasts, his tongue caressing mine, his hand between my legs. Can someone burst from so much wanting?

I should be thinking about Tarlia and what she told me about Sayanne, should be wondering what those men wanted, if Crisine really pretended she was kidnapped, should be thinking about where we are going. These thoughts are there, somewhere in my mind, telling me to pay attention to them, but the wanting is so much louder.

CHERRY CAKE SLOWS DOWN, gliding above trees. There's less wind now, but still a little chilly.

Marlak's hands move to my shoulders. "Cold?"

"A little."

He rubs my arms. "We'll land soon."

Soon is not that soon, as we keep flying in this dark night, under a trail of stars and above so many forests, down to a wide river near a village, from where I see a cluster of lights.

We indeed land at the riverbank and dismount. Marlak holds my hand again, and I can see that he's attentive, careful. This is not a safe place. We reach the outskirts of the village, where there are some five wooden row boats on the bank.

He gestures for me to sit on one boat.

"We're stealing a boat?" I whisper.

"*I'm* stealing. Don't take thieving credit when you shouldn't."

I sit on the boat, then he pushes it to the river, jumps in it, and it starts to move.

"Lie down," he whispers. "And silence."

I bet he wants to cross the village undetected, as if this was a boat taken by the river current.

He leans down beside me, speeding up my heart as I hear his breath so close, as I sense his warmth. Like that, we float by the village. All I hear is my own heart, the water, the wind on trees, and his not-so-steady breath. His dark eyes are focused on me, his expression inscrutable.

When I start to think I'm going to spend a week with a backache, he sits up and looks back. "We're safe."

I sit and stretch my arms. I would get up if I felt safe enough to do it, but I fear I could fall into the water. I'm still wearing the pretty multicolored dress, and at least the night is warm enough that without the wind, I don't feel cold.

The dress. I think about Lidiane. "I don't think anyone noticed what I was wearing."

He chuckles. "Oh, they sure did. I wouldn't worry about that." He stares at me. "What happened? With Crisine?"

Right. So this is the moment of truth. "She said she wanted to talk to me for just one minute, alone. That she wouldn't harm me. I thought she had something important to say."

He raises an eyebrow. "Did she?"

"Not really. She just wanted to tell me not to trust you, that you'd betray me."

"Did you believe her?" His voice is even lower pitched than usual.

"I think that was her truth, or how she sees things." I shrug. "She can't lie, right?"

"Do you think I'll betray you?"

"What's there to betray, husband?"

He tilts his head. "True. Where did she take you?"

"We were high up on a hill."

He shakes his head. "And she left you there."

"Like I said, two fae came, grabbed her, and she screamed."

"But you think she was pretending."

"I do."

"Then that's what it was."

"You're just going to take my word for that? What if I pushed her down that hill?"

He stares at me. "You wouldn't do that. And I know that you're telling the truth." He rubs his chin. "Now, I don't think she had anything to do with the Crystal Court fae who tried to take you... The death bees, maybe. It's just the beginning, Astra. Enemies surround me everywhere."

"Is she your enemy, though?"

"Her mother's dangerous. I don't trust either of them. You shouldn't have—"

"I know. I thought I was safe in the Court of Bees Castle."

Marlak fiddles with his rings and sets his eyes on me. "Is that how it's going to be? I won't be able to leave you for even ten minutes? You'll get into trouble?"

"Don't leave me, then." The words were meant to be a challenge, to tease him, to remind him that I'll be able to find out his secrets, but I don't think they came out that way. "I mean, do whatever you want."

His chuckle is soft and warms my heart. I need to tell that stupid organ to stop being such a Marlak fan.

He snorts. "If only. There's a gigantic gap between what I want and what I need."

"And you'll never tell me."

"There are things I can't. You know that."

All his mysteries. Maybe he can't really mention certain things, but it might be an excuse. Still, I don't want to confront him now. Not after everything. "The fae who tried to kidnap me, how did you know they were from the Crystal Court?"

Marlak shrugs. "Clothes, manners. And they have to be my brother's dogs." He rubs his eyes. "Speaking of dogs, what did Azur tell you?"

"That no torment lasts forever."

Marlak rolls his eyes. "Perhaps this was their way to try a gallant rescue."

Rescue. It makes sense. "Tarlia said my master hadn't given up on me."

"I know. I heard it, remember? But he can't go back on his word."

"The *king* can't go back on his word. My master..."

"True." He clenches his fist. "But he serves the king. And we had a deal."

"Perhaps they're willing to return whatever trinkets you gave them."

He huffs. "It doesn't work like that." He pauses then, his dark eyes on me. "Would you go back? If your master found a way?"

"I don't know." I swallow. I really don't know, or perhaps I don't want to confess I don't want to go. My own answer terrifies me, but I shrug. "Would there be a good reason? And I don't think it's possible. What's the point of dealing with improbabilities? Would you turn into a tree if presented with the possibility?"

He frowns. "Well, no. Who would do that?"

"Would you fly if someone offered you that magic?"

He's still frowning. "I would wonder about the cost first. Wife, there are answers for things."

Great. I'll ask *him* then. "Would *you* want me to leave?"

His eyes get wide and a little maniac. "That's not even a question. You think I gave away the Shadow Ring for you, just to see you go?"

Shadow Ring. The freaking Shadow Ring.

My breath leaves me. My thoughts and heart stop, then I blink. "You. What?"

24

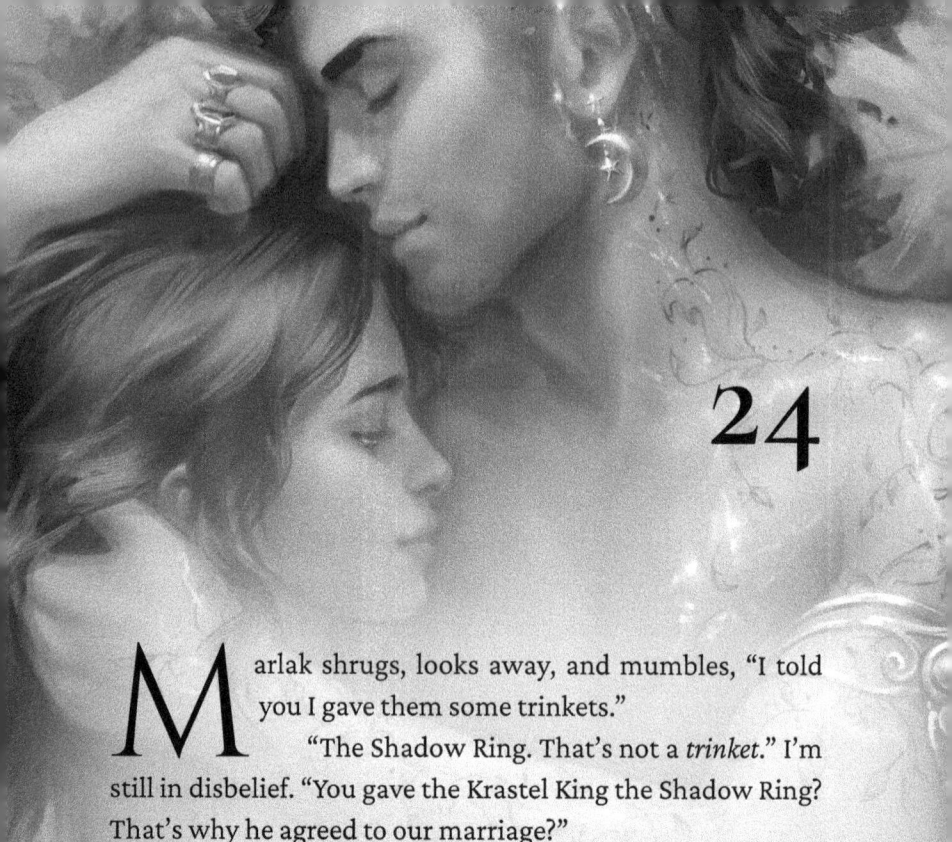

Marlak shrugs, looks away, and mumbles, "I told you I gave them some trinkets."

"The Shadow Ring. That's not a *trinket*." I'm still in disbelief. "You gave the Krastel King the Shadow Ring? That's why he agreed to our marriage?"

"I had to give them something. What did you expect?"

"You said I was traded like a cow, Marlak."

He raises a finger in the air. "A cow, not a chicken. Have you checked the price of a cow?"

I want to slap him, but instead, I clench my fists. "You told me you gave them some cheap trinkets, clearly implying I had no value, and you were lying."

He raises an eyebrow. "No. I said they traded you for cheap trinkets. You think a stupid ring is worth more than you?"

"It's the most powerful magical artifact in the world!"

"It's a trinket!" He yells.

I rub my face, still in disbelief. I can see now how they were so eager to have me sent off with him, why they entertained this mad idea in the first place. And now he doesn't have the ring anymore. "Can't it be used against you?"

He fiddles with his earring. "Humans don't know what it is, Astra. They wouldn't be able to wield it, and it's not like the Krastel King has some vendetta against me. Don't know if you noticed, but I have other magical artifacts."

I'm still unable to digest this revelation. The Shadow Ring? He gave the Shadow Ring to the Krastel King? I don't know what to think. I decide to forget it for now, and take a deep breath. "Where are we going?"

"There's an old fae who can peer into dreams."

Oh, ouch. Awkward. I grimace. "Peer into dreams? You want this person to see them?"

He laughs. "No. But she might help us solve our problem."

Yes, sexy dreams, what a horrific problem.

I wonder if he's hoping I'll tell him I love our dream sex, that in fact I love it so much we should try to make it real.

Haha. As if it wasn't partly true.

I want to disappear.

But there's something else I want to know. "How come you believed me? I told you I didn't create the dreams, and you believed me at once, when I'd been trying for days to tell you that."

He smirks. "There's a huge, huge difference. Before, you weren't trying to say you didn't create the dreams. You were lying to my face, saying you knew nothing about them. To my face, making me think I was insane." He rolls his eyes and changes his voice to a mocking tone. "*Oh, husband, maybe you should seek some treatment for your nightmares.*" He glares at me. "You know the worst part? I *believed* you. You're saying I didn't believe you, but I did. I started to think it was all in my head."

When he puts it like that, I feel a little bad, but at the same time... "What would you want me to do, Marlak? Say *hey, actually, I do dream about you.* Sexy dreams, in fact. You would mock me, you—"

"I would not."

Oh, how easily he forgets his words. "You called me unattractive, told me my attempts at seducing you were pathetic. I thought you would think I was trying to seduce you and then lash out at me."

He sighs and runs a hand over the burned side of his head. "I..." He pauses. "I didn't think you'd believe such crude lies, Astra. And I didn't think they'd hurt you. All I can say is I'm sorry." He looks up, thinking, then back at me. "Though it won't change much."

"It does. I also said things I regret." I squirm in shame when I recall calling him half roasted, especially after glimpsing his trauma. "I'm sorry."

He stares at me and I can hear my heart wanting to jump out of my chest, wanting to take over and get bigger than my entire body, and yet I can feel my stomach shrinking in fear of what might happen, of my own confused thoughts.

I have to change the subject. "Why didn't you go talk to this dream fae before?"

"As you can see, she lives far, also..." He raises one shoulder. "Is it that abnormal? To dream about someone I'm attracted to? I thought I was just very much interested in you."

Thought. "But you're not."

He waves both hands in the air. "How can I even know? How much is me, and how much are the dreams? And if you don't even want them... Who was it you kissed, wife? Was it me, or the man in your dreams?"

"Who did *you* kiss?" I snap back. I don't want to consider his question.

"I know very well who I kissed. And you know what? In my dreams you're much, much nicer."

"Oh, as if *you* were the same."

"I am!" He puts a hand on his chest. "It's me in the dreams, exactly the way I am. No difference."

"Of course not. The man in my dreams..." I was about to say, *loves me,* but I catch myself. "Is different." And then I recall something else. "It means that in the cave, when we first met, it was you."

He runs his hand over his hair. "That was different. That wasn't a dream. It was me, but..." He closes his eyes and sighs, then stares at me. "I wouldn't do it like that in our first time, but in the vision, it wasn't..." He frowns. "Do you really want to discuss this? How I would make love to you if it were real?"

The idea flashes through my mind. Before it muddles my brain with images of him undressing me on his boat, I say, "So you gave it some thought."

"Obviously. I spent my nights doing it. Who wouldn't think about it during the day?"

I swallow, surprised that he can be so candid about it. "It's not like you showed it."

"What would you want me to do?" His eyes widen. "Leer at you? Tell you all the thoughts crossing my mind? While you were staring at me like I was a monster?"

He can't be serious. "I wasn't staring at you like that."

"That's how it felt, and I didn't want to make you uncomfortable. Plus, I thought you were trying to seduce me, and didn't want you to think you were succeeding."

"I wasn't trying—"

"I know. Now I know. Then I didn't. I kept wondering if I was a hopeless fool caught in a trap I didn't even understand what for, or if my mind had just become sex-addled for some reason. Torment, Astra."

"You say it as if it was my fault."

"You could have told me, wife, told me it was happening to you too." I'm about to protest, when he says, "But I understand you were afraid. I can see I didn't help."

Perhaps I didn't help either, but then, the way he talks about it while keeping his distance, his composure, doesn't help me believe he was ever attracted to me. "You pretend well. I would never have guessed any of that."

"I'm telling you now. With my whole chest, Astra, because we can't fix something if we don't know what it is. And it's not as if I wasn't redirecting all that sexual energy."

"Redirecting?" With someone else. I feel as if there's a layer of ice under my skin, but try to pretend it doesn't bother me. "So you had lovers."

He frowns, then laughs. "Two, actually. The most wonderful and amazing lovers you'll ever find. They're fantastic, in fact."

It takes me a lot of effort to keep my face a mask, to keep my voice steady even though there's only emptiness inside me. I shrug. "Don't know why you were complaining, then."

He has a half smirk as he sets his eyes on me. "My loving time with them doesn't erase my thoughts about you, so there's that."

"That's gross."

He chuckles. "Are you jealous?" The delight in his tone makes me sick.

"Why should I be? And I don't know why you laugh at things that aren't funny."

"Actually, I think you *should* be jealous." He raises his hands in the air. "Let me introduce you to Righty. And Lefty, the roasted one."

Oh.

He's unbelievable. I slap his hands. "You're a crass asshole, did you know that?"

"Ouch. You *are* jealous." His laughter sounds relaxed and happy—but I'm still annoyed.

"Marlak. I don't care what you do with your hands."

And yet strangely, the image of his scarred, ringed hand moving up and down doesn't disgust me. If anything, I want to join his hands, feel him, then feel them caressing my body. Lefty and Righty. Agh. No.

He's looking at me as if he can see all these thoughts, then says, "I think you should care."

"We shouldn't be talking about this."

He tilts his head. "Maybe we should. I'm here being honest with you, and I have no idea how you... How these..." He makes a circle in the air with his hand. "... visions have been affecting you."

I take a deep breath. How honest does he want me to be? "I liked the dreams when I was dreaming them. They weren't unpleasant. But when I woke up, they felt awkward, especially when you were telling me I was pathetic."

"You make it seem like it was every day. I stopped, Astra."

"But once you made it crystal clear you'd never want me, did you have to repeat it?"

He chuckles. "The most ridiculous lie."

"So funny. You forget I didn't even know you could lie, husband."

"I wasn't laughing at you. I... find it puzzling." He rubs his chin.

"Hilarious. Here I was, with my captor—"

"Captor." He frowns. "Do you still see me like that?"

I see him in so many different ways now. I focus on one

fact. "I wasn't given a choice in our marriage." Then I add quickly, "But you're nice."

He rubs his hand on his face. "It was either me or Renel. He's prettier, sure, but he's cruel. I had no choice either."

"I don't think it would have been me."

"We've gone over this. I wasn't going to take the chance."

"I think it's going to be Tarlia. I'm worried about her."

He stares at me and bites his lip. "At least she knows what she's up against. I'm truly sorry you have to do that, sorry they force you..." He shuts his eyes. "I'm sorry, wife."

And it's not like Tarlia is willing to run away or anything. In fact, I think she wants this wedding, wants the opportunity to be in a position from where she might exert at least *some* power. Compared to none. She has such little choice, such little freedom. Not that I have much more than she does, and yet I feel I have more say with Marlak than I had at the tower. And in fact, there's something I need to tell him.

"Our dreams, they're not all bad." He raises an eyebrow, and I continue, "When you were poisoned—"

"Great." He points a finger at me. "So it *was* you. I asked you, asked you directly, and you denied it."

I huff and throw my hands in the air. He's impossible. "Are you going to keep repeating it? *You denied it, you denied it, you denied it.* Yes, I did. I already explained why. Now leave it."

He sighs. "It wasn't something to be ashamed of. You saved my life. Why would you deny it?"

"Because you'd think I was in love with you!" Oh. I need to remain quiet when I'm annoyed. I'm not sure what I confessed. My heart is punching me now.

He looks away, then down, and fiddles with his rings. "Oh, how horrific. I understand why you were terrified."

My heart is still all I hear. And I think he understood

something different than what I said. "Our shared dreams saved your life. So they can be useful."

"Astra, you said you didn't want those dreams. We'll get rid of them. If it's not my time to die, I won't die. I'll find another way."

"What about when I called you? When I was with Nelsin?" I'm not sure how to say it. "It might have been our connection."

"I'll find you, Astra. Wherever you are, I'll find you. I saw your light tonight. Even from afar, I knew it was you. I ran—and found you. We don't need the dreams."

I don't know how he can make such a romantic promise sound like he doesn't care for me, but he manages it. Marlak and his contradictions. And if I keep trying to read between his words, how much of it is him, and how much of it is what I want to see?

I nod, unsure of what to say. If I keep arguing, he'll think I'll want to keep having those dreams, or that I'm creating them on purpose, like he always suspected. He might even think it's some mischievous plan. Perhaps he's expecting me to tell him I love the dreams, but it's true that they also bother me. I don't like the awkwardness around them, that feeling that we're one couple when we dream and another when we're awake. The disconnect bothers me.

But what if he's right, and the dreams are an illusion confusing us? Confusing him? Do I need the dreams to feel what I felt tonight when kissing him? Perhaps there's only one way to know—by stopping them.

"Do you think it will work?" I ask.

"I hope so." He looks at me, then glances at the trees by the riverbank. "I'll improvise a bed for you. I think you'll be safe if I'm awake."

I'm not sure what he means. "Safe?"

"From the dreams." A current of wind brings some leaves to the back of the boat, and he points at it. "It's not great, but at least you can rest until we get to our destination."

It looks cozy enough for a nap. "What about you? Won't *you* get tired?"

"I can manage, wife. And I have to keep the boat going."

"I'm not..." I was going to say *tired*, but I'm stopped by an overwhelming desire to yawn, as if seeing the improvised bed made my body agree with his wish for me to sleep after all the overwhelming events of tonight. "Fine, maybe a little tired."

"You can just lie down and rest. You used a lot of magic."

He might be right. "I'll lie down. Thanks for the bed."

"You should be sleeping in a much better place. But I want to get there soon."

The leaves feel soft against my back as I watch the trail of stars above us. There's so much I haven't said, so much we should discuss, and yet my thoughts are drifting.

It's true that I used a lot of magic tonight, since the moment we walked into that coronation, when I shielded his mind from those horrific images—memories. Those images that revealed so much. I wish I could acknowledge how much seeing them changed my perception of him, but I don't know if I can breach the subject without poking at his open wound. And then there was so much more that happened. His words, our kisses... Tarlia telling me Otavio might still rescue me, Azur trying to provoke Marlak.

How could so much change in just one night?

A long night. And now that I'm here, lying down, I wish we hadn't stopped kissing, wish I could tell him that the dreams are all right, that they are part of our truth, but then he'll start thinking this is a ploy to seduce him or whatever scheming he believes I'm capable of. Perhaps it's better to get rid of the dreams, and then we'll look each other in the eye and know what we really think.

And if Otavio comes for me, what am I going to do? What am I going to say?

The leaves are soft, the movement of the boat is soothing, and perhaps I don't need to think about any of that just yet.

Dry leaves, dirt, and glass shards cover the floor, while wind keeps blowing through the broken windows.

Our palace—destroyed. There are no lightstones, no lanterns, just a glimmer of light from the stars outside, and yet I know he's not here. I know it. They took him. There's a hollow, cold chamber where my heart should be, and a bitter boulder lodged in my stomach, its horrid taste spreading to my entire body.

"Marlak!"

I don't know why I yell when I'm certain the worst has already happened, why I hope. Yelling might put me in even more danger, but if his captors find me, at least it's a clue.

"Marlak!" I yell again, more desperate than ever.

I don't know how long they'll keep him alive and where they took him.

"Marlak!" I'm just hoping for some miracle, some light perhaps.

I think back to our connection—but all I find is emptiness, darkness.

"Marlak!" My voice is hoarse and my hope is thin, but I'll have to find a way.

I feel a hand on my shoulder and push it off, but it holds me again, and now there are two hands shaking me. I want to fight, but I'm too weak. All I do is open my eyes.

Marlak is crouched in front of me, frowning in what seems to be worry, surrounded by a pink sky. "You were having—"

He looks so stunning and I'm so happy to see him that I wrap my arms around him, relieved to feel how he's real, solid. How *this* is real.

"—a bad dream," he finishes, then moves his arms slowly, until he's also holding me tight.

I lean into the embrace, and yet I can't shake the feeling of the dream, the terror I felt. "You were gone. Something terrible happened."

"I'm here," he says in my ear. "It was just a nightmare."

My heart is so loud that I wonder if he can feel it against his chest.

He caresses my hair and repeats, "I'm here."

All I can do is hold him tight, let him envelop me with his comforting presence, and his warm, gentle embrace.

He kisses my temple, then says, "I'm here, azalee, and I won't let you go."

I exhale, all my panic gone. Still holding him, I ask, "Why do you use a Tiurian word?"

He breaks the embrace to look at me. "Oh. You mean... Why not? Aramids uses it in some of his poetry. Mostly, to be very honest, it was dream me who said it." The corner of his mouth lifts. "Was it why you wanted a dictionary?"

"Hmm. Yes." Sure, it's embarrassing, but I'm not going to come up with a stupid lie now. "I wanted to understand why you were calling me that."

He chuckles. "It's just *wife*."

"In a forbidden language."

He tilts his head. "Why? Do you think Tiurian words will make things manifest or something? You're my wife already, like it or not."

"No, I... Like I said, it's forbidden."

The amusement vanishes from his face, and he says slowly, "This is not Krastel, Astra."

"I know. Where exactly are we, by the way?"

He pauses. "This is the Wild Forest. We're already in the Shadow Lands, but still close to the Dark Court."

Shadow Lands—where no court rules. "Doesn't sound safe."

"We'll be brief." His jaw is tight.

I can see that he's tenser than usual, perhaps more alert.

"I guess... we're getting there?"

His eyes are distant, his expression thoughtful. "Yes." He then turns and looks back. "I got our suitcase."

I see it lying in the boat behind him and smile. "You know, you could have summoned it in front of me. It's not like it's a secret or something."

"It doesn't work like that. But it means you can change now."

Indeed. I'm still wearing the multi-leaves dress, and I'm glad Lidiane's such an amazing dressmaker that all the sewing doesn't prickle.

The boat slows down, and for the first time, I realize Marlak has been using his magic to move it. What was I thinking? That it was the current? I was definitely tired.

He turns, opens the suitcase, then beckons me. "Put aside what you want to wear. I'll turn around, and you can jump in the water. The river's shallow up here and your feet will touch the bottom."

I could tease him and tell him he'd seen me naked innumerable times, but then I fear he'll get grumpy. Plus, I'm glad to have the space to freshen up. Then I recall something. "Aren't there nymphs here?"

He chuckles. "Not right here, no. Their magic protects us,

but they won't come to see you naked, Astra. There's nothing to fear."

"I was just wondering," I say as I search for the first hook on my back.

He chuckles and turns around. "If something scares you, yell."

"I will."

It's a little difficult to reach behind me and open my dress, but I manage it, and get rid of my clothes and the underwear, so that I'm standing here naked. Naked on a small boat with Marlak. What would happen if I breached the distance between us and touched him?

Well, he'd probably complain. With that thought, I jump in the river. The water isn't that cold, but it helps to waken me. My feet soon reach the sandy bottom, and I'm glad to have footing. Do I have footing in my life?

What happens if I decide I'm no longer a Krastel elite guard, that I'm no longer loyal to Otavio and the Krastel King? Do I even have any shred of loyalty left for them? At least I don't need to think about that now.

I pull myself up, back to the boat, then feel a current of air around me, making me shiver for some seconds, until I'm dry. Marlak's magic sometimes is impressive.

I smile. "Thanks."

"Not a problem," he says, still turned around.

I put on leggings and a loose shirt, then say, "I'm ready."

Marlak turns. I realize he has changed his clothes as well, and is now wearing a dark navy shirt. I'm surprised he's wearing any color other than black, wondering if perhaps he's run out of clean black shirts.

"Great," he says, and the boat moves even closer to the sandy bank of the river. He passes me Dusklight and its scabbard. "Take your sword. We can walk from here."

I strap the sword to my back, hold my boots and socks, and take a wide jump, so that my leggings don't get wet, but then my feet sink in the sand.

Marlak lands in front of me, displaying his control of air magic. I wonder if I could do something like that if I trained, if I got another taste of his blood. I don't know why I'm thinking about it.

"Let's go," he says, then gives me some bread. "We'll see her first, then we can go to a village near here and have an early lunch. You must be starving."

I nod. The bread is stiff and rubbery, but I eat it. Oh, how I miss Nelsin's and Ferer's food. I want to slap my past self who was disappointed because they never served anything hot. At least it was delicious.

I swallow the last piece and ask, "Who's *she*?"

"An old... creature. Not a fae."

"Does she have a name?"

"Some call her *the nameless*."

I chuckle. "Eerie."

"Wait till you see her."

"Is this meant to be encouraging? Or do you want me to beg you to turn around and just ignore the dreams?"

He snorts. "Please. You've faced death bees and blood-puppets. You've faced *me* without a hint of fear."

"Oh, you're a monster now?"

Tilting his head, he runs a hand through his curls. "Excessive magic can be frightening. For most people."

"You don't scare me."

"I know." He stares at me, something intense stirring in his eyes. "And the nameless won't scare you either."

The trees in this forest have wide trunks draped in vines and other foliage, while the ground is covered in roots, moss, and shrubs, making it hard to walk through.

Marlak steps in front of me and reaches out his hand, which I take. It feels natural, not strange to hold hands with him, and I feel a wave of comfort moving up my arm.

We walk in line like that for a long time, the only sound our feet moving between leaves, birds chirping and warbling above us, and something else, like a powerful hum coming from the forest; its breath and life.

After some time, we reach a clearing with an old stone well in its middle. I'm dreading having to go down in it, but all he does is sit on its stone wall and put a finger on his lips. I sit beside him, missing having our hands connected, wondering if this nameless creature is really going to break our connection.

As much as I'm already missing the dreams, perhaps getting rid of them will help me understand my feelings. My feelings. All I know is that I want to reach out and hold his hand again.

Then I recall my recent nightmare and the terror I felt, the feeling that something was wrong.

Perhaps we shouldn't be here.

I'm about to suggest we turn back when a strong gust of wind hits my face. It's magic, but feels foreign, strange.

I guess we'll find out if being here is a mistake.

25

I'm still sitting beside Marlak, on the well wall, still in the middle of this strange forest, but something has changed. The leaves are bluish and the sky is darker, even though the sun is in the same position. As to the ground, there's a black void around us.

I take Marlak's hand, too scared to worry about his reaction or opinion. To my surprise, he squeezes my fingers in a comforting gesture.

Then everything is the same as before. Same colors, earth and plants beneath our feet, normal light, but there's a woman in front of us.

She's wearing a dark gray hood covering her hair, and looks human—or fae. I'm not sure about her ears. With light hazel, almost yellow eyes, and a painted flower on her forehead, she looks like some kind of priestess of an ancient creed, bearing long forgotten stories, even though she doesn't look old. I'll need to ask Marlak how he knows her.

The Nameless glances at our interconnected fingers, in what I feel is a judgemental stare, and I let go of his hand. She then smirks and says, "So you summoned me."

Her voice doesn't sound magical or formal, but rather conversational, even somewhat annoyed.

"I wouldn't be so bold," Marlak says in that low, comforting tone I know so well. "But I was hoping we could meet you. For some advice."

Her stare is eerie and disconcerting. "Hmm, so there's something afflicting you."

"Yes," he says. "We—"

"No," the woman interrupts him. "I want to hear it from *her*." She has a smile that I feel is mocking me.

They both turn to me, and I sigh. "I wouldn't call it *an affliction*, but we have the same dreams."

Her face changes, and now she frowns, looking concerned. "Oh. Are those horrific dreams? Terrifying nightmares?"

I'm about to answer, but Marlak's faster. "They are fine dreams, but unwanted. We've also shared visions, when I tried to get into her mind. Unwanted as well. And therein lies the problem."

The woman narrows her eyes. "So you tried to see her mind, saw her thoughts—"

"No," Marlak says. "She didn't create those thoughts."

I feel heat rising to my cheeks.

"Hmmm." The Nameless still has that concerned tone. "Where did they come from, then?"

Marlak shakes his head. "I do not know."

The woman turns to me. "Do you have any idea?"

"If I had, would I be here?"

She stares at me. "Wouldn't you?"

I want to slap her, which I'm pretty sure is ill-advised.

"Lady," Marlak says. "We wish to stop these shared dreams, that's all. If you can help us understand how they came to be, it might be helpful, but for now, we just wish to stop them."

She still stares at me. "Do *you* want to stop them?"

Why is she putting me on the spot? "Well, they're awkward," I say.

"Awkward." The woman paces back and forth. "And what's in those dreams? Is that something unpleasant?" At least she asked both of us.

"That's not the point," Marlak says, his voice rising. "If my wife doesn't want them, I don't want them."

She stares at him. "Shared dreams are proof of a powerful connection, young king. You cut that connection, you cut a part of you, you cut your power. It's not advisable. Instead of making this journey here, to speak to me, you should rather look into your own hearts."

"I know my heart!" he says. "And I don't want her to have unwanted dreams."

"But that's like cutting a part of you. Would you cut a finger for her?"

He raises his hand, showing his pinkie. "This? For her? That's not even a question. I wouldn't think twice."

I feel my heart beating faster.

She turns to me. "Would you—"

"Cut a finger for him? If I was sure it helped, of course. If it was an arm or something, I'd try to see if there was any other way."

She laughs. "This wasn't my question. I wanted to know if you'd be happy if the dreams stopped."

"How can I know?"

Her stare cuts right through me. "Let me see if I get this straight. Both of you would go to great lengths for each other, and yet you want your connection broken. Is that so?"

"I just want the unwanted dreams to stop," he says. "That's all. And if you know if there's any malicious intent or mind magic behind them, it would be helpful to let us know."

"Your mind magic helps you connect to each other, prince." Funny that she calls him both king and prince. "Other than that, all that you're seeing are your combined desires. There's no malice, no magic, nobody trying to manipulate anyone."

I exhale and sit up straight as I realize he came here to learn whether this was part of some plan. At least he got his answer.

The woman now turns to me. "Are the dreams unwanted?"

"I've said it before; they're awkward."

"Awkward is not the same as unwanted. Don't you know how the dreams came to be?"

For a second, I'm back at the tower, lighting a candle, asking the Almighty Mother to connect me to my kindred soul. I *asked* for this connection. I wanted it. But not like this, when we're one way when sleeping and another way awake, when I have to feel ashamed of my own dreams, when he can peer into my desires. *My desires.*

"No answer?" The woman smiles.

Marlak stands partly in front of me. "You're embarrassing my wife, and I'll ask you to stop."

"Your wife." The Nameless laughs. "The one you'd definitely never have dreams about. The one you don't think about day and night."

"What if I do?" His tone is flippant, but I notice he's shaking. "It doesn't mean I want her to share my dreams."

"Don't you want her to share your bed?"

"What if I do?" he asks.

"Then invite her like a grown man."

He clenches his fists. "It doesn't mean she needs to have unwanted dreams."

The woman shrugs. "Well, then you never had a problem to begin with. None of the dreams are unwanted, none of the visions are unwanted. Like it or not, you both created them. Perhaps you were not aware of what you did, but you did it. Now deal with it."

"So that's your answer," Marlak says.

"The truth can be uncomfortable sometimes." She stares at me. "And awkward, quite frequently. There's no reason to evade it. But the truth will help you." She turns to him. "Sometimes only darkness reveals light. Don't lose hope. There's protection for you. I'll go now." She turns to me. "Trust your power."

With that, she disappears. Only then the forest comes alive with sounds of birds and leaves in the wind.

Marlak turns to me. "She's been more helpful before."

I'm glad for the opportunity not to discuss what the woman just said. "When did you come? Was it the Nymphs who told you about her?"

He nods. "Yes, it was them. But I can't tell you what she helped me with."

"Part of your big secrets."

"Unfortunately, yes." There are shadows in his eyes. "And I'm sorry. I thought..." He looks away and shakes his head, then reaches out and holds my hand. "Let's go to the village. There's a place where we can eat. We'll need to be quiet in the forest."

Like that, we walk away, hand in hand, with so many unsaid words between us, so many unsaid truths. I feel that the only truth lies in our connected hands, but what truth is it? And where will it take us?

Our hands are clenched together as we walk by the riverbank towards a group of wooden houses with hay roofs, the wall of silence between us still standing.

It's no longer the silence of the forest. For me, it's the silence of not knowing what to say, or maybe just trying to process all that happened. He wouldn't think twice before cutting a finger for me, and yet, he won't say what it means. We're holding hands, and yet, we won't talk about it.

Dusklight is secured on my back, the sword he gave me. I have to force myself to remember that it's a replica, not the real thing. Not everything is what it seems.

The river curves inward, and once we walk by that curve, I see a small wooden pier and a stone path leading into the forest. We take the path and reach a clearing with five houses forming a semicircle. I'm assuming this is the heart of this tiny village, and yet all the windows and doors are closed and there's nobody in sight.

Marlak turns to me. "I think we're early."

It must be eight already, but then, if it's a fae village, they're probably fast asleep. It only reminds me that Marlak has been awake for more than a day now. "Aren't you tired?"

He stares at me, then takes a deep breath. "If you want to know if I need to sleep, not yet. If you want to know if I'm tired... Yes, I'm tired, wife. Tired of running, tired of chasing false trails, tired of hiding. But I can be tired and still keep going. Are *you* tired of this life?"

That's a weird question. "We just started. How can I be tired?"

He chuckles, then pulls my hand and kisses it. "Tired of my secrets, maybe. It won't be like this forever."

A door opens behind him, screeching as it moves, and an old fae with deep blue skin comes out of a house.

"What are you doing here?" he asks, his voice raspy, accompanied by a deep frown.

Marlak turns to him. "Sterin. I was hoping to see you."

The fae glares as if he's planning the most painful way to murder us. "Now?"

Beside me, Marlak is relaxed and smiles. "Yes. This is my wife, and she wanted to taste some of your delicious—"

"Come in, come in," the fae beckons.

I would describe his tone as somewhere between extremely annoyed and absolutely furious, but I don't think Marlak would bring me to a psychopath's house. Inside, there's a small wooden table for two people in a corner, and a counter with three high stools separating us from the kitchen.

Marlak gestures for me to sit at the table.

Sterin stares at us, then yells, "Fish stew. And grape juice." He grins, showing pointy teeth. "Too early for wine, huh?"

Marlak inclines his head. "True."

The fae goes behind the counter as I watch him, still a little stunned that we just came to the smallest tavern in the world, where it seems that the owner is the one who chooses what we eat.

That said, fish stew is a great idea. I turn to Marlak and smile. "Well, I *was* getting tired of bread."

"And I was starving."

Our eyes meet, and I feel the pull of the unsaid words, of those thoughts I've been pushing down for so long.

He takes my hand and runs a finger on its palm in a gentle, circular motion. "I'm sorry she wasn't more helpful."

He means the Nameless. "At least now you know I'm

not... Not trying to..." I don't know why I'm stumped for words. "Manipulate you."

His lips form a line, and he raises his eyes from my hand to my face. "I... Can you blame me?"

I don't know if I have an answer, if his assumptions were fair, but if he didn't think I was trying to seduce him, what else would he think?

The truth, my own voice whispers to me.

What truth? I want to ask myself.

He interrupts my thoughts. "And we'll find another solution."

"For the dreams?" I'm surprised he's still considering it, and try to pull my hand, but he holds it.

"For everything."

The blue fae then comes from behind the counter, holding a tray with the three largest bowls I've ever seen. He puts a bowl of fish stew in front of each of us, and one with toasted manioc flour in the middle of the small table. He then returns to the counter and brings us cups and spoons.

"No talking while eating," he rasps.

I'm pretty sure that if anyone values their life, they'd better do what he asks. This has to be the smallest tavern with the worst service in the world. But then, I'm so glad to finally eat some hot food that I'm about to forgive it all.

I take a spoon of the broth, just to taste it. Oh, wow. It's warm, comforting, sustaining. It's like tasting a family history passed down through seasoning. The food in the castle was never bad, but it was made in a huge kitchen. This, this is art.

I let myself be taken by the contrast of the dry flour and the broth, the softness of the fish flesh on my tongue, the taste filling my mouth, then warmth reaching my stomach. It's satisfying and fills a void I didn't know was there. I wonder how many unknown voids we have, hiding and waiting until we realize they exist. Voids.

I glance at Marlak, eating calmly. I think he also likes hot food, and maybe we could figure out a way to have a stove on the island and perhaps light it when he's not home.

Home. A different warmth fills my stomach.

It's no longer the castle; it's the island. Perhaps I don't need to wonder who I'm loyal to. But can I really trust Marlak, with all his secrets?

He finishes eating after me, then gives the grumpy fae some strange copper coins, and we leave the little house, back to that silent heart of a remote village.

His hand reaches for mine, and I take it, even though I know it says so much more than what I've allowed myself to say.

When my fingers reach his, I feel an energy moving from his hand to mine, and then I see a huge chamber, like a palace or temple, with columns decorated with sculptures of snakes and other animals, and a shallow water pool in the middle.

I turn to him. "Did you send me a thought?"

He widens his eyes and looks paler than usual. "What kind of thought?"

"A large chamber. Underground, I think. Not sure why. With huge columns."

His chest moves down in a long exhale. I'm afraid to imagine what he was thinking I'd seen.

He hesitates and bites his lip. "There is a place, but..." He frowns. "I can't send thoughts like that, and I wasn't even thinking about it." He looks at me, glances into the forest, then back at the river, and takes a deep breath. "That said, I *am* looking for something." He chuckles. "A few somethings."

He swallows and turns to me. "It's why I spent some days away. I guess you know that."

I remember then my dream when he was poisoned and he was in an underground chamber like that, but that one was different, longer and wider, with different columns. So there are many of those places, and we're near one of them.

Astra. A voice calls me, compels me, a voice coming from the forest, inviting me to a place where there's power and magic and wonder. Magical voices are dangerous, and yet there's something familiar about this one.

"Astra?" Marlak's deep voice startles me. His gaze is intense. "You want to see the sanctuary?"

"Sanctuary?"

"The place you saw—in my mind."

"I didn't know what it was."

"It's a Tiurian sanctuary."

I freeze. "They had sanctuaries? All the way here? I thought they lived mostly in the Krastel area."

"There are Tiurian remnants all over the continent, and one here."

"Can I see it?" I know it's foolish, but it's a piece of my past, my people. Perhaps they did horrible things, but still... To step foot in a place like that would be magical.

He stares at me and smiles. "Come. Come learn some of my secrets. I guess you deserve that. Silence in the forest, though."

With our fingers entwined, he pulls me away from those houses, away from the river, towards a mysterious place where I might find a hint about my past—the past I've never tried to face.

A CURSED SON

THE RUSTLE of leaves and twigs cracking under my feet compete with my anxious heart as we walk in a thin trail in the forest.

What does a Tiurian sanctuary entail? Master Andrezza would certainly tell me it's a place where evil beings commune with evil spirits, and for years I let those words enter my ears and pass through my head without any filter, fearing the pain in recognizing the truth, or perhaps the danger in challenging those words. Of course, an old, abandoned sanctuary won't give me any answers. It won't tell me if they drank blood or murdered children.

Astra. I hear that voice again—and sense no malice in it. But I could be wrong. Then again, if Marlak has been to many Tiurian sanctuaries before, and if he's taking me to one, it's probably safe. The weight of Dusklight comforts me for some reason, even though I can't yet fight with it properly.

The truth is that Marlak's presence also calms me, not only because he can defeat most threats. I guess being with him makes me feel at ease, comfortable; it gives me the courage to peer into this window into my people's past.

My people. I feel a shiver down my spine. I don't know if it's fear, anticipation, or something awakening.

Or maybe I'm being silly, making such a fuss for what is probably just some abandoned ruins. Abandoned Tiurian ruins—which I never even knew existed.

And yet I still feel that voice calling me.

We're deep in the trail, surrounded by thick vegetation, when Marlak stops and crouches, then touches the ground near the roots of an enormous fig tree.

I crouch beside him and whisper, "Looking for the sanctuary?"

He nods. "I need to find the markings."

I think I know where the sanctuary is, except that I might

be mistaken, and then perhaps I'll reveal more than I should. Well, it's time to stop hiding things. "I think I know where it is." He stares at me, his eyes wide, and I add, "I feel it calling me."

"Where?"

I sense it further down, near the trail, and point in that direction.

He gets up. "Guide me, then."

We walk some more steps, and then I understand his confusion, as we're by another fig tree, this one gigantic. The place calling me is near the trail, but further down, buried amongst the exuberant vegetation.

Marlak points in the exact direction I feel calling me. "There?"

I nod, even if I'm still unsure why I can find it. He walks ahead of me, in a thin, almost imperceptible trail, enough that we can move amongst such thick vegetation, in a forest so dense I fear it could swallow us if it wanted.

We come to a huge stone, standing out against the forest around it. I feel that this is the place, and yet I don't know how a sanctuary can be here. Right as I think that, Marlak closes his eyes, as if concentrating, and then the stone detaches from the ground and floats, revealing a thin staircase underneath it.

"Go ahead," he says.

I try to do it as soon as possible, fearing that the stone could fall over us. I wonder what magic he's using, since I can't sense any wind or strong air current. Marlak descends after me, then I hear a loud thud, and we're immersed in darkness.

"Keep going," he whispers, then ignites a lightstone behind me.

I descend slowly, stepping on my elongated shadow on

the narrow stone stairs, until I find myself in an underground chamber. The bluish light illuminates the exact same place I saw earlier, the place I must have glimpsed in his thoughts, the place that called me.

It's odd how Marlak's tiny light can illuminate so much of the sanctuary. Everything is more vivid than I imagined, the columns thicker, the ceiling higher, all made of some granite or other stone. On the ceiling there are many huge, long crystals forming a strange circular structure.

There's a dais or stage in the front, and several niches on the sides, covered with something soft, like cushions, reminding me a little of the Court of Bees castle, with those beds in nooks. I'm still not sure what kind of place this was or what they did here, even though it feels familiar.

Marlak stands beside me and asks, "How did you know it was here?" He's no longer whispering, and I'm surprised his voice doesn't echo.

I turn to look at his face, even more striking in the bluish light.

"I... truly don't know. A hunch. I'm surprised, too."

He stares at me. "You need to develop your magic, Astra. Whatever it is that made you sense this place, it might be useful. You don't know when you might need it."

"Do you have any tips? On how I should develop it?" It's a sincere question.

"You start by identifying your magic slowly, noticing when it happens, what causes it. You feel it first, then you can try to replicate it on purpose."

I dread even the idea of accepting that I have magic, but perhaps he has a point. "I'll pay more attention. And you? How do you know about this sanctuary?"

He shows me his right hand. "One of my rings can help me locate... beacon stones. And where they were made."

I look around me. "Beacon stones? Here?"

"Well, Tiurians made them. You can always find one or two in their ruins."

That doesn't make sense. "I thought..." What did I think? Nothing, actually. "I didn't know about the origins of the beacon stones."

"What did your Krastel teachers tell you?" His chuckle is warm and comforting, even though I know he's making fun of me. "That they came to be spontaneously?"

"No. Just that they're really old. It's why even inactive beacon stones are valuable, as they're considered relics of an ancient time. I guess they are."

"They're all Tiurian, wife, and only Tiurians can activate them. I'm guessing Krastel overlooked this little fact when they killed them all. Or else they didn't want more magical stones."

"Why haven't they told me that?" The question was more for myself, and yet I'm surprised I voiced it.

Marlak shrugs. "I guess thieves thieve. You can't steal something and keep claiming someone else made it." He sighs. "Sorry. I know Krastel's your kingdom."

In reality, I don't know anymore. "It's fine. I like to learn about the past."

"You should read the book I left you, then. I'm guessing you didn't touch it."

"It says the Tiurians created beacon stones?"

"And some more, yes. I thought you were interested in the fallen kingdom when you asked for the dictionary, but I realize now you just wanted to know what *azalee* meant."

I feel my heart pausing for a second. Part of it is wondering if he really doesn't know what I am, if he didn't notice I tasted his blood, and part of it thinking about the dreams. "Why are *you* interested in Tiurians?"

"Where do you think most of the Crystal Court relics come from? Krastelians aren't the only thieves out there. And Tiurian sanctuaries are great hideouts."

"We could live in one."

He nods. "Sometimes I spend time in them, but I prefer the nymphs' protection and the freedom of the outdoors."

"I meant in theory. I love the island house. Are we really going to have to leave it?"

He tilts his head, thoughtful. "For now, it's safe, so we could stay."

I wish I could kiss him, wish we didn't have this distance between us. Perhaps most of all, I wish I could have a place I could call home.

He gestures to one of the nooks. "Come. I want to show you something."

He approaches it, and with air magic, blows away the dust to reveal soft brown suede. Following his lead, I sit on this ancient sofa or bed, where many of my people might have rested, slept, sat, or maybe even made love. It's so much to take in.

Marlak pulls a strange dagger from his belt, with a black blade and three clear crystals on each side of its silver hilt.

"One of the relics," I mutter. By now, I should have gotten used to Marlak's magical artifacts, but the power emanating from this dagger still awes me.

"Yes. Obviously."

"You never carry it, though."

"Well, I believe you've noticed that I don't drag all the Crystal Court treasure with me everywhere."

"You don't have to. You could just…" I extend my hand, as if a relic could just land on it.

"Sort of. True." He chuckles, then looks down and takes a deep breath. "But this, it can cut through magic." Cut? I'm trying to understand what he means, when he adds, "Undo deals." His voice is heavy, solemn.

"Like what?"

"Deals can be quite complex, wife, and involve many stipulations. For instance, if the deal is important enough, quite often the parties are not allowed to mention it to anyone. Sometimes you can't even talk about the circumstances involving the deal."

"So you can't tell me."

"I didn't say that."

But he sort of did, except that I think he can't mention it.

He puts the dagger in my hands and shows me the encrusted crystals. "These are Tiurian stones." I'm surprised, and he notices and nods. "Yes. You'd call them beacon stones, I think, but they're more like opus stones. Without them, this is just a dagger. A stunning dagger, for sure, but it won't cut through magic. I need to either find a way to activate these stones, or find the original ones."

So he's trying to undo whatever deal he made, a deal that relates to what happened years ago, when his family died. It means he has been looking for beacon stones or some kind of magical solution to activate the stones he has. Beacon stones. A thought hits me.

"Was that why you attacked my carriage? Were you after that beacon stone?"

He sighs. "Put yourself in my shoes for a moment. You have these random visions of this Krastelian girl, and you don't understand why. One day, out of the blue, you see her in a carriage, staring at a chalice with a beacon stone, close to the Fae Shortcut. I mean, I thought it was a sign."

"I was right that you wanted the cup, then."

His brows rise. "You were. But that beacon stone could be a pebble for all the power it had."

"Then you thought maybe I'd have the secret for you to find your stones."

"I just wanted to understand why I kept seeing you in my mind. I thought... I don't know what I thought. I guess maybe yes, you could lead me to a stone, or maybe there was something else. I didn't know."

I take the dagger and look at it. "Was that really what you wanted? The explanation as to why you kept seeing me?" I turn to him, even though I feel heat rising to my face. "Did it ever cross your mind that you *saw* the explanation?"

"It was easier to believe you were manipulating me."

"So you decided to come and marry me? Like *wow, I think she's manipulating me. Let me step into her trap.*" I set the dagger between us.

He chuckles. "I was proactive. Trap you before I'm trapped."

"You think someone's controlling me?"

He fiddles with his rings as he looks at me. "You are—or were—loyal to your kingdom. Grew up in a sheltered environment, hearing only what they told you. I mean..." He shrugs. "And I saw you in some of your training. They teach you to seduce."

"*Try* to teach me. I'm not good at it."

"I'll have to disagree with you, Astra."

I can't suppress my laughter. "Oh, yes, I'm incredible."

"You are. And yet you're still your king's tool for... I don't even know for what, to be very honest."

"I'm nobody's tool. And I think the goal with the substitutes is an alliance, something that would improve my master's social position, while at the same time protecting the princess. It's dishonest and deceiving, but... You make it sound more insidious than it is." He's staring at me, and I realize he might think I'm defending Master Otavio, so I add,

"Not that what they're doing is right. But either way, you're not part of it. My master wanted to help me escape and commit treason rather than marry you, so he can't have been plotting to *trap you*. And the dreams weren't my fault. You heard the Nameless."

He's thoughtful, stroking his chin. "I did." He looks at me. "And I still wish you had been more honest with me from the start."

"We've gone over this, husband. And I'm being honest now. I'm just what you see. An orphan raised in Krastel. And you're right. I was raised to be used as a tool." The words rasp against my throat, an ugly truth I avoided facing for so many years. "But I was also taken care of: fed, clothed, protected. I love my sisters, and they're my sisters, even if not by blood."

"True."

"I don't love my masters, but I... have some respect for them. Still, I have my own mind."

He's so close to me, peering into my eyes. "And what's in that mind?"

"I'm still curious about you. I know you didn't kill your family, I—"

"Do you?" He raises an eyebrow.

"Not on purpose, at least. I know you want to kill your brother, though, and you might have made some kind of dangerous deal with him or someone else. But... where is that Amethyst Palace? And what's in that tower? The tower I saw you looking for in our dream? The dream that drove you running to Krastel, afraid I'd spill your secret."

His chest moves up and down slowly. "I don't know about that palace, Astra, and I also wonder what or where it is. And the tower... it's part of the things I can't talk about. I'm sorry."

"Where's the Pit of Death?"

He shakes his head. "I can't. Can't, Astra. Please never mention this to anyone."

"But you know where it is?"

"I..." He raises his hands and clenches his fists. "Have a theory. Please don't ask about it. Please."

I sigh. It's possible he can't say anything, but it's also possible he's hiding the truth. And there's something I need to know. "Is it truly dangerous?"

"I wouldn't take you there."

"I'm worried about *you*."

"Danger surrounds me everywhere, Astra. You'll have to get used to it."

"I won't. You'll have to avoid danger, Marlak."

He snaps his fingers. "Oh, yes, it's that easy."

"Make an effort."

"Trust me, I already do. Especially now, that there's also you to worry about."

"Apologies for inconveniencing you. Maybe you should have considered it before snatching me—"

"From the monsters who would exchange you for a trinket."

He has a point, even if I hate it. I shake my head. "I still can't believe you gave them the Shadow Ring."

"What would you do in my place?"

"Offer something else?"

"It would need to be something valuable. The Shadow Ring is legendary, meaning they would accept it, and it can only be worn by a fae, meaning that they can't use it. It was perfect. I don't know why you're upset about it."

"Not... upset." In my dream, I was furious, but that's not how I'm feeling. "Just... puzzled that you'd give away something so valuable, that's all."

"A strategic trade, Astra. You know, when I was a young teenager, having recently run away from home, the word going around was that I'd squander all the Crystal Court treasure. But I didn't. I kept it. Kept it from falling into the wrong hands. But when the moment came, I was able to trade part of it. I don't regret it. You're here."

My heart beats faster, sure that he considers me more valuable than the Shadow Ring itself, while my mind is searching for the trick, the lie, the catch. Well, indeed it wasn't for me, but to protect his secret about the tower and the Pit of Death, whatever that is.

I force a smile. "And your secrets are safe." Something else comes to mind. "I don't know how you didn't try to stop our dreams before, if you were afraid I would betray you."

He pauses and takes a deep breath. "I tried to find ways to block my mind. I did. Nothing worked, though. This time, with the Nameless, was my last resource. I thought if both of us wanted it... Didn't work either. I'm sorry. We can try to sleep at different times, maybe. That could help."

"The dreams aren't bad." He raises an eyebrow, as if surprised, but that doesn't stop me. "Not anymore. And dream Marlak is really nice."

He chuckles. "Unlike me, I suppose."

"You said it was you."

He fiddles with his rings. "Felt like me."

I realize now what I'm doing. I'm poking and searching, trying to get him to say he cares about me, hoping he'll open up and we'll no longer have to live two different lives when awake and asleep. I want to hold him like I do in my dreams.

I need to tell him, tell him everything. Tell him he's my kindred soul, tell him how much these dreams meant to me, before I met him. And yet the idea feels like jumping from a height when I don't know how far I am from the ground. To open myself like that... There's a chill all over my body, but there's also a fire burning deep down, yearning to come out. The truth. If I can make it brave my constricted throat, if I can trust that I won't be hurt, it will come out.

Trust the truth. Perhaps I should tell him part of it. I inhale, hoping there's courage in the air reaching my lungs. "The dreams, they had been going on since before I met you."

He pauses. "For me too, but you were... different. They started a year before."

"Then how come you thought I was manipulating you?"

"I thought you were transforming something in my own mind, or changing something that already existed. I wasn't sure. I couldn't see you clearly before, then I met you, and boom, it was you, had always been you. Apologies, but it felt... suspicious."

"I..." I want to tell him everything, but I'm afraid of what he'll think. Maybe I should say it. "I was sad, but then I learned this trick of faith to see my kindred soul, and burned a strand of hair on a candle, thinking about the strands connecting souls. Then the dreams started. All I saw was the star on your chest. Until I met you."

His breath hitches and his lips part. His eyes bare no accusation, no playfulness, just surprise.

I'd better say the whole truth while I'm at it. "It was *you* I kissed," I blurt. His eyes look even darker in the dim glow of his lightstone, and make my heart beat faster. "You," I continue, even though my throat is about to close. "The man who gave me my sword, who cared enough for me to make sure I was well clothed and fed. I mean..."

I swallow. Giving me a gift and clothing me isn't why I kissed him, and doesn't sound the least romantic.

"I kissed the man who worried about me, worried about my heart being broken—despite invading my thoughts."

This is also terrible. He's staring at me wide-eyed, perhaps thinking I'm a lunatic. I need to fix it. "The man who tried to encourage me to find my strength. The man who showed me his humanity and let me reach out to him in his most vulnerable moment." Maybe I need to simplify it. "I kissed *you*. Do I need a reason?"

He's just staring at me in silence. I fear he'll brush me off or tell me I'm pathetic. Maybe he'll burst out laughing.

Finally, he takes my hand, then strokes my palm in a circular motion. Perhaps he'll tell me nicely that my feelings are appreciated, but not returned.

He says, "I don't know if a reason is needed, but you do excel in asking for mine, wife." He chuckles. "You keep asking me why I married you, why I traded the Shadow Ring for you. Oh, the Shadow Ring, why?"

I pull my hand. "Great. Mock me."

"I'm not mocking." He takes my hand again, brings it to his lips, and kisses it. "Fine, maybe I was." He pinches my nose, then whispers in my ear, "You're my wife, Astra. You don't need any reason to kiss me. All you need is to tell me that this is what you really want."

The low rumble of his voice brings shivers all over my body, and yet my mind doesn't love his words. "You still think I'm trying to manipulate you?"

"No. Just that you might still be confused, afraid, uncertain..." He looks up and down my face slowly. "I wish everything was different, wish we had all the time in the world. I would have courted you—if I could. I agree you were snatched from your castle. While I can tell myself it was justified, it doesn't wipe away the fear you must have felt. I'm... not sorry. I can't say that. I'll never say that. But I want you to be comfortable, happy." He closes his eyes and inhales, then looks at me again. "Despite all the danger following me. The danger that will follow you too."

I touch his soft, wonderful hair, bury my fingers in his lovely curls. "Danger is a paltry price, Marlak. And if I'm in danger already, what difference does it make if we—" I swallow. Kiss? Make love? Become a real couple? Why do I still struggle with words?

His face is so close, his lips just a breath away, as if inviting me. Perhaps words just complicate everything.

I reach out and kiss his lips, and then he's holding my face with his hands and kissing me deeper, his soft lips pressing into mine. It's a freeing kiss, tearing down the dam that kept my feelings restrained for so long. Too long.

26

I caress his hair with one hand, his chest with the other, that lovely chest where I rested my head so often.

He breaks the kiss, still holding my face, so much care and love in his stare.

"Be my wife, Astra. Be my wife in earnest."

A happy laughter escapes me. "Make me. Make me your wife."

He chuckles and kisses my temple. "I have to redeem myself. The worst part of these visions and dreams is that you must be thinking I'm some kind of deranged animal who doesn't know how to make love."

I laugh again. "That's not true, and you know it. And I don't mind..." I swallow. "... the deranged animal."

He chuckles and kisses my cheek. "Fair. But we'll do it right. First, I'll kiss you a million times, hold you tight in my arms, shower you with loving touches. We'll take a week to get there."

I'll die if I have to wait a week. He might be joking, but I'm not sure. I pinch his arm. "It's not a performance, you know? And you won't be graded. There's no beginning or end. Just now. And us here, apart from the rest of the world. Does anything else matter?"

He caresses my face. "Not right now, no. Tell me, Astra. Tell me you're my wife in earnest."

"What about you?"

"I've been your husband from the day we got married, in case you didn't notice."

That doesn't make any sense. "Kind of hard to notice when you kept telling me I was unattractive."

He shakes his head. "You'll never forgive me, will you?"

"I just want to understand!" And it's true.

He sighs. "I thought you were pretending and wanted you to stop it, but it was a lie, Astra. A clumsy, absurd lie. But I'm sure you weren't lying when you told me I was *half roasted*."

Ouch. The memory still makes me cringe. "If it helps, I regretted saying it immediately. I regret it even more now."

He runs a finger over the left side of his head, over the scars, and shrugs. "Truth is truth. Not saying what you think won't change what happened or the way I look."

I pull his scarred hand and kiss it. "You're beautiful."

"I'm glad there are still people with odd taste in this world."

"Why do you have to be silly right now?"

"Not silly. Tell me you're my wife, Astra," he insists.

I sigh, but then smile and look into his mesmerizing dark eyes. "I promise to honor and protect you, love and appreciate you, cherish and respect you." I can feel the power in the words, the energy in them, and our bond getting stronger.

He holds my face again. "From now until forever, we're bonded in light. I'll do everything I can to keep you safe, wife." He leans closer and whispers in my ear. "Do you still hate that word?"

A warm, pleasant shiver runs down my spine, and I can swear he's using some air magic. I whisper, "No."

He unhooks my scabbard and pushes Dusklight aside, then wraps his arms around me and holds me tight, just like in the dreams. I want to feel the skin on his chest, touch him, so I push up his shirt. He pulls it above his head and tosses it to the ground. In front of me is the chest I've seen so many times, the star that comforted me for so many nights. I run my finger softly over his scars, where the skin feels thinner, smoother and hairless, with a few bumps.

"Your scars are brilliant in my dreams," I tell him.

He looks at his hand and chuckles. "In real life it's just ugly, stretched skin."

"There's nothing ugly about you. And it was your choice not to glamour or cover up your scars, wasn't it?"

He huffs. "What's the point of hiding the outer scars, when the inner ones are so much deeper? It's who I am."

"I like who you are."

"I thought you preferred the dream Marlak."

"You said it was you! And I'd rather have you here, real and solid, even if imperfect, than those intangible dreams. I mean, ideally I'd like to have both, without the confusion of awakening in a different reality."

He moves a lock of my hair away from my face, then kisses my forehead and holds me tight, then says, "I like this reality."

I run my hand over his star, that beautiful star, even if it's a sign of all the unbearable pain he's gone through. I kiss it, then kiss his stomach. With every kiss, his breath gets more ragged.

He's still wearing the belt from where his dagger hung. I

think I want to open it, undress him, but then he lifts me and lies me on the cushioned platform. It's his turn to kiss my neck, my collarbone, then, slowly, one by one, undo the buttons of my blouse, and push it down my shoulders and off my arms. His eyes are dark, reflecting the glow of the lightstone. I could swear there's a light dancing in his eyes, a light between us.

His fingers brush my skin softly, something about that touch making me shiver and warming me at the same time. Such a lovely touch over my stomach, above my breasts. I close my eyes, delighting in the sensation of such a simple touch, and whisper, "Make me your wife, Marlak. Now. I'm not going to wait a week."

The rumble of his laughter caresses my entire body, and then he plants a kiss on my collarbone. "You've always been my wife."

I have to laugh too, perhaps laugh at my previous folly, at all the time I avoided facing my own feelings. It's so much easier to surrender to them, to let my heart take the reins.

He lowers my breastband and I feel the wet touch of his tongue on my nipple. My breath hitches and my back arches, while I feel a pool of warmth in my core. He undoes my breastband, and then kisses my body slowly.

Power ripples from each of his kisses as he opens and lowers my trousers then kisses my inner thigh, something wonderfully magical about his soft lips and the tips of his lovely hair on my skin.

Slowly, he undresses me, until I'm only wearing my undergarment. He runs his hands over it, then, slowly, touches under it, his rings grazing the skin near my slit, teasing me. I feel as if there's fire in his touch, and a fire awakening in me, an ember about to become a gigantic, brilliant blaze.

He's so beautiful with his wide shoulders, brilliant hair, and even his scars. Our eyes meet and I sit up again. He moves closer and kisses my face, then whispers in my ear, "Lie down. Lie down and let me adore you. You want me to make you my wife, let me make you."

I run my hands over his chest, and together, we move back, until I feel soft leather caressing my back, his chest against my nipples. I close my eyes as he kisses my neck and caresses my core, close my eyes as he pulls down the last piece of fabric covering any part of my skin.

I'm naked in body and mind, I have nothing to hide, nothing to fear. My chest is moving up and down, so much air coming in and out, so much feeling renewing me.

He stares at me like I'm the most precious thing in the world. "You're more magnificent than even in my dreams, wife."

"I thought I was the same person."

He runs his hand over my shoulders, then descends slowly, caressing my ribs, hips, until he reaches my thighs. "You're real. And I'm not going to say you're solid." He pinches me softly and chuckles. "You're quite soft." The corner of his mouth lifts in a happy smirk. "And mine."

"Always."

He kisses my lips. "Always."

His body is over mine now, and even though he's resting on his arms, part of his weight is over me. It feels as if he's securing me in place, grounding me, reminding me that this is indeed real. And even though he hasn't removed his trousers, I can feel something else real in there.

I smile. "You, on the other hand, are quite solid. Rock solid, I'd say."

The low rumble of his laughter is a soft caress that reaches my core.

Our lips meet again, as my hands explore his back, drinking in the feel of his skin against my hands. I touch his waistband, his belt. I want everything off right now, I want him inside me, I want to feel his entire body against mine.

He parts our kiss and goes to his knees, his eyes so dark and yet seeming hot like embers, as he opens his belt then undoes the laces. I want to help him, get him undressed as fast as possible, and yet I'm mesmerized watching his ringed fingers open his trousers, then finally seeing the member that I've only glimpsed—and touched and kissed—in dreams before.

I'm ready. I want this, him, everything, and I think he knows it as he lies over me again. Our faces are so close that our breaths mingle. Our bodies are so close that our souls intertwine.

There's something magical in the touch of his fingers, in the feel of his skin, in the kisses he claims from my lips. I could melt in those kisses. Die and come back again a thousand times. Become a new person in his arms.

He kisses my cheek, my chin, then sets those lovely eyes on me. There's fire in them, a fire that's life, love, a fire that's the complete opposite of destruction.

"Astra," he rasps. Why does it feel so good to see him breathless, see him losing control? "You need to tell me what you like."

I can't help but smile. "I like you, Marlak."

The tips of his fingers stroke my face gently, so gently. "You undo me when you say my name like that."

"Like what?"

"You said it the first time when we were headed to the Misty Court. I wondered then if I imagined it, wondered if the dreams were addling my mind, but I heard a current of tenderness, of sweetness, lacing the word." He swallows. "It was when I thought—or hoped—this could be real." His hand moves from my face to my hips. "Now you're here. My wife, my love, my azalee."

My breath gets caught in my throat and my heart pauses for a second. *My love*. I want to reply, tell him he's my kindred soul, and yet I can't find my voice. Perhaps I want to leave his words echoing in my mind, their energy filling the silence surrounding us, our wordless declarations.

I think he understands what I say with my eyes, as he kisses the corner of my lips.

No, I know what he wants me to say. A single word.

"Marlak," I whisper. I'm still not sure if I took that long to say his name, but I can believe him when he says I let my feelings slip through the cracks of my ridiculous armor.

His chuckle is light, happy, relaxed, and he kisses my throat, then moves his hands to my thigh, in slow caresses, a fiery magical touch of his fingers igniting something inside me. He kisses my collarbone in slow, adoring kisses that make me feel I'm precious. A loving energy surrounds us, that same energy that was faint in our wedding, now bindings us together. How could I ever doubt it was real?

I feel his lips on my breast, his hand cupping it, the graze of his rings against the soft skin sending a rush of pleasure down my body. When his warm mouth takes my nipple, I'm undone. I close my eyes, taken by the sensation of his body against mine, of his hands trailing my skin, of his tongue… There's nothing but here and this feeling, this moment, this eternity condensed in kisses, whispers, and so many tender caresses.

I bury my fingers in his soft curls, while the tip of his hair caresses my chest, right above my fluttering, content heart.

His kisses trail my stomach, and then his lips reach my core, the twirl of his tongue a spark igniting a fire inside me.

"Marlak," I whisper.

His chuckle is warm and comforting, its low rumble vibrating throughout my body, a powerful wave of pleasure tearing down all my remaining walls. His lips and fingers and tongue are magical. A healing, renewing touch, an enchanted fire shattering me from the inside, uncoiling me.

I'm here, lying on an ancient bed, and I'm also floating above clouds. I'm here, under my husband, and I'm the entire universe. I'm lost and found in his touch.

And yet I want more. I want him.

"Marlak." My voice is a rasped breath, a plea, a prayer. There's fire in my lower belly, a fire that's about to explode. "I want you." I don't know how I even gain my voice. "Inside me," I moan, because I can't form coherent sounds anymore.

The kiss he gives me down there is soft, gentle. It's loving, cherishing, adoring. I understand now what he means, understand what he's doing. It's for me, not for him. But I want him.

"Marlak," I whisper, and I'm rewarded with that lovely low chuckle that always speeds up my heart, always reverberates through my body.

He moves up again, his hands trailing my skin slowly, until his chest is against mine, his dark eyes so wonderful looking at me.

"Are you sure?" His voice is soft, breathless, sweet.

Silly, happy laughter escapes me and I nod, then I wrap my arms and legs around him, as if to keep him as close as possible, as if my body wants to make sure that he's indeed mine, wants to press as much of my skin against his as possible.

He pinches my nose, then kisses my cheeks, my chin, my lips. Soft, fast kisses. Loving kisses.

And then I feel it: the tip of his member against my

entrance, teasing, caressing it. I raise my hips and feel a part of him inside me, then slowly going deeper and deeper. He's careful, giving my body time to open up and make room for him, gentle, so that there's not a tinge of pain. Slowly he enters me—until he's all mine.

Our eyes meet and my heart pauses.

We're one. Together. In real life.

He moves his hips back, then thrusts slowly, and we rock back and forth together in a soothing, hypnotizing motion. It feels good to have him inside me, filling me, to feel the warmth of his skin against mine.

My heels are crossed over his back as we move together, his hair caressing my neck and collarbone. My body and his are one, moving like the up and down of a river current, or the movements of clouds. Perhaps we're leaves rustling in the wind, or the movement of day and night. Back and forth, the way it should always have been. Back and forth, because it's who we truly are. Back and forth, together at last.

His hands move down to my lower back, to my hips, claiming me, those beautiful hands I love so much, their firm touch sending a brilliant energy to my entire body.

I can't believe how much I wanted him, how much I still want him, so much want that seems to come from a bottomless pool the size of the universe.

He kisses my ear, my neck, my breasts, while I run my hands over his back, his soft skin warm against my fingers.

I never imagined sex could be so tender, so loving, so sweet—not even in the wonderful dreams with him. It's as if the cords uniting souls no longer have to strain from being apart, so they just envelop us in a loving light.

From slow and steady, our movements speed up to urgent, frantic. I feel as if there's fire inside me, some magical fire about to burst and consume everything—except that this fire heals, and never burns. I want him more and more. I want everything.

Each of his thrusts is a burst of sensation, a torrent of pleasure, a rush of power. We move faster and faster, speeding like the blood in our veins, our bodies becoming one pulsing heart. A frantic, furious heart, furious that it had to wait this long to exist.

Above me, Marlak's breath is ragged, his movements unbridled. I love to feel him claiming me with so much urgency and want, plunging into me without restraint, thrusting like *a deranged animal*. There's something powerful about seeing him losing control.

Control. There's nothing to control. There's nothing, in fact. And then I'm gone. I'm nowhere and everywhere, nothing and everything. But I'm not alone. He's with me, within me, around me. We're bound free.

Around us, there's nothing but stars. And light, so much light uniting us, binding us, so much light around us. All my muscles are loose, all my thoughts are gone. I'm in my body and outside it. Perhaps we have both become pure light, and it's not that I can sense it illuminating us, but that I have become it.

From that state of pure contentment and bliss, it's hard to come back, to look at the world again, and yet I open my eyes and see his gorgeous face, his magnificent smile. He kisses my lips and caresses my hair, then stares at me with those brilliant eyes. Loving eyes, like a balm to my heart, filling it with a warm, comforting feeling.

Something's different, though. There's light around him, light everywhere. I look beyond him, and realize that the ornament with crystals in the ceiling is casting a purple light, like a magical chandelier.

He turns, looks at the crystals and the sanctuary, then at me again, his eyes wide, his mouth open. "You lit it."

"I..." I'm not sure I can comprehend this. "How?"

He sits, looking so impossibly good looking. "I think... They're beacon stones, Astra. That's what they are."

I sit as well. "But purple? I thought they could only be clear or red."

"It's not common knowledge, but they *can* turn purple. Sometimes. I myself only learned about it a few days ago."

"What does purple mean?"

"It's obvious, isn't it?" He smirks. "Love."

I punch his arm softly. "Very funny."

He laughs. "It's true. Do you want to bet?"

"No, I..." I look at the crystal formation again, its long filaments emitting light in several shades of violet, purple, and lilac. Of course I want to believe it's love, our love manifested in the ceiling, lighting this sanctuary, but I'm pretty sure the explanation isn't as magical. That said, I do take in his meaning, his words. Love.

I look back at him, but his smile suddenly fades and the light in his eyes dims.

"You're an orphan, right?" He asks. "They said nobody knew who your parents were. Is that true?"

What an odd change in subject. "Yes. Why?"

He bites his lip. "I think you're Tiurian, Astra. Partly, at least." He closes his eyes and shakes his head. "I can't believe it, can't believe I didn't see it. Get dressed." His voice is dry, harsh.

My legs tremble and I feel cold all over, unable to process his reaction. It's true I never told him I'm Tiurian, but I never expected him to react like that—especially now, after everything. "What if I am?"

27

Here I am, stunned, my Tiurian origin revealed and slapping me in the face.

Marlak's already putting on his trousers. "Tiurian magic can be traced. The worst type of people and creatures will chase Tiurians hoping to activate magical stones. The rivers must have kept you concealed, and I think this sanctuary might be safe, but I'm not sure. That day, with Nelsin, do you remember casting any magic before the creatures showed up?"

"No. And after they came, it was just light. That's not Tiurian magic."

He sighs, while putting on his shirt. "I bet you wouldn't even know it. You have no clue what kind of magic you have. Isn't that right?"

"I..." I don't know what to say. I'm feeling stunned, dizzy, nauseous. "It's not my fault." Not my fault that I am what I am, not my fault if I don't understand my magic. I stare at my clothes scattered on the floor, unsure what to pick first.

He lifts my chin and makes me look at him. "Wife, I'm not angry at you. I'm worried. Imagine if you, by accident, cast some magic on our way here or when we spoke to the

Nameless. Just imagine it. There could be bloodpuppets or mercenaries out there looking for you. We need to get back to the river. Right now."

I'm trembling as I put back on my underwear.

"We'll look at your magic, Astra," he adds, his tone soothing. "And figure out a way for you to conceal it more effectively. There must be a way to do it."

"I've never heard that Tiurian magic could be traced." I can't imagine that Otavio would have kept something like this from me. "Maybe you're exaggerating." I'm trying to put back my leggings but struggling as it's sticking to my skin.

"Am I?" He raises an eyebrow. "Every time you used magic outside a river, someone tried to attack you."

"When we met, I used it."

"Incredibly, that day you used most of your magic while on a bridge, Astra, and maybe my magic concealed yours."

"Go out there and do some strong magic, then," I say as I put on my blouse.

"Right, because nobody's trying to find *me*. We're too far from the river or from any place with lots of fae and magic, so it would draw attention. We'll get back home, where it's safe, then check your magic, and I'll find a way to protect you." He steps closer and caresses my hair. "And I'll hold you tight every night."

I exhale, a lot more relieved than I imagined. "You don't mind that I'm Tiurian?" I don't even have the strength to pretend I'm surprised or suggest he could be wrong.

"Of course not. But we'll need to be ten times more careful." He takes a deep breath, then chuckles. "I'm guessing dream me already knew that, *azalee*. And maybe you're right that he's nicer."

"You two are the same." *And I love you both.* I don't know why I hold back those words.

He passes me my sword and helps me strap it on my back, then holds me close. "I think real-life me has just panicked, and might have scared you. It's just... I've sworn to protect you, and now everything's a lot more complicated than I imagined." He kisses the top of my head. "We'll have a lot of time later, when you're safe."

"I know." I'm leaning on his chest, comforted by the sound of his beating heart, when I hear a loud thud.

The colors are different. I look up and notice that the crystal formation has turned red, making the sanctuary eerie and strange.

Red. If they're beacon stones, it means danger.

My eyes meet Marlak's but all I can see is pain—and horror.

Now I can understand Marlak's panic. We're far away, in a chamber with only one way in or out. If there's something dangerous out there, about to come in, we'll be trapped. That said, I still think his magic is strong enough to defeat most foes.

He's pale, trembling, his eyes distant. There's either something horrific and incredibly powerful out there or he's again reliving a painful memory. I reach out to touch his hand, but he steps back and laughs.

Laughs. He's laughing.

His reaction is so strange that it petrifies me. "What's the joke?" I manage to ask between gritted teeth.

He's laughing so much that it takes him a few seconds to reply, "Oh, Astra, do I have to spell the answer?"

"Just say it," I hiss.

"You, Astra, you are the joke." For some reason he looks amused as he says that.

I don't like his tone, his words, his posture. "Explain, husband."

He widens his eyes. "Husband? Oh, you surely didn't take any of that seriously, did you?" He shakes his head. "Oh, you did. Poor, little, innocent Astra."

My stomach sinks and my mouth is overcome with a bitter taste. "It's not funny."

"Oh, no." He laughs. "It's sad. Did you ever think I liked you? Did you?"

My insides feel cold and hollow. I'm too stunned, too shocked to even try to comprehend what's happening, and stupid tears are pricking my eyes and closing down my throat.

He laughs again at his own idiocy, at his own cruelty. "I can lie, Astra, and lie incredibly well, so make sure you don't forget that."

There's a whirlwind in my stomach and a loud buzz in my head. "Great." I can't believe I was able to find my voice. "Just open this sanctuary and you'll never need to see me again."

"Why? You truly don't want to understand what happened? Don't want to learn from your mistakes?"

I swallow, then force words through a lump of ice in my throat. "I don't care."

He shrugs. "Unlucky for you, I do care, so I need to tell you." He stares at me. "I used you, got what I wanted..." He points to the nook where we just had sex. "And I don't mean that. I don't mean the blandest, most boring fuck ever."

"It takes two to dance. If it's boring, it's because you're boring."

He gestures to me. "Well, hard not to be boring with

someone like you. I lied a lot, Astra, but at least I was honest when I said you were unattractive."

"At least I'm not half roasted, asshole. Poor you, so ugly that you need to create elaborate schemes just to have sex, since nobody wants you."

For the first time since he started his farce, he has a smile that isn't cold or cynical. Only a mad person would look so genuinely relieved to hear he's ugly.

He pulls his dagger from the scabbard. "It wasn't for sex, Astra. You think I'd waste my time with a bland human, when gorgeous fae fall at my feet?"

Human. He still dares call me human, knowing what I am, having used me for what I am. I'm guessing somehow I activated his dagger's beacon stones. What I can't understand is how he knew I'd be able to do that, how come it took him so long to bring me here. It doesn't make sense.

He narrows his eyes. "If I were you, I'd be more careful with your secrets. And I'd stop opening my legs to any fool who's mildly polite to you."

Before I can even digest his absurd words, my hand moves to his face. For some reason he doesn't block it, and my palm slaps his cheek so hard it leaves a white mark.

He touches his face, but sneers. "That's it? That's it? Can't even slap properly, Astra?"

"I won't soil my hand with you anymore. You don't even deserve my anger."

I want to leave—disappear, and never see him again, and yet I doubt I can even remove the rock blocking the sanctuary's entrance, let alone find my way back to Krastel. My legs are trembling and my stomach is revolving, but I stand still, chin up. I'm not the one who needs to be ashamed here. Not that it helps me feel any better in this reality that doesn't make any sense.

The corner of his mouth lifts, and then he stares behind me. I turn to look, but my eyes must be going crazy. It can't be.

Coming out of the stairs, I see Otavio. Otavio, of all people, then Azur, and a tall, dark-haired fae man, followed by six blue-skinned pixies with translucent, shimmery wings.

"Let her go!" Otavio roars.

I don't know if I'm flattered or puzzled. It's not like anyone's holding me. Right as this thought crosses my mind, strong arms pull me back, and then I'm pressed against Marlak's body, a sharp silver dagger against my neck.

"Or what?" he asks. "Let me go or I'll kill her."

My hearing is muffled, my vision blurry, my senses numb, so numb. Fear hovers around me, but it's distant, strange. Everything is strange. Still, I realize Marlak's grip is quite loose. So loose, almost like he doesn't know how to fight.

The tall fae walks towards us. He has black hair and eyes... Those eyes. They're brown, but the shape... That has to be Renel, Marlak's brother. They're so similar, except that Renel's hair is wavy and long, and he doesn't have any burn scars. He's also tall and slim, whereas Marlak is bulkier, even though he's also tall.

Renel says, "Stop it. Let her go and I won't kill you."

Marlak chuckles. "You think you can?"

"Oh, yes, I do." Renel raises his hand, showing a ring on it. A ring with a stone that looks like a stormy sky.

Shit. The Shadow Ring. I mean, I don't know why I'm thinking *shit*. Let's rephrase it: yay, the Shadow Ring. It means Marlak can't use his magic. He still has a dagger, though.

I can deal with a dagger. I elbow and headbutt Marlak at the same time, then crouch to escape his clutch, and run towards Otavio, like a little girl rushing to the safety of one of her parents' arms, except that I don't want to hug him. I still have my sword, but I'm not foolish enough to try to fight Marlak with it.

"You're safe, Astra," Otavio whispers.

I nod, then turn to look at Marlak. He's on the ground, kneeling, while Azur has a sword pointed at him, while three pixies surround them.

"Fight me, brother," Marlak says. "One to one. No magic. Fight me, and let's end this once and for all."

"I don't have anything to prove," Renel says.

Marlak's eyes are pure hatred staring at his brother. "Or any honor to uphold."

Renel clicks his tongue. "Don't you dare talk about honor. Don't you dare talk about upholding anything. You know nothing about responsibility, duty, integrity." He points at me. "You took advantage of an innocent girl for your selfish goals, Marlak. You should be ashamed of yourself."

"Then fight me," Marlak insists. "Prove you have honor, prove you deserve the crown. Let's end this nonsense here."

"We just got started, brother. Nothing's ending. And I'll make sure you'll never threaten me again." Renel turns to the pixies near us. "Take our guests back to the castle."

Two pixies come to me and Otavio.

"It's fine, Astra," my master says. "Don't be afraid."

He follows one of the pixies, and I believe I have to do the same, but I want to stay and see what happens, I want to... I don't even know what I want, but my heart is beating fast inside my chest. It's the stupidest heart of all time, because it's afraid they'll hurt Marlak. It's better for me to leave.

I go up the stairs and dare to look back one last time. Marlak isn't looking at me. It's as if I didn't exist. Azur and a pixie are putting something on his wrists, some kind of armbands made of some black metal. I'm surprised to see him subdued like that, defeated. Without his magic, it makes sense. And it still strikes me as wrong, illogical, as if there's something I need to notice.

"Astra, let's go," Otavio says.

I turn and follow him. Some things need to be left behind.

What I thought we had was a lie, and at least the lie is over now. Am I even married? I don't want to wonder if he ever liked me, if there was ever any hint of truth to anything, because those are silly thoughts that won't change the past.

But it doesn't make sense.

I want to smack myself. I'm stupid, that's all. Things don't need to make sense. But Otavio's presence in front of me reminds me of his teachings, of the importance of understanding people's motivations. Well, Marlak's motivation was activating his dagger.

It doesn't make sense, though. Why did he wait so long to bring me here? Why did he cut leaves for my dress? That was for his friend. His need for my magic even explains why he wanted Nelsin and Ferer to protect me. It doesn't explain why he took me to the Nymph queen and introduced me as his wife. What does it change, though?

Outside, by the entrance, the huge rock is shattered, and two more pixies stand by two round silver carriages. I can't imagine how they got here, through this dense forest, considering there are no horses or trails. Otavio leads me to one carriage and we enter. Through the window, I see three pixies putting on some kind of harness, then flying. A few moments later, we soar into the air.

The pixies are carrying us with those thin, delicate wings. This is worse than wingless Cherry Cake.

Otavio's expression is serious. "How are you?"

I'm not even sure what to say, or if the question makes sense. I just shrug. "Fine."

He sighs. "I told you not to go ahead with this wedding, Astra, I did. Thankfully, despite your foolishness, we were still graced with luck and were able to save you from that maniac's grasp. He almost killed you!"

I don't think my life was in danger at any moment, but that's not a point worth arguing. I give him a polite smile. "Thanks for saving me." I should be more thankful, I know, but there's a void where my heart should be.

I look out the window, see clouds below us, and can't believe how high we are. On top of everything, I'm feeling queasy wondering what could happen if those pixies decide to let go of this carriage. Useless thread of thought.

Otavio's still staring at me as if I had failed a test. "It was so close. Now listen to me, and listen carefully. We'll need to play it right this time. King Renel knows you're Tiurian, but other fae don't. Not yet, at least."

I tremble. "Yet?" I must have misheard him.

He nods. "I had to... adapt the plan. You'll learn more about it soon. For now, all you'll have to do is seduce the fae king."

I don't know how to reply. Why is it that he talks to me as if he had the right to tell me what to do? Perhaps because my life has always been that way in the Elite Tower. I was raised as a tool, and it's no wonder he sees me as one. But this is not the time to try to defy him or to change a dynamic that goes back nineteen years.

There is something I need to point out, though. "But he knows I'm not Driziely."

Otavio laughs and waves a hand. "Driziely. Krastel. Fae don't care about human nobility. But he'll want a Tiurian bride, one with purple hair and royal blood."

My heart pauses. My breath hitches. I feel cold all over, then I blink, stunned. "You know who my parents were?"

He waves a dismissive hand. "Of course not. Tiurians don't have kings or queens—but Renel doesn't know it. It's all a game. All pretend. And it doesn't matter. Use your skills and seduce him. That's your assignment. For glory and revenge, we'll need the might of the Crystal Court."

I was too stunned to think, too brokenhearted to feel, but it's time for me to smarten up and try to understand what's going on. "Whose glory?"

He holds my hand. "You have no idea for how long I wanted to tell you, how much it pained me to see you alone, sad, unaware of your own power, unaware of... everything. I'm Tiurian too, and we'll regain our glory. You'll be welcomed by your own people, and you'll be yourself again, without any fear."

My people. I've always wanted to meet my people.

No. I've always been ashamed of my people. "And yet you let me grow up thinking we're monsters, darksouls. You told me my magic was dirty, dangerous. You never told me my magic could be traced."

"I had no choice. You raise a snake in a mouse nest, you need to make sure it looks, thinks, and talks like a mouse. You think it's easy to raise a purple-haired Tiurian in the castle of her enemies? A child? What can you tell a child?"

"I haven't been a child for years."

"Enough of this."

"Or what? You'll replace me? Are Tarlia and Sayanne

Tiurian as well?" My heart bleeds as I consider how much we could have shared, all the ways we could have supported each other.

He snorts. "Of course not. Those girls are distractions. I had to hide you, Astra. Again, it wasn't easy, but our effort will be rewarded."

I sigh. "So that's it? All I have to do is seduce him? Without any other information, right? I'm guessing you want me to whore for you while you keep the plans to yourself."

"Whore? Women *dream* about marrying a king, Astra. It's your chance for glory, for everything you've always wanted. Don't make me change all my plans."

Maybe upsetting him when we're so high in the air and he could toss me out the door is not a good idea. I shake my head. "Sorry, I'm just... traumatized."

"I know." There's sadness in his eyes. "Did you take any precautions? Not to get pregnant?"

"I was taking the tonic you gave me."

"Good, good." Oh, great. That's all he cares about. "We'll double check. You'll need to give Renel an heir."

Exactly. Whoring. But I swallow my words, and think about another issue. "Wouldn't he want to marry a virgin?"

"Fae are not like us. And if anything, that will draw his interest even more." He sniggers. "At least he'll be able to claim he took *one thing* from his brother."

Thing. Charming.

"What's he going to do to Marlak?" I ask. "Kill him?" I don't know how to feel about that.

"I think not. The brothers have a deal or something."

A deal. A deal Marlak wanted to break. But if it was keeping him alive, then he wouldn't break it now. "I see. And how did Renel find us?"

Otavio sniggers again. "Renel. That kid is incompetence personified. And quite stupid, frankly. It's going to be so easy, Astra."

"Who found me?" I insist.

"You need to give me more credit. *I* found you." He points to my hair. "The color tincture was enchanted." He frowns. "You were hidden for days, though."

Hidden because of the river, but when I was outside the island... A chill runs over my body. "You sent bloodpuppets after me?"

He frowns. "No. Bloodpuppets?"

"There were also Crystal Court mercenaries. In the Court of Bees."

"That wasn't me. You'll need to tell me everything in detail, so we understand. The magic of the coronation in the Court of Bees also hid you, and I couldn't take you from there. Now I finally found you." His voice cracks with emotion. "I never gave up on you, Astra."

Of course, he's all emotional about his plan, not about me. Still, I don't even know what to do with my life, so I'd better play along—at least for now. I give him a smile, paying attention to smile with the eyes as well. "Thank you. I... should have listened to you."

"Sometimes what we need are hard lessons. You'll be stronger now, and we'll have the Crystal Court by our side."

Something else comes to my mind. "Are there others... like me?"

"With your hair, no. Tiurian, yes. The time for you to meet them will come. Focus on your task for now, Astra."

Lovely task. "Sure."

"Once we control the Crystal Court, then things will change."

We. He thinks *he*'ll control the Crystal Court. The worst is that until a few days ago, I wouldn't have seen anything wrong in that, wouldn't have realized I was being manipulated. Perhaps I needed a hard lesson. Hard. That only reminds me of Marlak. It felt good, though, to feel his hardness inside me, feel his body against mine. Now it's all so tainted that I want to swim in a pool of alcohol to get rid of the memory of that touch.

Otavio then points to the sword on my back. "What's that?"

Can't he see what it is? "A sword."

He chuckles. "What for?"

Right. He thinks I'm incapable of wielding it. "You see, this is an interesting weapon." I pull it from the scabbard and show the blade. "This part is pointy and sharp. You can stab or cut enemies." Then I show him the pommel. "This part you hold." My words sound so much like Marlak's sass that I feel I'm squeezing my heart. Stupid heart.

Otavio's mouth is wide open, his eyes wide, staring at it.

I'm starting to think he has never indeed seen a sword, and say, "Impressive, right?"

"Is that... Dawnshadow?"

I almost tell him it's a replica—when I notice the pommel.

The stones are red.

They were never amethysts, and Dawnshadow never had rubies: they were beacon stones.

The real sword. I had the real sword all along.

28

Marlak

If I flinch, Renel will notice. If I glance her way, he'll notice.

I laugh instead, even though I can see her disappearing up the stairs from the corner of my eye. I laugh even though I'm pretending I'm subdued, even though I'm letting my brother's dog clasp dark bracelets on my wrists.

"Fight me!" I yell at my brother. I know he'll never agree with that, but it draws his attention.

The bracelets are heavy, so heavy that I can't even move from this position. There's definitely some dark magic weighting them down. A strange magic, and it can't come from my magicless brother, his fae friend, or the pixies.

"Dabbling in dark magic, Renel?"

He stands in front of me. "I have no wish to fight you. Never had."

Something then connects with my ribs. Azur's boot. I take the opportunity to pull his leg and knock him to the ground. In a second, I'm above him, a dagger against his throat.

A CURSED SON

"Marlak, stop," Renel pleads.

Azur's eyes are wide. Can I kill him? Can I kill my brother's best friend?

The coward fae then says, "Stand down or I'll kill them."

Them. Them. He knows. He means Astra as well. I feel cold all over, while at the same time, that dreadful fire threatens to burn everything. I kick his balls hard enough that he'll be immobilized for a while, then get up and advance towards my brother.

"I'll kill them!" Azur yells.

It's when I realize he means the pixies. Three pixies, drugged and enslaved, gasping for air. As if their lives were not miserable enough, he wants to kill them. If they die, all I'll have to deal with is Azur and my brother. I have a good chance, even without magic. For Astra, for my sister, I have to escape. I have to keep going.

What are three lives? And then, where does it end? Where do I draw a line? How many lives are worth it? Where do I lose my humanity?

"Stop it!" I raise my hands, even though it feels like lifting boulders.

The pixies breathe again, but I realize Azur could suffocate me just as easily, and his air magic is much more powerful than I thought.

I say, "Aren't you ashamed? First you enslave other fae, then threaten to kill them?"

Azur gets up and rolls his eyes. "It's clear you don't know anything about politics. Don't know anything."

"Marlak, just come with us," Renel says. "I won't hurt you. If anything, this is for your own good."

"What, you're *saving me* now?" My voice is such a roar that I fear I might spit fire. "Like you saved our sister?"

"One of us has to carry the weight of the world, and that's obviously not going to be you."

I have to laugh. "Weight? What weight?"

Weight. I can't stand anymore, and fall to my knees.

Renel crouches in front of me. "One day you'll understand."

"I doubt it."

He takes a deep breath. "You'll have a lot of time to think in the Blue Tower."

Blue Tower. Is he really going to take me to the place I've been looking for? Is he going to give me that gift? Perhaps I'll finally learn where this Pit of Death is, and what lies beyond it. What kills me is leaving Astra behind, leaving her after hurling hurtful words at her, sharp enough to wound her where she's most vulnerable. Each word was a dagger slicing into my heart.

"Time to repent from your evil deeds," my brother says, then shakes his head. "Taking advantage of innocent girls, Marlak? I couldn't imagine even you'd stoop so low."

Advantage? He doesn't know that my soul and Astra's are intertwined, that our hearts are connected, even if she might never forgive me. But she'll be safe for now. Her hatred for me will protect her.

Until I find my way back to her.

Astra

We barely arrived at the Crystal Palace, and they gave me a room, a big room with a huge double bed and windows leading to a misty hill. I wonder if the view changes when the castle moves, and if anything here is real. I wonder if any part of my last days was real.

The castle is filled with low fae with creepy empty eyes, and two of them are preparing a bath for me, following Otavio's instructions. Otavio, who's eager to take over my beauty routine again, and make me his doll. Otavio, who took away my sword and is going to present it to Renel.

All I can do is dance to his song, at least until I can find my own. And to be fair, I was eager for a bath.

The water is deliciously warm, the smell of herbs fresh, relaxing. I haven't had a warm bath since forever, and never had such a luxurious bath. I lie down, letting the water caress my naked body, letting it wash away my shame, my anger, letting it wash away everything.

Alone for the first time with my thoughts, I look back and think about what happened.

Otavio's voice is the one that comes to mind. *Understand people's motivations, what makes them tick.*

What was Marlak's motivation? Activating the stones, of course.

Was it?

I swallow. Marlak's words are the ones that come to mind. *I made an oath to protect you and I take it seriously.* I remember him at the coronation. *Whatever happens, my brother can't notice how much I care for you.*

Whatever happens, my brother can't notice...

I recall his face, his panic, his fear when he realized I was Tiurian. I recall his panic when the stones turned red.

Which is more likely: that he'd been pretending for several days?

Or that he pretended for five minutes, when he must have known what was about to happen?

I sit up and exhale, fast. My heart is making a racket in my chest. I'm partly relieved, partly furious.

Marlak played me.

Tricked me.

I was so overcome with my own fears, my own insecurities, that I didn't notice it.

I clench my fists. Couldn't he have winked? Have whispered in my ear? Couldn't he have trusted me? We could have fought together. Perhaps he had no more magic, but I still had mine.

Right, the magic I barely understand and have no idea how to use. I still want to strangle Marlak. We could have tried.

And that was exactly what he wanted to avoid.

Still. Even if we were to fake this, he didn't have to say all those things to hurt me, to make me believe he used me.

Would I have walked away, would I have let them take him, if I thought he was pretending?

I don't know.

What I know is that his brother took him, and I'll have to find a way to free him. Then I'll yell at him.

Oh, I'm going to yell so much.

THERE'S MORE!

Thanks so much for reading this book!

The series continues in *A Traitor Sister*.

Sign up for news, updates, and even some freebies at dayleitao.com

If you're on social media, make sure to follow me. I love to connect with readers:

- instagram.com/day_leitao
- tiktok.com/@day_leitao
- goodreads.com/dayleitao
- bookbub.com/authors/day-leitao

ACKNOWLEDGMENTS

I'd like to thank my readers for their incredible support and enthusiasm. Special thanks for my wonderful beta readers and proofreaders, as well as my author friends, who helped me so much this year.

Finally, thanks so much to all my Kickstarter backers. You've made so much possible!

Milton Keynes UK
Ingram Content Group UK Ltd.
UKHW020808130524
442628UK00004B/323